AF140155

Florian P. Wallner

The House of Time

Bibliographical information by the German National
Library: The German National Library has registered this
publication in the German National Bibliography; detailed
bibliographical data can be accessed on their website
http://dnb.dnb.de.

Production and publishing
BoD – Books on Demand, Norderstedt

ISBN: 978-3-7392-2194-6

I would like to offer my heartfelt thanks to those who gave so generously of their time to help me with the publication of this book:

Beate Kinzer for her translation

Margaret Grant for her proof-reading

Tamara Faye Creed for her cover design

Introduction

Chan was in charge of the excavation. Today he had been informed about a special find and he had sent his people to the site to take a look; he was happy that he was able to go there as well. This bloody traffic jam was going to drive him mad. Near a mountain a human skeleton had been discovered. According to the first results it was around 1000 years old. Chan, getting bored, turned on the radio. The presenter was making a joke. Chan couldn't laugh about it; he never really could laugh about jokes. The presenter was announcing a song when Chan's mobile started ringing. He turned off the radio and answered "Yes?" A female voice greeted him.

"Hi, Chan." It was Susan, his assistant at the excavation and a close colleague.

"Hi, Susan! What's up?"

"Chan, where are you? You have to get here as fast as possible. We have made an extraordinary discovery. The skeleton carried a driver's licence and an ID card."

"I can't get there fast. I am stuck in this damned traffic, for goodness sake, but hang on a sec, what did you say just now? A driver's licence?"

"And an ID card. It's totally crazy!"

"They don't necessarily belong to our body, do they?"

"We've checked. They certainly do belong to our body." Chan didn't know what to say. "Chan, this is totally weird. It won't be long and the press will get wind of this." He was shocked; years ago he had read something like this in a novel.

"Do your best to keep out the press."

"The police are here to keep journalists and the curious at bay as best they can."

"I'll be there as fast as I possibly can, Susan."

"Please hurry!"

"I'll try!"

"See you in a bit!"

"See you, Susan!"

Chan put down his earpiece and put the mobile in his pocket mumbling: "Crazy!"

So, what was the story in that novel he had read all those years ago? Something about a hole in time or something along those lines. Could that be possible?

This might be his breakthrough as archaeologist and professor. This skeleton was worth millions and it was his team that had got hold of it. This was his chance to leave the company and work at the university. Unless Sool was going to raise his salary. Chan turned the radio back on. Slowly, slowly the slip-road came closer and Chan could finally leave the motorway and reach the dig via back roads.

It was a road full of twists and turns and the old Honda groaned ominously at every bend, but with his raise Chan would be able to buy a new car. He had always wanted to buy a German car, an Audi or maybe a BMW.

Meanwhile the excavation area had been expanded tremendously. There were tents, cars and people everywhere. The police were bustling around and chasing down reporters attempting to trespass. Professors were shouting advice at great distances while business people tried to get a grip on the situation. Droves of excavators who had nothing more to do celebrated their find by drinking champagne out of plastic cups.

"We found a jeep!" cried Jack, the senior field archaeologist.

"What?" Susan had come out of her tent and tried to spot Jack.

"Hello, Susan." Suddenly Chan stood next to her.

"Do you see Jack anywhere?" asked Susan without greeting. Chan looked around and saw him outside the barriers.

"Over there. What is going on?" he pointed with his finger at Jack.

"Come along, Chan."

In the following weeks a company called Sool purchased the whole excavation area as well as thousands of acres around it. The purpose of the company was changed. Workers were made redundant, new ones hired. A giant building complex was erected on the newly purchased land at huge cost, the research began...

Jason's car danced through the air in a cloud of fire and black smoke. It went up vertically, wrapped in flames, losing its rear end to another explosion that catapulted it through the air in a wide arc. Unrecognisable parts rained down on the road. The once beautiful sports car landed on its roof, the fuel tank exploded. Jason, watching the scene from a safe distance behind a tree, was horrified and at the same time his opinion of people did not improve, quite on the contrary it deteriorated. Impatiently, Jason searched his coat pockets for his lighter and cigarettes. Finding both, he lit a cigarette. The wind carried away the smoke through the treetops into the setting sun. The landscape turned orange and red. Jason flicked the butt into the grass. At once he lighted another one, his lungs filling with the biting smoke before gliding out through his mouth. His thoughts drifted. He thought of his brother Eugene and his father, who had discovered the hole in time and had both paid for it with their lives. That damned Sool...

400 years later
A big battle raged on the yellow sand of the desert. "We cannot hold our position, go to the gate and travel immediately to 1998. Tell Sool to muster all available

troops at the time gate." Jackson, the general of the army founded by the powerful businessman Sool and calling itself the "gatekeepers", had just passed the order to Jason Hanks, who was now on his way to warn Sool. The gatekeepers, with a large part of their army, had travelled to 2420 to avert the extinction of humankind. Now far greater damage had thereby arisen. The political conflict had spread far beyond their solar system. The army of the United Dark Planets fought the warriors of Sool. Endless gunfights took place. Positions were abandoned, human lives ended. Jason ran as fast as possible to the building complex. He was nearly hit by a grenade, and then he stormed through the door and towards the time gate.

"Report, General," prompted Sool.

"We're falling back. The UDP's army is too strong."

"Damn it! How close are they to the time gate?"

"So far, we've been able to keep them at a distance but they are going to reach it in about three hours."

"Unless a miracle happens within the next two hours and we do win the battle, you know what you've got to do."

"Yes, I know. I shall personally initiate and execute 'RedDeath'."

"Take care! I sure hope we'll meet again."

"So do I, so do I!"

August 2420

The gatekeepers were virtually wiped out. General Wilson started to initiate "RedDeath" as agreed with Sool. At 10:43pm GMT a gigantic fireball would be swallowing the Earth. Heavy rocks would be catapulted into space at incredible speeds. Once the chaos will have subsided, nothing would be left of Earth. People who hadn't been present on Earth during its destruction were rounded up by UDP soldiers and sent into slavery. Some employees of the Sool Company were able to save themselves by jumping through the time gate seconds before they would have been torn apart. But they, too, were found later.

The government of the day took over the responsibility for the time gate. Sool had to step down as director of his company and was sentenced to lifelong imprisonment. The government had an administration block built around the gate to keep it secret from the public and to protect it. Internally the building was known as the "House of Time." Since the destruction of the planet was unavoidable and an evacuation was impossible, the government allowed people to go about their daily business until in 2440 the end finally came.

2388 years after the destruction of Earth on the desert planet Tattau

"Eugene! Run, run!"
"No!" he grabbed his arm.
"You can make it! I am too weak, leave me."
It cost him a lot of effort to leave his old friend behind. Drads came running round the corner. Eugene looked back at his friend and saw the drads stabbing him with their storm lances. Two followed him. He quickened his step, he could feel the sand beneath his feet, it was night. The drads dropped back, he was too fast for them. He had acquired too many muscles thanks to the heavy work he had had to do. He had escaped; he started to laugh, flung his hands in the air and screamed.

He was dirty and his eyes would soon give in to tiredness. Each step required an enormous effort. Eugene was totally exhausted. His long black hair was hanging dishevelled into his face. He ran and ran and yet he didn't seem to get anywhere, the horizon was retreating in front of him. The heat flowed around his body, there had to be more than

140 degrees Fahrenheit. The sun must have reached its zenith, it was high noon. In the distance the volcanoes peaked over the horizon and filled the air with their plumes of stifling smoke. Eugene put one foot in front of the other until all his energy was used up.

The sun slowly approached the horizon and gave way to the moon. A sign for Eugene to start looking for a cosy place to sleep in. The ideal hiding place would, of course, be a recess or a cave where he would be hidden from soldiers and fighting robots, so-called drads, who were looking for him everywhere. A cave or at least a small hole in the sand where he could cower was not to be found anywhere near, but at least a tall rock sheltered him from the moonlight. The long march in the blazing sun had sapped his strength. He tried to make himself as comfortable as possible on the dry cracked soil and fell immediately into a deep sleep.

A house painted black without windows but with a door painted in the same dark colour as the house. The sky as black as the house, the moon red as blood. What was he doing here? Bewildered he looked around. He was going to go into the house. "I know!" called an unfamiliar voice. He entered the house, the black, dark house. Into the living room, as black as the walls outside, just without the moonlight that helped the eyes to make sense of his surroundings. Bats were hanging upside down from the beam that kept the roof from collapsing. Woken by the intruder they winged outside into freedom, into the cold dark freedom. A breath caught Eugene's hair. One, two, three steps into the unknown and a fall into the depth of hell. Fire everywhere. Heat that drove you to distraction….

Eugene started from his dream soaked in sweat; the sun had given him an almighty sunburn, how long had he slept for goodness' sake? And why was there this buzzing in his head? No, it wasn't a buzz, it vibrated. Eugene ran around the rock behind which he had found shelter for the night and spotted a legion of drads, the whole desert seemed to be covered by them. There was a sea of black robots with just the one thought… to kill. To hide from them, Eugene backed behind the rock again, but that couldn't hide him forever. He needed to get to the volcanoes as quickly as possible. There would be more possibilities to hide there. But the drads were too close to reach the volcanoes without being discovered. His only chance was the hills not too far into the prairie, a quarter of an hour at most to get there; that might work. He could not remember this outcrop but he had probably not noticed it out of tiredness and the sudden darkness. Trying to stay under cover of his rock, Eugene was running towards the hilly area. His clothes stick to his skin with sweat. The army could not see him yet but he would not be able to hide behind the rock much longer, he was quite aware of that.

How glad he would be if it had still been night, but the damned sun would kill him yet with its heat. Not much further and he would have reached those hills.

Not far now… not far….sweat and strength, where is his strength? It was used up. Eugene put one foot in front of the other. He dimmed out all the pains. A few more yards still separated him from the place that would shelter him from the drads. He made it. Jumping over the little rocks he collapsed behind a big chunk, his breath came quickly and his heart was thumping. His eyes, caked with the dust of the relentless desert, glimpsed a path leading through the boulders. It wasn't the sun that was dead as in his dream, it was him. With his last bit of energy he started following the path. He stumbled more that he actually walked. The path was small and in some places hidden by debris and impossible to see. It looked as if it hadn't been used for years. Eugene saw a cave, quite low but apparently very deep. He slid into the cave feet first; it was dark until his whole body had vanished inside. Inside, there was a steep downward gradient, but it was not long before he stubbed his toes against something. Now he had to stay here until the legion had passed the outcrop. He hated not seeing where he lay or stood. Oh, yeah, how he hated that. The soil started to vibrate, first only a little, and then more and more. The UDP's drad army was very close to the rocks if not right among them. He had to remain in his position for a long time. Only when the vibrations started dying down, did Eugene dare to give a furtive glance outside. He put his head out of the entrance of the cave but saw nothing but rocks and the ubiquitous sand. The heat momentarily took his breath away; out here it was much hotter than inside the cave. Eugene decided to remain in hiding for a while longer to allow the distance between him and the army to grow. He closed his eyes to relax. Don't fall asleep…

A house, painted green, no windows, a door however, yellow, just like the lawn in front of the house, crazy ... the sky is orange and the sun green. It is bitterly cold. Shaking, he drew up his coat to his chin. Strange, he'll go into the house. "I can feel it…" the unfamiliar voice mumbled. He enters the house, inside yellow walls, the roof is missing, the sun is shining through, it is blue, the sky red. The wooden floor under his feet is rotten. A step, a fall into the heat of hell… A scream, and then it is HOT!

Bugger, he had known it, he had fallen asleep and he had dreamt again. The cave was like an enormous oven, the sun stood right outside the entrance. Eugene hurried to get outside. Soon it would be night. He followed the path until he came to its very end. In front of him was a wide desert, nothing but sand, sand, and more sand. The army had nearly vanished from view. Refreshed by his sleep, but weakened by hunger and even more by thirst and the sun, he started out towards the volcanoes, not that he had any real destination anymore. The sun slowly vanished. Because it wasn't quite as hot during the night as during the day, the march to the volcanoes was less exhausting.

He reached them after not too long a march. He allowed himself a rest and sat down next to one of the many rocks. All his limbs were tired. He was unable to move. What should he do now? If he walked on, he would die of thirst or get fried by the relentless heat of the scorching desert sun. But hang on, what was that noise? The sound of rushing water. Rushing water? Yes, rushing water, there definitely was the sound of rushing water. Eugene forced himself to listen more closely. It had to be water, somewhere there was an underground stream. Eugene tried to pinpoint the origin of the noise. After a short while he succeeded. It came from the ground directly in front of him. He started to dig till the sand became moist. Then for a last shovel with his hand, and the water shot out into his face. He had found a subterranean spring. Water, finally. Eugene drank, his head stuck into the ground. When his thirst was quenched, his craving for something to eat had weakened, too. Had he been a believer, he would have thought it a miracle.

He hated drads. Slowly, he walked along the path, without haste, passing rocks and little gorges walking beneath natural rock bridges like tunnels. Passing innumerable volcanoes until, finally, the path came to an end. Eugene looked up and saw the drad army standing on the sand not a hundred yards in front of him. That could not be possible. The sky was peppered with many little spaceships, there was a battle brewing. Eugene had no choice but to hide yet again. He ran back in the opposite direction to find another cave or some other hiding place. He left the path, ran over hills and stones until a crater blocked his progress. A shot sounded. Eugene was sure that the battle had begun Not long afterwards the air was filled with deafening noise and screams. Eugene found a little recess where he could somewhat barricade himself and where he was also sheltered from the noise of the battle. The war cries and the shots were suddenly far away and seemed strangely familiar to Eugene.

Time passed and the battle was still raging. The air vibrated with shots from cannons and guns. After some time dusk fell and night slowly came. The shots grew farther apart until there were none at all, the battle was over.

Eugene forced himself to leave his shelter, shook the dust off his clothes and started walking again. After leaving the volcanoes behind him, he had an unlimited view of the battlefield and came to the conviction that the drads must have won. There was blood everywhere, oil, severed limbs of human beings, of other creatures and of robots. Smashed spaceships, burnt fighter jets destroyed beyond any hope of identification, some were still burning. Legs of drads that ran around without body. There were coups de grace by firing shotguns and the fires were extinguished. Robot paramedics ran about and tried to save what could be saved. They were followed by drads who chucked all the still usable parts of their comrades into a huge wheelbarrow. There was nothing left to see of the airborne attackers. It seemed that they had been utterly defeated or had fled in time to avoid further losses. Eugene started walking again, he passed the battlefield. Nobody took any notice of him. Maybe he wasn't close enough to be noticed. The drads were probably too busy to see anything but their victory. His legs carried him past severed heads and other things, past incomprehensible, dubious and mysterious equipment and past burning spaceships. Eugene had never seen anything like it in his life; it was fascinating but also frightening and intimidating. He could not take his eyes off the spectacle and kept spotting new objects. Drads whose head was missing. Drads whose upper bodies were engulfed by flames and whose head had already melted into a shapeless lump. Drads who swam in a puddle of oil and drads who screwed on their own legs or arms. The air was like a veil, it had never been that hot, at least 140 to 160 degrees Fahrenheit. The sky looked like a huge sun, it gleamed yellow. Eugene mopped his brow with his left hand, but a few seconds later it was just as before, his hair was clinging to his head, his clothes seemed to have become one with his skin.

When he finally left the battlefield behind, he was immediately faced with another problem: the border post. He saw the towers with their black cannons on the horizon, they were bathed in red light, the sun being about to disappear behind them. The towers and walls stretched into the sky and blocked the path into freedom. He was faced by an intractable puzzle. How could he pass the guards without being noticed? The walls were at least forty feet high, the towers three times taller. It was impossible, he needed a miracle. Half a day's march still separated him from the walls and since he only had a chance to pass the guards in the dark, he decided to wait until the sun had completely vanished behind the towers and walls.

In order to rest for his night-time adventure, he lay down on the sandy ground and stared at the sky. The grains of sand crunched under his back. The sky was cloudless and its colour had turned a dark blue, here and there the first stars showed.

Not until the sky had become black and the moon had risen, did Eugene get up, full of energy, shook the grains of sand out of his clothes and set off for the border post. He had to make it somehow. The question was how?

Eugene had not quite reached the post yet when a spotlight was pointed in his direction. Maybe they had heat sensors or night vision devices. Blinded by the strong beam of the spotlight, he put up his hands as a sign of surrender and to protect his eyes that had become used to the dark. A warning shot was fired and hit the sand in front of his feet, then guards rushed out of the gates of the towers, strange creatures with long, very long heads and very thick legs but virtually without neck, as if their bodies had fused with their heads without a neck in-between. Eugene fell to his knees. He hadn't managed to escape. It had all been for nothing. The strange creatures handcuffed him; one of the guards hit him on the back of his head with a club. He fainted.

A house surrounded by thick fog, painted white with yellow shutters and black windowpanes. The unfamiliar voice sighed. As always he will step into the house....he will. Squeaking hinges announced him. One, two, three steps, no fall. No, no fall, quite unusual. A man stood in front of him. "Hey! I know you! You are the guy who... Yes, yes, that will cost you dear! You can rely on it! You are a bad person! Yes, yes, these things, they will be expensive, expensive." There was a funny smell...

Screams, rustling chains and the smell of death buzzed in the air…

Eugene woke from a weird dream. He was surrounded by black walls. His head ached intolerably from the blow he had received. His eyes hurt. He discovered a door with a small square cut out at eye level; the square was covered with mesh. Eugene looked around, but couldn't see anything except a bench made of old, nearly rotten wood supported by four frail thin legs. He sat down on it and hoped that it would carry his weight. It did but protesting a little with a loud "Creak!"

From the frying pan into the fire, he had screwed up, his whole escape, his exertions in the desert, all for nothing, why hadn't he run away? They would have shot and killed him, so what? Better than this! Now he sat on a bench with legs like four toothpicks surrounded by four bare, naked walls with a wooden door with a meshed hole. The door was his only chance to escape from his prison. The walls were too thick, the floor like a piece of concrete. All that was left were the few inches of wooden door to get out. And even these proved an insurmountable obstacle. It seemed as if the dice had been cast.

Shots, screams, pain and death, these sounds had become familiar to Eugene and they were just outside the wooden door with its meshed hole. The shots did not go on for long. It seemed as if the guards had been beaten. Intruders. Have they come for him? Do they want to free him? Or kill him? After some lengthy key jingling, the door to his cell was opened and, it seemed quite incredible but was still true, a human being entered. Eugene sat there befuddled, suspicious but also a little bit scared on his bench with the toothpick legs. With a gesture he was prompted to get up, as he very politely did. Then the human spoke to him in a language Eugene did not understand. "What?" he asked.

"I am sorry; we didn't know what language to use so we can understand each other. But it seems you even speak the old Earth language, still the official language in many places."

"Sounds like it. Have you come to free the prisoners?"

"Only one, you, Eugene."

"Why do you want to free me?"

"Because you are the only human being who has ever been able to flee from slavery. And now come quickly before reinforcements arrive."

"But you are human as well."

"Me? No…. but please come along."

Eugene and the human who apparently wasn't one walked through the door of the cell and entered a wide passage full of the same kind of bizarre doors, some with windows, some without. There were parts of destroyed drads everywhere. No sound could be heard.

"Everyone else is outside already. Hurry up, we don't have much time left. The drad army has nearly reached the post," somebody said. Another human. He had just joined them passing the last cell in the passage close to the stairs. He hadn't put his life on the line for nothing after all; the risk he had taken had been rewarded. How relieved he was, he, Eugene, who had spent his life in horrendous work camps and had to share his bed with three others, provided he was lucky enough to grab a space in a bed. Since there were more than a million human slaves on Tattau and only a little more than a hundred thousand beds, it was difficult to get one. All in all there were no more than five hundred sleeper blocks each holding dozens of dormitories. It was awful. Eugene couldn't believe his luck, but would his luck hold in the future? Through one of the great wooden gates from which the guards had emerged to capture him it was now his turn to walk, under very different circumstances. For the second time he had managed to escape from the drads. It was absolutely incredible.

It was hot outside under the blazing sun. With quick steps they hurried along, he and the two humans who weren't human, even though he couldn't be sure about one of them, he might be human or he might not be. They hurried along to the spaceship that wasn't far from the post. The hatchway had been lowered and they could easily go aboard. Inside the ship, it was a space jet, the temperature was pleasant and it felt good not to be exposed to that lethal sun any more. The part of the jet where they were was bathed in very bright blue light; there was no furniture in this room, only a door at one end. The light came from neon tubes on the ceiling. The human or non-human, as the case might be, put out his hand. Eugene took it and the "human" shook it and introduced himself.

"My name is Jim. And this guy next to me is Slow. You think we are human. You're not entirely wrong. We are Homo Sapiens 3000. When humans became scarce on the planet, we helped out as so-called substitute humans."

"Well then, you are robots? Just like those damned drads? Why did you free me?"

"We freed you because it is our task to find a human being who is able to undertake a strenuous mission. Who is able to work long hours without a break and who doesn't fear any type of work. Someone with courage, who loves action, without fear of change or even death."

"And that brought you to me?"

"Of course, but to be honest, it did not necessarily have to be a human. But we happened to hear about your escape and we just had to help you." Eugene looked at them doubtfully; he didn't understand at all what those two Homo Sapiens 3000 were getting at.

"Why me?"

"But that is absolutely obvious. You fulfil our

requirements."

"What are these requirements that I fulfil, I would like to know. And why do you risk your lives?"

"Those requirements help us to complete our crew and to make it perfect, so to speak. But allow me to tell the whole story. Many thousands of years ago a hole in time was found on your planet, the Earth and abused for the wrong purposes. The United Dark Planets tried to gain power over the time hole. People destroyed the Earth before they succeeded. Once the Earth had been destroyed and the time gate along with it, there was no reason for the UDP to go on fighting. Their plans to use the gate for military purposes had failed and therefore they looked for other ways to gain control over the universe. They started to create and perfect the drads and thus bred a huge army in just a few years. These drads were then stationed on every single hostile planet to solve the problem and convert the civilians. Something they did quite well. The drad army is controlled by a main ship and a control ship, but it can also function quite well when left to its own devices. Both spaceships are connected in such a way that they are virtually one vessel. In order to bring the unlawful rule of the drads to an end and to restore peace to the universe, this spaceship must be destroyed. And that is our order. Without their drad army, the UDP will lose its hold over the universe and will be far less powerful than they are today."

"Now let's recap that very slowly. You want me with my wonderful extraordinary ability to be strong and courageous to help you to destroy the drads and thus ultimately the UDP?"

"That's it."

"What if I don't want to?"

"Well then tens of billions of lives will continue to be in danger. Cultures and whole planets are threatened. And just like Earth all those years ago, whole planets will be destroyed time and again. Nobody can oppose the UDP. The outcome is always deadly and usually the innocent are made to suffer."

"But what do you suggest we do? To me all this sounds very much like a suicide mission."

"Everything has been planned very carefully right down to the tiniest detail, don't worry. We are not going to force anybody to be part of our plan. You are welcome to return to Tattau, if you like. Is that what you would like to do, Eugene?" Jim looked at him with his robot eyes. Those damned robots.

"Okay, fine. I am with you, even if it's the last thing I do." Relief spread over Jim's and Slow's faces.

"We are relieved. Eugene, we'll now enter the heart of this little jet."

Until now the door at the end of the room had been closed but now it opened and a large room presented itself. They entered and once everybody was inside, the door closed again of its own accord. Inside the temperature was pleasant and the room apparently occupied the whole width of the jet since there were windows on either side. Five people were seated round a small round table in the middle of the room. Eugene looked around, greeted everybody, they nodded a response.

"These are the warrior robots of the rebels; they have no language chip and no intelligence chip either. They can only distinguish between friend and foe and eliminate the foes. Really they are only prototypes yet, but in a few years they will be deployed for war purposes."

Eugene, Slow, and Jim settled at a table close to the windows. The room also held a small galley, two more doors and a big cupboard bolted to the floor with three doors, one of them with a mirror. In one of the four corners there was a pot with a plant, the plant had light green

23

leaves and a dark red stalk. On top was a very beautiful yellow flower with blue stamina and a red floral cushion. After a period of silence and futile looks around the room as if looking for something incredible nobody in the room had noticed so far, Jim finally spoke.

"Down there is Mike. It is the smallest planet in the solar system. Once it was known as Pluto but after the destruction of the blue planet it has been given another name for whatever reason."

"Tell me, where will our journey end?"

"We are on our way to the rebels' mothership."

Slow stood up and disappeared through one of the doors.

"I'll go and check how far we still have to go. We should get there soon."

Eugene stayed behind, stared out of one of the many windows into nothingness. Far away he could just make out some stars. He still couldn't believe what he had got himself into.

"Eugene?"

"Yes?" Startled, Eugene sat up. He had fallen asleep and had dreamt once more of this house. Jim stood in front of him. His head, what had happened to his head? It was missing. Impossible. Eugene closed his eyes again, opened them. His tiredness and his nightmares had played a trick on him. His thoughts buzzed unchecked through his head. It took him a while to control them.

"Eugene?"

"Yes, what is it?" Didn't he see that he had opened his eyes?

"We are in the mothership."

"Already?"

"Yes, and now come quickly, the nation of rebels is waiting for you."

Eugene stood up, he could feel every bone in his body,

painfully so. Following Jim, he stepped through the door and then walking down the hatchway he had used to enter the ship, he now left it.

The jet had landed in a big hangar; obviously they were now inside the mothership. The high-ceilinged, very wide and long hall was covered in metal panes. High above, right at the top, near the ceiling, Eugene could glimpse some windows where people could be seen. The windows were huge and milky; they had to be very thick. Maybe it was bulletproof glass?
By now Eugene and Jim had reached a door covered with metal just like the walls. They crossed the threshold.
A seemingly endless corridor with innumerable doors to the right and left opened up in front of Eugene's eyes. The corridor was empty apart from Slow. The three of them walked along side by side. The silence made Eugene nervous. Something felt strange. And this woefully long corridor just never seemed to end. Some distance away, Eugene could see that the corridor led to a huge door. It was as wide and high as the corridor itself. This door seemed to be their destination and finally they were right in front of it. It was really breathtakingly big. Jim stepped up to it, cranked a lever, and with a loud creaking noise the mechanics of the door were put into motion. The door swung open. Eugene, Slow and Jim stepped through the door into a gigantic hall boasting windows as big as houses. Eugene looked up. Apparently, they were at the highest point of the hall because the ceiling was right above their heads. The ceiling was full of windows as well and you could see the stars. In front of them was a simple balustrade, they took another step and looked down. Eugene was thrilled and speechless. He had never seen anything like it. The hall was more than three hundred feet high. Eugene heard a creaking noise. At such a dizzying

height a creaking noise isn't terribly welcome, but in this case it was just the elevator they stood on and that now slowly moved downwards to the floor of the hall. It was a wonderful and heavenly view; the hall was filled with people, computers and huge screens. There was a big hustle and bustle; you could find anything in this hectic turmoil. Eugene even saw someone cutting his nails. With a spirited braking manoeuvre the elevator finally reached the lowest point of the hall. The balustrade moved sideways a bit and with a low humming noise glided into little slits in the floor. After the whole iron railing had disappeared, they stepped into the huge hall that now appeared even bigger and, what really surprised Eugene, was utterly silent. No sound could be heard, no coughing, no sniffing and no desperate rustling caused by someone urgently looking for something important. Deep silence surrounded him and his two mechanical companions. By the wall, many yards away there was a big pedestal on which stood an old man holding a microphone in one hand and a sheet of paper in the other helping him to find the right words. He cleared his throat and everybody's attention was on him. After clearing his throat once more, he lifted the microphone to his mouth and began his speech.

"Today, my dear fellow campaigners and inhabitants of this ship, the war against the UDP officially starts." The old man had to interrupt his speech because the audience started to applaud and some looks swayed towards Eugene then back to the old man on the pedestal. The latter now lifted his hand, the clapping died down. He waited a moment until the last murmurings were hushed.

"A squad sent out by me has succeeded in finding the first person for the team and rescued him before the drad army had a chance to kill him. He is here right now. Ladies and gentlemen, I welcome Eugene to our ship!" Everybody looked at Eugene and he didn't know what to do. So he just stood still, smiled and said an occasional "thank you" which was drowned out by the audience's clapping. Hesitatingly, he raised his hand to show his gratitude.

"Enjoy it, Eugene, it is well deserved." The old man nodded at him appreciatively. "As you know, the crew, the team is not complete yet, not by a long shot. Therefore Jim, Slow and you will set out to find the other three members. You will set out to find Aecey, Lyon and Rob. With their help, you will destroy the control ship of the drad army. With them, you will be an invincible squad!" Again the crowd cheered. The old man bowed and left the pedestal through a door behind him. With a queasy feeling Eugene realized that all eyes were upon him again. Jim, who stood next to him, prodded him in his side and hissed, "Let's get out of here quickly before everybody comes over to wish us good luck!"

Eugene nodded and they walked off to the other side of the hall, the crowd parted in front of them to allow their passage. Some nodded towards them as they hurried past, others called out good luck and still others just stood and watched them. Eugene saw the most unusual life forms; some looked like plants, weird leaves and tentacles growing all over their skin. Others looked comparatively normal if you ignored the black-red eyes or the arms that were three yards long, but most of them seemed to be these strange Homo Sapiens 3000 androids. By now they had reached the steel door, it was light grey and had a big round spyhole made of glass in the middle. The door opened inwards with a quiet humming and they could easily enter the next room. After they had all passed through, the door closed behind them with the same quiet humming. They now found themselves in a small square room that had a door in each of its four walls. All four doors had spyholes like the one they had just passed. In the middle of the room were small stools placed around an even smaller table and there sat even smaller creatures. They were very thin und their heads could hardly be distinguished from their bodies. Jim and Slow hurried past them towards the door on the opposite side. Eugene followed them while he kept staring at the little creatures. They didn't look up. He saw that there were cards or something like that on the table and they had some in their hands. It looked like they were playing a game. Eugene just tried to have a sneaky look at the cards when Jim pulled him into the next room.

"Leave them alone. They feel watched if you look into their cards. They don't look it but they can get quite nasty."

"Okay." Eugene found that difficult to believe. They could get nasty? A likely story! The room they now entered held paintings and benches. It was fairly long and a part of its floor was covered by a runner. The runner was very nicely ornamented and shone purple, blue and turquoise. Jim, Slow and Eugene walked along the elongated room and Eugene noticed how, with every step, he sank a few inches deep into the carpet. Finally they reached the end of the room and stepped through a dark-red door with an old-fashioned doorknob.

"Our leader has a weakness for antiques even if some of the pieces are just old-fashioned rubbish," explained Jim. One after the other they walked through the dark-red door. This area was full of doors. There were grey, red, blue, green, black and pink doors. Some were made of wood, some of iron or plastic. The floor was dark grey and dirty from the many feet that trampled over it every day.

"Are there several of these corridors in the ship or is there just this one?" Eugene's interest was aroused.

"Well, there are a main corridor and fifty minor corridors per level, as well as three secret corridors only the boss and his immediate staff know." Jim pointed at a light green

door. "These are the doors leading to the minor corridors."
"Are we in the main corridor?"
"Oh no!" he laughed. "The main corridor is almost twenty yards wide and has more than eight hundred doors. There is so much traffic that we introduced the fifteen lane system. Seven lanes for one direction, seven for the other."
"I understand. What about lane number fifteen?"
"Very good; finally someone who is actually thinking. The last lane is reserved for emergencies and is marked red."
"I see." Eugene nodded. Somehow it all felt like a dream. Maybe he was going to wake up in a few seconds' time? Surrounded by rocks and sand?
"We are in corridor 23; we call it the *boss level*."
"Why do you call it *boss level*?"
"Because that's where all the generals, directors and so on have their offices."
Eugene realized that they had been walking for quite a while. He also realized that there were very few people around. Now and then they met someone carrying a pile of papers or talking excitedly into a telephone. Eugene didn't know the language, however.
"Where are we actually going?"
"We are going to see our director, Hesson Lachopp.
"That old man on the pedestal who gave the speech?"
"Correct, that's him."
Eugene was just avoiding a creature without eyes that had nearly run into him. After walking some more, they finally stopped outside a door with a wooden appearance. Jim stepped up to it and knocked three times. A moment later it was opened from the inside and the old man stood in front of them and asked them to come in. They found themselves in a very large, tastefully decorated office just as you would expect a director's office to be. Being invited to sit down in three leather armchairs opposite an enormous desk, they did just that. The man took his seat

behind the desk, leaned back and said, "Welcome, Eugene. I am most grateful that you accepted our offer to be part of our team since at the moment it consists only of you, Jim and the good Slow, doesn't it?"

"To be honest, director, I am not thrilled at the prospect of destroying the control ship of the UDP," said Eugene and saw no reaction in the old man's face. He waited a moment. "But someone's got to do it, don't you think?" Hesson nodded slowly but firmly.

"We will do our very best, director," promised Jim and the man nodded his thanks. Jim, Slow and Eugene stood up. The man shook their hands and wished them good luck for their journey. This done, they left the office. Once they were back in the corridor, they walked just as long a distance as before until they passed a door into a big hangar. In the middle of the hangar was a space jet. They approached the jet walking side by side. Eugene felt a sense of pride and self-confidence. And he was sure that Jim and Slow felt just the same. Time stood still at that moment, all consciousness of slavery had disappeared from Eugene's memory. His brain freed itself from the unpleasant memories, now he was truly free. Past machines and gas containers they finally reached the space jet. The hall was bigger than it seemed. As if by magic a hatch was lowered so they could board the jet quite comfortably. Once they were inside, it was raised again. The jet was quite different from the flying object in which Eugene had travelled to this place. It consisted of a corridor that after three yards branched out into tree more corridors. One went straight on and ended after a while in the engine room. The other two led to the cockpit and the leisure rooms. All three chose the corridor leading to the cockpit. There were two seats, one for the pilot and one for the person commanding and activating the guns on the jet roof and bottom or taking care of the speed of light mode.

The role of pilot was taken by Slow and Jim was responsible for the weaponry. Eugene stepped behind Jim's chair that looked more like an armchair and held on to the back while the big gate of the hangar opened and the way into space was clear. Slow started the engine and seconds later they were surrounded by the all-encompassing blackness of the airless space.

"Where are we going to pick up our fourth member?"

"Our first destination is Mars where we'll pick up Lyon, a native of Mars."

"I thought Mars was destroyed along with the Earth."

"No, you are wrong there. It still exists, but in only half its glory, so to speak. It has only one hemisphere now. The inhabitants of Mars can call themselves lucky, that their oh so beloved Mars wasn't thrown out of orbit when it was hit and half squashed to dust."

"It is a single hemisphere?"

"Yes. I have read up on it. Nowadays there are about three million inhabitants, a third of them lives in towns and cities, the others in the country and a few live beneath the ground. Besides, they never got round to building sewage drains, so be prepared for some pretty awful smells."

"We will be there within a few hours."

The Black Circle

The animal was goaded by its hunger and by the plebs pitilessly wanting to see the death of its still living prey. The Colloscoseum shook and the mob shouted incessantly "Death! Death! Death!...." The predator satisfied its hunger because it knows very well that it might take some time before there will be anything more to chew on....

"We need some disguise for Eugene. We cannot take him to Mars the way he is." It was Slow who suggested this to Jim. He nodded, but didn't reply instead he got up and

31

beckoned Eugene to follow him. While Slow was busy piloting the space jet to Mars, Jim and Eugene went to the big room with the hatch. The area lit by neon lights was quiet and its peace was only disturbed by the humming of the jet engine. Jim opened one of the doors; all sorts of clothes were hidden behind it. Jim pulled out a particularly ugly piece of clothing and with an encouraging look he gave it to Eugene, who took it and looked it over. Then he looked at Jim and said, "Why do I have to dress up?"

"Please forgive us! We are quite aware that you cannot know anything about all of this. We simply forget now and then, however. Well, here goes. After your planet, the Earth, had been destroyed, the UDP sent the survivors into slavery. Some of them, actually quite a lot of them were handed over to the inhabitants of Mars as compensation, so to speak, because half the planet had been smashed by humankind. There have always been fairly barbaric customs on Mars and they have used humans for their amusement for a long time now. They constructed a building where they stage the killing of humans to entertain the people. That's its sole purpose. It's called Colloscoseum. You can see that name as an homage to ancient Rome, on Earth, you know. The Black Circle, that's what the locals call it, holds about two million spectators. It's got an area of about half a square mile. To make the most of that huge space, several humans are executed at various places within the arena at the same time. Any human being, who is on the planet illegally and is found out, will be taken there and killed for the amusement of the locals."

"I don't know what to say, only that I already despise this planet. How are humans killed in the arena?"

"Oh, there are endless variations. Humans are run over, shot, quartered, impaled, drowned, eaten by animals while still alive, tarred and feathered and so on and so forth."

"How wonderful, I don't really want to know more."
Eugene took the moth-eaten garment that Jim held under his nose again and had a closer look. It had to cover legs, arms and body completely. And so it did. After Eugene had put it on with some difficulty, only his head was still visible. But not for long because Jim found some colour and started to paint his face green to go with the outfit. Then his lips were given a dark-blue colour and his hair was tinted blue as well. Eugene looked at the result of Jim's handiwork in the mirror. It was awful.
"What exactly am I?"
"The way you look right now, you are a Saphorian."
"A Saphorian? What's that supposed to be?"
"Saphorians live on the moons of Jupiter. Each moon has its own city with one exception. 99.8% of the biggest moon are covered by plants and that provides the oxygen necessary for the other moons."
"Is it inhabited?"
"Robots live there. They look after the oxygen stations and maintain the plant diversity of the moon. We'll have to pick up one of our crew members there, the other one we'll find on one of the urban moons called Aqua."
Eugene was just looking at himself again in a tall mirror that slid out of the wall as Jim pressed a button. Once Eugene had finished studying himself - it was hopeless anyway, he had never looked so ugly in all his life, the perfect Halloween costume - they returned to the cockpit. Through the windscreen, the red planet already slowly became visible in the darkness, it was surrounded by a dust cloud and the closer they came, the bigger the small rocks became. In fact the planet was badly damaged. The once round sphere had become a hemisphere. Rocky, full of cracks, uninhabitable. Hot, bright red magma came to the surface at some places on the damaged side. It looked incredible. Half a planet.

"When are we going to land?" Eugene wanted to know.

"In ten or fifteen minutes." Slow avoided some lurching rocks. They were now quite close to Mars even though they still seemed to be far away. A big red rock passed their jet very closely and threatened to crash into them. A sheet of dust settled on the windscreen and by and by everything outside looked red. They were now passing through the second layer of Mars dust and slowly but surely reached the so-called particle-free zone. They didn't speak a word until the jet was brought to a standstill after having been safely landed by Slow. Once the dust thrown up by their jet had settled, they disembarked. To avoid unnecessary interest, they had parked their jet outside the capital. In the capital, Mars City, stands the equally famous and infamous Colloscoseum much feared by humans. Slow, Jim and Eugene waited silently until the hatchway had been lowered completely and it was safe to disembark. They left one by one and stepped onto Mars soil. Their shoes didn't leave any prints in the red sand of Mars, the air, however, was full of fine red flour-like dust that burnt in their lungs. In the far distance they could just see Mars City with its tall towers, red buildings and the great oval of the Colloscoseum in the background with its many decorations, ornaments and statues. Everything around them was red. No other colour was visible, even the sun seemed to have adapted. It was setting behind the mountains and spread red light on the planet making it seem even redder. It was not without reason that humans called it the "Red Planet."

Walking side by side they approached the capital that slowly disappeared into the darkness of night. Behind the city the mountains now shone bright red. Eugene was fascinated; it was a truly beautiful spectacle to watch the nightlife of this enormous city slowly coming to life. The sun now only lit the distant mountains and part of the

Colloscoseum. It would take them half the night to get there. Their new team member was to be met at his home. "Tell me, Eugene, how did you manage to escape from Tattau?" Jim wanted to know.
"That wasn't easy. I had a really tough time."
"We have a long march ahead of us, your story will pass the time and we will be in the middle of a busy city before we know it."
"Right, I'll tell you."

We slaved away underground all day and hoped to be released from life this time round by a collapsing tunnel. But I always got away and had to go on working day after day. We got up early in the morning and returned from work late at night. There was never enough to eat and many of the robots that brought our food soiled it with their oily fingers but we ate it anyway. What choice did we have? Many died of hunger, others didn't return from the tunnels because they had fallen victim to the heavy work and yet others died of diseases or rammed their tools into their bellies to kill themselves. I had a pal; we worked in the same tunnel and got along famously. We hatched a plan that was to lead us into freedom. We continued to do our work to their satisfaction until the day came when we made our bid for freedom. While everybody was asleep, and to make sure of that we waited till long after midnight, we sneaked out of bed to the door. Using the stairs, we would flee to the ground floor and from there, with all the alarms ringing by now, into freedom. But that was not to be. In front of the exit, we came across some drads; we had to choose another way. Twice we ran in a circle until we saw that the door was free, but before we could reach it, my pal was shot.
"Eugene! Run, run!"
"No!" I screamed and grabbed his arm. But he was

adamant, "You can make it, I am too weak, leave me!"
It cost me quite an effort to leave my friend behind. Drads
came running round the corner and I set off to the exit. I
looked back at my friend and saw the drads stabbing him
with their lances. Two followed me, so I ran faster, out of
the door. Finally I felt the sand beneath my feet. It was
night. The drads fell back. I was too fast for them. I had
acquired too many muscles what with all the hard work I
had to do every day. I had escaped, flung my arms in the
air and screamed. Then my ordeal through the desert
began, you know the rest."

When the three companions finally reached Mars City,
Eugene was surprised and shocked. The biggest city of the
planet was covered in piles of rubbish and junk. On every
corner girls stood, waiting to sell their bodies. And it was
loud and noisy. The streets were overcrowded with
people. The stench was incredible, and many, to Eugene's
eyes abnormal creatures walked about. Eugene, Slow and
Jim pushed their way through the crowded streets in single
file. There were such weird, grotesque creatures out and
about on Mars at night. They passed a house brimming
with neon advertisements. A house floodlit by spotlights
had a tall tower. On top stood a naked man singing
undefinable words in a loud voice to the passing crowd
below. Eugene couldn't help laughing. They pushed past
the onlookers who were congregating outside the house
with the tower and stopped not long after in front of a little
house with a front garden. A front garden should not be
imagined as a green paradise. Like everything else on
Mars, the front garden is all in red because the few plants
that grow on Mars have adapted to their home planet and
glow in strong red colours. The house had a small front
door and a window on either side. The roof was very flat
with two chimneys. The little group walked through the

garden gate one after the other and followed the winding cobbled path their team member to be had obviously laid himself right up to the red front door. A bell was dangling on a string from the overhanging roof. Jim grabbed the string and swirled it. The bell rang. After a few moments, a dog opened the door. Well, a sort of dog. He had a black head like a jackal with golden eyes, his clothes were simple and round his neck was a turquoise collar - and he walked upright. In his mouth were dangerous looking pointed teeth, his hands were hidden inside black gloves. "Hello, Jim. Hello, Slow," said the jackal head.

"Finally, Lyon. Eugene, this is Lyon, our fourth team member."

"Delighted." Eugene was unable to say more.

"Me, too. Come on in," replied Lyon and stepped aside to allow them to enter his house. Inside it was dark and Eugene couldn't make out anything. That was why he just stopped after a few paces and hoped Lyon would guide him or at least put on some light. Lyon, having closed the front door, now flicked the light switch next to the door much to Eugene's joy. The walls were slightly yellowed; the floor had dark-red tiles. After entering the house, they had followed a short hallway that ended in the living room. Eugene entered, Jim and Slow had already settled in brown armchairs. Now Lyon also came into the room and sat down in the last free armchair. Saying nothing, they sat there until Lyon broke the silence.

"How was the trip? Would you like a cup of tea?"

"I'd quite like some tea," said Slow.

"That would be nice," the others confirmed. Lyon got up from his chair and went through to the kitchen. Eugene noticed that there were no doors in the house apart from the front door.

"We'll stay here overnight and tomorrow we'll continue our trip to the Forest Moon of Jupiter," Jim said to Eugene, who just nodded. Lyon returned with a tray in his hands. He put it on a round glass table with dark wooden legs standing in front of the chairs. They all took a cup of tea and started drinking. It tasted of lemon and had an aftertaste reminiscent of almonds. Eugene, who tried hard not to look at Lyon's head all the time, was delighted with the tea. He had never drunk anything like it.

"We should go to bed, tomorrow will be a tough day," said Jim. Lyon guided them to another room with three mattresses and a bed. Eugene, Slow and Jim lowered themselves onto the mattresses and Lyon lay down in his bed, and soon after they had all gone to sleep. Eugene slept fitfully. As he so often did.

"The house! The house! The house!" The unfamiliar voice shouted so loud and so long until it lost its teeth. Then its eyes fell out and from the eye sockets shot fountains of blood. But it kept on screaming until the arms fell off and then the feet. "House! House!" The screams became ever more shrill and unbearable. The man next to it had meanwhile taken a drill and bored holes into his own head. He was laughing incessantly....

Eugene started out of his sleep and again was soaked with sweat. These nightmares would finish him off eventually. Through the window above Lyon's bed the stars sparkles and bathed the bedroom in a cold pleasant light. It was incredibly silent. Eugene was only aware of the breathing of his three roommates. He hadn't had time to think. So much had happened in the last hours. If only he knew who he was. What had his childhood been like? Where had he grown up? So many questions and no answers in sight. Eugene closed his eyes and tried to collect his thoughts. When he opened them again, it was getting light. The sun would soon shine through the window. Lyon's bed was empty. Eugene stood up and entered the room with the armchairs. Lyon occupied one of them and wished him a good morning. He returned the greeting and rubbed his eyes. He couldn't suppress a yawn.

"Would you like some breakfast?" asked Lyon and pointed to the table where different kinds of jam and marmalade, honey, fresh rolls, toast, and butter were on offer.

"Very much so," replied Eugene and took the chair opposite Lyon. In silence, Eugene spread honey on a slice of toast. Lyon sat and watched. He probably had eaten already; still, it made Eugene nervous. What did he want?

"Lyon," said Eugene, his mouth full, "What is the matter?"

"You are not a Saphorian, but a human being," he answered. Eugene froze. Hang on, he is one of us, so it didn't matter if he knew. It wasn't as bad as all that.

"How did you know?"

"My nose doesn't just look big, its sense of smell is as good as its size suggests and as far reaching." Lyon raised his cup and sipped.

"Is that supposed to be a joke? But you are right. I managed to flee and those two picked me up, outlined their plans and convinced me fairly quickly to help them. I ought to mention, however, that the alternatives would have been worse."

"It's not good that you're here. It's not that I mind but last night I heard the screams of those dreaded devils yet again."

"Of the devils?" Damn it, what devils?

"The dreaded devils of Mars. They also go by the name of "trackers", quite self-explanatory, really. They track down humans on Mars, outlaws, slaves, drifters, whatever you want to call them. Once they have found one of them, he or she is doomed. They emit deafening screams and alert those bloody hunters. Hunters are truly evil creatures who will knock you out right away and carry you to the Colloscoseum."

"What a sweet story for breakfast, Lyon. And how do they track down humans, by our looks, I hope?" Eugene knew while putting the question that that was wishful thinking.

"No, they use their noses, they smell humans." By now Lyon had taken a roll and spread jam on it. Now sounds could be heard from the bedroom. Soon Jim and Slow appeared in the living room. With a sleepy "Good morning!" they collapsed into chairs and took a slice of bread each. While the others were eating, Lyon explained, that Eugene's presence on Mars wasn't terribly clever and that they should return to the jet immediately.

Suddenly the walls shook, the windows vibrated. The tea in Eugene's cup made waves. A kind of alarm signal rang over Mars City with eardrum splitting intensity. Lyon sprang up and hectically pulled the curtains to cover all the windows in the room. Eugene wondered how that would help against this weird noise. Then the noise died down.

"We have to leave instantly!" called Lyon. "That was the signal for the games to begin in the Black Circle! More importantly the devils will be sent into town to find more humans. As if they didn't have enough in their dungeons already," explained Lyon.

"Let's get to the jet before they find Eugene."

"Well, hurry up!"

For a brief moment there was complete mayhem in Lyon's living room, one of the tea cups was broken. Nobody paid any attention. They all grabbed their gear and burst outside through the front garden into the street. The streets of Mars were not half as busy as they had been the night before.

"We better be quick, they might turn up any second," called Lyon.

"We should run." They ran, followed by the shrill screams

of the devils.

"Damn it! Run! They are already in the neighbourhood!"

Gasping for air, they hurried past the red buildings, the house with the tower and the many pubs and restaurants. Passers-by had already correctly interpreted the scene and jeered and laughed about them. Not very helpful when you are on the run. A few more yards and they would have reached the city limits but their hopes were dashed when, a couple of blocks away, two devils emerged from an alleyway, a cloud of dust in their wake. Their eyes were red as blood; slobber ran out of their big mouths brimming with sharp teeth. Their long noses had a weird shape and twitched all the time from left to right. Eugene and the others stopped and looked back, the road was clear. But if they returned to town, they would be stuck there.

"Damn it, now what?" There was an alleyway next to them. They looked at each other and ran into it, closely followed by the devils. The devils were fast, their twitching noses wouldn't leave Eugene's trail until they had caught him. The lane they had entered proved to be too dark to run quickly because they kept bumping into things, knocking their feet or arms. Old rusty barrels, stinking puddles, oil drums, old bricks and tyres cluttered their path. Eugene, who started to trail behind because he had caught his disguise on a rusty nail, looked back and saw the red eyes of both devils jump over tyres and stones. He careered at full speed into a barrel full of foul smelling liquid. His impact made the barrel tumble; he himself was catapulted away and landed between food leftovers and empty whisky bottles. The devils burst into incredible screams and this time Eugene thought he recognised some sort of howls, only much higher pitched. He closed his eyes, got up out of the trash but it was too late. The devils had surrounded him and sniffed him with their noses. At close quarters, their eyes were very sinister. Eugene saw that the claws on their front legs measured at least three or four inches. He decided not to move, under any circumstances. Eugene's companions had disappeared into the darkness of the lane. He felt abandoned and fearful, he slowly sank down into the rubbish, the devils didn't stop him and after a while the hunters arrived. The hunters had yellowish skin and carried batons in their hands. One pulled a cart with two wooden wheels that was full of humans, badly beaten, smelling, entwined and stacked one on top of another, nearly dead.

"I am not human! I am a...." Eugene hesitated, what was he? A Safarian? No. "I am a Saphorian! You mustn't hurt me!" A hunter stepped up to Eugene, looked at him and said, "A devil is never wrong!" He grabbed Eugene by his collar and knocked him out with a well-aimed blow. The last thing Eugene was conscious of was the fact that more devils started screaming in other neighbourhoods, then the world went black and he fell to the floor. The hunter threw him over his shoulder, left the alleyway and threw him onto the cart.

His friends had not run away, of course. They had watched from a safe distance what the hunter had done.

"That's not good," said Lyon.

"We have to save him," added Jim.

"But how? In the end we will all end up in that awful Colloscoseum and be slaughtered. What about our mission? We must not fail!" retorted Slow.

"Are you crazy? We cannot leave him to certain death!" Jim looked surprised at Slow's coolness. Slowly they emerged from behind the barrel where they had been hiding and headed out of the alleyway.

"Lyon? Is there anything we can do without endangering ourselves?"

"Without danger? Absolutely impossible, everything on this planet is dangerous."

"You see? Forget about him, we must not endanger our mission!"

"Slow! Shut up! We are going to rescue Eugene." Jim gave a grateful nod towards Lyon. He had known Slow for ages. His reaction had been totally unexpected.

"Our only chance is one of the entrances they use to bring humans into the Colloscoseum," said Lyon.

"Let's go then! What else can we do?"

"That is suicide!" They ignored that remark

They emerged from the dirty and dark alleyway into the blinding sun. It was noon. The red buildings seemed even redder than usual and the sand on the street had heated up to over 140 degrees. Hardly anybody was in the streets now and even the buildings were empty. Everybody had gone to the Colloscoseum. That was where Lyon, Jim and Slow were now heading as well, past the usual splendour of Mars, to the city centre. The closer they came to the Black Circle, the noisier it grew, the ground seemed to shake and the streets were full of people. Everybody wore red hats shaped like the Colloscoseum; others wore t-shirts embellished with a black circle in the centre of which was a picture of a human being penetrated by a spear. Suddenly there were no more buildings around them, only the enormous, feared, and impressive mass of the Colloscoseum in the distance. It was at the centre of a huge beautiful open space. The sand beneath their feet was now no longer red but black, the black circle surrounding the Colloscoseum giving it its popular name. Here the crush of people was no longer as bad and after all that pushing, squeezing and bumping they had finally made it. They stood right in front of the terrible and yet fascinating round building.

"Listen!" Lyon had to shout to make himself heard by Slow and Jim. "All in all there are seven entrances on this side, four for the spectators, one for the staff, and the last

two are for the animals, humans and the other prisoners and, if necessary, for the devices of execution!"
"We are going to use the one for the prisoners. Normally that should lead into the dungeon!" Jim shouted in his turn. They nodded and walked along the Colloscoseum looking for the prisoners' entrance.

Eugene woke up in a dark damp room. It was extremely hot, his costume stuck to his skin. He sat up and tried to remember the last minutes. The hunter had knocked him out und now he was in the Colloscoseum! This realisation felt like another blow to his head. His eyes, slowly getting used to the darkness, started to take in his surroundings, a small room. In front of him was a door made out of old dirty wood, still, it looked too solid to break down. In one of the corners of the room, hay and straw had been piled up presumably to serve as his bed. Eugene sank to the floor and leant against the door, his head aching. The floor was damp and grimy. Distantly the spectators' shouts and yells could be heard. He tried to concentrate on that noise. Trumpets, drums and screams mixed with clapping and laughter. He closed his eyes. He could hear rattling chains behind the door, screams of pain and creatures sobbing, the noise of lashing whips. He hoped that Lyon, Jim and Slow would rescue him.

Lyon, Jim and Slow looked at the entrance for humans from some distance. It was watched by a guard. He was an ugly big bloke with a spear in his hand.
"These guards aren't terribly clever. They are quite stupid to be precise. The government uses them as cheap labour for jobs nobody else wants to do. We can outsmart him and it doesn't have to be too spectacular or even extravagant."
"Not spectacular? Well, if that is so, we volunteer. Let's

say we are criminals on the run who hand themselves in," suggested Slow.

"Not bad, not to say that is quite simply ingenuous," said Lyon.

"Will that guy buy that? I can't see it," objected Jim.

"Didn't you hear what Lyon said just now? These guys have virtually no sense in their drained-out brains, they're the size of a peanut!" retorted Slow.

"It is going to work, Jim. Don't worry. I know these guard types," said Lyon.

They started to walk towards the entrance with its guard. The ground shook, in the Colloscoseum the executions were apparently already in full swing. People wearing Colloscoseum hats kept crossing their path, others wanted to sell those hats. Politely they declined again and again. The guard, who now had realized that they were approaching him, started to pay attention and tried to stand to attention, an attempt that just made him look ridiculous. They stepped up to him; he blocked the small door-less entrance with his huge muscular body. He emitted a bad smell.

"You can't enter here," he grunted loudly, slobbering.

"Why can't we? We are here to make the people of Mars happy," said Slow smiling.

"How do you want to make them happy?" asked the guard and with the word "happy", he flooded his tunic with slobber.

"With our death," said Lyon simply and looked into the guard's black bug-like eyes.

"My order says not to allow anybody into the dungeon!" he drooled quite unimpressed. "And now get lost!"

"Your boss won't be happy with you once he realizes that you allow merchandize to get away."

"You are not merchandize. You do not look human."

"We want to die for the good of the people! And you

45

prevent us from doing so!"

"I must not allow anybody to enter the dungeon without permission. That is my task!"

Lyon laughed an artificial laugh. "Your job is not to allow anybody inside who frees the prisoners. We, however, are not here to free prisoners but to become prisoners." That gave the slobbering monster pause. Lyon kept looking into his eyes.

"Are you trying to fool me? Why should you want to become prisoners?"

"We want to hand ourselves in. We are criminals."

"I don't believe that. You should get lost."

"We will not get lost. We want to go in and you are going to allow us to do so," said Lyon. The plan seemed about to fail. It seemed as if they had met with a reasonably intelligent specimen.

"Go away or you're going to have a problem with me!" Slowly he became angry. Now they needed a quick solution. Lyon's eyes looked around. Slow and Jim just stood there and obviously didn't know what to do. Lyon was on his own.

"Well, then. We are going to leave and complain about you." Lyon turned around. He was just about to turn back and push the guard down the bloody stairs when he said, "Wait!" Lyon turned around. "Where are you going to complain?"

"To your boss, of course. Where else?"

"Go inside quickly." The guard stepped aside. "Quickly! Please, no complaint."

"We have to thank you. We owe you a favour."

"Won't do me much good. In a few hours you are going to lie dead in the sand of the arena." They entered and descended the steep staircase, one behind the other. At first, the light flowing in from the entrance helped but the further down they went, the harder it became to see the steps. After a while there was a torch mounted on the wall. Lyon took it to shed light on their way down. They now walked side by side, the stair had become very wide and the further they descended the wider it became. The air was stifling and carried many different odours, a musty odour, the odour of putrefying bodies, the odour of rot and decay and many other unrecognisable odours of the dungeon of the Black Circle. At last, Slow interrupted the endless clanking of their shoes on the steps of the dirty stone staircase.

"I just realized something. Interrupt me if I am saying something stupid or if I have missed something, but do we have a weapon? I mean we are in the Colloscoseum on Mars and in the dungeon to boot. Did we bring a weapon, for heaven's sake?"

"Slow, you are obviously not aware that weapons are only allowed in the arena of the Colloscoseum but forbidden on the rest of Mars. Where should we have got a weapon?" replied Jim.

"We're finished! When we find Eugene's cell, we might as well join him and wait till the henchmen come."

"Now don't lose your head, guys! Of course, we have a weapon. Do you honestly think I'd leave the house unarmed on this crazy planet?" Jim and Slow looked at Lyon. Lyon reached inside his coat with his gloved hand and pulled out a silvery, beautifully curved laser pistol.

"Thank you, Lyon. Thank you. You do not only save our lives with this but you also calm my nerves," said Slow. Jim shook his head. "How did you get that gun?"

"That's a long story, my friend."

They continued their descent, the staircase stretched before them, black and fathomless like a gorge. Their steps echoed from the walls and the echo died in the darkness ahead of them. Their breath came in jerks and hung in the air like fog. From the depths they were heading to, they

47

could hear rattling chains, slurping steps and other sounds that gave them goose bumps. Screams interrupted their steps and the torch in Lyon's hand had burnt down fearfully low. Several times they tripped because the steps beneath their feet were breaking away or because the next step was smaller or further away than expected.

Finally, hours later or so it seemed they could make out the end of the staircase. The floor was trampled down by the multitude of people who had walked across it over time. The air left an unpleasant taste in the mouth. It was cold and caused a strange damp and dumb feeling in the lungs, the smell had become worse as well. Lyon moved the torch to and fro to lighten up the room. It was a long wide passage. At its end was an arch lightened by torches. To the right and left were columns. They walked in the middle of the room where there was a big trapezoid stone with an inscription that was barely legible. Lyon shone the torch onto it.

Here rests our beloved king
and creator of the Black Circle

Edward Korte, King of Mars
760- 812 n. DoM

"They buried the creator of the Colloscoseum down here," stated Jim.

"He wasn't only the creator of the Colloscoseum. He was King of Mars. And yes, his remains were indeed buried down here," said Lyon patronisingly.

"What do you think DoM stands for?"

"DoM means: Destruction of Mars. The King lived from 760-812 after the Destruction of Mars or to be more precise after the bisection."

They proceeded to the entrance they were able to see in the

48

glow of the torch. Their shadows danced over the dark walls. Again and again, they could hear eerie sounds from the depths of the dungeon. Their steps on the hard ground, however, could hardly be heard. The entrance proved to be a big arch. After Lyon had swapped his torch for a new on, they passed through and found themselves opposite a wall. There were passages to the right and left.

"Which way shall we choose?"

"Good question. We go where the dungeon is."

"And where is the dungeon?"

"I don't know. That is why we are going to look for it."

"I know that. So, right or left?"

"We'll go to the left," decided Jim

They turned into the passage on the left. Everything was well lit by torches so that Lyon's torch wasn't necessary. Here and there a wall was covered with blood, on the floor lay dead rats. The passage went round a small bend and they found themselves in a hall with all sorts of paraphernalia. Above them, the crowd jeered, the air vibrated as did the walls and floor. They must be right beneath one of the spectators' stands.

The closer they came, the more they became aware of the uses of what they saw. There were torture machines, sinks, ropes, swords, posts and some indefinable instruments the uses of which were better kept hidden. Carefully they wound their way through the maze of instruments, always expecting to be discovered. It smelt of rotten meat and old stale water. At the end of the hall, they could see a ramp which certainly ended in the arena. They had to go back.

"We should have turned right," cursed Slow and kicked against one of the instruments which answered with a resounding "clunk" that echoed through the room.

"Slow! Stop that nonsense! Do you want us to be discovered?" Jim couldn't understand him. He was usually a very relaxed calm guy. Lyon gave the entrance they had used a worried glance. But it stayed calm.

"If they have heard us, they will be here within a few minutes."

"Who will be here?"

"Guards, hunters, anything and anyone that was close enough to hear you blowing your top."

"If that is the case, let's stop quarrelling and get going," suggested Slow and headed off. The others followed him. They ran back, past the instruments of torture. They looked carefully round the corner; nobody was visible in the passage. Slowly they emerged and then walked ever faster until they reached the crossroads where they went straight ahead. Still nobody came to meet them. There were more and more stones on the path. In parts, it was uneven; they had to be careful in order not to trip. Eventually the tricky path became a smooth pavement; the walls, however, were still bare and dirty. To shed light in the passage, torches were placed at equal distances but not enough to dispel the uncanny atmosphere. They walked carefully and quietly to avoid attracting attention. After a while the passage gave into a larger passage where there were dungeon doors on either side. The passage was filled with moaning and rattling, screams and bangs. Nearly every cell was occupied by a human being, maimed, young, old, deformed, wounded, fat, there was everything and they all had one thing in common, they were dirty and unkempt. The air was damp and when breathing, it felt like disgusting, stinking syrup. Everything smelled of decay and excrements. In the middle of the dungeon were sewage drains to wash away the prisoners' discharge as effectively as possible. Since the floor sloped towards the drains, everything floated in the middle of the room. Therefore the stench was unbearable and the floor was unimaginably dirty. There was a passage on either side of the room, which led to even more cells.

"I'd say we split up. Lyon, you go to the left to look for Eugene. Slow, look around here and I'll search the passage on the right."

"Okay, but what are we going to do if devils show up or something of that kind?"

"Run and scream to warn the others."

They looked at each other and nodded in agreement, and then they parted.

Lyon walked to the right. He had trouble to keep his balance on the slippery floor. Green water was running down the walls and disappeared gurgling into a drain. Because of the damp conditions, a thin slimy film had started to cover the ceiling. In some places it dripped down at regular intervals. His steps made a smacking noise and a thick crust of dirt stuck to his shoes. Lyon entered a room that held yet more cells and he started to run along the cells, looking inside, trying to find Eugene. The room was similar to the previous one in virtually every detail. Even the smell had stayed the same. Some humans were close to death; others were still young and had only just been captured.

"A dog! Hey, Bello! Come here, I have a nice juicy bone for you!" called an old man from his cell. He was stark naked and covered in his own excrements. A woman called out to him: "Don't listen to the old man! Come here to me, I know how to treat a cute doggy."

"Be quiet, you stupid woman! He is mine!" called the man. They must have gone mad or crazy over time.

"Don't listen to them," said a boy in the cell right next to him, "They are loonies, they have spent half their lives in here. You aren't an employee of the Colloscoseum, are you?"

"No, I'm not."

"Have you come to set us free?"

"No, I came to free a friend."

"A friend? What does he look like?"

"Blue hair, muscular. Looks like a Saphorian."

"I am sorry, I can't help you. But couldn't you free me, too?"

"I am on an important mission which must not be jeopardized. If they catch me, everything can go wrong. I am sorry, my boy."

"I understand. But let me tell you one thing for the road, I am going to die tomorrow. By a wooden post. Just like the crazy guy in the cell next to me." Lyon looked into the cell next to the boy's and saw a man without hair on his head who incessantly knocked himself on his head with the palm of his hand.

"It's about time that they kill him before he does it himself."

"I have to go on," said Lyon and went to the next cell. If he had stayed any longer, his kind heart would have ended up rescuing the friendly boy. But he couldn't risk their mission so foolhardily.

"Save me or I shall haunt you in your dreams! Damn you! Go on! Save me!" screamed the boy after him and rattled his iron bars like mad, "I shall haunt you in your dreams! You dirty dog!" Lyon ignored him. He had to find Eugene. They had already spent too much time down here.

Jim had a bad feeling. He didn't like these rooms at all.

"Ha-ha!" laughed a man with long dirt-encrusted hair in a cell. His hands were full of blood. The awful smell was unbearable. Here, too, every liquid the prisoners excreted flowed to the middle of the dungeon room and from there into the sewage containers underneath the Colloscoseum. The floor was slippery and like Lyon Jim had problems keeping his balance. He walked along the cells and looked inside, but there was no trace of Eugene. Slow came over and said, "I didn't find him. Lyon is still looking."

"He isn't here either. He must be where Lyon is. Let's go there." They nodded at each other and walked over to the third room of cells where Lyon was searching, always alert not to slip and land in the dirty mush. They spotted Lyon at the end of the room where he was looking through the bars into the cells.

"Lyon!" called Slow.

"Are you nuts? Don't shout like that or do you want them to catch us after all. What is wrong with you?" Jim scolded him. Lyon looked across and came towards them.

"Are you crazy, don't shout like that!"

"Don't tell me, tell that noisy brat here!"

"Doesn't matter now. Have you found him?"

"We actually thought that he would be with you."

"He wasn't here. Damn, where can he be?"

"In your dreams! Listen! You bastard!" shouted the boy.

"Who was that?" asked Jim.

"I found a boy. I asked him if he knew where Eugene was. But he didn't. He will be executed tomorrow."

"A boy?"

"Yes, do you think we could help him? He looked clean and cared for and I had the impression that he hasn't been here for long."

"We cannot endanger our mission to save a human being. If we fail, millions of other people and nations will suffer for it."

"You are right, but I feel sorry for him. And he could be useful for our mission."

"First we have to take care of Eugene. That is our first priority and if we then have a chance, we might just consider it," said Jim.

"That really means, not a chance," opined Lyon.

"We'll see. Eugene wasn't in Slow's room, nor in yours or mine. Therefore he must be somewhere else, in a fourth room. That must be here somewhere in the Colloscoseum."

"Let's look for him. But quickly, I have a bad feeling about this."

"About what?"

"About staying in here any longer, in this building of death. We have been undiscovered for too long, that cannot last much longer."

Lyon, Slow and Jim walked back through the passage that had taken them to the cells. After some yards they found a recess they had overlooked when passing earlier. They decided to enter. The passage they now followed was narrow and low so they had to walk behind each other. After a few steps, they reached a rotten wooden staircase. It was flooded with bright light that shone from above. Jim who was first in line stepped onto the staircase to test its stability by stamping on it. It was stable enough. The staircase ended far above at an arch through which very bright light flooded in. When they had climbed about half the staircase, Jim decided to go on ahead to check if there were enemies or other creatures up above. Quietly he hurried up the stairs that were no longer quite as rotten and stopped below the last five steps. He ducked and crawled up the last steps. Then he carefully glimpsed over the edge and tried to see something. There was a long passage with big light shafts on either side. The floor was sandy and the air dusty. At the end of the passage Jim could make out a wooden gate. Jim turned around and looked down to his companions. They stood there and looked up to him, he waved and they waved back to show they could see him. Jim gave them a sign to follow him. When they both reached Jim, they stepped into the passage. The sand crunched under their feet and the air scratched unpleasantly in their lungs. The light shafts provided the passage with enough light for them to see where they put their feet. Lyon removed some sand with his shoe to show wooden planks underneath.

"We must be on one of the top floors of the Colloscoseum."

"Why do you think that?"

"Look at the wooden floor. That is only used above the basement. So we are either at the same level as the stands or the arena, but not below it."

They heard a sound. A slurping and stamping. It came from the staircase they had just climbed. Smacking sounds, hissing and growling. Jim. Lyon and Slow ran to the wooden gate at the end of the passage and tried to open it. There was no handle or lever. The snorting and panting came closer; it must have reached the end of the stairs when the gate opened in front of them. Without looking what was approaching them, they ran through the gate....

Eugene wasn't in good shape, he was hungry and thirsty. The odours of rot and decay that were prevailing here drove him nearly mad and the darkness made him feel depressed. Leaning against the wooden door, he had fallen asleep out of exhaustion and pain. And now, as he woke up, his back ached. He got up groaning and rubbed his back with his left hand. One of the torches shed some light through the bars and made it easier to look for a more comfortable place to sit. The cell wasn't very big, but not that small either. He preferred to avoid the straw and hay, already rotted black. Opposite the door stood a shabby bench reminding him of his brief sojourn at the border post. He sat down on it. The hay and straw were now right next to him and the stench that emanated from there was simply dreadful and abominable. He took the bench and pulled it towards the door, away from the rotting hay. Then he sat down again, leant against the cold wall and closed his eyes. He had to think of food. What wouldn't he give to sit in Lyon's house eating a warm slice of bread and honey, drinking a nice, hot, sweet-smelling cup of tea. He had to think of the armchairs, the sun shining red behind the windows and the front garden with its equally red plants. Simply everything was red. How much he would love to know what the Earth used to look like. Had everything been red as well, or blue, maybe that was why it was called the Blue Planet? He had to do some research into that some time. With this thought in mind, he fell asleep.

Lyon, Slow and Jim were welcomed by a deafening roar. They had burst right into the arena. The sun was right above them and burnt down hot on their heads. The sight was breath-taking, but at the same time frightening. The Colloscoseum was incredibly huge. The stands were full of people and the noise was tremendous. They looked back and saw the gate through which they had entered. It was black, cracked and seemed to grin. "Damn it, we just sacrificed ourselves," cursed Slow.
"We've had it," remarked Lyon.
"We have an even bigger problem." Jim pointed at the gate, it was still open. A hunter emerged holding a leash in his hand. The leash led to a collar and this was round the neck of a lion-like creature. The lion roared as he saw the three standing on the sand and the hunter had to use all his force to keep it back. The crowd in the Colloscoseum shrieked with joy as the lion suddenly bit its master's thigh. Some leaned across the parapet to get a better view. Meanwhile the lion had taken another bite out of the bawling hunter's leg. The pain made the hunter collapse and the beast started to tear his innards from his belly and devour them. The sand took on the colour of Mars. Its brown mane flapped while it devoured its meal. Its beautiful golden coat was splattered with the hunter's

blood. The hunter groaned and tried to chase away the lion with weak punches, but the lion bit even harder. At the sight of his own entrails, the hunter lost consciousness which was probably for his own best.

"What are we going to do now?" asked Slow

"Beat it, while it is still busy with the hunter, I'd suggest."

"Yes, but it will easily catch up. Just look how big the arena is. Just to reach the other side will take us fifteen minutes. If we run, it'll take at least five minutes."

"You are right, but we have to do something. I am not going to allow a lion to eat me alive. No, painful thanks."

The lion was lying with its back towards them. Its munching could not be heard over the spectators' din. But they were sure that was what the animal was doing.

"I could shoot and kill it with my laser gun."

"Sure. That is it! Shoot it dead!"

"No, the guards would come and arrest us. If they arrest us, we cannot free Eugene and our mission is doomed."

"If we die, our mission is doomed as well!"

"We have to do something before it loses its taste for the hunter and comes after us."

"I suggest we run as far away from the lion as possible. That way we escape from it and you may not have to shoot it."

"Fine then, let's run to the other side of the arena."

"This discussion was unnecessary if I may say so," said Jim.

Hesitatingly, they started walking to avoid alerting the lion to their presence. When they were far enough away, they started running. The audience jeered. Stones were thrown at them but they were out of reach. The sand flew up beneath their feet and mingled with the air. The thick boards below the sand shook and trembled with a muffled sound under their steps that must have even been heard in the dungeon. The sun was unbearably hot.

"I am finished," Slow called over the roaring of the crowd.

"Come on, we're already half way there," shouted Lyon.

"If I run another step, I'll break down."

"The lion has not noticed anything yet, but if it does now, we are still too close." Slow had sat down in the sand, Lyon sat down next to him, and Jim gave a worried look at the lion that sat next to its victim far away, happily devouring its lunch.

"We have to go on!"

"No, let's just have a little breather," begged Slow.

"Oh well, it will be your fault if we all have to snuff it." Jim gave in and sat down in the sand opposite the others to keep an eye on the lion.

Now and then some stones were still thrown into the arena but for the most part spectators had realized that their victims were too far away from the stands to be hit. Slow lay down in the sand and closed his eyes. Jim lost his patience and sprang up.

"Guys! That is enough! You are lazing about in the sand while over there, not a hundred yards away there lies a lion tearing somebody to pieces."

"Now don't make a fuss! It is awfully busy, by the time it notices anything, we'll be long gone."

"Keep turning your backs on it if you like, and wait till it comes for a visit. I'm going on. Lyon, be reasonable!"

"Go on if you have enough breath to run all the way over there. We won't stop you," Slow retorted impudently.

Jim turned round and left, slowly to begin with, then faster and faster until he started running. He didn't look back, that was a favour he didn't want to do them. They shouldn't think that he was worried about them. He wasn't going to look back until he had arrived at the other end.

"Let him run if he enjoys it." Slow was irritated.

"Slow, seriously now, what is the matter?"

"What should be the matter?"

58

"You behave really strangely."

"Rubbish. Do you know what I think? I think he likes acting the boss. But he is not the boss."

"Who is the boss?"

"Nobody, nobody is the boss!" Slow shouted in a cross voice.

"Let's go on running. We are too close to the lion."

"No."

"Slow, what is up with you?"

"Nothing is up with me! Jim has gone mad. He acts like he was the boss. I should be the boss! I could lead you!" Slow's eyes started to shimmer and his pupils darted crazily to and fro. Lyon got up, looked at Slow nervously, and then looked at the lion. But it wasn't there anymore. The dead body lay lonely and savaged in the sand. The lion was approaching them in full gallop. It trailed blood, the sand whirled in its wake and its mane flew in time with its steps.

"Slow! The lion is coming, we have to run!" Slow turned round and saw the lion heading towards him. He gave a small choked shriek and sprang up.

"Run for your life!" Lyon called and started to run after Jim who was already at a distance. Slow stood still as if hypnotized and looked at the approaching lion.

"Slow!" Lyon called, "Come on!" And Slow gave a start, looked at Lyon and ran for it.

Far ahead ran Jim. By now he was quite close to the stands and the spectators started again to throw stones. Jim spotted an open gate to his right, he ran towards it trying to avoid the stones as best he could. One of the stones hissed past close to his ear and landed with a muffled thud in the sand, the boards underneath making it skip. He had nearly reached the gate, just a few more steps and he was safe. A stone hit his shin and he fell to his knees and collapsed. The enormous pain made him black out briefly. He felt his leg with his hand. Now a hail of stones was raining down on him. Groaning Jim got up to reach the gate as quickly as possible. He covered his head with both hands for protection. The entrance was very close now when another stone hit him. The pain hissed through his body and the punch made him lose his footing. The stone had hit his shoulder and its impact sent him tumbling into the sand. Another stone hit him on his forearm. Jim cried out in pain, the audience started to cheer. Crawling, he moved closer to the gate, stones dropping into the sand around him. Some found their mark but he no longer felt the pain, he was fully concentrated on the gate. Unsteadily he stood up, avoided a stone and ran towards the gate. The people in the front rows leaned over the parapet to take better aim. With a dive he saved himself through the gate. The crowd started to jeer again.

Lyon was now dangerously close to the audience, his chest ached and he started to lose control over his legs. Slow was far behind, the lion was catching up with him frighteningly fast. Lyon didn't look back even though he hadn't heard Slow's trampling steps behind him for a while. Jim waved from the gate and called his name. Lyon tried to guide his feet but they didn't respond any longer. Stones were falling down into the sand nearby, Lyon called up new strength, closed his eyes. He opened his eyes again and ran with his last bit of strength to the gate where Jim stood and waved. Just a few more big steps and he had done it. He ducked a stone that came dangerously close to his head. The crowd roared. Another three steps, the spectators leaned over the parapet yet again and shouted. A stone hit Lyon's thigh. He fell into the sand and held his leg. Jim rushed out, grabbed his arms and pulled him towards the gate. Stones rained down on them. Three more stones hit Lyon's back, one hit Jim's shoulder.

Finally they were safe.

"You're okay?" Jim asked.

"I think so." Jim knew he was lying but didn't contradict. Lyon's thigh was bleeding.

Slow ran towards the gate and screamed. The lion was dangerously close now. Jim started to wave. Slow ran towards him. Stones rained down on him. The lion roared and Slow speeded up with what was left of his strength.

"He won't make it," Jim said to Lyon, still lying on the floor. Jim started to wave again and to signal that he had to run faster.

"Slow told me he wants to be the boss. And he said that you are not the boss. And he started to shout. That was really frightening. I thought if I didn't agree he would attack me," said Lyon while trying to minister to his thigh.

"He has become weird," remarked Jim.

Slow ran and tried to avoid as many stones as possible. But it was impossible, he didn't have a chance. A stone hit him in the stomach and forced him to his knees. Groaning he tried to get up again when another stone hit his shoulder forcing him back down on his knees again and nearly toppled him backwards into the sand. In a moment the lion would be upon him.

"Lyon, your gun! Quickly!" demanded Jim.

"Jim, you know our mission must not fail."

"Yes, I know but we must save him."

"No. We cannot save him."

"What the hell, Lyon, give me your gun. That is an order!"

"I am sorry but we cannot risk that...."

"Lyon, please!" pleaded Jim.

"No..."

Slow felt the sun on his neck, the warmth. He felt the hard wooden floor underneath the sand, warmed by the sun. And he felt the pain in his stomach and in his shoulder.

Why hadn't he listened to Jim and had run? A third stone hit him in the chest and took his breath away; another heavy one hit his forearm. He was trying to get up again when two more stones hit his thigh and he sank back to the floor. He looked up to the sun, smiled briefly and closed his eyes. His thoughts wandered. Suddenly he felt a sense of freedom. The lion ran towards him. Slow wasn't aware of it anymore. With a powerful jump, the lion leapt and threw Slow heavily to the floor. Then it rammed its powerful teeth into his neck.

"Lyon, Slow is on your conscience! You bloody bastard of a dog!"
Lyon looked at Jim appalled as the latter ran past him into the passage where the darkness swallowed him.
"Jim! Wait! You do understand, don't you, why I couldn't give you the gun. We discussed that earlier! Now wait for me! Thanks to you, the whole mission might fail yet!" Lyon tried to get up and after several futile attempts he eventually managed to do so. Limping he hurried after Jim. Finally, after a few steps, darkness surrounded him and he couldn't see anything. Blindly he ran on until he perceived some light at the end of the passage. He speeded up. The air took on its familiar damp and musty odour. Panting he stopped because he had reached the end of the passage. Lyon was holding his side, leaned against the wall and took deep breaths. His side and his thigh hurt. When his stitch subsided a little, he peeked round the corner. There was no-one to be seen. He entered the room. It stretched for a long way to the left and gave into a smaller room. There was nothing in this room, it was absolutely empty. The muffled sound of water could be heard from somewhere.
"Where has he run to?" Lyon talked to himself. He rubbed his face with his black gloved hand. Then he adjusted his

black coat and made his way to the next room hoping to meet Jim there.

Jim ran. The walls flew past him He didn't pay attention if hunters or guards were in the room. Right then, he didn't give a damn. "How could he not give me the gun? How could he let him die?" He slowed his steps. He stopped, rubbed his face with his hands. In the room where Jim stood, there were shelves on the wall. They were made of the same greasy old wood. They reached all the way to the ceiling and were brim-full of weapons, helmets and shields, lances and daggers. There was nobody around, so Jim walked on to the door at the other end of the room. He looked at the weapons and other things lying on the shelves and wondered if they might not come in handy. Finally he decided that some of them might serve as disguise and protection at the same time. Jim approached one of the shelves and looked at the equipment. A silver helmet to hide the face caught his eye. He took it and put it on. It fitted like a glove. One of the torches that lit the room flickered. Jim looked around, but couldn't see anything suspicious. He felt queasy. The torch flickered again. Jim looked at the door where he had come from, it was open. Had he closed it after entering the room? He couldn't remember. He went to the door and closed it firmly. He felt very queasy now. Jim turned around to go back to the shelves when Lyon stood suddenly in front of him. Jim started.

"Lyon! Are you nuts? Do you want to kill me, too? Isn't it enough that you have Slow on your conscience?"

"Jim, you have to understand. I couldn't give you the weapon. We had discussed it. The guards would have arrested us and our mission would have failed. What happened to Slow is regrettable but it happened and we cannot make it undone."

"That is not easy to understand. Especially not, if you have to watch your best friend die."

"I am sorry, Jim. I wish things had been different. Don't blame me, but blame those who sit on the stands and laugh and shout," said Lyon.

"I don't want to talk about it anymore. Let's rescue Eugene and get away from this damned planet!"

"Okay, Jim. What about the helmet?" asked Lyon. Jim realized that he still held the silver helmet in his hand.

"I thought if I put on a disguise, I'll not be recognized so easily. And I'll also arm myself with it."

"Good idea."

Both stepped up to a shelf and chose the things they liked. Many items were rusted or broken. But most were still functioning. Jim put on the silver helmet, a coat of chainmail and a sword belt. Now all he needed was a sword. Lyon had chosen a bronze helmet that went perfectly with his golden eyes. He put on a belt with two swords in it. Meanwhile Jim had found a sword that fit and put it in his sheath. Lyon took a beautifully decorated dagger and put it in his pocket. Now they were properly equipped. The quest for freedom could begin.

Jim opened the door and had a look what was behind it.

"Another dungeon," he said.

"Eugene has to be here," stated Lyon.

"You take the cells on the left; I take those on the right."

"Will do," said Lyon and they started looking for Eugene. Lyon tried to take shallow breaths, the poisoned air turning his stomach. Some doors were made of wood and only had small barred windows. They had to call inside and hope for an answer. As in the other rooms earlier, the excrements were running to the middle of the room and through the drains to the collecting tank. The air became stuffier, the closer they came to the cell doors. Jim was convinced that they could have held only little oxygen.

Lyon stopped in front of a wooden door, stretched himself to be able to shout into the cell and nearly lost his balance. When Eugene's head suddenly appeared behind the bars, he fell irrevocably to the dirty floor.

"Oh damn it!" he shouted and Jim looked across.

"What are you doing there?" Jim couldn't keep back a grin.

"Stop looking so stupidly and be kind enough to come over here. I have found him."

Jim came across. "At last! How do we get him out of there?"

"We have to force the door open."

"Lyon, couldn't you use your gun to shoot it open?"

"I might injure Eugene."

"Eugene?"

"Yes?"

"Lyon is going to shoot the door lock open with his laser. Can you protect yourself somehow?"

"Not directly. But do it anyway, I want to get out of here!"

"There you are, Lyon, shoot that damned door open."

"Well then, if you want me to. Take cover!" Lyon reached into his black coat and pulled out a gun. It was long, black and had a silver butt. Lyon took aim and fired. The laser beam penetrated the wood of the door and destroyed the lock. Bits of wood flew through the air like dangerous projectiles. Lyon fired three more times and then let the gun drop. Around the points of contact the wood was charred. Eugene kicked against the door from the inside, it didn't budge. Jim and Lyon took a step backwards. Eugene kicked it again, a crack opened near the lock. Eugene kicked yet again with all his might. The door burst open and fell with a loud bang on the muddy floor.

"I am so glad to see you. I started to think I would meet my end in this hole."

"Did you think we would let you down? You won't believe the things we have been through to save you."

"Where is Slow?" Jim's head drooped.

"He didn't make it. We tell you everything once we are safe," said Lyon.

"I am sorry to hear that."

"We have to get out of here, quickly."

"You are right but where is the exit?"

"We'll have to look for it."

Carefully they approached the passage, always trying to avoid slipping on the wet floor. The gateway opened into a passage lit by torches. They followed it; it was wide enough to walk side by side.

"Be quiet!" Lyon ordered suddenly. "Do you hear that?"

"What? I don't hear anything."

"Shush," Eugene this time, "I can hear it, too. It sounds like a cold. I mean as if someone was sniffling."

"Those are sniffers! Go on, follow me!" Lyon called.

"What are sniffers?" Eugene asked and looked at Jim who shrugged his shoulders. They followed Lyon running down the passage. Eugene looked back and could just make out some small four-legged creatures that were following them into the passage. Then there was a bend and the sniffers disappeared from view. Now they were running toward a stone staircase, Jim and Eugene had caught up a bit with Lyon and they were nearly abreast again.

"Sniffers are smaller versions of the devils. They have long legs and therefore can run faster. Their eyes glow red and their teeth are pointed and long, their bodies are sinewy and very small. They cannot stand sunlight and live in caves."

They ran up a flight of steps. There were only a few steps, then there was a bend and they ran along a passage. They reached another staircase running up those steps, too. It was very steep and they tripped several times, often clutching each other to avoid falling down. At the top all they could do was turn the corner and run up some more stairs. Behind them the sniffers started screaming. They were sharp cries, very short but constantly repeated. Their screams echoed on the smooth walls and stung the ears of the fleeing trio. At the top of the stairs another steep small staircase descended into the darkness and there were passages on either side.

"What do you suggest?" Lyon asked wheezing.

"We should be at the same level as the stands. We have to go back down," said Jim.

"Oh great," Eugene groaned.

Followed by the sniffers and their sharp cries, they rushed down the small stairway into the darkness. The stair was only sparsely lit and they had to move slowly to avoid falling down. The steps were becoming red with sand. Once at the bottom they ran straight to a gate. The red sand beneath their feet was damp. After crossing half the room, the sand turned to a red muddy mass. Slipping and sliding they came to a stop in front of the door. Lyon turned the door handle and the door opened. Quickly they stepped through. They turned to the left and ran down yet another passage until they reached a gateway. They entered quickly. It was a similar room to the one they had passed on their way into the Colloscoseum. On the left and right were columns and in the centre there was a square stone block lit by torches. On the other side of the great hall there was a small staircase like the one where they had entered.

"Come on, we've nearly made it!"

"How can you be so sure?"

"I can feel it!" Lyon called and ran ahead.

Jim and Eugene followed him, one after the other they stormed up the small stairway. The sniffers had caught up and their screams were louder than ever. Far away, they could discern a square spot of light.

"Look, there is the exit!"

"I very much hope that you aren't wrong."

As quickly as the steep stairs allowed, they rushed towards the spot of light. The sniffers stood at the bottom of the stairs and looked up, their red eyes sparkling eerily in the dark. They had stopped pursuing them.

"Why don't they follow us?"

"Sniffers are overly sensitive to sunlight. Their realm is the darkness. The light up there must be sunlight. We have found an exit, guys!"

Slowly it grew warmer and the air fresher. Soon they were able to see the steps and put down their feet securely without slipping or stumbling. At the top they stepped out into freedom. The sun welcomed them with his bright rays; the three comrades leaned against the red ornate wall of the Colloscoseum in exhaustion and caught their breath. Eugene was sick from running, Lyon held his side and Jim hung his head and breathed heavily.

"Come along, I want to get away from this damned building and off this planet," said Eugene.

"He is right, we can have a rest in the jet," agreed Jim. Lyon nodded and they started their way across the city. They put some distance between themselves and the Colloscoseum and the Black Circle and returned to the city with its narrow streets and little houses. Nothing had changed. Vendors were trying to sell their caps, the square full of people selling drinks and hot dogs. As quickly as possible they squeezed through the crowd till they turned into a street that was somewhat less busy. The further they moved from the Colloscoseum, the emptier the streets became until finally there was hardly anyone about.

"If you don't mind, I'd like to know now what happened to Slow," said Eugene cautiously.

"Fine," was all Jim said. Then he started to recount how they had gone to the Colloscoseum to free him, how they had outwitted the guard and searched the dungeons, how they ended up in the arena, fled from the lion and finally how he had argued with Lyon about the laser-gun while Slow was being torn to pieces. Once he had finished, nobody said a word.

There were only a few houses now, the street hardly deserved to be called that. Soon they were surrounded by red desert. Far away their space jet reflected the sunlight.

Once they had reached the jet, they decided to take a rest to recover their strength. In the two-storey jet each team member had his own room. In the main room there was a spiral staircase leading to the upper floor. The few windows that were in the jet had been covered to keep out the heat of the sun and its light. When Eugene woke up, he went to the single window in his room, opened the blind and looked outside. The sun had already gone down and it was dark. Far away the stars twinkled. He turned around and left his room. The doors to Jim's and Lyon's rooms were closed. Probably they were still asleep. He sneaked to the top of the stairs and quietly went downstairs. If they were still asleep, he didn't want to be the one to wake them. At the bottom he crept through the common room and slid through the door leading to the galley of the jet. Here the blinds were not pulled in front of the windows and the stars bathed the steel cupboards in a silvery light. Eugene crossed the galley and opened the walk-in fridge. Shortly after opening the door, the neon-lights came on and showed him the way. Eugene was impressed as he slowly entered the voluminous fridge, cold air filling his lungs. There were drawers on either side reaching up to the ceiling. Eugene pulled one open indiscriminately and looked inside. There were frozen rolls and other bakery items. Eugene took a bag of strangely shaped croissants and opened the next drawer. Here he found frozen cakes and pastries. He closed it again and opened another one. There were hundreds of different kinds of cold meats and pâtés. Yet another one was full of jam jars. With arms full of meat, jam and bread, Eugene returned to the exit. In the galley he put down his booty on the wooden table and closed the fridge door with a quiet "plop". He went to a drawer in the galley and pulled it open. From the cutlery therein he chose a knife and cut open the bag with the frozen rolls. He took a couple from the bag and put them in the oven to bake them until they had a nice crust. How much he was looking forward to a really nice breakfast.

"A wonderful good morning, Eugene. You are awake already?" Lyon stepped through the door and yawned while stretching himself.

"The same to you, Lyon. Breakfast? I am baking some rolls for myself. If you'd like some, too, I'll put some more in the oven."

"That would be nice. I'll help you. Let's make breakfast for all."

"Shall I help you?" Jim now joined them coming in through the galley door.

"Of course."

They all looked for something to do and started to prepare a delicious breakfast. After spreading the table with loads of delicious food, they started to eat. There was something to suit everyone and after a while they all had had enough. It had been a very long time since Eugene had eaten that much. Thinking about it, he couldn't remember ever having eaten quite so much.

"I am going to start the jet. We're flying to the Forest Moon of Jupiter to pick up our fifth member."

They all looked at the floor, embarrassed, thinking about Slow. Jim got up and left the galley to go to the cockpit. Lyon and Eugene started to clear the table and after finishing, moved into the common room.

"What do you think, will he cope with it?" Eugene asked Lyon while sitting down on the simple couch.

"It will take some time till he can cope, he will never forget," answered Lyon and sat down on one of the chairs. "Jim is quite angry with me because I refused to give him the gun."

"You couldn't endanger your mission," said Eugene but didn't sound very convincing. "Besides it was my fault. If I hadn't ended up in the Colloscoseum, Slow would still be alive."

"Nobody is to blame. Slow could still be alive if he had listened to us."

"It happened the way it happened. What's done is done. You cannot change anything; he has to cope with it. Slow was on a mission, he could have died any time. It happened to be here. Maybe we all have to die. Our future has not been written yet. We don't know what to expect."

"Don't say that. My plan is to use the money we get as a reward to go looking for a beautiful planet and live there. Away from Mars. To live on Mars is awful. Everyday those deafening trumpets. At night the streets are teeming with unpleasant types and during daytime everybody is in the Colloscoseum. Eventually you either go absolutely bonkers like everybody else or you lock yourself into your home until you rot."

"I've had enough of Mars already. I never ever want to come back here," agreed Eugene. Somewhere in the jet the engine hummed.

"I'll go and check on Jim," said Lyon, got up and went to the cockpit.

What was it about the house he always dreamed about? What was it called, the House of Time? Why did he always dream about it? It seemed to him that he must have been there at some point. Why did it look different in every new nightmare? Well, that was because it was a dream. Dreams are often confusing. What was the House of Time after all? To whom belonged the strange voice in his head? He had to question Jim about that.

Lyon came through the door and interrupted his thoughts. "We are going to land soon on the Forest Moon of Jupiter," he said and disappeared again into the cockpit. Eugene got up and followed him. Jim sat on a chair and piloted the jet. Lyon sat next to him.

"We are going to land in a few minutes," said Jim. Eugene looked through the windscreen into space and saw Jupiter. After some time he spotted the Forest Moon, it gleamed in a green colour.

"Who are we picking up?" Eugene wanted to know.

"He is a forest guard and has lived through many adventures. You ought to know, however, that he is a robot. An older one. He is made of metal, not like the newer models that are all made from organic materials and even bleed and feel pain when they are injured."

"Do we have to go and find him or is he expecting us?"

"We're arriving unexpectedly. Unfortunately it was impossible to contact him beforehand. But we know where he works on the moon and when. We know where he lives, when he finishes work, and we also know where his friends live."

"Finding him shouldn't be too difficult then," said Eugene. There was silence and they all looked at the green moon as they approached it and Jupiter slowly disappeared behind them. Soon there was only forest ahead of them. Then they could make out individual trees and eventually they were able to see individual branches.

"We are flying to the only town on the Forest Moon. It is called Hio and is in the middle of the jungle. Only robots live on this moon because they don't need oxygen. As you know, all the oxygen produced by the plants is diverted to the four urban moons."

"How many robots live on the moon?" Eugene wanted to know.

"They have never been counted, but at a guess I would say about three thousand."

"How long are we going to stay here?"

"Until we have found our team member."

"Why do you always say our member and do not call him by his name. He does have a name, doesn't he?"

"Yes, he has a name. A very stupid one. He finds it embarrassing to bear that name. Maybe he should tell you himself."

"Come on, tell me. I am not going to laugh."

"You must promise me to pretend that you don't know his name. Can you do that? You are not going to call him by his real name until he has introduced himself."

"Fine, now tell me, I am dying with curiosity."

"His name is Rob."

"It's not that bad to be called 'Rob' as a robot." Eugene couldn't help smiling but it wasn't that funny after all. Jim exaggerated a bit.

"Oh yes, it is very bad, believe me." Jim looked at him with an earnest gaze.

In front of them the silver, golden and glass points of high-rise buildings towered into the sky like swords sticking out of the green carpet around them. As they approached Hio, the runway came into view. Jim prepared to land. He parked the jet in one of the parking spots for "Long Stay", and then they proceeded to the common room and walked down the hatchway onto the Forest Moon. The air was incredibly fresh and in the truest sense of the word unbreathed. A light breeze blew through the tree tops and made the branches tremble. Accompanied by the slight rustling of the trees, they walked to the square building at the end of the runway. There was total silence. On the roof, the helium lamps pronounced "Welcome to Hio."

"What are we doing in the building?"

"Everybody who lands on the Forest Moon has to register. He is assigned a hotel and a means of transport."

They entered the building through a very creaky revolving door and found themselves in a dark room. Jim stepped up to the wooden counter and rang the dome-shaped bell. On the equally wooden ceiling a ventilator did its lonely laps. Eugene wondered who it was going round for. Robots had certainly no use for it. Shortly afterwards someone came clattering from the backroom.

"Welcome! I am Jack. What can I do for you?" asked the robot. He sounded a bit tinny and his mouth didn't move when speaking.

"We are travellers and want to visit a friend who works on this moon. We're planning to stay two days," said Jim.

"Very good. Please sign your names here." Jack the robot pushed a thick book across the counter. Each page was split into columns. Everybody signed their name in the column, and then Jack took the book back and said:

"I am going to call you a taxi that will take you into town to your hotel."

"Thank you." They sat down on a dusty bench in the corner and the robot disappeared into the backroom.

"Who is going to pay for our stay in the hotel?"

"Our boss. The whole operation is paid for."

"Where are we going to find Rob?"

"He is on reconnaissance in the forest all day. He will be back home in the evening or at night. Then we are going to see him."

"Are there any rules of conduct I have to follow?" Eugene ran his fingers through his black hair and looked about the room. All furniture was made of dark wood, even the floor was dark brown. On the ceiling next to the ventilator there was a small lamp with two lightbulbs, one of which actually worked.

"Not really. Just be normal, behave appropriately."

"Good to know. I don't want to end up in a damp dungeon again."

"That is not likely to happen here. The town is very clean, there is virtually no crime and even accidents are very rare."

"That is reassuring. Is it a big town?"

"No, there are many high-rise buildings but the town has only an area of about two square miles."

"What are we going to do till tonight. I mean if Rob only comes home at night, we have to wait for him all day."

"We are going to visit a few sights, go to a few shops and have a meal. There isn't much to do, this is no tourist destination, you know."

"I don't understand that. This paradise out there could easily become a superb holiday spot."

"This moon delivers air for four cities that are so big that each covers a whole moon. The central government of the Jupiter moons particularly protects this moon. Not even fires in the grate are allowed."

"How are we going to move about?"

"With horse-drawn cabs and coaches. Sounds a bit unusual for a moon inhabited by robots but nothing else is allowed. Only means of transport that do not pollute the air. Electricity is produced by photovoltaics."

Outside the revolving door, a cab stopped. Up front sat a robot, glittering silvery in the sun, looking out of blue shining eyes. He waved haltingly with his hand. On his chest was a sign saying "Taxi Service HIO."

"There is your taxi. Have fun in town," said Jack and disappeared again into the backroom.

"Thank you," Jim called after him but they didn't know if

he had heard it. They stepped outside.

"A very good morning to you from your Taxi Service in Hio. I am Julo 4 and will take you to your destination. Please tell me your destination."

"Town centre, Hotel Golden Forest," said Jim and got in. Eugene and Lyon followed him. Once they were all seated, they started. Over a small bumpy road they left the airport area. The road became wider and less bumpy until they were finally able to go at a fair speed. They passed trees that were so high that their tops seemed to brush the clouds. All kinds of plants were represented. On the ground, flowers bloomed in all colours. Mosses and dark green grass sprouted up in-between and gave the forest a colourful face. There was a sea of flowers. In-between towered the brown trunks of the monster trees. Conifers, deciduous trees, trees with fruit, trees with flowers, or trees with red leaves, every imaginable type was there. The black tarmac road ran like a straight line through the jungle until Hio suddenly appeared before them, with its high-rises they had already seen from the jet, its milky white air containers and other remarkable things. On both sides of the road there were huge skyscrapers, there didn't seem to be a single building that was less than three hundred feet high. The pavements were decorated with trees and flowerpots. Everything was very clean. They approached the town centre and thus the old town and their hotel. The road turned into a cobbled street. There were fountains everywhere, shooting their water jets into the air. There weren't many cabs going the other way. Finally they stopped outside a prettily decorated building. There was beautiful tall writing above the entrance: Hotel Golden Forest. The cab stopped in front of it.

"Thank you," said Jim and they got out after having paid, of course.

"I wish you lots of fun on our moon," said the robot and

drove away.

On a red carpet they entered the hotel. The walls were partly painted red. The upper half was painted in white. The entrance hall was expensively and beautifully carpeted and the walls were hung with lavish oil paintings by famous artists. The ceiling was decorated with white stucco and a golden chandelier gave out a warm light.

They approached the wooden counter decorated with notches and were welcomed by a robot dressed in a dinner jacket.

"I wish you a wonderful good day and a warm welcome to our Hotel Golden Forest. What can I do for you?" said the robot without tinny accent and with real lip movements.

"Good morning. We've got a reservation for a room for three and would like to register and to collect our key."

"Well, what is your name?" The robot looked at the computer screen in front of him.

"Jim, Lyon and Eugene," said Jim.

"Yes, we have the reservation. One moment, please, I'll go and get your room key."

"Of course."

The robot turned around and walked to a cupboard with glass doors. He opened it with a bronze key and extracted a little silver key.

"There you are. Your room is on the thirtieth floor and has picture windows with a view over the air containers and the forest. Kosjor will show you the way."

"Thank you." They turned round. Behind them stood a robot in red clothing. He took Jim's suitcase. Then he started walking and they followed him. They walked beneath the resplendent chandelier and passed designer chairs and tables on their way to the elevator. Once there, Kosjor pressed the button and only seconds later the cabin came to a standstill on the ground floor. The automatic door opened and they stepped inside. Kosjor pressed the button for the thirtieth floor and the bronze coloured door closed again. The elevator started with a slight jolt. Eugene's stomach seemed to sink to his knees. He felt dizzy as if all his organs were sliding down to his legs. With incredible speed the elevator shot up to the thirtieth floor. Arriving there the elevator slowed down and everybody's heart seemed to jump into their heads. Dizzily they left the cabin. They had trouble following Kosjor who had already walked on. Swaying slightly they rushed after him. To the right and left there were the most expensive doors set into the wall. The floor was carpeted and kitschy baroque lamps hung from the ceiling. They turned into a corridor and saw Kosjor standing in front of a door. They hurried to him. He unlocked the door and entered, the others following him. The reception robot had not exaggerated. The room had three four-poster beds decorated with light blue hangings. The window took up the whole wall and offered a view over a quarter of the town, including air containers and forest. The floor was made of light-coloured wood and covered with beautiful carpets. There were also a desk, a shelf filled with books and a chest of drawers. Kosjor put down the suitcase at the end of the bed and showed them the room.

"This is the door to the bathroom," he said and opened it. The walls of the bathroom were covered from top to bottom with tiles in a warm colour and boasted a washbasin surrounded by marble. The shower cubicle was made of marble as well. The toilet was in a separate room with a ventilation system. The heated floor was covered with a soft carpet and a white shelf was filled with white towels embellished with the hotel logo. Handing him a tip, Jim thanked Kosjor who retreated with a slight bow.

"This room is absolutely fantastic," stated Lyon and Eugene nodded in agreement.

Jim stood in front of the bookshelf and looked at the

78

provided books.

"Who wants to sleep where?" asked Eugene and lay down on the bed next to the bathroom door.

"I'll sleep next to the big window!" Lyon went to the bed he had claimed and as he dropped down onto it, he rebounded.

"Jim, I think you have to sleep in this one," said Lyon and pointed to the one next to the room door. Jim looked up from the bookshelf and nodded. Lyon started again to bounce on the bed.

"It's like being a child again," said Lyon and laughed.

They headed back to the elevator to go to the top floor. On the roof of the hotel, there was a rotating restaurant. Since it was lunchtime and they felt hungry, they decided to eat there. The elevator door opened and they entered. Jim pressed the button for the ninetieth floor and the elevator started moving. Before leaving, they had all taken a shower and washed their hair in the marble cubicle. That had been more than necessary after the ordeal on Mars. The elevator stopped and the door slid sideways. The corridor in front of them was hung with pictures and lined with palm trees. The elevator door closed behind them and they walked along the corridor. It ended in a big dining room. Most of the tables were taken, nearly all of them by robots. A robot dressed as a waiter approached them.

"Good day, gentlemen. Can I help you?" he asked politely.

"We'd like a table for three by the window, please."

"Of course, please follow me."

The dining room was even bigger than it had seemed at first. There was a bar with bar stools and about a hundred tables. The waiter guided them to a table next to a window. Eugene looked outside. There were high-rises outside. Some were taller than the hotel. The forest behind the city stretched to the horizon. The streets were small lines.

Coaches and cabs were undistinguishable. To their right at a fair distance, Eugene was able to make out the airport where they had landed a few hours ago. The restaurant moved round slowly in a circle so it was possible to see all parts of town.

Jim, Lyon and Eugene sat down at their table

"What would the gentlemen like to drink?" asked the polite waiter.

"We would like to have a look at the drinks menu, please."

"Very well, I am going to fetch it for you." The waiter left and disappeared between the tables and palm trees.

"I like it here very much. Why there aren't more tourists here, I don't understand," said Eugene and smoothed the white-and-red chequered tablecloth.

"That is a mystery to me as well. But we should be glad, so we have some peace and quiet."

"Tourists just aren't wanted here," said Jim.

"Gentlemen, the drinks menus." The waiter gave each of them a menu and thanking him, they took them. Jim opened his. There were many exotic things like oil on ice or Robocola. But there also were normal things like water or juice and even lemonade, wine or whisky.

"I would like water with ice, please," Eugene ordered.

"And for me a cold beer," said Lyon.

"I'll have some Hiobian wine and a small glass of water, please."

"Thank you." The waiter disappeared again.

"These buildings are magnificent. Compared to them, the buildings on Mars are like snail shells," observed Lyon and looked out of the window.

"Talking about houses and buildings. Jim, have you ever heard about a building that is called the House of Time?"

"I don't know but I have a feeling that I have heard that name before. What makes you ask?"

"I dream about it nearly every night."

"Eugene, you mustn't believe everything you dream about. Dreams grow out of your imagination. They are fiction," said Lyon.

"No, this is different. It is as if I had experienced it."

"As if you had experienced it? Experienced what?"

"I don't know. But I am going to find out, somehow."

"What do think about going to the library? After lunch. It should be nearby. We could walk there. Maybe we find a book that tells us something about the House of Time. We have to wait till evening anyway to go looking for Rob."

"Good plan."

Meanwhile the waiter had served their drinks and taken their food orders. After a short while, their food stood in front of them, giving off delicious aromas, and they consumed it with good appetites. The revolving restaurant moved very slowly and when they had finished eating and Jim paid the bill, they had a good view over the old town. There the buildings weren't quite so high and many were made of stone and not of iron and concrete like the modern ones. They said good-bye to their waiter and took the elevator to the ground floor. With the sound of a bell, the door opened and they stepped out into the lobby.

Their lungs filled with fresh air while they walked along the cobbled path past bubbling fountains, crowded cafes and shops to the library. It was about twenty storeys high and richly decorated. On the square outside the entrance, a splashing fountain provided a relaxing atmosphere. The entrance was reached via a staircase and the door was seven feet high and two yards wide. The stairs were made of stone and there were lanterns on its banister. Jim, Lyon, and Eugene ascended the stairs and the door opened automatically. A red carpet showed them the way into the library. The entrance hall was very high and the marble floor was covered with beautiful old carpets. On the left wall were windows as high as the room; on the right wall were pictures of all the librarians. In front was the reception. Lyon looked up at the ceiling, which was impressively painted with a scene of bygone days. The air was cool and smelled of printer's ink. Together they approached the stone counter of the reception.

"How can I help you?" asked the reception robot.

"We need information about famous buildings."

"Buildings on certain planets, moons or in cities?"

"We don't know that. That is why we are here to find some information."

"Do you have the name of the building?"

"The House of Time."

"I am afraid I cannot help you. But maybe you'll find something about it on the eighth floor."

"Thank you."

They went to the only other door that led out of the room. Jim opened it and walked through. The room behind it was incredibly high, too. In the centre there were stairs that ended on a square platform. There were tables with reading lights and chairs. Around the top of the stairs the whole room was filled with bookshelves all the way up to the ceiling. There was total silence, apart from the occasional rustling of paper. The elevator was on the other side of the room. They turned right and walked across the room. Eugene pressed the button to call the elevator. It arrived after a moment's wait and they stepped inside once the door had opened. The elevator had a mirrored wall. Eugene looked at himself in the mirror all the way up. He was tanned and his black hair hung openly in his face. Meanwhile they had become used to the speed of the elevators. The upstairs room wasn't like the one at the bottom at all. It was low and had no tables with lights or chairs. There were no stairs that met to form a square. Ahead of them were endless rows of shelves that ran all

the way to the opposite wall, filled with books, of course.
"This will take us a few hours."
"Then let's better make a start." And so they started. Each
of them took a row of shelves. Once one row was finished,
they moved on to the next.
"I've got something. *Famous Houses of our Time*." Eugene
held up a dusty and faded brown book. Some pages had
come loose and threatened to fall out. He pushed them
back into the book.
"Read it out loud," said Jim. Eugene looked up the list of
contents. The pages were yellowed and he had trouble
reading the old script.
"Nothing about the House of Time."
"Let's go on looking," said Lyon and flung his arms in the
air. With the draft this gesture caused, he whirled up a lot
of dust. He had to sneeze. While searching they found
more books with similar titles:

- *Famous Cities.*
- *Destroyed Cities of Earth Vol. 1.*
- *Destroyed Cities of Earth Vol. 2.*
- *Cities with More than Twenty Million Inhabitants.*
- *Cities with Famous Buildings.*
- *Buildings of 2789.*
- *Buildings Everybody Should Know Vol. 1.*
- *Buildings Everybody Should Know Vol. 2.*
- *Buildings Everybody Should Know Vol. 3.*
- *Buildings Everybody Should Know Vol. 4.*
- *Buildings Planned but Never Built.*
- *Houses on Mars.*
- *Cities without Inhabitants Vol. 1 & 2.*
- *Cities without Inhabitants Vol. 3 & 4.*
- *Everything about the Colloscoseum.*
- *All Buildings on Hio and Their Uses.*
- *Capitals of Earth.*

- Buildings Built Without Plans.
- Why Neptune Is No Longer Called Neptune.
- The Smallest House of the Universe.

They found many more books but none of them was of any help in their search for the House of Time. Finally they gave up. Outside the sun was setting and their eyes hurt from the constant reading. They took the elevator back down to the ground floor and left the library. Once outside they decided to eat an ice-cream before starting their search for their fifth member. They went to the ice-cream parlour next to the library and sat outside under a sunshade. A robot came to take their order. The glass fronts of the high-rises shimmered red in the setting sun. Everything was quiet, there wasn't even a breeze, and only now and then some voices could be heard. From inside the cafe the scent of ice-cream and waffles wafted outside and mingled with the scent of the nearby forest. Only now did they realize how hungry they were.

"It's a real shame we didn't find anything. Maybe the House of Time only exists in your imagination after all."

"I'll keep on looking till I have found an answer."

The waiter returned with a tray and placed the ice-cream sundaes on the table.

"I know that I have never eaten ice-cream in all my life and yet I have the strange feeling that I have done it," said Eugene.

"One thing I promise, Eugene, should we survive this mission, I'll help you to find out everything there is to know about your past," said Jim. Eugene thanked him. He really hoped very much that that day would finally come. After they had finished their ice-cream and Jim had paid for them all, they set off for Rob's apartment to pick him up. Lyon called a taxi and they got in after it had stopped next to them.

"To the eastern side of town, guard centre, street number eight, house number three," Jim told the driver. Lyon and Eugene sat down next to Jim and the cab started moving. At the next intersection they took a left turn.

"These are the apartments for the guards. The guards check the quality of the air and the state of health of the forest," explained Jim and answered the questions Eugene and Lyon had on the tip of their tongues. Finally the taxi stopped and they got out. To reach the front door, they had to climb small shallow steps. At the top, Jim rang the bell. Shortly afterwards the buzzer hummed. Jim opened the door and they entered.

"Which room does he live in?" asked Eugene.

"That is what we have to find out, we don't know everything after all," said Jim and approached the counter that stood forlornly in the big room. The floor was covered in white tiles; the walls were painted white as was the ceiling. There were spotlights on the ceiling that illuminated the room. At the counter sat a robot reading a newspaper.

"Excuse me?" Jim announced himself. The robot took the newspaper from his face and looked at each of them.

"How can I help you?"

"We are looking for a guard called Rob."

"One moment, I'll check the staff list."

"Thank you."

The robot opened his laptop and started looking.

"I have several Robs. Does the one you are looking for have a number or a second name?"

"No, not that we know of."

"The first one lives on the third floor in room 323. The second in room 334, also on the third floor. The third one lives on the eleventh floor in room 1142. And the last one in room 3588 on floor 35."

"Thank you," said Jim again. They went to the elevator and went up to the third floor. With a quiet clicking the door opened.

"He said room 323. That is to the left."

Up here everything was kept in white as well, even the doors.

"Here it is, room 323." Jim knocked. Nobody answered, Jim knocked again. Again no-one answered. After another five futile tries, they gave up and decided to move on to the next one, room 334.

Once there Jim knocked. It only took a moment for the door to be opened.

"Hello." A female robot had opened the door.

"Hello, we'd like to speak to Rob."

"I am Rob, what is it about?"

"I am sorry, we must have mistaken the door. We are looking for another Rob. Sorry."

"Don't worry."

"Good-bye." She closed the door and Jim, Lyon, and Eugene went back to the elevator to go up to the eleventh floor.

"I didn't know that there were female Robs as well."

"Nor did I. But why not?"

The eleventh floor looked like a perfect copy of the third floor. At room 1142 Jim knocked and after a few seconds the door was opened.

"Hello," said Rob.

"Hello, Rob. These are Eugene and Lyon," said Jim.

"Hello."

"Can we come in?"

"Of course." Rob stepped aside. "I have already been informed about everything, but didn't expect you until tomorrow."

Rob's apartment was sparsely furnished and in some places a bit run-down. The air was fresh thanks to an open window. The wall was painted white; the floor was laid with parquet. The three doors of the room were red and looked new. The kitchen to the left of the apartment door was directly next to the bathroom door and on the other side of the room was the bedroom door. A cheap spotlight adorned the ceiling. The table was packed with useless stuff and had probably become the second bin of the apartment quite a while ago. A pretty chest of drawers stood between bathroom and kitchen, on top of it was a clock.

Rob closed the equally red door behind them. In some places the fresh paint had already started to crack.

Rob pulled out three chairs away from the bin table and put them in the middle of the room. They sat down.

"What is the latest information?" Jim asked.

"I have been informed that a secret, extremely dangerous mission is taking place, the destruction of the drad control ship. Because of my qualifications, I am member number five."

"Right. We need your technological support with computer communication and the like. We have made a long and arduous journey and had to live through some adventures before we were able to sit here in front of you," said Jim. "You are a professional in your field. This project is extremely important for the future well-being of our universe. We have only the best in our team."

"Understandable. Which hotel are you staying in?"

"Hotel Golden Forest in the city centre."

"I am going to be there tomorrow at 11am." Rob opened the door. Jim, Lyon, and Eugene got up from their chairs and left. Quickly they went to the elevator and descended to the ground floor. There they asked reception to call a taxi.

"An odd bird, that Rob," remarked Eugene. "Most geniuses are strange," answered Jim. They were driven back to the hotel, went to their room and enjoyed a refreshing sleep in their blue four-poster beds.

Slowly he approached the gaudily gleaming house; he entered through the big gate that served as an entrance.
"I knew it!" The voice shouted, shrill and croaking. People walked around in all sorts of different clothes and bent their heads before him. The ground shook. The walls moved towards him, first slowly, then ever faster until they threatened to squash him. Screaming he shrank back and tried to go back outside but the gate was not there anymore. The walls kept moving towards him. They touched him, broke his arms, then his ribs, his pelvis and finally his skull. He screamed... the voice laughed.

Eugene woke early. Why did he always dream of this house?
He got up and left his warm soft bed. He shivered despite the pleasant temperature in the room. He tiptoed to the bathroom and switched on the shower. His eyes fell on the clock, it was 6:35.
After having showered and dried himself off, he left the steaming bathroom and had a closer look at the books on the bookshelf.
He pulled out an encyclopaedia and began to leaf through it. When he came to the letter E, he got stuck there; there was written in big letters, beautifully decorated and richly coloured:

EARTH
Counting from the sun, the 3rd planet of the solar system. The Earth circles the sun in 365 days. The Earth has an inner core that is solid and reaches a temperature of 4900°C. The outer core is liquid and reaches a temperature of 4700°C. The lower mantle is viscous and

has a temperature of 3500°C. On top of the upper mantle is the crust. On this crust life is able to sustain itself. There are forests, lakes, rivers, cities, towns, villages, meadows and oceans. The Earth was created about 4.6 billion years ago. 29% of the Earth is dry land; the rest (71%) consists of water, the various oceans.

Eugene let the encyclopaedia drop and thought about what Earth used to look like. The encyclopaedia had no pictures. The information in the book gave no clue how Earth had been destroyed. He closed the book and put it back in its place. Behind him he heard a yawn.

"Good morning," said Eugene.

"Good morning," said Lyon returning the greeting, "Why are you up so early?"

"I would have liked to sleep longer," said Eugene.

"What book were you looking at?"

"An encyclopaedia, I wanted to find out a bit about Earth, but it doesn't say that much about it."

"What exactly would you like to know?"

"How was it destroyed?"

"I can tell you one reason," said Lyon after some thought, "They needed slaves and the dark ones wanted to gain power over the universe."

"That much I already knew."

"Maybe that was the only reason."

"I don't believe that."

"I don't know why the Earth was destroyed. I'd much rather know what it is about the House of Time you keep dreaming about."

"We are going to solve the mystery in the end. Let's go for breakfast. Do you want to?"

"Should we wake Jim?"

"Let him sleep."

"Good morning, you two," said Jim, joining them at the breakfast table.

"Good morning."

Jim ordered a breakfast of toast and honey, fried bacon and eggs and a salad. Eugene and Lyon had already eaten.

"Eugene and I have discussed Earth ever since waking up. We have concluded that the House of Time must have been on Earth and that the Earth might have been destroyed because of it."

"What gave you that idea?"

"Pure speculation."

"So you thought it up?"

"No, we put two and two together."

"Ah yes," Jim took a bite of his toast.

"It is quite possible."

"It is possible but it could also be quite different. They are just dreams. We are going to get the relevant information in the main library of our mothership."

Rob stepped through the hotel entrance and saw Lyon, Eugene, and Jim sitting on a bench. With quick steps he approached them.

"Let's get going." They got up, Jim fetched his suitcase. They announced their departure and took a taxi to the airport. Together they walked to the parking jet and entered via the hatchway.

"I have a question. How many will participate, apart from the four of us?"

"We used to be four, you are our fifth member. But one of us had to be left behind on Mars. There is one member still to be picked up. Her name is Aecey and she is an Aqua."

"That means we are only five in total?"

"That has to be enough. After all we are the best."

"Very optimistic. Where does Aecey live by the way?"

"As I've said already, she is an Aqua; her home is the Aqua

moon, a three day journey by jet."

"What are we going to do during the three days?"

"Recover our strength, relax and memorize the plan."

"I should hope so. I intend to survive this."

Jim took his place in the cockpit and started the jet and soon they were on their way to the Aqua moon.

"Send us some hunters to chase these rebels, they mustn't become a danger to us, the more we eliminate, the less trouble they'll be for us."

It was still very early when they all got up. They had been travelling for a day by now. After their communal breakfast they got together in the common room and started to tell Rob everything that had happened so far. Then Jim proceeded to lay open their plans to Rob.

"We're going to pick up Aecey on the Aqua moon and fly to the control ship of the drad army of the USB. We'll use the parking deck and Eugene, Lyon, Aecey, and I are going to get in through an air vent. You have to explain to us where to go. We'll stay in touch by radio and we'll also carry tracking devices. On the screen in the jet you'll see us as red dots. The enemies will be yellow dots but some of them might not show. You'll steer us through the ship. Our target is the main engine room. Any questions?"

Rob didn't beat an eyelash after Jim had finished.

"Where is the parking deck?"

"The parking deck is on level one." Rob nodded.

Eugene went to the computer and entered "Earth" as a search term. The computer returned two full pages of information.

Lyon passed the time throwing a ball against the wall and catching it on the rebound. Jim read a book and Rob recharged his battery. He had a big battery in his body and had to recharge once every other week for about an hour.

They had travelled for 50 hours and would soon land on Aqua. After breakfast they met in the cockpit and each chose a seat.

"I don't know why but we're losing electricity," said Jim suddenly.

"Does that matter as long as we have fuel?"

"It does matter quite a bit. The engines that power our jet use fuel but everything else is run on electricity. That means we freeze in the dark without water and food and the controls won't work either."

"What can we do?"

"We'll have to make an emergency landing. We cannot risk flying through space without the means to navigate."

"But there isn't anything close-by, apart from a few asteroids. We cannot land on such a rock."

"If need be, we can."

"How much time have we got?"

"Not much, maybe four hours."

"Look out for an asteroid we can land on," commanded Jim. They all looked out of the window and Jim switched on the big searchlight. There were rocks all around them but most of them were too small. Big rocks measured no more than a yard. Time was slowly running out and the crew was getting nervous.

"We're going to die out here."

"Calm down, we're not going to die."

"I hope you're right."

Jim steered the ship through some more rocks when suddenly a huge rock came drifting along. It had a diameter of nearly a mile and looked like a good place to land.

"See, what did I tell you, Lady Luck is on our side," said Jim.

"Well then let's go down before she changes her mind."
Jim guided the jet carefully close to the big rock and the closer they came, the better they could see its surface. There seemed to be buildings.
"Do you see that? There are houses, maybe it is inhabited."
"Unlikely, there is no oxygen down there."
"Maybe robots?"
"No, all robot settlements are registered in a book. There are none on asteroids."
"But there are still houses down there."
"Get ready for landing."
Those who didn't have a seat held on to whatever was close-by because they didn't want to float around and hurt themselves. The landing was smooth, they had come down outside the settlement to avoid raising the alarm just in case it was inhabited.
"Two will be enough to go and explore. We keep in touch by radio. Volunteers?"
"I'll go," said Lyon.
"I'm coming with you," added Eugene.
"Good, there are your radios." Jim put them in their hands.
"Be careful!"

Only moments later, Eugene and Lyon stood outside the jet in their spacesuits. The ground was hard and covered in strange brown fibres. In some places round columns came out of the soil and grew up into a crown-like structure. A lot of scrap metal was lying around. Everything was brown and dark. Slowly they walked towards the settlement, carefully and always watching out not to step on anything sharp-edged or to trip. There really was a lot of rubbish lying around.
"Looks like a space scrap yard," Eugene reported to Jim via radio.
"I agree," Lyon added, a lot of interference in the

background.

"Report, please. What does it look like out there?"

"Fairly dreary, the ground is covered in rubbish. Everything has the same colour. We can see the settlement from here and are going there."

"Okay, be careful that no inhabitants catch you unawares." They were quite close now to the settlement and could make out individual buildings but ruins as well. The rubble piled up to several feet in height and they had to walk around it to get to the other side.

"There is nothing left. If that has ever been a settlement, it is not any longer," Eugene radioed back to the jet.

"Look out for batteries."

"Okay."

Feeling their way, they advanced. The deeper they got into the settlement, the taller the buildings became and unfortunately for them, the heaps of rubble. Climbing one of the heaps, Lyon slipped. Desperately he tried to find a footing in the loose rubble. But instead of carrying him, it caved in and crumbled on top of him.

"Argh!" he shouted desperately.

"Here, Lyon, take my hand!" Eugene held out his hand and climbed back down to keep up with him.

"What is going on out there? Answer me!" Jim called into the radio repeatedly. Lyon grabbed Eugene's hand, who pulled him back to his feet.

"Thank you!"

"You are welcome."

"We are fine, Jim."

"Be careful, for goodness' sake. A small hole in your spacesuit and we'll have to bury you here," came Jim's response. They kept on scrambling. On the top of the heap, they had a wonderful view over the settlement. The small houses were behind them and the tall ones were around them. Ahead of them was the centre of the settlement.

There was a colossal square building with a blue inscription above its entrance:

SOOL

There didn't seem to be any windows in the building.

"Wow. I wonder what that used to be. This building is bigger than all the other buildings put together and it is the only one without a window or any other openings." Eugene mumbled this more to himself than to the others. Lyon agreed anyway.

"What is it? What have you found? Please tell me that you have found some source of electricity," Jim spoke into the radio.

"Sorry, Jim, no electricity. But maybe there is electricity in the building we're facing."

"Well then don't dawdle, get busy and find electricity."

"We're on our way." Carefully they started descending. There were no more heaps of rubble ahead of them; there was only some rubble here and there that was easy to walk around. As they approached the building, they became aware of just how huge the building really was. Finally they stood right outside it.

The doors were rusty and their glass panes dirty but intact. Eugene advanced and tried the door handle. The door didn't move an inch. Lyon had a go as well. Dust rained down on them but the door stayed on its hinges. Eugene picked up a stone and began to knock out the glass from its frame. Bits of broken glass fell to the ground. Now they could just walk through the door. Inside, darkness surrounded them and only the pale light falling in through the broken door showed them the way deeper into the building. The floor was littered with glass and paper. Eugene switched on his torch and moved the small light beam around the room they found themselves in. It was a kind of entrance hall, to the right and left stairs led up to a gallery that circled the room. There were windows everywhere that separated the former offices. The broken glass crunched unpleasantly under their feet and the sound echoed eerily from the dark walls. Lyon, too, had switched on his torch and swung it around to see more of the hall. Somewhere on the gallery little red lights became visible, and then disappeared again into the darkness.

"I suggest we look for stairs going down to the basement. If there is any electrical power supply here, it has to be on the lower floors."

"Sounds logical."

They turned right and walked along a hallway lined by offices. The corridor ended in a hall. Eugene shone his light into the middle of the hall and the light fell on a pedestal covered in broken glass. There was a panel. They stepped up closer to read it:

Our Museum
What you see here, is a SUV. Manufactured in 1970. Excavated in 1976, at the age of 1000 years.

"Strange. Why 1000 years?" wondered Lyon.

"Where is the SUV?"

"I see it. It must have slipped through the room. It's over there." Lyon shone his light on the SUV that stood lonely and covered in scratches and dents in one of the corners of the hall.

"Let's go back. There are no stairs here."

There was a humming and shuffling but Eugene and Lyon didn't hear it. The red dots wandered down the basement steps quietly.

Lyon and Eugene went back to the hall with the stairs and the gallery.

"You have a look here, I'll go over there," said Eugene and pointed to the other side of the room. Lyon nodded. They walked up and down their respective sides, looked behind doors and searched for a way into the basement. The red lights watched them all the time. A humming startled Lyon. He looked up to the gallery, but didn't see anything. He shrugged his shoulders to calm himself and continued searching. The red lights disappeared into one of the upper rooms.

"Eugene, I think I've found something," radioed Lyon. Eugene went to join him.

"What is it?"

"Here is a stairwell."

"Perfect, come on, let's go downstairs and have a look." They stepped into the grey square room. The stairs to their left went up, those to the right went down. The banister was rusty and bent. The floor was covered in pitch-black dry dirt. Lights shone from below and watched Eugene and Lyon. There were lights shining down from above as well. Eugene looked up; the eerie red glowing lights disappeared.

"Did you see that?" asked Eugene and shone his light upstairs. "What?" asked Lyon.

Eugene couldn't see anything. "Nothing. I guess I was seeing things." Carefully they started to descend into the darkness of the basement. With the help of their torches they were able to see where they put their feet. They shone their light on the walls and steps. They could hardly see the steps under all the rubble and the walls were cracked. At a safe distance a couple of red lights followed them. With every step they took on their way down, the dirt rustled beneath their feet. Finally they came to the end of the first part of the stairs and found themselves in a corridor. The stairs continued further down to their left, ahead of them were two open doors. The ceiling crumbled

97

and the floor was covered in dust. They took the first door and found themselves in a laboratory.

Everything was white; computers were on some desks, here and there some microscopes as well. The ceiling was full of ugly neon lamps. Some desks and computers were on the floor across the room, broken. Lyon radioed Jim to keep him informed. They left the lab and inspected the next room. It was long and it was absolutely empty. They walked to the other end of room but there was no door. They started returning to the entrance but the door had closed. They rushed towards it and banged with their fists against it, but the room started moving. Finally it dawned on them that they were in an elevator.

"Unless I am wrong, we are going down," said Eugene.

"I think you're right," replied Lyon. They didn't know that at that very moment several red lights were hurrying down the rubble-strewn stairs. Since the elevator was very fast, Eugene and Lyon would arrive at the bottom two minutes earlier. The elevator stopped with a jerk, the door opened and they stepped outside.

"Do you hear that?"

"What?"

"That sound. Here is something that makes a noise."

"You're right, I hear it as well, it comes from the stairs over there." Lyon pointed to the staircase in front of them. Down here there was no rubble at all. They had to be several feet below the surface. It was dark all around them. Eugene sent the beam of his torch into the darkness and discovered a long passage. To their right was another long passage.

"What is that?"

"I don't know, but I have a feeling that we are not alone in this bloody concrete monstrosity."

"Darn, what do we do now?"

"Not a clue, maybe they are peaceful creatures. Maybe

they can help us find electricity."

"Shall we risk asking them?"

"No, what if they are hostile after all?"

"That's a good point. Let's go back upstairs, get out of this bloody building and run back to the ship. I won't be torn to pieces for a bit of electrical power."

"Let's go then." They went back into the elevator or rather they wanted to but the door had closed. Eugene banged it with his fist. There was a sense of panic. The clattering and rustling noises the creatures with the red glowing lights made grew louder. Lyon shone his light to find a switch but there was none.

"We're going to die in here, we're about to die now, I know it."

"No, we are not going to die. I've found the switch. Here it is." Lyon pointed to the door. There was a quite inconspicuous switch of the same colour as the door. Eugene pressed it and the door opened. Quickly they rushed into the elevator. It took a moment, and then the door closed. But not before they saw some robots with thin bodies, narrow heads that were elongated at the back and sinewy wired feet on sprockets rolling down the stairs. The red eyes glowed so brightly that the whole passage shimmered in a red glow. They emitted droning and squeaking sounds.

"What sort of creatures are those?" said Lyon and his panting owed more to the shock than any actual physical effort.

"No idea and I don't really want to know."

"Let's hope that they don't manage to get upstairs first."

"This must be a goods elevator or something like that," said Eugene and looked around.

"Probably, watch out, we're nearly there." Lyon had hardly spoken these words and the door opened. They stormed out, rushed up the stairs and ran through the dead town back to the jet as fast as their legs would carry them.

"Now tell us, what happened?" asked Jim. Eugene and Lyon were lying on the floor of the common room and recovered from the sprint they had just done. Finally Eugene started talking.
"We went into this big square block because it was the only building left that wasn't badly damaged. It was totally dark inside, everything was dusty and broken. We went down to the lower levels in an elevator hoping to find electricity there. Obviously there still is some. When we arrived at the bottom, we heard some noise. We went back up, when we eventually found the button for the elevator. Just as the door was closing, we could see through the gap what had made those sounds." Eugene took a deep breath. Lyon was lying next to him rubbing his calves. Rob and Jim stood over them looking at Eugene expectantly; keen to learn what had caused the noise.
"Now don't keep us in suspense like that!" Rob finally demanded.
"They were bloody robots! They only had one foot and ran on funny wheels. Like chains. The back of their head was quite long and the body fairly slim. Their eyes glowed dangerously red," said Lyon. Eugene nodded in agreement and lay back again.
"You relax now. Rob and I are going to question the computer about this building."
"I can help you with that. There was something written above the entrance. I think it was *Sool* or something like that."
"Rob, can you do that? Meanwhile we'll have something to eat."
"Sure," said Rob and went to the computer. The others went into the galley, Jim serving the others.
After a while Rob joined them.

100

"What have you found out?" asked Jim.

"You won't believe it. We have actually landed on a chunk of Earth," said Rob.

"What?" exclaimed Eugene leaping to his feet.

"It is as I tell you. You better believe it."

They stared at Rob in astonishment. Nobody uttered a word. They got up and went together to the computer.

"Here, read for yourselves," said Rob finally and pointed at the screen. And there it was:

After the Sool Company had closed down, the USA built a huge structure around the time hole to avoid causing even more damage. They called it the House of Time. Since it might pose a danger to people, special robots were developed to protect the building at all times. They were called the Guardians of Time. The House of Time was open to visitors, of course. There were the museum and the projection rooms. In 2140 Earth time, the Earth was destroyed and its inhabitants became slaves. All over space, there are still pieces of Earth floating around. Some legends tell about a piece of Earth where robots live, in a concrete house called Sool. In fact, this piece has never been found.

Below the text was a picture of Earth.

"Incredible, we have discovered a piece of Earth and a hole in time."

"What do you mean by a hole in time? How do you know there is such a thing?"

"It's obvious. We were in the House of Time where there is a hole in time."

"Maybe the hole no longer exists."

"Of course it still exists or do you think it just disappears from one minute to the next?"

"Stop arguing. It would be wiser to find a solution to our

problem."

"I suggest we'll do that tomorrow. I am far too tired to think about anything."

"Lyon is right, let's think about it tomorrow."

Jim and Rob gave in and they all went to their separate rooms. Eugene reflected about the House of Time. Why did he feel there was any connection to himself? It had something to do with him if only he knew what it was. With these thoughts on his mind he finally went to sleep.

The next morning Jim was the first to wake up. He went down the steel spiral staircase and into the galley. There wasn't much light coming in through the window, just enough for Jim to see where he was going. Since he wasn't sure what to do, he sat down at the galley table and waited until the others woke up. If only their radio had worked, they would have been able to radio for help. The only question was, of course, if anybody would have found them. That rock kept changing its direction. How else could it have stayed hidden for so long? By and by, Lyon, Eugene, and Rob turned up.

"Okay, problem number 1, we have no electricity. And why do we not have electricity? Because the generator of our jet has packed in. So what are we going to do? Get another generator, of course. Problem number 2, how do we get one? The only place on this rock where there might be generators is guarded by mysterious robots with red eyes. How do we get past them? Well, maybe they are friendly and give us a battery if we ask politely. But there is always the possibility, of course, that we ask for electricity and get our heads blown off by way of reply. Problem number 3, what are we going to do if there are no generators or any other source of electricity?" Jim concluded his opening address, there was no reply. Each one of them thought about what had just been said and wondered what he could contribute.

"You can forget about problem number 3. I am a hundred percent certain that there is electricity in that building," said Lyon finally.

"How can you be so sure?"

"We went in an elevator."

"Our only way to get electricity are those robots. Either we wait till someone finds this rock and by extension us or we try to befriend the red-eyes," suggested Eugene.

"I agree with Eugene," said Rob.

"But what if they kill us?"

"We don't exactly have a choice, do we? Either we starve here or we die trying to save ourselves. Now what do you prefer?"

"Let's talk to the robots!"

"Fine, breakfast first and then we get going."

After breakfast they got ready. Lyon took his loaded laser pistol and released the safety catch. Then they were off, hoping the robots would be friendly and communicative.

"I don't know if it is a good idea to go and talk to the robots. They looked really vicious," remarked Lyon as they climbed one of the bigger rubble heaps.

"It is our only chance to get electricity," Jim countered and that was that.

Slowly and carefully they descended the heap on the other side. Part of the extraordinary building was already visible from their position. Though part of it was still hidden behind heaps of rubble, its size, however, was already obvious. Jim and Rob were amazed; they hadn't imagined it that big.

"Wow, it has no windows, how did light get in?"

"There are probably light shafts that go down from the roof and lots of artificial light." They were circumnavigating some hills that blocked their path to the House of Time. And finally they stood in front of it. They had a queasy feeling in their stomachs and none of them dared make the first step towards that sinister structure. They stood like statues in front of it, surrounded by rubble, and the unnatural whiteness of their spacesuits set them apart from the brown junk.

"Let's go!" said Jim and they started moving. The ground gave under every step and they sank in up to their ankles. Finally, after what seemed to them half an eternity they stood outside the door leading inside. Eugene went ahead, followed by Lyon. Then Jim and Rob stepped through the broken door. The rubble under their feet made a lot of noise and crunched unpleasantly on the floor. They stopped in the middle of the entrance hall and looked around. This time they had brought more sources of light. They looked around apprehensively in search of the red eyes. They couldn't see any, so Eugene and Lyon decided to show the museum to Jim and Rob. They followed the corridor into the big room. Jim and Rob looked at the pedestal in amazement and then at the ruined SUV. The walls were lined with display cases. They were full of all sorts of things, a skeleton among them and a plaque below explained:

Joe, our first find. He was 1000 years old, like his jeep, but he was only born in 1945. His wife died of cancer in 2007, their two children, Jason and Eugene, are still alive. Jason worked for the Sool Company until it was closed down.

"This is fascinating," declared Jim.
"Yes, this is totally crazy. This Joe must have been the first to go through the hole in time, and it looks like he got killed, unfortunately," said Rob.
Eugene had a funny feeling inside. Something was going

on and it had something to do with him. And why was his name there? If he only knew why he felt connected to this house. Was Joe his father? Thoughts went round and round in his mind, they came and went in no time and he had trouble remembering any of them.

He was in a museum. Everything around him sparkled and looked new. In the middle of a big room was a SUV surrounded by glass that was so clear that it was barely visible. The floor was so clean you could see yourself in it. There stood a man in front of the SUV. Eugene realized that they resembled each other. He quickly approached the man who noticed him and turned towards him. It gave him a shock; he was his mirror image...

"Eugene, wake up!" Jim slapped Eugene's cheek with the palm of his hand. He finally opened his eyes and held his reddened burning cheek.
"At last!" said Jim and sat back.
"What happened?" Eugene asked.
"You just fainted. You were out of it for nearly ten minutes."
"But, we are still in the House of Time. Why have you taken off your spacesuits?"
"The life-support computer tested the air, imagine, there was still enough oxygen in the air for us to breathe without any problems." They were still in the museum. He breathed in, the air smelled old and musty. It was also quite thin, not as chock-full of oxygen as on the Forest Moon of Jupiter. Eugene stood up and brushed the dirt off his spacesuit. After a moment's hesitation he took it off like the others had done. They could move more freely now, without the suits. Every sound was audible and the weird smells of the building tickled their noses. It smelt of chemicals and cleansing agents, of leftovers and burnt

plastic and of stale water. In the light of their torches everything seemed grey; there was no colour, as every thing in that building was black, white, or grey. On their way back to the entrance hall, Eugene spotted a lamp on the ceiling of the corridor. It was still in one piece. If they could find a generator or something like that, they could possibly illuminate parts of the building. Then it would be easier to find the robots. They forgot about one thing, however. The robots had been watching them ever since they had entered the building. The red eyes scurried about, but remained unseen.

Jim walked up the stairs ahead of the others. Once they all stood on the gallery, their eyes roamed around. The big entrance hall was in front of them, above them were more galleries. On the opposite side was a glass wall behind which were rooms for various purposes. They walked along the gallery to a door half way down, there they entered. Jim shone his torch around the room to see where they were. The room had blue walls and white tiles. There were two rows of chairs. They stood at a single table behind which was a big blackboard. Obviously this used to be a conference room. There were no other doors, so they returned to the gallery. They turned right and stepped through the next door. There was another conference room. The next three doors brought the same result. Finally they reached a bend in the gallery. The next two doors were locked, but the third one opened and they entered. It was a storage room. They found old computers, monitors, keyboards and other now useless electronic gadgets.
"If we go on checking every single room for robots or this generator, we'll use up the remaining oxygen before we're through," opined Lyon.
"I agree, we should shout to attract the robots' attention or

try somehow to establish contact."

"But how? Our problem is that we probably don't even have a common language."

"Of course they speak our language; otherwise we wouldn't have been able to read the descriptions in the museum."

"Absolutely correct. I am in favour of calling them."

"How should we call for them?"

"Robots! Robots!" Rob mocked them.

"Be serious, Rob. No, we'll do as we've planned. We'll go looking for them, ask them about electricity and then get out."

"Then let's go looking." They passed through the next door and found themselves in a corridor that ended at a steel door. Jim rattled the handle but it was locked.

"We'll have to split up," said Jim.

"That might be dangerous."

"We'll form two groups. Rob and Lyon, you go together. Eugene, you come with me. Each group takes a radio. Let's go."

"Lyon and I go left," said Rob. They nodded at each other and walked off

Eugene and Jim walked silently side by side and checked the doors. Most of them were locked. It seemed hopeless to look for the robots. Maybe they had a hiding place or an assembly point. The chance to find them in this building was quite small. The communicator crackled in Jim's hand and a moment later Rob's voice came out of it.

"We're at the end of the corridor and going through a room to a door on the other side. How are you doing?"

Jim pressed the button to talk and spoke into the microphone, "Our corridor seems to go on forever. Most of the doors are locked and the others just lead to a lot of junk. We're still looking."

Rob answered, "We'll be in touch again in half an hour."
Jim put the communicator back in his pocket. Eugene opened the next door and entered. It was an office. The air smelled of rotten meat, salty and somehow disgusting to breathe. Jim followed him into the office. On the left was a set of shelves, as high as the ceiling, full of books, to the right was a chest of drawers. The floor was littered with pieces of glass. Opposite the door there was a desk, a smashed computer in front of it. There were no more doors, so they left the room. The sight of a skeleton lying splintered under a monitor on the floor gave Eugene the creeps. The dry air ached in his lungs and he had the feeling that it drew the water out of him. He and Jim continued to walk along the corridor. Eugene kicked a piece of glass lying on the dusty floor and sent it flying against the wall where it shattered with a tinkling sound. Jim gave a start and gave him an angry look.
"Sorry," said Eugene and looked at the floor.
"Have you noticed that someone has been following us for a while?"
"No," said Eugene and looked frightened back at the dark passage they had been walking along for quite a while.
"But I have, something is following us and somehow I have a feeling that it's not Lyon and Rob," said Jim conspiratorially.
"If anybody is following us, it must be the robots."
"What should we do?"
"We could go back and thus towards them."
"They would go back, too."
"What do you think of calling to them?" asked Eugene.
"It is worth a try. But how?"
"How do you know that someone is following us?"
"Sounds and red eyes. When we came out of the door, I looked down the passage and for a brief moment I saw two red lights flicker then they disappeared in the darkness

followed by a slurping sound."

"I suggest we continue walking and disappear into a room. We wait there for a bit. Maybe they will come closer to look for us, and then we pounce."

"What else can we do?" replied Jim and they moved on, not knowing that every single word they had just spoken had been overheard. Silently they walked down the corridor, the walls hung with pictures. The wooden frames had started to rot and the glass supposed to protect the pictures was broken or cracked. Some pictures were crooked. Eugene looked at one of them walking past; the frame and glass were undamaged. It was a funny picture, a rectangle of black at its centre emanating bluish wave-like bows that disappeared in the yellow outline. A red sun gave it an exotic look. Jim stretched out his hand and straightened it. Now the picture hung straight on the wall. They walked on and disappeared through a door. Eugene shone his torch through the room they had just entered. It was littered with broken glass. Finally they realized where they had ended up, the toilet. They stepped deeper into the room and after a few careful steps they stood outside the cubicles. The stench was devilish. The broken glass under their feet made an unpleasant noise and Eugene felt a shudder run down his spine every time he heard it.

"Be quiet," said Jim and put a finger to his mouth to signal silence. Eugene nodded and stopped moving. His breath came quickly and the air he exhaled was grey with humidity. After a long time without movement, his legs started to hurt. He looked to his left and saw himself in a dirty mirror.

"I cannot stand still much longer," he whispered to Jim, who nodded and shifted into a more comfortable position. Eugene did the same. After the crunching of the glass had died down, it was again utterly silent in the small room. There was no sound from outside. Slowly they became impatient, what if the robots didn't come after all?

"I have an idea. If I radio Rob and tell him to come here, we could virtually surround the robots."

"Do that. I cannot stand up much longer."

Jim took the communicator out of his pocket and spoke into it: "Rob, this is Jim. Please come." After some crackling, Rob answered, "Hey Jim, what's up?"

"We have the feeling that we're being followed and have a favour to ask."

"Why don't you talk to them?"

"They won't allow it, besides we don't know really what to say to them."

"What do you expect us to do?"

"You and Lyon could come down that corridor after us and trap the robots between you and us." More static.

"That is...we....wait for us..."

"Rob, the connection is breaking up. Could you repeat that?"

"I that we....Okay then...."

"You're coming?"

"Yes."

"Good. We're waiting. See you in minute." Jim took down the communicator and put it into his pocket.

"Well, that means, we have to wait again. We can only hope that the robots don't get away."

"Or we end up on the barbecue," said Eugene more to himself than to Jim, who nodded anyway. They waited silently. Eugene was leaning against the wall. It was impossible to sit down unless they were keen to have pieces of glass sticking out of their flesh.

"Tell me, Jim, why do I have the feeling that I have been here before?"

"You should know that better than I do," replied Jim, running his fingers over his hair.

"You know what I dreamt when passing out earlier?"

"Tell me."

"Well, it's really weird and just fits in with everything that happened. I was in the museum. I mean the museum here in this building. Everything was brand-new and tip-top and clean. On the pedestal in the middle of the room stood the SUV we saw in the corner just now. But it looked just as damaged. I stood in the entrance to the museum and stared at a man standing in front of the SUV with his back towards me. I slowly approached him and just before I reached him, he turned round. Then I woke up because of you slapping me."

"Sorry about slapping you but we were worried about you and didn't know how to wake you up again. In the end I thought of something that might do the trick."

"That is quite alright."

"Do you remember who the man was?"

"I saw him, got a fright and woke up. But I believe I saw myself."

"Yourself?"

"Yes, just somehow different. Younger and well-groomed, but the features were similar."

"Oh, I suspect something. I've been wondering for a while where you've actually come from. Most slaves are born by other slaves and from the age of ten depending on their build they are assigned to different types of work. But I remember that many humans were discovered on a meteoroid many years after the destruction of Earth. It was assumed they were fugitive slaves and they were taken along, of course. Finally it was found out that no human had ever managed to escape and thus it was assumed that they were survivors who had settled there over the centuries. But many were sceptical. There were rumours that it was the meteoroid where the hole in time was located and, of course, there were attempts to verify that. But the meteoroid could not be found anymore and over time the story sank into oblivion. That was nearly twelve years ago. That is why I wonder if you couldn't be one of those who were found on the meteoroid? Maybe that is the reason why the building seems familiar. Because you have been here before. But why don't you remember it? Can you remember anything else, your childhood, for example?"

"All I remember is my captivity, to be honest." Eugene looked to the door; he had heard a sound outside. Jim now looked in the same direction. He shone his torch into the passage. The noise stopped. Jim gave Eugene an anxious look. He realized that his hands were shaking. Everything was dark except the small part of the corridor that was illuminated by Jim's torch. Then the entrance to the toilet darkened then it was bright again as if something big had walked past.

"Oh bloody hell," whispered Jim.

"What do we do? What the hell should we do?" Eugene whispered back.

"I'll radio Rob," said Jim and pulled the communicator from his pocket. He gave the torch to Eugene.

"Rob? Are you there? Answer us."

"Rob, come in. Rob, Lyon, please answer." Jim tried again. Eugene watched Jim and hoped fervently that nothing had happened to Lyon and Rob.

"Rob, answer, please."

"...Rob. What's happening?" Rob finally answered. Both heaved a sigh of relief.

"What's up, where are you?"

"If we knew that I'd tell you! We walked along the corridor and about half way down we heard some noise ahead of us. We walked faster. But we couldn't see anything. We haven't heard anything for a while now.... Walk towards us so we can m....."

"Okay, we're coming." Jim put the communicator back in

112

his pocket and he and Eugene left the toilet to find their way back to meet Rob and Lyon.

Jim told them about the figures walking past the toilet entrance and they decided at once to follow them as quickly as possible. Since the corridor wasn't wide enough, they had to walk in single file. Up front were Jim and Rob followed by Eugene and Lyon.
"These robots are playing with us. They lie in ambush somewhere and are going to tear us apart."
"They won't tear us apart."
"But as we know, they are guardians. What if they are programmed to kill intruders?"
"They would have done that long ago."
"Right, so they're playing with us."
"As you like. I rather think we are dealing with intelligent robots."
They now passed the toilet entrance where Eugene and Jim had been hiding only a few minutes ago. There were no robots to be seen.
"I have a feeling we've lost them."
"I share your feeling but we mustn't give up. Remember how many lives depend on our success."
"That is exactly what I am worried about."
"We'll be alright," Jim reassured his downcast team mates. The corridor ended in a wide loop. They circled it and stepped through a double door. Now they were in a room that was a least 20 feet high. In the centre stood a large conference table. The chairs that had once stood around it now lay broken all over the stuffy room. Slowly they entered. On one side they could make out the outline of another door. They headed for it. Jim and Rob showed the way with their torches. Lyon knocked his foot against a chair leg. Quietly he cursed and kicked the chair. The darkness was getting to them. Jim, who had already

arrived at the door, another double door, opened it slowly. The hinges squeaked and protested with eerie sounds. A corridor led off to the left. It was very wide and after a few yards there were glass windows with a view of the lower levels. In amazement they looked out and tried to spot red eyes somewhere in the darkness. In that wide passage it was possible to walk side by side.

Silently they walked on, the unrelenting fear and darkness preying on their nerves. Nobody wanted to talk. They were just passing a badly damaged door when they heard a noise not far ahead of them. It was grinding and echoed unnaturally. The dusty air tickled Lyon's nose, and he struggled to suppress a sneeze.

"Did you hear that?" asked Jim. Lyon rubbed his nose to stop it itching. No way did he want to sneeze right now.

"Yes. What are we going to do?" asked Eugene.

"Continue." They crept along the passage.

"Maybe we should go to the basement. It was when Lyon and I went down there that they started chasing us," suggested Eugene.

Buzzing loudly a creature appeared in front of them taking their breath away. It was one of the guardians. The eyes gleamed down on them in a menacing dark red.

"We have been watching you for a while and have found out what you want to do," said the robot in a tinny voice accompanied by a constant buzz that seemed to come from inside it.

"Yes...," said Jim haltingly and took a step forward.

"Right. I think we should introduce ourselves. My name is Jim and these gentlemen are Rob, Lyon, and Eugene." Jim pointed at them in turn.

"You are looking for electricity? You are in the wrong place for that," said the guardian and his eyes flickered.

"We are looking for an electric power supply. That is

correct. There is no electricity here? But there must be, we used the elevator and that only works with electricity."

"That was no elevator. It's a floating room, an invention of the technicians and engineers who used to work here before everything was destroyed."

"Do you mean that there are no generators or batteries here?"

"No. All we have is a hole in time. That is where we get our energy to survive."

"Is it possible to transfer energy to our ship? We need it urgently or we are marooned here, maybe forever."

"I am afraid that will be difficult. You'd have to travel through the time gate to a point in the past to get a generator."

"Into the past?"

"Of course, it is virtually impossible to travel from the present into the future. Only when you travel into the past, you can return to the present. The Sool Company, however, managed to break this rule of the gate. They travelled into the future. Nobody knows how. It would be best for you to travel to the 20th century. It shouldn't be difficult to get a generator there."

"Could you guide us to the gate?"

"Of course," said the robot and started rolling on his chainlike wheels. Jim, Rob, Lyon, and Eugene followed him. Through corridors, rooms and over stairs they were led by the robot. Eventually, they stood outside a steel-plated door.

"The unnatural friendliness of this guard robot makes me nervous," Lyon whispered to Eugene, who nodded in agreement.

"My name is RB8, by the way. But usually I am just called 8."

"How many of you are there?"

"In the beginning there were forty robots operating and

twenty in reserve. Only nineteen survived the catastrophe."

"By catastrophe you mean the destruction of Earth?"

"Indeed." 8 had unlocked the door by now and invited them to enter. Eugene had a queasy feeling. Lyon, too, felt uncomfortable about the whole situation. They were in a long grey passage that ended at yet another door. Here 8 had to key in a number code whereupon the door opened automatically. They entered a big hall where a huge ramp had been placed in the centre. There was nothing else.

"We can make it visible by using paint that was specially developed for the purpose. Normally the hole in time is invisible, as it is right now," explained 8.

"Unbelievable! We can just walk through there and whoops! We are in the 20th century?"

"It is not quite so easy, some scientists did indeed try to connect the hole in time to a computer and thus make it easier to control, but they failed and after several vain attempts the project was finally abandoned. So you will have to use the conventional method – jump at the right moment."

"And how are we supposed to know when the right moment has come?"

"You don't have to; a travel guide will accompany you. That's the way people had to travel in earlier times when the Sool Company still existed."

"The Sool Company? The company that used to organize trips through time?"

"Correct. After it had been closed down, the USA built this block around the hole in time and banned its civilian use. It could still be used for scientific purposes, however."

"And then Earth was destroyed?"

"Yes. Some fled through the hole. I don't know where they landed. They never came back."

"Do you know who managed to flee?"

"No, after panicking began, most people who happened to be in this room just jumped into the hole. A few years ago spaceships landed here on the meteoroid. After a day they left again. We stayed hidden. A few days later we went outside for the first time. Up until then we had spent all our time inside the House of Time. I'll introduce you to my friends now."

"We're looking forward to it."

Out of the darkness red lights approached from the right. The other robots came to see the visitors.

"This is guardian number 2, guardian number 4, guardian number 23, guardian number 11, guardian number 6, guardian number 9, guardian number 14 and guardian number 39," said 8 and pointed at each guardian when pronouncing his name.

"Delighted to meet you, my name is Jim and these are Eugene, Lyon, and Rob," said Jim indicating them in his turn. The robots nodded. Eugene felt queasy, he looked at Rob and noticed that he stood very relaxed and at ease. Lyon, too, seemed unconcerned. So Eugene did the same or at least tried to.

"Colour time hole," said 8.

They stood next to the ramp and had an excellent view into the time hole. It was really fascinating, it shimmered like water. Blue was running into green and became blue again. Now and then a red bolt flashed.

At last everything was ready for the trip into the past. 8 had agreed to accompany them. But he could only accompany them until they reached the Earth because he would be too conspicuous on the old Earth. He would pick them up once they had acquired a generator or a battery and were ready to return. They stood side by side on the ramp of the time gate and stared spellbound at the shimmering hole. 8 stood in the middle, between Jim and Lyon, and then came Eugene and Rob.

"Hold hands," ordered 8. They each took their neighbour's hand. They walked up to the gate together. Eugene felt his stomach churn. What was waiting for him? After all he had learnt, he had a queasy feeling, as if there was a connection to his past. They were very close to the time gate now. Reverently they stepped through it and disappeared without a sound.

They whooshed through time as through a tunnel. It gleamed green and purple. As in a maelstrom they were being sucked in by an unexpected force. They were rushed through a round tunnel at an incredible speed, its walls shimmering in all colours, past turn-offs and other tunnels leading somewhere else. They were sucked into another tunnel with a jerk. Floating they tumbled about. They were still holding hands. Past all sorts of colours and shapes that were mirrored on the walls of the tunnel, 8 guided them into a tunnel on the left. They slid into it with a small jerk. Shortly afterwards 8 pulled them to a blue shimmering spot that wound down like a funnel into the deep and as they came closer, they were sucked into it, one after the other and disappeared into the colourful time tube.

With a dull thud they landed in grass. Eugene rolled off his shoulder elegantly to get out of the way of the others who now seemed to appear from nowhere above him and landed next to him in the soft grass.

"I am going to leave you now," said 8.

"Where can we find electricity?" asked Jim.

"There should be a small city over there," said 8 and pointed to the plain that lay in front of them.

"Okay, if everything goes well, we'll meet at this very spot in three days' time," said Jim.

"I'll be here waiting for you." 8 turned away.

"One more question, what year are we in?"

"In 1989 according to Earth time," he answered and disappeared with a quick wave and a "Good luck" back into the time hole. They turned around to start heading for the city. There was a building site ahead that took up nearly the whole area around the time hole. There were workers everywhere surrounded by bulldozers, cranes, diggers, caterpillars and concrete mixers and innumerable workers performed their daily duties. Nobody had noticed the four time-travellers.

"What next?" asked Lyon.

"I suggest we walk around that building site in a big loop and start heading into town."

"Agreed but I guess that the march to town will be long and exhausting. What do think about my organizing a means of transport?"

"You want to steal a vehicle?"

"Why not?"

"We cannot risk to be caught and maybe even get locked up afterwards."

"You won't be able to stop me," said Lyon and vanished in the direction of the car park. The ground was covered with heaps of soil. Trucks arrived full of bricks and left full of soil. A board big enough to be seen from a plane advertised in huge letters:

WE CONSTRUCT A NEW HOLIDAY CENTRE FOR YOU AND YOUR FAMILY.

"What are we going to do?"

"We walk to the road. If we're lucky, Lyon won't get caught." They turned right and at a safe distance headed for the dusty road.

"This building site is incredible. It must be as big as the one on Mars when the Colloscoseum was built."

"You could be right there," agreed Eugene watching the

119

work going on at this outsize building site. Meanwhile they had nearly reached the road. There was a lot of traffic. Trucks went past constantly and threw up thick clouds of dust; there was no pavement for pedestrians. Eugene, Rob and Jim crossed the road that was yellow with desert dust and started on their way to the city. Lyon had not returned yet, but they assumed that he would pick them up along the road should he succeed in finding a vehicle. If he got caught, they had a problem.

"I hope Lyon doesn't do anything stupid," said Jim and threw a worried look at the building site near them. Dust churned up by the constantly passing trucks was blown into their faces. They had all narrowed their eyes to the size of slits to prevent the dust getting in their eyes.

"What is keeping him; I hope he didn't allow himself to get caught."

"If he did, it's his own fault. This sort of thing threatens the entire mission. And if it fails, you know what's going to happen," said Jim. Eugene looked back and realized that they had already walked a fair distance. A passing truck blew a big cloud of sand into his eyes; he cursed and rubbed his eyes which started to water. In silence they covered an even longer distance when the wind picked up and the air became misty with the whirling dust. After ten minutes they became despondent.

"Find us a car, Lyon. Otherwise I'll never reach that city before that damned sand eats my eyes out of their sockets."

"I couldn't agree more, we should have joined him in his enterprise and we might have a car already."

"Or we might be prisoners," said Jim looking reproachfully as if the sand didn't bother him at all and they were but snivelling cry-babies who were just wailing to get their daily bottle of milk. But it wasn't like that. The wind grew into a storm, they wouldn't be able to see the road and might get lost or disappear into the sand forever. "Don't be so suspicious. Together we would have had a better chance of finding a vehicle. I hope he's coming soon."

Full of hope and hopeless at the same time, they kept on walking towards the city that would appear on the horizon eventually while waiting for Lyon and his car. They soon gave up thinking about a vehicle and kept a lookout for Lyon. They decided to wait. The sand storm was getting worse when a van stopped beside them and the passenger door opened.

"I am sorry you had to wait for so long. But it was not easy to find a vehicle without one of the workers seeing me," said Lyon sitting behind the steering wheel on the driver's seat. Eugene and Rob got in and took the backseats. Jim got in on the passenger side. As Jim closed the door, Lyon started driving. Since the fog lights were on, they were able to see about ten yards along the road.

"We are so glad that you are here. We had virtually given up believing in getting transport."

"Nonsense. But I am here. I have to tell you something. I heard how workers talked about money and I remembered, what are we going to pay with? I mean we don't have money that is valid on Earth."

"Indeed, now that you mention it. We'll have to think of something. But that can wait till we actually have a generator."

"Of course."

Silently the drive continued. Everybody looked out of the window even though there wasn't much to see. After some time the wind slowly died down and the sand settled back down. Vision improved and soon Lyon could even switch off the fog lights. Houses appeared along the horizon.

"We'll soon be there, the city is over there," said Jim and pointed at the tiny houses visible in the distance.

"How do you suggest getting a generator? Do you think there are shops that sell them?"

"Quite possibly, we'll just ask. None of us has ever been on Earth. - On Earth! I can hardly believe it, on Earth."

"Talking about which. We are on Earth, my ancestors lived here," said Eugene full of wonder.

"And maybe you, too, it looks like it anyway."

"If I only knew, but I'll find out eventually."

The city slowly got bigger. The air was clear and no longer full of sand. Lyon looked in the rear view mirror and saw the cranes of the building site with the mountains in the background. They were now in the middle of the prairie. Lyon hoped that nobody missed the stolen van yet. Jim started fiddling with the controls on the middle console and murmured, "Interesting, all the things they had on Earth. What are those buttons for?" He pressed his finger on one of them and the answer came immediately in form of a voice singing "...to sing it note for note. Don't worry be happy..." Startled Jim had pressed the same button again and switched the tape deck off again.

"That is a tape deck," murmured Eugene. They all looked at him. He answered Jim's surprised look.

"What?"

"I said this is a tape deck." Now Lyon looked back as well. Unfortunately his movement had an impact on the steering wheel and the vehicle veered into the sand of the desert.

"Lyon, are you crazy? Look at the road for goodness sake!" Jim scolded him but kept looking at Eugene. Lyon veered back onto the road.

"How do you know that it is a tape deck?" asked Jim.

"I don't know. I just remembered it," replied Eugene.

"Just like that?"

"Just like that."

"How can you just remember something that you have never heard of before?"

"I don't know. You played around with it and suddenly I knew the name of the thing."

"What did you say it was called?"

"Tape deck."

"Ah yes. Eugene, I'm slowly becoming convinced that you are not a descendant of Earth dwellers but that you are a real inhabitant of Earth. One who was born on Earth before he vanished into the future through the hole in time," Jim put forward a bold theory.

"I have often wondered about what you've said just now. But I can't really believe it."

"We'll do some research. And we have three days. When we are in town, we get a generator and then we'll try and find some information about you."

"And what if I'll not be born for another hundred years?"

"In that case we won't be able to find anything about you but we can at least try."

"Fine."

"Good. Once we're in town we need to get new licence plates for the van. After all it will be our home for the next three days."

The sun burnt down hot when they finally arrived in the outskirts of town. Little houses stood along the street decorated by front gardens covered with flowers. They decided to go into the centre as far as possible and then ask a passer-by for a shop selling electric goods. It wasn't a very big town. The highest building that Jim could see had about ten floors. Most buildings were family homes. When they arrived in the town centre, Lyon parked the van in a carpark outside a supermarket. They all got out and rubbed their backs and stretched their legs. At the entrance to the supermarket was a little van advertising *Roast Chicken!* At the back of the van chickens were being roasted on spits and the man inside the van shouted constantly: "Chicken! Roast chicken! Fresh roast chicken!

Chicken!" Some people, humans, as Eugene noticed with pleasure stood before the van and bought something. They were all equally enthusiastic. Nobody had had any idea what life on Earth was like. After all, hardly anything had been passed down.

"What are chicken?" asked Rob and made them all grin.

"What?"

"Nothing. It's just that your question is funny."

"Yes, very funny."

"Funny!"

"Really? My question was funny? Since my question was so funny, I am sure you can answer it easily, or can you?"

"Get off it, we don't know ourselves what chicken are. How about just having a look?"

"Okay, good idea. Maybe we can eat it. I am absolutely starving."

"I would assume that chicken can be eaten," opined Eugene

They marched to the stand. The man had stopped yelling like a nutcase and kept staring at Rob and Lyon. Jim looked at Rob now, too, and finally at Lyon and he realized something.

"Oh, pardon us but we're not from here, we picked up those two from a fancy dress party and are passing through. We got hungry and stopped here in town." At the words "fancy dress party" Rob nodded and so did Lyon. They had realized that they didn't fit into the human world.

"Oh, of course. Great costumes. You're hungry? You've come to the right place. Would you like some chicken?"

"We would, after all we would be eating it for the first time. But we don't have money, unfortunately."

"For the first time? Incredible. You know what, you can have a chicken for free. What do you think of that?"

"That is awfully nice of you but that won't be necessary."

"But sure you get it for free." The salesman put the

chicken in a bag and gave it to Jim who thanked him profusely. Then the guy started yelling again: "Chicken freshly roasted! Chicken!" With quick steps the little group went to a bench and sat down. Jim tore open the paper and the delicious smell of roast meat streamed out of it and mingled with the fresh air of the trees around them.

"Everybody, take a piece and try it. I am curious to see what chicken tastes like."

"Me too," said Eugene and tore away the leg.

"We need to do something with the two of you; we cannot have you walk through town the way you are. People would get suspicious. Just think about how that guy looked at you, I think this gift was an apology for staring at you."

"Rubbish. I think he gave it to us because we had never eaten chicken before. It seems that chicken is something like an international mass food here on Earth," said Lyon with his mouth full.

"What the hell? Whatever, what are we going to do with you?"

"I could disguise myself," suggested Rob.

"Yes we could do that, but how? Should we disguise you as a human? I guess that won't be that easy. With you, Lyon, it will be easier, your, well, bowels are better hidden."

"What do you think, should Rob guard the van and fix the new licence plates while the three of us go looking for a generator?"

"That will probably be best. Do you mind, Rob?" asked Eugene.

"No, I can keep myself busy, no problem. Now that I know how to work a tape deck." He got up and left.

"He does mind," said Lyon.

"He'll get over it," said Jim to Eugene. Rob crossed the road and went to the supermarket carpark. Jim put the chicken bones and the paper it had been wrapped in in the bin next to the bench. Eugene's gnawed-off leg went the same way.

"I am sure they sell make-up in that supermarket. What do you think about a little detour in there?" asked Eugene and pointed at Lyon.

"Good," agreed Jim and they went towards the electric sliding doors of the supermarket vanishing inside shortly afterwards.

"So much for your disguise, Lyon, there is nothing that can cover your nose," said Jim. They sat down on one of the benches and sighed. Rob sat in the van.

"If anybody asks, we'll just say that Lyon comes from a fancy dress party. I mean he has the shape of a human unlike Rob," said Eugene. Jim nodded; they got up and started walking to the pedestrian area.

"How did you like the chicken?"

"Well, a bit bland but not bad," said Lyon. Eugene nodded in agreement but didn't say anything. Again he had this feeling of having been here before and having met the person selling the chicken. Perhaps he had really travelled through the time hole to the future as Jim suspected.

In the town centre the buildings had been very prettily restored. Everything was spick and span, presumably for the tourists who would soon come to travel through the time hole. After the next bend the street turned into cobbles, the beginning of the old town. A sign announced the pedestrian area. They walked past shops selling clothes, second hand bookshops, restaurants and food stalls. They were fascinated by it all. To all intents and purposes they were the first tourists to arrive through the hole in time. Outside most shops were tables piled with the goods for sale. The air was redolent of tea and trees stood in regular intervals, surrounded by small circles of grass.

Above every door a wooden or brass sign advertised the goods for sale inside. Above one door there was no nicely decorated sign but a clean neon sign that read *Electric Shop*. Just what they were looking for! They walked over and entered. There was bright light inside and it smelled of plastics and chemistry. A bell at the door chimed and announced their arrival. Eugene looked around, electrical devices everywhere. On the left was a wall of TV screens that all showed the same channel without sound. The floor was covered with a grey fluffy carpet that went well with all the electric knickknacks. The shop assistant came towards them. His hair was oiled; he wore a suit and had a silver watch on his left wrist. His teeth shone like freshly polished ivory in his sun-tanned face. As he approached, he impressed Eugene and the others with being a bit naïve and boastful.

"How can I help you?" he asked politely and smiled. He didn't look at Lyon at all.

"Well, we're looking for something unusual," said Jim.

"Has it anything to do with electricity?"

"Oh yes, definitely."

"Then tell me, our selection is larger than it may appear."

"We are looking for an emergency generator," said Jim, and the assistant wasn't sure if he should laugh or throw them out. Did they take him for a fool?

"What? You want to buy a generator?"

"That's it."

"But we don't have that in stock, we're an electric shop."

"Begging your pardon, but we didn't know where to look for it."

"I understand but I can't help, that is, hang on, maybe I can get you one. It'll probably take two days and most definitely won't be cheap."

"That would be very kind. Could you do that for us?"

"Of course. What is your name and address, please?"

"Jim, Eugene and Lyon. We are travelling through. As soon as the generator has arrived, we'll pick it up," said Jim.

"Okay, if you'd care to come back the day after tomorrow," said the assistant as he looked up from his notebook.

"Good-bye and thanks again. We'll be back in two days."

"That went rather better than expected."

"Really incredible. Now we can actually spend a couple of days looking into Eugene's past."

"Something I am really happy about. It's starting to get on my nerves that I don't know where I've come from."

"That's what we are going to find out since we have enough time."

"I suggest that we borrow books from the local library and have a look at them in the van."

"Have you thought about how to pay?"

"That is a problem indeed we have to try and bypass somehow. What do you think of an IOU?"

"That is the perfect solution to the problem."

They strolled a bit awkwardly along the street looking for the library. In a colourfully decorated souvenir shop, they asked the way to the library. With no further detour they went straight there.

Inside the library it was nice and cool and the lights were dimmed. Eugene was excited and hoped eagerly for a past he could identify with. Wasn't it possible that, as a younger person, he was wandering around somewhere in this time, that is in his past? Would his younger self be able to cope with meeting him? He just hoped that he had led a good life or was he, in fact, leading a good life right now. Would it matter if his life was a mess or if he was a beggar? Would it matter if he was a criminal or if he was in prison? What would Jim, Lyon, and Rob think of him? He was afraid of his past, he was afraid to learn what and who he used to be.

2 days later

They had spent a total of sixteen hours in the library and had learnt a few things but nothing about Eugene. Finally they had decided to check in the town hall. But they didn't know anything about him either. They didn't know what else they could do. They had had a unique chance to uncover Eugene's past and had done their best to use it but they had failed. Eugene was downcast and relieved at the same time. The thoughts that his past might have been awful still tortured him.

Rob was in an extremely bad mood, oversensitive and not communicative. After all he had spent the last two days in the van. He had changed the license plates to cover the fact that the van had been stolen. The sun burnt down relentlessly on the little town and had heated up the driver's cab until it was like a deadly sauna. The only one who wasn't hot was Rob. Even Lyon was sweating although he was able to endure exceptional heat, in fact needed it.

"I feel awful. We haven't learnt anything about Eugene's past and I can't stand this hothouse any longer."

"Let's go and get that damn generator. It should have been delivered by now."

"Excellent idea! Why didn't we all think of that? This heat is going to drive us nuts." Jim opened the driver's door and jumped out. Eugene did the same on the passenger side. Lyon followed them and banged the door shut. Rob had to stay behind as usual.

The air was sticky and uncomfortably heavy to breathe. It spread like molten lava in the lungs and burnt from the inside, that what it felt like anyway. The heat had increased and nobody was on the streets. Only Eugene, Lyon, and Jim were walking in the pedestrian area. Finally they turned the corner and stepped inside the grey electric shop where the temperature was kept at a pleasant level thanks to the quietly humming air conditioning. They entered and heard the familiar tinkling to attract the attention of the shop assistant. He stood bent over the counter but now looked up. A smile spread over his face.

"A very good afternoon! I had started to worry you might leave me in the lurch with this generator," he said and smiled at Jim.

Sool's high-rise

"How's the work going so far?"

"Good, most likely we'll meet the deadline for completion."

"How wonderful! As soon as the profits start rolling in, we'll start building a hotel complex around the main building with the time hole. But first we have to make sure that I and my projects are left alone. Those two cops, James and Henry their names are, I believe, need to go."

"I understand. I'll let Jason know."

"No, we cannot trust Jason anymore. He is unreasonable, stupid and too careless. Tell Albert, he'll take care of it. And send Eugene to the building site to check that everything runs as planned. And if he can manage it, he should persuade his brother Jason to come and join me at the office in New York. He can get rid of one of those time travel opponents for me, his last task."

"Certainly," Okasti quickly said good-bye to his boss Sool and disappeared through the outside door. Reaching the ground floor he took his mobile out of his trouser pocket and called Eugene. After a long wait Eugene finally answered.

"Yes?"

"Hi, it's Okasti, the boss asked me to send you to the building site. And tell your brother to get to New York to see Sool a.s.a.p."

"Okay. I'll be at the building site in an hour. See you then." He hung up. Okasti put the mobile quickly into his jacket pocket and left the high-rise through the revolving glass doors. He hurried down the steps and called a taxi. As soon as he was inside the taxi, he called Albert and gave him the necessary information about Sool's request. Albert agreed to take care of the two cops, provided the payment was adequate. This was the end of the working day for Okasti. He leaned back into the soft seat of the taxi, relaxed and watched the houses and pedestrians speeding past.

"Of course we wouldn't let you down," said Jim to the shop assistant.

"I managed to get you a generator but it is not going to be cheap."

"We can pay," Jim assured him.

"And how?" Lyon whispered into Eugene's ear so quietly that only he was able to hear it.

"Very good," said the assistant and asked them to follow him. They went into the back part of the shop and stopped at a big brown box.

"There you are, your generator," he said pointing proudly at the box. How on earth were they going to transport this to the hole in time?

"It wasn't easy to find one in just two days."

"Wow, we didn't think it would be so big."

"What did you expect? This is actually quite small."

"Of course." We are in the 20th century on Earth, pull yourself together, Jim. Of course the generator is small for that period of time.

"How would you like to pay? Purchase on account, cash or

by credit card?"

"I would prefer purchase on account."

"In that case I need your name, home town and account number."

"What would it cost to have the generator delivered to the building site at the foot of the mountains?"

"There would be a delivery charge but it's not that far to go out there. Twenty dollars should do it."

"Good. We'll meet you on the road outside the building site in two hours, okay?"

"Fine, the total price adds up to two thousand dollar."

"Okay. See you soon." They left the shop and walked quickly back to Rob. The sun still burnt down on the town and their heads. The pavement they walked on was so hot that the air above it started to shimmer. Luckily they all wore shoes. Eugene imagined what it would be like to walk on this boiling pavement without shoes. On the other side of the street they could see the van sitting in the car park. At long last they were able to continue their journey although they had liked Earth better every day.

They had been waiting for some time before the van with "Your Electric Shop" written on it finally appeared on the dusty road. They indicated to him to follow them and got back into their van. They drove along the building site for quite a while until they reached the spot where the hole in time was located. Before they could reach it, however, they suddenly caught up with a big black limousine. Unable to overtake they had no choice but to remain behind it. Eugene nearly had a heart attack when Jim said: "The driver looks very much like you, Eugene."

"Holy shit, don't say that," said Lyon.

"What if I do say it? Look in his rear view mirror and have a good look at his face, just like Eugene only younger."

"You think so? Oh man, what if that really is me!" he

exclaimed. He didn't know if he should be delighted or if he should cry. Finally he might learn something about himself and his past.

"We'll follow him."

"Of course we'll follow him."

Jason had left his bed very early this morning and had driven out to the building site in his new company car. Why did he have the feeling that something was going on in this damned company? Of course he knew that people who might be harmful to the company were eliminated and it was common knowledge that Sool was the instigator but nothing could be proven. And of course he was the one who frequently carried out these jobs but he still had the feeling that something bigger was about to happen. After an exhilarating trip to the building site in his new car he found that work was in full swing. He joined the engineer and had a cup of coffee with him, pretty awful coffee.

"How is it going?" he asked and took another sip from the white plastic cup.

"We're making good progress. So far we haven't had any problems, only a van got stolen a few days ago."

"Doesn't matter. Anything else?"

"No, sir."

"Good, I'll get going then. If there are any problems, I'll be in my container."

"Understood."

The limousine turned off the road after a while and drove down a little hill leading to the car parks and the workers' trailers. They were red and painted with the blue logo of the Sool Company. Down here the soil was brown but still bone dry. Jim parked the van a few yards away from the limousine. Finally the door opened and the man who looked like Eugene got out.

"Holy shit! That is Eugene! No doubt about it, we have found him," said Lyon.

"Do you think so? I think he is not as much alike as all that. He has short brown hair and his clothing is totally different."

"Never mind the clothes! The hair has grown over the years and as a slave he wasn't able to have them cut." Jim looked at Eugene who nodded in agreement.

The man who looked like Eugene went to one of the containers, knocked on the door and was allowed in after a few seconds. As the door fell shut behind him, Eugene, Lyon, Jim, and Rob got out of the van and crept up to the container. Once there they listened, hoping to overhear parts of the conversation.

"What? Can Sool not tell me himself? This bastard is up to something. I tell you it's time to get out."

"I don't know but I do hate working for these criminals and you know as well as I do that I owe it to you that I have to work here."

"So? I beg to differ, my dear brother."

"Perhaps you do. Anyway I'd get going if I were you. Sool has a very important job for you."

"Slave driver! It won't be long and he'll be history and I'll take over the company."

"You shouldn't dream about taking over, not even in your wildest dream."

"What do you mean? They owe it all to our father."

"You're way out, you have always been a bit crazy but it looks like it's growing into megalomania. Take care, Jason."

"You'll come to me on your knees once I've turned this club into a global venture, my dear brother."

The door opened and nearly knocked Jim on the head. Rob and Lyon had quickly gone into hiding behind the container. Jim who had to dodge the door had nearly knocked over Eugene who now tried to keep his balance teetering on one foot. The man who had just been talking with his brother Jason stared at the two men staggering in front of him. Jim couldn't stop himself from looking at Eugene's face.

"Can I help you?" asked the man.

"Well. Does this gentleman here by my side look familiar to you?" asked Jim and pointed at Eugene. The Eugene of the past looked at his older self.

"Should I know you?"

"Certainly, just imagine him with short hair, other clothes, younger."

"I don't have the time to play games."

"Do it or you'll regret it."

"Are you threatening me? I have you removed from the premises if you don't leave of your own free will now."

"I am not threatening you. Just imagine it. Do it, just for a moment."

"Okay, I imagine him. And?"

"Don't you see it?"

"No. What should I see?"

"Wow, Eugene, you were a bit thick in the past," said Jim and kept looking at the man.

"I'll have to admit that he bears a certain resemblance to myself. He has the same name as I."

"Not just that."

"Pardon?"

"Well, Eugene and you are like one and the same person. Just a slight difference in age."

"Very funny. You are real comedians, aren't you? Now get lost or I'll have you removed."

"That is no joke but the plain truth," said Jim and stopped the man when he stepped forward. "We travelled through the time hole back to this place to get a few things organized."

"And you expect me to believe that?"

"Yes, you'd better."

"Why are you here?"

"That is a long story, probably. What's your name?"

"My name is Eugene Hanks. I am one of the many directors of the Sool Company."

"Pleased to meet you," said Jim and shook Eugene's hand. Eugene shook hands with Eugene as well.

"Tell me something about you."

"Why should I, you have lived through all of this in the past."

"That is my problem. I cannot remember anything about my past."

"Oh well, I'll believe you even if I find it difficult to believe. I am you. Jason is our brother; he is a bit nuts, maybe because he is a big cheese in this damned company."

"Jason," murmured Eugene. Pictures of his childhood appeared. He was on a swing with his brother in the playground. His mother laughed in the background. Something was wrong about that picture.

"Yes, Jason. Jason's father died shortly after he was born. I have a different father, but I have never met him."

Eugene murmured something again. It was wrong, something didn't fit. He didn't know what it was. But something was amiss.

"Nice talking to you, guys. Have fun on your way home and I hope we'll never meet again."

And quicker than they had wanted him to, Eugene had got into his car and driven off, engine howling.

"So, I think now we know who you were, Eugene. A bloody idiot!" He nodded. He wasn't convinced. Without a word they walked back to their van. The delivery van with their generator was waiting for them.

After off-loading the generator outside the time hole, Rob suggested to knock out the shop assistant. Eugene and Lyon had protested but had finally accepted that they had no choice. Shortly afterwards, number 8 appeared in front of them. His red eyes still frightened Eugene and he was sure that the others felt the same.

"Nice to see you again," said 8.

"Nice to see you, too, 8," replied Jim.

"Let's go then." 8 took the box containing the generator, his strength was astonishing, and jumped into the time hole but not without calling out first:

"Hold on to my feet." And that's what they did. Like a snake, they flew through the cheerful colours in the time tunnel. They turned corners a few times and finally 8 steered them to the exit. Suddenly they were back in the hall of the House of Time. Most guardian robots had assembled to greet them. Slowly they stepped down from the platform.

After a big send-off from the robots they walked through the rusty brown metal and stone rubble back to their ship. At last they were able to continue their journey. They were really happy to leave this last desolate chunk of Earth. When the ship's battery had been reloaded with the help of the generator, they took off and flew away from the rock and back into spacc.

"I assume we're on our way to the moon of Aqua to pick up our sixth member."

"Yes, but there is a little problem, the rock we landed on has moved while we were on it and now we are even further away from our destination than we were at the beginning of our trip. That means we'll have to travel at the speed of light."

"Well, then off we go."

"It will take an hour. Hold on tight."

As fast as lightning the jet hissed through the dark nothing. Eugene looked at the stars.

Jim throttled the engine to go down to half the speed and finally he stopped. Ahead of them was a really small moon, Aqua also known as water moon. Only seven percent of the planet was above water level. There were also underwater cities, of course, but they were rare and mostly very crowded. Aqua was inhabited by 2.5 million souls. Slowly they approached.

"What's the name of member number six?" asked Rob.

"Aecey."

"A girl?"

"A woman, yes."

Silently they hissed over the surface of the sea. The sea glistened crystal blue below them. Now and then a kind of dolphin broke the unruffled surface, did a somersault and disappeared gliding back down into the depth of the cool waters. It was mesmerizing to see nothing but water as far the eye could see. On the horizon shone the sun, red and warm. It was mirrored in the water. Small waves gave the sea now a unique glitter. Like liquid crystal the sea shimmered below them. They flew in their jet across the ocean as fast as the wind. It took a long time for land to appear on the horizon. A coastal city, surrounded by forests, emerged ahead of them when they approached the island. The tall sky-scrapers stretched towards the sky and gleamingly mirrored the blue of sea and sky. Through the gaps in-between the sun sent its rays in a warm glow. They still had some way to fly across the sea until they finally saw sand below and the city grew up in front of them. Jim made a right turn to one of the big runways and moved the jet into landing position. A little while later they landed.

"I want you to start a search for these rebels and eliminate them. They have become more dangerous than we had expected in the beginning."

"Yes, milord." The messenger turned around to pass the message immediately to one of the eagles, small spaceships equipped with laser weapons. Contentedly, the lord of the UDP turned around; the rebels were as good as lost. If only he hadn't destroyed that bloody Earth all those years ago. He still got upset about it. They would have been powerless after the war anyway and it would have been such an ideal base for himself and his prospective army. But he would manage without it. Once the rebels had been eliminated and Mars had been taken, it would be easy to conquer the rest of the universe. Laughing quietly he retreated trailing his long flowing cloak.

They had safely come to a standstill and Jim had parked the jet in one of the free parking bays.

"Aecey said that she wanted to meet us in her favourite cafe in the city. We can eat there and then we leave to finally start our actual mission," explained Jim.

"Okay, no objections to some yummy ice-cream from me."

They left the jet through the hatchway and made their way into the city. The path was cobbled and a wooden bridge took them over the river without getting their feet wet. Beautiful trees had been planted along the path. After a while the path gave way to a sealed road. Now they were inside the city centre surrounded by high-rises and cars. They turned left and set down at one of the iron tables with matching chairs. Big red sunshades protected them from the sun. The waiter had only just disappeared inside the cafe when Aecey joined them at their table. She had nearly white skin and blond nearly white hair. Her nose was small and pointed, her eyes green. They introduced themselves one after the other. Then Aecey ordered ice-cream as well.

"I have a feeling that something is wrong. One is missing, right?"

"Yes, unfortunately we had quite a few things to get done hence the delay. I am afraid Slow lost his life while trying to save Eugene and all of us."

"I am sorry."

"It's okay, don't worry about it."

"May I ask how he died or do you not want to talk about it?"

"We were on Mars to pick up Lyon when Eugene was carried off into the Colloscoseum. We saved him but during the rescue we happened to stray into the arena. There Slow was torn to pieces by a lion while we had to watch from the exit." Jim stared at his ice-cream. Aecey started to poke about in hers and Eugene and Lyon started feeling guilty. Eugene because he had been abducted and Lyon because he had refused to hand Jim his laser gun.

"Let's talk about something else," said Jim.

"Wonderful idea," agreed Lyon instantly.

"Let's talk about our mission."

"Good, we are going to land on the parking deck and then climb through air vents to the different levels. There we can deposit a bomb that will explode after a specified interval. And then the dark ones will be history."

"That sounds a lot easier than it is going to be."

"You better believe it!"

"Rob will guide us from the jet. We will be in touch with him via radio and we are going to carry tracking devices. Rob will see us as red dots on the screen in the jet. Our opponents will be seen as yellow dots. Rob will guide us to the engine room. It will be pretty hard to get there. The ship has several engine rooms. The bomb will be most effective in the main engine room where we will place it. And then we need to get off the ship a.s.a.p."

"When do we start?"

"As soon as we've finished our ice-cream."

Everybody quickly took another spoonful of ice-cream. Aecey put down some Aquarian coins on the table; they got up and walked back the cobbled path to the ship. On board ship Aecey first got a guided tour. Eugene showed her the room where she was going to spend the next few days. Then they all went to the cockpit and Jim started the engine. They set off for the main ship of the UDP.

"What is that?" asked Jim and looked bewildered at his radar screen.

"What do you mean?"

"I have other spaceships on my radar screen but they are too small."

"I have a bad feeling about this. The UDP aren't stupid; I would be surprised if they didn't know we're planning an attack against them."

"What do you think? Are they eagles?" Lyon looked at Jim nervously.

"Quite possible. If they are, we'll look pretty stupid. We stand no chance against them in our jet."

"I am afraid they are eagles. Get ready!" said Aecey suddenly. In front of their spaceship three little spacecraft called eagles had suddenly appeared.

"Oh, shit, we've had it!"

"Not if we act normally and prepare for an attack."

A big jolt shook the jet. They had taken a hit. Jim was busy stabilizing the jet.

"I'll try and lose them!" called Jim. The eagles kept shooting at their jet while it rushed on expertly steered by Jim. Soon the engine would fail and that would be the end. Jim flew some acrobatic manoeuvres to avoid the shots but didn't stand a chance. All warning lights on the instrument panel started flashing. Jim lost control of the jet. They raced aimlessly through space chased by three eagles shooting incessantly. "We don't have a chance; the gravity of that planet over there is pulling us in!" Jim gave up trying to steer the jet. They hurtled with ever increasing speed toward the planet.

"What planet is that?" asked Eugene.

"I think it is Jaffadurr," answered Aecey.

"We're heading for it; maybe we can do an emergency landing."

"It is worth a try. Maybe that way we can also lose those three eagles."

"Isn't Jaffadurr the planet where hundreds of millions of slaves used to work?" murmured Lyon.

"Yes, indeed," answered Aecey in a low voice. "They all worked in underground mines. Jaffadurr has more minerals in its soil than any other planet. Ten percent of its soil consists of gold, three percent of diamonds, ten percent of brown coal and twelve percent of bituminous coal. Only about thirty eight percent of the planet consists of real soil or sand. Considering its size, that sounds less than it actually is. The planet has a diameter of forty five miles."

"Fascinating," Lyon was impressed. The jet shook again under the fire from the eagles. Meanwhile they were quite close to Jaffadurr. Jim tried to manoeuvre the jet into the right position for entering the atmosphere to avoid burning up during their descent.

"The mining industry has left quite a few scars on Jaffadurr. There are more disused mines here than on any other planet. It is dissected by more tunnels than any other planet as well. Because of its enormous diameter, some of these tunnels go down for miles," Aecey continued. Lyon listened to her with interest but his mind was on their life-or-death struggle, really. They entered the atmosphere, there was a big jolt and Lyon and Aecey quickly had to hang onto something to stop them from falling.

142

"It could get quite uncomfortable now for those of you at the back," called Jim over the noise of the shots and the beeping of the flashing instruments. Eugene, who was in the co-pilot's seat, invited Aecey to sit down.

"You're quite the gent," said Lyon to Eugene as the latter stood next to him and held on tight.

"Thank you," retorted Eugene. The eagles fell back and stopped shooting. They probably assumed that the spacecraft they had been firing at was going to crash on the planet. Everybody held on tight in order not to be thrown around during the expected impact. In front of and behind the jet a tail developed. From up there the whole planet, or at least the bit that was visible, had the same colour, a brownish grey. Jim pulled up the joy-stick to bring the jet into the best landing position. Finally he succeeded but they were still way too fast to bring it down safely. Jim kept trying to slow down. It was in vain, there was too much damage.

"We are going to crash on the planet!"

"Not if I try to turn the jet when we touch down. If we're lucky, it gets slowed down. Then I can activate the brake pads without them getting twisted into a vertical position."

"What choice have we got?"

They flew only some thirty feet above the ground of Jaffadurr. Closer and closer Jim lowered the jet towards the ground. Many miles ahead mountains towered into the sky. Dust was hurled in all directions and obscured the view. They were so close to the ground now that they could hear how the rocks of Jaffadurr scratched the underbody of their jet. Then they touched down. Everything shook and shivered. The noise seemed unbearable, everything on board screamed and screeched. Jim had problems to turn the jet. The jet kept bumping into rocks, they didn't slow down. The red lights on the instrument panel kept flashing, everything was beeping and bleeping and emitting all kinds of warning signals. Jim was desperate. They were too fast to operate the brake pads and the jet was heading for a rock towering up in front at tremendous speed. The constant skimming on the ground had already caused a small hole to develop in the outer hull of the jet. They slithered over a bigger rock and the jet did a leap. Eugene held on tight to Jim's seat; Lyon and Rob clung to Aecey's. The nose of the jet stayed in the air for a split second and then crashed down to the ground with an enormous impact. Eugene, Lyon, and Rob were flung into their seats. The instruments showed a leak in the fuel pipe. It appeared to have been damaged despite being installed beneath the third layer of the hull of the jet. But it looked as if even that had been scoured away by now.

"If we don't manage to stop soon we'll smash into that rock we're heading for or the jet is going to explode!" called Jim at the top of his voice to make himself heard over the din of the jet. There was a small rise ahead. Jim had now managed to turn the jet a little bit.

"If we slide over the rise in this position we might end up on the roof. I have to deploy the brake pads now."

"Just do it!"

Jim did it. Slowly the pads were deployed and at once made a difference. With stones and dust crashing into the hull, they slowed down. The rise came closer and closer, the speed decreased abruptly. Slowly the jet slid up the rise but still didn't come to a standstill. As if in slow-motion the nose of the jet and thus the cockpit skidded over the edge and Jim, Aecey, Eugene, Rob, and Lyon looked fifty feet down into nothing. The jet had nearly stopped. There was a rumble; two thirds of the jet were still on firm ground. They stopped – at last! There was total silence, they didn't dare move.

"Right, we get up very slowly and walk to the main room and then we'll leave through one of the side doors," said

Jim. Lyon, Rob, and Eugene were the first to move and waited in the main room for Aecey and Jim. Once the group was complete, they walked to a door that looked so much like a part of the wall that Eugene had never noticed it before. Jim pressed a button on a panel and the door opened. Air floated in. It smelled of soil and metal mixed with the smells of petrol and fire. The jet wobbled. Jim tripped, fell backwards and pulled his comrades with him. They fell back into the main room and knocked against the wall. The stern of the jet got lifted up and for some seconds the jet was balanced on the edge of the hill before tilting into the abyss. Slowly it slid towards the bottom and finally crashed, nose first. Now the stern was pointing towards the sky and the nose was in the ground. Getting out of the upended jet might get tricky.

"Everybody okay?" asked Jim.

"Yes, I think so," replied Lyon. Aecey moaned but nodded.

"I am fine," said Eugene, and Rob, too, declared to be in one piece. The door was blocked by a rock so the hatchway was the only way out. The lamps flickered and briefly the lights went out before they came back to life with another flicker.

"When I open the hatch, we may have to jump," explained Jim and put his hand on the button ready to press and lower the hatchway.

"That's okay," said Rob and everybody waited for the hatchway to lower. They really did have to jump. Jim went first and did an elegant roll off his shoulder on the rocky ground. Rob jumped next, and then Lyon who rolled off his shoulder as well. Now Eugene got ready.

"You want to go first?" he asked Aecey.

"I'd rather you caught me when I jump," she said and Eugene nodded. Then he jumped, too, and also rolled off his shoulder. He looked up and saw how Aecey looked down apprehensively. He opened his arms to show her he was ready. She jumped and he caught her in his arms. Carefully he put her on the ground and she pushed her hair out of her face. Their eyes met briefly then Aecey turned away. Jim and the others had already assembled at the side of the jet and inspected the damage that was quite substantial.

"Remarkable parking," opined Lyon to lighten the mood.

"We are going to need help to get it back into working order," remarked Jim.

"No kidding! We need spare parts and a crane to lift it back into a decent position," said Rob. Aecey sat down on a rock and sighed. Eugene caught himself staring at her and quickly looked away before she could notice.

"We have to find a town or settlement and get help."

"This is a pile of bloody junk how do want to put that back together again?"

"I'll manage, you'll see. It's going to take a while, though."

"Maybe we could contact the mothership and have them send us a new jet."

"That would take too long. We'll have to get it fixed ourselves."

"I know Jaffadurr a little bit. That is I was here before, once, and know the capital but only the downtown area. If I am not mistaken, this is the famous pinnacle rock." Jim pointed to a mountain with a sharp peak in the far distance.

"We saw that from our hotel room. What I mean to say is that it must be quite close to the capital. I'd say we'll use it as a point of reference."

"That's fine by me."

"Shouldn't we take some provisions?"

"I agree but how can we get back inside the jet?"

"That shouldn't be a problem. The panes in the cockpit have been smashed. We can get in no problem."

"I hadn't noticed that."

"I'll get provisions," said Rob and climbed through the broken window into the cockpit.

They were ready to go. Eugene, Lyon and Jim had each picked up a backpack full of water, sandwiches and food cans. They marched off in single file. Their surroundings were bleak, brown, grey and dry. A small path led the little group down a low hill. Little pebbles kept coming loose and rolled whispering down the slope. They had to tread carefully because losing one's footing would end in a rush downhill that would be a lot quicker than was desirable. Eugene took a long look down and found that a wide desert of brown sand awaited them at the bottom.

"The air here reminds me of Mars," said Lyon wheezing. Nobody liked to be reminded of Mars. Lyon stared at the floor in embarrassment. Without speaking they continued walking. They were nearly at the end of the little path.

"Keep an eye out for that rock."

"Of course. But how long do you think it will take to get there and to find the capital?"

"Capitals tend to be fairly big; that shouldn't be a problem."

"First we have to walk across this desert," said Jim and started trudging into the wide single-coloured plain to set an example. The others followed walking side-by-side. The ground was still brown but also greyish in places. And it was quite hard despite its soft appearance. Pitch-black thunder clouds were gathering over the mountains in the distance.

After walking through the wide open plain for several hours, their feet began to hurt. Rob was in the vanguard and the others fell back more and more. Second came Eugene, who was used to cope with such forced marches. Jim and Lyon waddled a few yards behind him, side by side and supporting each other. Aecey brought up the rear and had fallen nearly fifty yards behind.

"Rob, let's have a rest," called Eugene

"I don't mind." Rob sat down on the ground. When Eugene caught up, he sat down beside him and took off the backpack to rummage through it looking for a water bottle. Thirstily he gulped down its liquid contents. Jim and Lyon had now arrived as well and sank to the floor with a loud moan. Eugene looked back the way they had come.

"Where is Aecey?"

"No idea." Now they all looked back. Aecey had disappeared without a trace. There was nothing but brown sand as far as the eye could reach. Here and there the wind picked little sheets of sand that vanished again in an instant.

"That is impossible, how can she disappear around here?" Eugene jumped up and ran back.

"Aecey!" he called.

"Aecey!" They all jumped up now and ran back to find Aecey. Eugene had stopped. In front of him gaped a hole in the ground. Jim, Rob and Lyon stood next to him and looked down into the black hole.

"Aecey!" he called into it. No answer.

"Maybe she is injured."

"What are we going to do now? We don't have a rope."

"We all have to climb inside and find an exit."

"How do we know there is an exit?"

"Don't you remember? We talked about Jaffadurr being full of tunnels."

"I remember."

"My guess would be that this is a tunnel that has caved in. We all walked over it and destabilized the construction. So when Aecey walked across as the last person, the timber broke and the roof fell in and so did Aecey."

148

"Makes sense."

"Aecey!"

"Here," came a hushed voice out of the hole. There was a musty odour and the damp air touched their faces as they bent over the hole.

"Aecey, are you okay?" called Eugene into the hole.

"I think so."

"Can you tell us what it looks like down there?"

"The ground is muddy and damp."

"Can you feel rail tracks?

"Yes, but they are quite rusty."

"Did you hurt yourself on them?"

"I don't think so."

"Blood poisoning is the last thing we need now."

"I knew there was a damned tunnel. Aecey, we're coming down. Step away from the hole so we don't jump onto you."

"Okay."

"Be careful about those rusty tracks," warned Jim.

Eugene jumped. It was deeper than expected. Suddenly it was cool and the air was stale and smelled of damp soil. Eugene landed in the mud and had to balance himself with a hand in order not to land on his face. He saw Aecey standing next to him. His look went back up the hole.

"Okay," he called up. Seconds later Lyon landed in the mud, then Jim and last but not least Rob. Their eyes needed some time to adjust to the darkness. Jim rummaged in his backpack to find a torch and switched it on. They really were in a tunnel. Jim shone his light into the darkness ahead, specks of dust dancing in the beam. After a few yards the darkness swallowed the torch's beam. The ceiling was supported by wooden beams; the floor was muddy and laid with railway tracks.

"This is going be an adventure," said Lyon.

"Indeed. Which direction do we walk in to emerge as close

as possible to the city?"

"The city lies in the east that means we'll go this way." Jim pointed at a path no-one had paid any attention to so far.

"Let's go." One after another they got started; Jim first with the torch, Rob next with Eugene and Aecey behind him, Lyon bringing up the rear. Each sound echoed eerily off the walls and mingled with the sucking noise of their footsteps on the muddy floor.

"I just hope that we get out of here in alive before we've used up our food and water," said Aecey.

"So do I."

"Do you think that this tunnel is still in use?"

"No, I don't. Just look at the tracks. In some places they have rusted away so much that you have to look closely to see that there used to be any."

"You're right."

"Have you considered that the tunnel might split into several passages?"

"No, we haven't."

"Then it is time to do so. Well then, what do we do if the tunnel curves?"

"Follow it."

"And if we have a choice of two or three tunnels, which one are we going to take?"

"The one we like best," said Jim.

Their shoes were drenched in water and mud. The air was damp and clung to their clothes. Without a word they continued.

"Don't you notice something?" asked Jim after a while.

"No, what should we notice?"

"It's all downhill."

"What does that mean?"

"That means that the ground tilts downwards and that the distance between us and the surface of Jaffadurr is growing."

"I know what downhill means. I want to know what it means for us."

"It means for us that we are walking down," said Jim. Lyon snorted irritably. The layer of mud became deeper and with every step they were up to their knees in it. The tunnel went down more and more steeply and slowly it became difficult not to slip and slide down.

Finally it was over, the tunnel levelled out and it was flat again. Relieved they took a deep breath. At least none of them had to slide down the path on their backside. Finally the mud became shallower and they could walk normally. The air had deteriorated. Jim moved his torch to throw some light on their surroundings. The wooden beams above them were greenish and the walls had a red tinge but as soon as the bright beam of light was back on the track, everything else became black again. They followed the tunnel at their by now accustomed speed.

"There is the end of the passage!" called Jim.

"What do you mean? I don't see any light."

"It gives into a room!" said Jim by way of answer. He was right, the tunnel ended in a room. Jim moved his torch around and showed them the surroundings they were in. The floor glittered golden and was even throughout the hall. The ceiling was covered in stalactites, some of them so big that they touched the golden floor, some as small as a little finger. Their steps on the smooth hard floor echoed on the walls. Strangely enough the air was fresh and cool. There was a constant dripping of water in their ears, sometimes they also took a direct hit. Jim shone his light to the other end of the hall and found a wooden door. He beckoned the others to follow him. They walked towards the door. Once they stood in front of it, they realized that it was much bigger than they had first thought, more like a gate. Jim looked for a handle to open the gate and was lucky. They turned the handle with all their force. With a noisy squeaking and eerie squealing the gate opened inwards. With a last look at the hall and its stalactites they slid through the gap.

Drad control ship
"Did you destroy the jet of the rebels who were getting too close?"
"Yes, we did. We executed the order. They crashed on Jaffadurr."
"Very good. You may leave."
The two pilots bowed and left. The Dark Ruler started to laugh and laughed so hard that the spaceship started shaking and everyone knew why he was so powerful.

The tunnel they were in had about the same height and width as the gate they had just passed. The floor was virtually even, the ceiling was supported by old mouldering wooden beams.
"Most likely, the workers found the hall during the excavations."
"Maybe."
They walked on. The air became fresher. Eugene had the feeling that they would soon reach the exit. But maybe that was just wishful thinking because he hoped for it so much. Finally the tunnel took a left turn and a staircase came into view leading upwards. They had found the exit even faster than they had hoped. Quickly they ascended the steep staircase. It was fairly long and after some time they had to slow down for their legs to keep up.
"Damned be whoever cut these stairs out to the bloody mountain!" grumbled Lyon. Jim laughed. Eugene grinned and had to balance himself with his hands in order not to trip over the many uneven and crooked stairs. Finally the stairs came to an end and they found themselves in another passage that ended, Lyon noted with a sigh, at the bottom

of another staircase. Looking up the stairs, they found the warm rays of the sun shining down on them. They had made it after all. Jim switched off his torch and ran up the stairs two at a time closely followed by the others. It was good to feel the rays of the sun on the skin. Eugene stretched and opened his arms to show the sun that he was happy to see it again. Jim looked around for Pinnacle Rock, but couldn't see it anywhere. Lyon tapped him on the shoulder and pointed to his back. They had stepped out of a massive mountain range. Behind the mountain from which the staircase emerged, the sharp peak of Pinnacle Rock towered into the sky. They looked around and made out a city not too far away. First it was downhill and then on a small path towards the city. Aecey walked in front of Eugene and he kept looking at her golden hair until he nearly tripped. Then he paid more attention again to the path. Aecey looked back and gave him a fleeting glance, and then she turned round again. Eugene blushed. Was he in love? No, no, absolutely no way. He tried and guessed the distance to the city and concluded that it was about half a day's march away. The sun would set soon but for the moment it still lit up the city and its copper roofs reflected the light and made the walls and streets look like red rubies and warmly shimmering diamonds. It was a wonderful sight and turned the dreary landscape they were in into something special. Somehow this landscape reminded him of his life as a slave. Eugene turned round and saw Lyon who was scanning the area and didn't notice Eugene's look. Eugene turned back and looked ahead.

The city didn't come closer; they hadn't felt their feet for hours. The city had been further away than they had guessed. Everything glittered in the last rays of the setting sun, soon it would be dark. Eugene tried to imagine sleeping on the sharp pebbles that lined the path and covered everything around it. Slowly the moon rose on the horizon and the sun had disappeared from the now black sky. Then the dull light of the sun-lit moon lay over the area and made it shimmer. Despite its dreariness, Jaffadurr was quite an impressive planet.

"I can't walk anymore. What about getting some rest and continuing tomorrow morning?" Those were the magic words; they all dropped to the floor, totally exhausted. With their bare hands they cleared away the sharp pebbles to sit more comfortably. They were only just able to pull out the bottles filled with water and take a refreshing gulp. Nobody said a word; all they wanted was to go to sleep to be fit for whatever lay ahead of them the next morning. Their backpacks serving as pillows, they fell asleep.

Due to Jaffadurr's rotation the moon always followed the same path over the night sky and bathed this dreary world into eerie black shadows on grey-white light. There were no sounds. When, creeping and menacing, two yellow pairs of eyes approached, none of the peacefully sleeping travellers stirred. Scurrying noiselessly, the eyes came closer and closer. It was impossible to see what they were. Lyon groaned in his sleep and the two pairs of eyes turned towards him. He didn't open his eyes but had certainly attracted the attention of the creeping eyes. Sniffing, they approached Lyon. Howling shattered the black silence around the team's sleeping place. Nobody moved. Somewhere far away and many feet below the surface water dripped regularly from the ceiling of a gallery into a small puddle. Slobbering and doing their best not to wake their prey, the nocturnal creatures came closer. The group emitted an attractive scent; they wouldn't be able to defend themselves. The creatures were two huddus. Huddus had lived on Jaffadurr for centuries and hunted only at night. Their hunting instinct was strong and no other animal on this planet was their equal. One would attack Lyon from behind, the other from the front. He wouldn't stand a chance. With their eyes on their prey they were in place. A huddu flattened his pointy ears and crept closer. He used Eugene's head as a cover. His hot evil-smelling breath hit Eugene's face. Eugene's nose twitched and he opened one eye. Unbelieving, he looked into the yellow eyes. Shit, what a load of rubbish was that? If he screamed, would that scare those two animals? They had crept up dangerously close to Lyon. The huddu that had woken Eugene had passed him and approached Lyon from behind. Eugene decided to scream and hoped to put them to flight. With the speed of lightening he jumped up and screamed some incoherent syllables at the top of his voice, waving his arms and hopping up and down. The huddus hadn't reckoned on this and were momentarily a bit thunderstruck. When they saw the hopping and screaming jumping jack approaching, they turned tail. Eugene dropped his arms. With his screaming he had frightened the rest of the group. They looked at Eugene in consternation. Only Lyon had seen the huddus run away.

When they woke up the next morning, the sun was just rising and bathed the whole landscape in red light. After much yawning and stretching they were ready to depart. They remembered the events of the previous night but nobody said a word about them. In fact nobody said anything at all. Staring at their feet they approached the city. They hoped for some helpful mechanics, whom they could ask to help them fix their jet.

Their progress was faster than they had expected. After about two hours the little dirt track turned into a sealed road. It wound its way through the buildings that had gone up next to it. There were no people about.

"They must be still sleeping the sleep of the just," murmured Lyon.

"I rather think that they are at work," retorted Jim. The

further they advanced into the city, the wider the streets and the taller the buildings became until they reached the city centre. Here the streets were bustling with activity. Traffic jams of so-called cars extended as far as the eye could see through the downtown area; impossible to see the end. The people on the pavement trampled on each other's feet if one didn't get out of the way quickly enough and the noise was so great as if there was an ongoing explosion. The businesses were the same as in every city, ice-cream parlours, clothes shops, grocer's shops, book shops, cinemas, and casinos, everything was packed with customers. The buildings around them were so high that they kept out the sun but that didn't mean that it was cold. In fact it was quite warm. After some time they decided to ask where they might find a garage for jets. They saw a man sitting at a table in one of the many cafes and approached him. Jim enquired politely whether he knew a suitable garage. The man replied with equal politeness that they should try Jonny's garage. They were the best in town. Directions having been given, Jim thanked the man and they set off.

Finally they stood outside the garage. It was a simple house with a garage door and a simple wooden door and above was written in neon letters: *JONNY'S GARAGE*. The garage door was open. Inside was a chaos of screwdrivers and other tools. Had they really found the best? Lyon, Jim, Eugene, Rob, and Aecey entered, careful not to step on and break any of the things lying about on the floor.

"Hello?" called Jim into the silent garage.

"Yes, I am coming!" came the answer from the back of the building. A few seconds later a man appeared in the door next to the crammed shelves of the garage. He had greasy shoulder-length hair and was covered in oil stains. He grinned about five persons in his garage giving him a horrified look.

"Can I help you?"

"Oh, yes, of course, I am sorry. A friendly gentleman recommended you very warmly. Our jet sits out in the desert and we need a really good mechanic to fix it."

"You do? What is broken?" asked the man and stepped into the garage. Lyon wrinkled his nose.

"We crashed. I wouldn't be at all surprised if more or less everything was broken."

"A challenge for me, very good, very good! My name is Hense by the way."

"I am Jim, and these are Eugene, Lyon, Rob, and Aecey."

"I'll fix your jet for you but will you be able to pay me?"

"Of course. Money is no object!"

"How wonderful! I'll pack my gear as quickly as possible." Hense scuttled off and started to throw the scattered tools in a grey dirty suitcase. At last he was ready to go.

"We'll take my company car. It'll be quicker in the desert," said Hense and beckoned them to follow. Through the door they stepped into a backyard where they saw a rusty old car. With some effort they all squeezed inside. Then they drove off. Since the suspension seemed to have stopped working long ago, it was a fairly rough ride and on the bumpy desert ground it was hard going. The bends were the biggest challenge. Eugene wondered how a mechanic could drive around in a vehicle without intact suspension. It didn't make for a good impression, he thought clinging to his seat in order not to slide off.

On arriving at the jet they all got out shakily, except Hense who obviously was used to this. Aecey was quite pale and disappeared behind a rock, staggering. Hense got to work instantly and started to scrutinize the jet. Shaking his head he walked around it several times, gave the jet hull some knocks with his hand, sighed and bent down. Finally he joined the others who had sat down together to watch him.

"I can fix it." Jim heaved an audible sigh of relief. "But it might take a while and it definitely won't be cheap. This thing is just a pile of scrap."

"Main thing is that it'll fly again when you're finished. Get to work, man. Money is no object." And he started working immediately to get the jet back into working order.

Dusk started falling and Jim began to get worried about the mechanic because he had been working on the jet for hours without a break.

They decided to get a campfire going and have a barbecue. Once the news had spread, there was no stopping anyone. They wanted to start the barbecue as soon as possible. Jim lit the fire that caught quickly on the dry ground and in the dry warm air and soon it was big enough. The sparks danced through the air and died away. The air was filled with the crackling sound of wood in the dark red and bright yellow flames.

"I've read somewhere that the barbecue was invented on the moons of Irinus. But on Earth they had barbecues as well, mainly with electric or coal fire. There were even gas barbecues," remarked Lyon.

"Really?" asked Jim, got up, and clambered into the jet to get sausages and steaks to roast over the fire.

"Yes, really," said Lyon more to himself.

"Shall I tell you about my everyday sort of customers?" asked Hense. They all nodded.

"How nice," said Hense with a grin. "You won't regret it, it'll be the best laugh you've had for a while, I promise."

And he was right, Hense told one story after another and there was much laughter. They each grilled their meat or sausage over the fire and listened to Hense's stories. It happened that they were so caught up in a story that the meat got burnt on the spit. Finally when the moon had already finished half its nightly cycle, they decided to sleep. Tomorrow would be another tiring day as the jet had to be towed to a runway.

Hense's grotesque face was indescribably evil, frightening and disgusting. Eugene sat with him by the fire and they were on their own. Eugene held his hand into the fire to grill it until it was crispy. Crazy. Had he lost his mind? With a confused look on his face, he took it out of the fire and pressed against the black crust with the fingers of his other hand. It broke up; pink flesh could be seen underneath. Suddenly it started bleeding heavily. Hense started to dance like a madman and shouted incessantly: "The House of Time is waiting for you, Eugene!" Jim showed up suddenly and held Lyon's head in his hands. "I am going out hunting to get something to eat for tomorrow," he said and shot a hole in Hense's head with Lyon's laser gun. Laughing he took Hense's limp body and threw it into the campfire. With a small piece of wood Jim poked about in the fire. "Nice and crisp," he murmured. He had Lyon's cut-off head under his arm. "Go on, Eugene, take a bite!" he called with eyes screwed up and threw Lyon's head into Eugene's arms. Lyon's eyes looked up at him, dead.

Eugene woke up soaked in sweat. He had had another nightmare. How he hated that! In a bad mood, he flung his blanket aside and sat on the edge of his bed. To get rid of the picture of Lyon's cut-off head was impossible. He got up, sneaked into the galley and took a sip of water before going back to bed. For the rest of the night his sleep wasn't disturbed by any more nightmares.

Drad control ship
"How are we progressing?"
"Good, good. Things are proceeding very well. Our drad

159

army has doubled by now. There are about five hundred thousand in this ship. The others are on their way to our secret command station."

"Very good. Everything is going according to plan and soon I shall rule the entire universe!"

"So you shall!"

"Very good. You may leave."

Thick fog wafted through the many gorges and over the countless mountains of Jaffadurr. The air was cold and tasted of metal. Lyon stood near the jet and looked at it. In his hand he held a cup of hot cocoa, the steam whirling up and mixing with the fog.

Carefully he took a sip, mindful not to burn his lips. How much he missed his beloved Mars, not so much its inhabitants but the familiar climate and his house. Shivering, he took another sip.

"Good morning," Jim joined Lyon who hadn't noticed Jim getting out of the jet.

"Morning," he answered. Jim, too, held a cup in his hand. Lyon sniffed, coffee. He didn't particularly like coffee.

"Why are you up so early?" asked Jim and sipped from his steaming cup.

"Couldn't sleep. And you?"

"Same here."

"Funny weather today, don't you think?" Jim looked at the fog. "And the air tastes bitter, a bit like metal."

"Yes, you are right. I hope we can leave today." Lyon emptied his cup in one gulp. "Let's go inside, it's cold out here."

"Sure."

When they entered the galley, Eugene was up, too, making toast. "Good morning," he wished them as soon as he noticed them. They replied politely.

"Would you like some toast as well?"

"Yes, thank you."

Eugene put some raspberry jam on his slice and took a bite. The bread for Jim and Lyon was in the process of being toasted. Jim took his second cup of coffee while the toaster hurled its two slices of toast a foot up into the air. Eugene nearly choked on his toast and had to cough; Jim spilled half the contents of his cup. The two slices of toast that had just been catapulted out of the toaster were now lying on the work surface. Eugene took them and put them on Jim's and Lyon's plates, one each. Running her fingers through her hair, Aecey came into the galley and as a greeting yawned with her mouth wide open. Blinking her eyes she studied the general mayhem reigning in the galley at that moment. Jim wiped away the coffee with a cloth, Eugene was still red in the face and toast crumbs were everywhere. Lyon couldn't help laughing. Aecey shook her head and sat down at the galley table next to Lyon.

"Do you like toast?" asked Eugene studying her naked legs.

"Yes, I do," replied Aecey.

"Eh, shall I make you some?"

"That would be rather nice," smiled Aecey. Eugene nodded, got up and put two more slices of toast into the toaster. Silently they sat at the table. Eugene tried hard not to get anything down the wrong way again. Lyon and Jim put jam on their toasts and Aecey rubbed her tired eyes to wake up.

"I can hardly wait to get away from here," said Lyon. They all agreed, nodding their heads.

"Hense should show up soon as well. He said he'll try and get here as early as possible and that he'd bring reinforcements," remarked Jim.

Just then there was a knock at the jet door. Hense had arrived to get the jet ready for take-off.

"At last," sighed Lyon almost inaudibly. Eugene smiled

and Aecey took a bite off her slice of toast strewing crumbs all over the table.

"Good morning everybody or as we say on Jaffadurr: mogons," said Hense and waved in the direction of the galley before he disappeared with Jim. Lyon put his cup in the dishwasher and disappeared outside as well to watch what Jim and Hense were doing.

"How do like our trip so far?" asked Eugene shyly.

"Oh, apart from the fact that our mission seems pretty hopeless, quite well," replied Aecey and put the remaining bit of toast into her mouth. With quietly humming joints Rob came into the galley. "Morning," he said.

"Morning," said Aecey and Eugene simultaneously.

"Well, see you." Eugene got up and headed off to join the others outside. Aecey who didn't fancy staying behind with Rob and his funny ways followed him quickly.

Jim, Hense and Lyon stood side by side in front of the jet and talked about how best to move it into the starting position. Eugene and Aecey joined them.

"If we get a few guys from town, we could use ropes to pull it onto the runway."

"How many guys? A hundred? Forget it!"

"A crane would be easiest."

"I can get one though that'll take at least three hours," said Hense.

"A crane would be perfect."

"Perfect," repeated Hense and set off for his car. "I'll get one," he called back, got in and drove off in the direction of the city.

"A few more hours and we'll be on our way to the control ship of the dark ones," said Jim with a sigh.

Trailing a cloud of dust, Hense's car came to a standstill. Far behind a slowly moving crane could be seen. But move it did and soon the heavy crane stood in front of the jet. It was orange and the engine noise was deafening.

"We never doubted you, Hense," said Jim and patted his shoulder appreciatively. That wasn't entirely true, though. They had already started to lay bets if he was going to show up before sunset. The crane driver, Fleur, had got out to talk to Hense about the best way to drag the jet onto the runway. After some discussion, he eventually got going.

Ahead of them stretched the wide dusty runway in the middle of the desert of Jaffadurr and they were ready to head off into space with the newly restored jet. They had solemnly said their good-byes to Hense and the crane driver Fleur and were glad to be able to continue. After all they had an important mission to accomplish.

Rumbling and noisy, they took off, Hense and Fleur shielded their eyes from the sun and waved. Jaffadurr grew ever smaller below. The brown planet with its mountains, mines and the little city in the middle of the desert. Now they found themselves in the cold endless space on their way to the drad control ship, where the ruler of darkness could be found.

"As you no doubt remember, we are going to park the jet on the parking deck of the control ship. Rob is going to stay in the jet, replacing Slow to report our positions, to guide us and to warn us if there is any danger, which is highly probable," said Jim. Before anybody was able to comment, he continued; "Aecey, Lyon, Eugene and I will get into the interior of the control ship via an air vent. That won't be easy since there are strict safety rules in force on the ship. At the entrance of the vent there is a hatch that opens every five minutes. It stays open for twenty seconds. Each of us has five seconds to get in. Since the entrance is large, that's not a problem provided we're quick enough and don't dawdle or do anything stupid."

"When are we going to arrive?"

"In two days' time."

"Does anybody have any idea how we are going to spend our time over the next two days?" asked Aecey and looked round with her big eyes.

"By elaborating our plan and memorizing it. Nothing must go wrong and to fail in our mission is not an option!" said Jim. They realized, of course, that they mustn't fail.

Eugene looked in the mirror; his eyes were swollen and surrounded by black rings. He hadn't expected that so much planning would be necessary. He counted on his fingers the number of hours he had slept so far, a total of three. With a sigh he rubbed his eyes with the backs of his hands to wake up. Twelve hours to go before they reached the control ship. He decided to use these few hours to get some more sleep. What would be the point of all this planning if he'd fall asleep on the mission?

The others hadn't fared any better. Lyon had swallowed a few of his "Stay-awake" pills and given some to Aecey as well, with the result that she fell asleep more quickly than ever. Jim was as alert as ever, just like Rob. But in the end they all had decided to take things easy before the grand finale. The jet moved on autopilot.

He quickly climbed up the wall, higher and higher. But it seemed as if he didn't get away from the ground instead the ground seemed to come closer and tried to gobble him up. A big mouth formed out of the black soil and snapped at his heels. In the end it caught them and pulled him into the darkness. A red house appeared in front of him and it had cracks and holes everywhere. Outside, the door stood an old woman, smiling. Quickly he approached her. The woman stretched out her hands towards him. Claws reached for him and tore into his body. Sharp and thin as threads, they tore through him. They had grown out the woman's fingers.

Bathed in sweat and certain that he had screamed in fright, Eugene woke up. He went to the sink and with his hands threw cold water into his face. He hated these nightmares, especially since they never made any sense and visited him virtually every night. Quickly he dried his face with the towel next to the sink and walked through the door out into the hallway and down to the galley. He was the first to wake up by the looks of it. The reason was surely that he was the only one who was visited by nightmares nearly every night. With a sigh he made himself some cocoa. He wondered all the time if they would survive their mission. And Aecey... he took another spoonful of cocoa powder from the silvery round can and stirred it into the milk. Aecey, if she and he might.... rubbish, he sat down at the table and took a sip. Had he really fallen in love? No, there was no time for that; the mission had to come first. Once it was all over and they were still alive, he would think about it again. But he didn't succeed until Jim came into the galley and took Eugene's mind off Aecey. When Aecey stepped into the galley, Eugene blushed and had the feeling that he had already talked to her but he had only thought about it. Pull yourself together! Quickly he took another sip and in his haste he nearly swallowed the wrong way.

"Two hours to go," said Jim. What he meant, was, that it would take them another two hours to reach the ship.

"Yes." Eugene couldn't think of anything else to say. Rob came into the galley followed by Lyon, yawning and showing all his teeth. Now they all sat together at the galley table saying nothing. Eugene stared at his hands.

"I hope we discussed our plan in enough detail," said Jim. "I would never dare doubt that," said Lyon. Eugene remembered the last two days. They had done nothing but discuss the plan from front to back and back to front, they changed it, improved it and discussed it again. With a tired look he glanced at the clock on the wall of the galley. Only ten minutes had passed since he had got up.

"I have a suggestion to make. Since we are going to start our mission in two hours' time, a little snack would go down well. We're going to need all our strength after all," said Lyon. "I could cook for you, some special dish of my home planet."

"Sure, that would be great", Aecey was the only one to reply. The others nodded in agreement. Lyon went to the stove, put two frying pans on it and started to take all kinds of things from the fridge.

"What if we don't survive?" asked Rob.

"What do you mean?"

"What do I mean? Isn't that obvious? What if we don't get out of this mission in one piece?"

"Well, then the universe will fall into the hands of the UDP."

"Obviously, but what about us? What are we going to do if one of us gets caught?"

"Difficult to say. If it is possible to free that person, we're going to try, of course. But that mustn't endanger our mission."

"Ah," said Rob and nodded. Eugene had listened to Jim's words like the others. The team had to be prepared to die to destroy the ship. The mission was more important than each of their lives.

Lyon's home-cooked food had been excellent and they all had had enough to eat. Jim went into the armoury that was under a hatch in the jet cockpit. He handed a laser pistol to every member of the team, except Lyon who carried his own.

Now the moment had come. In a few more minutes they were going to land on the parking deck of the ship. After

166

some discussion over the intercom with the parking attendant of the ship, they had permission to station their jet. Jim steered the jet to the appointed deck. From there they would go into the vent as planned. With a dull thud they landed on the grey concrete floor of the deck. Jim looked at his watch. "The air vent will open in exactly fifty seconds." Everybody nodded.

"We can park as long as we like." Rob sat down in the cockpit and switched on various computers and monitors to be able to follow all the actions inside the ship. The others got out of the hatch and stood in front of the jet. The air smelled cold and filtered. Aecey took a deep breath, at home there was a similar smell. The stale air of the jet had begun to cause her problems.

"Rob? Can you hear me?" asked Jim into the micro-transmitter on his wrist. He didn't wear the receiver visibly in his ear.

"I can hear you very well," replied Rob.

"Good, let's go." They set off together. There weren't many jets parked on this deck. Theirs was the only one apart from two small red jets and a two-seater that was black and decorated with chromium controls that gave the impression of the jet consisting of a single thin line.

"The vent will open in five seconds," said Jim. Eugene could already see it. Being light grey it was silhouetted against the dark grey floor. They quickened their steps. Just as they arrived at the vent, the hatch opened. Jim slid into it without a word. Lyon followed, Eugene was next and Aecey was last. Just as Aecey pulled in her legs, the hatch closed with a hum. They were inside. Their mission had finally begun.

"Rob?"

"Okay, I can hear you loud and clear and I can see your position on the screen."

The air vent was not high enough to allow for upright

walking. That meant they had to crawl on their hands and knees to advance. They only made slow progress. It was dark, therefore Jim moved in front with his torch. When they passed a grid, Eugene looked through. The air vent was inside a wall. Eugene looked through the grid in the wall into a big hall where weapons were stored. They were piled on big shelves that stood in rows. In every passage in-between there was a drad on patrol. Quickly Eugene crawled on. After some time they came to a turn-off.

"Rob? Where do we have to go?" whispered Jim carefully into the transmitter.

"You have to turn right. Next you'll get to a hatch that leads downwards. You have to go down there."

Jim turned right and the others followed. When they reached the hatch, Jim opened it and shone down his lamp. There was a ladder with iron rungs on one side. Jim reached for it and climbed down. Next came Lyon, then Eugene and Aecey was last. Aecey closed the hatch as soon as she stood on the ladder. Meanwhile Jim had reached the bottom. He shone his torch around; they were now in a larger shaft and were able to walk in a stoop.

"You better hurry up. The animal section is right above you," Rob let them know.

"Are you sure? We can't hear anything."

"I am sure. Move on quickly."

They walked on quickly as Eugene heard a strange scratching noise. Lyon heard it, too.

"Oh, shit!"

"I think they've noticed us, damned bastards."

"Keep going, fast!"

A long drawn-out scream echoed through the shaft. Now they had to move on quickly before the animals could smell them. They only just made it, turned the next corner and according to Rob's instructions they were no longer below the animal section.

"That's not exactly a good start," wheezed Lyon.

"Go on, move on. Everything is going according to plan," said Jim and kept on moving through the tunnel system.

"So far," murmured Aecey.

"You are now approaching section 4. That's where the kitchens and store rooms are," announced Rob.

Eugene rubbed his neck with his hand. It started to hurt because of their walking in a stoop all the time. Aecey groaned behind him as well and wished she were able to stand up straight. Lyon lifted his nose. "Do you smell this?"

"No, I don't. What is it?"

"It smells of food," said Lyon.

"Where does it come from?"

"Haven't you heard Rob? The kitchens and store rooms are around here."

"Guys! Please, concentrate on our primary mission."

"Meaning?" grinned Lyon lopsidedly.

"Concentrate on your mission!" Jim started to become impatient.

"It's all right," said Lyon.

Carefully they moved on to avoid suspicious noises on the tinny floor. The shaft came to an end ahead of them and gave into a black room Jim shone his torch into it. The room was full of pipes on the walls and on the ceiling.

"I have a funny feeling about this."

The floor was black with oil. The further they moved into the room, the louder the indefinable noise became. They hadn't noticed that noise before. It was the droning of machines.

"Rob? Where are we?" There was no reply.

"Rob? Please come in, do you read me?" Again no reply.

"Guys, I am afraid we don't have reception, that means no contact with Rob," declared Jim.

"Perfect," remarked Lyon.

"The quicker we get out of this weird room the better," said Aecey. Eugene nodded.

Jim walked on. The room turned towards the left. Eugene screwed up his eyes. "Jim, turn off the torch."

"What?"

"I said turn off the torch!" Jim switched it off.

"Do you see the light beam? At the end of the room?"

They all looked into the darkness searching for the light.

"Yes, I can see it," said Lyon. Carefully they walked towards the light. It came out from under a door. They drew their pistols and held them in their hands ready to use. Jim took a step and put his hand on the handle. With a jerk he opened the door. Eugene saw a corridor. Grey floor, grey walls, grey ceiling. The light was sent out by some neon lamps that were fixed to the ceiling at regular intervals. The corridor was empty. Eugene went in first followed by Lyon, Aecey and finally Jim, who closed the door. They advanced carefully. If anybody should open one of the many doors and step out into the corridor, Eugene would be forced to kill that person. One of the neon lights on the ceiling flickered and bathed the corridor in a sinister flashing and twitching light. Their shadows danced on the walls and seemed to mock their mission. Far away there were sounds, so quiet that it was impossible to identify them.

"Stop," said Jim.

"What is it?"

"The corridor is very long and we have to reach its end. I am in favour of doing something to make those neon lights go out. That would lower the risk of someone discovering us," explained Jim in a low voice.

"If we destroy them by shooting, the shots will be heard."

"We smash them," said Lyon, reached up and hit the light with the butt of his pistol. The lamp burst into a thousand pieces. They ducked and avoided the flying shards. At once there was darkness but after a few steps the next lamp shed its light into the corridor. Lyon walked along the passage on his own until he was right underneath the lamp and hit it with a well-aimed blow. That way he advanced along the corridor until they stood in complete darkness. In the dark Eugene could hear his steps echo on the walls. They moved closer until Lyon was in front of them and Jim switched on his torch and shone it along the passage. Slowly they walked on. Although they made hardly any noise, their steps were audible. Jim's torch danced wildly along the corridor. One of the doors opened and a ray of light illuminated a small section of the corridor only ten yards away.

"What's going on? Why the hell has the damn light been switched off?" echoed a voice along the passage. Jim crept to the door, the torch switched off as he waited for the man to step out into the corridor. He would make short work of it. Jim had his gun at the ready. A beam of light reached the opposite wall and the man walked out of the door. Using his gun like a club, Jim hit him on the head and the man went down on his knees. Jim hit him between the shoulders, there was an unpleasant snapping noise and the man, who was now out of action, sank to the floor. Jim slowly closed the open door and turned his torch back on. The others joined him.

"What are we going to do with him?"

"We have to take him with us. If we leave him lying here, he'll be discovered."

"But how are we going to take him with us?"

"We'll drag him to the next air vent and leave him there, tied up and gagged." Nobody contradicted, so Eugene and Lyon took the man on their shoulders and carried him. Jim stopped outside the last door of the corridor and shone his light back at his team mates. Eugene and Lyon stopped next to him and let the man glide down to the floor to relax their shoulders. Aecey stopped next to Eugene. Eugene smelled her wonderful silky hair. Only with a lot of concentration did he manage to take his eyes off her.

"Okay, I am going to open the door. Eugene, Lyon, you storm into the room with your guns drawn and shoot down anybody who might be in there." Eugene and Lyon nodded and drew their guns. Jim switched off his torch. With a powerful jerk he opened the door and Eugene and Lyon were temporarily blinded by the bright light of the neon lamps. Nevertheless they stormed side by side into the room, spun round in a circle with raised guns to check every corner of the room in a few seconds. There was no-one in it. Jim and Aecey followed and Jim closed the door behind them. They were in a room with round walls. There was an air vent above them. The room was about thirty feet high. The vent crossed the room about six feet above them. There were pipes everywhere climbing up the walls or thrusting through them. Some were very thin, no thicker than a finger; others were as thick as a thigh or even thicker. There were three doors in the room, the one through which they had entered and another two.

"Rob? Are you there?" said Jim into his microphone.

"Yes, I can hear you loud and clear. Good, glad to be in touch again."

"Rob, give us a report."

"You now are in a pipe room. A lot of the pipes of the section you're in run through there. There are countless rooms like this in the ship. You see two doors ahead of you. One leads into the animal section, the other should be locked," said Rob. Aecey went to the door and moved the handle. The door opened and an incredible noise wafted out, accompanied by a stench that turned Eugene's stomach. Aecey slammed the door shut.

"Damn it! Aecey, why did you do that!" shouted Jim at her.

"Aecey opened the door to the animal section," reported Rob.

"Climb up into the vent above you at once." Jim climbed up, opened the hatch that covered the shaft and got into it. He reached down with his hands and Lyon and Eugene lifted up the man towards him. It smelled abominably of excrements and something undefinable. The screams became louder and Eugene was sure they would soon notice what was going on. Jim had now lifted Lyon into the vent. Now it was Aecey's turn. He pulled her carelessly into the vent and quickly reached down to grab Eugene when the door opened and smashed against one of the thick pipes with a loud thud. Two stinking creatures crawling on all fours came rushing in and tried at once to grab Eugene's feet. They jumped and snapped with their slobbering mouths. Their teeth were black and rotten but as sharp as knives. Eugene kicked them. Lyon had his work cut out not to lose his safe hold on Eugene. Eugene writhed, kicking at the creatures and finally placing a hit. With a loud smacking noise, Eugene had rammed his shoe into the creature's eye. Whimpering, the creature was thrown against the wall and slammed to the floor face down. Dark red, nearly black blood flowed out of the wounded eye. The other creature had stopped to snap at Eugene and sniffed its companion. Lyon pulled Eugene up and out of reach of the still healthy creature. The air vent was low but so wide that they were able to crawl two abreast. Lyon closed the hatch once Eugene lay in the air vent.

"You're okay?" asked Aecey and pushed a strand of black hair out of his face. Eugene nodded. Aecey turned to the others. "I am really sorry," she said and seemed to be close to tears. Lyon nodded but his expression was unfathomable. "Move on, let's go," he said finally. Jim crawled in front, followed by Eugene and Lyon. Aecey brought up the rear. The whimpering and snarling could still be heard.

"Rob? We are in the shaft now."

"Good, follow it until there are branches to right and left. There you turn left. Then you have to go one at a time, the shaft is free-floating. And make yourself light because if that shaft caves in you fall down at least a hundred feet."

"Understood."

Once they reached the spot, Jim crawled first. Once he had arrived on the other side, he shone his light at them as a sign that it was the next person's turn. Lyon was next, then Eugene, Aecey last. The shaft wobbled dangerously. Aecey gave a little cry and stopped.

"Keep crawling, Aecey, don't stop," called Eugene. Carefully Aecey crawled on. The shaft crunched and dropped down by an inch. Aecey screamed and Eugene's blood froze. She mustn't fall, not now. "Come on, carefully, you're nearly there," he called encouragingly. Aecey nodded and sniffled. There were still ten yards to go. Behind her were twenty yards. There was no going back, either she made it to the team or she fell a hundred feet to her death. She had no choice. Slowly she crawled towards Eugene who stretched out his arm encouragingly as if he might save her like that. She was still a good seven yards away. The shaft held. She had nearly reached Eugene. With a loud cracking, the shaft dropped another half inch and they could hear the dust raining down a hundred feet into the depth. Aecey caught her breath; she wasn't even able to scream. She closed her eyes and expected to fall down at any moment. But she didn't fall, instead her teammates called to her to continue. So she moved on. She pushed herself off and grabbed Eugene's outstretched arms. She landed on her flat stomach on the shaft floor with a loud smack. Eugene pulled her towards him and past him and she was safe. At the back the shaft dropped further down and clattered over the edge into the deep. They could hear it whistling through the air. Then it hit the floor and a tinny noise wafted up. But they didn't hear that anymore. They had already moved on, as fast as possible.

"Rob?"

"Good, you're safe. This shaft goes on straight for about a hundred yards. Then there should be a ladder to climb down, and from there you can climb through a hatch into a security room."

"I'll be in touch as soon as we're there."

With a last look at the screen, Rob made sure that his friends really had nothing to fear then he got up from his chair where he had been sitting for the last three hours and went to the galley. There he had a drink. When he returned, he saw that his friends had nearly reached the security room.

Eugene thought he would break down soon. His knees were raw from the metal he had been crawling on for hours and his back ached. Secretly, he looked forward to climbing down the ladder.

When they finally reached the hatch above the security room, Rob radioed. "Listen closely! There are five guards in the room underneath. They all sit at their computers and presumably don't expect anything to happen. But every single one of them can raise the alarm by pushing a button. So I recommend that you shoot quickly and shoot to kill. Three are on the right, two on the left." Jim kicked the hatch with his foot and jumped. Lyon jumped next and Eugene could hear shots being fired as he jumped.

The room was filled with grey smoke and Eugene saw two dead guards on the floor. They both had been hit in the chest. Eugene heard Aecey hit the floor behind him. He rushed on and started shooting. Jim and Lyon had already done a good job. All guards were dead and it seemed that none of them had managed to raise the alarm. As the smoke lifted and the view became clearer, Eugene was able to see what had happened. The three guards that had been on the right had all been killed by shots in the chest or stomach. The two on the left, however, had had time to fight back. One of them had jumped up from his chair and was hit in the shoulder; the other took a hit in the thigh. Both were out of action but suffered severe pain. Jim killed both with neat shots to the head. The groaning and wheezing stopped at once and the light of life died in their eyes. Jim sat down at one of the computers. Eugene looked around the room. It was rectangular; a square column covered in cork protruded from the floor in the middle of the room and was apparently used as a blackboard. There were only a few notices. On the wall to the left stood five monitors each with a swivel chair in front of it. On the opposite wall where Jim now sat were five more monitors and computers. The other walls had a door each. Above the monitors were two rows of screens, presumably showing live pictures from security cameras in various rooms of the ship. Eugene had a closer look but wasn't able to see anything interesting. He especially watched for running guards or drads. But there were none.

"What are you doing exactly?" Aecey asked Jim.

"I am getting a fix on the exact position of our target and try to install a worm in the computer network of the ship," he murmured looking at the screen in deep concentration. Lyon, meanwhile, checked the door through which they were going to leave. "Once you're finished, you can take care of the electronic locks," he said to Jim and turned to Eugene who was still staring at the surveillance screens. Lyon joined Eugene.

Aecey, Eugene and Lyon had settled into the soft swivel chairs. Jim was still rather busy. Suddenly there was banging at the door behind them. It shook with further blows.

"Damn it! Jim, how much longer are you going to take? It looks like there's trouble coming," called Lyon to Jim.

"Nearly there. Give me five more minutes."

"Sure, I just hope that we've got them," retorted Lyon. The door shook again and there were first dents in the metal. It looked like the whole of the animal section was after them. Eugene could smell the odour wafting in underneath the door and he was sure that Lyon smelled it, too, because he pulled a face.

The screaming wasn't too bad but they all knew that soon they would have to put their hands over their ears. Jim's fingers flew over the keyboard.

"Faster!" the door had started to buckle menacingly and nearly jumped from its hinges.

"Nearly there!" A flash shot over Jim's face reflecting the many changes of light on the screen in front of him. The door creaked. It had been bent so far by now that the wild blood-smeared claws of the sniffers and searchers on the other side appeared through the gaps at the side of the door. They could be flooding the room any second now. Another tremor shook the door. "Done!" called Jim and they all rushed to the other door as it opened a crack with a loud humming noise. Jim pushed it open completely and they slipped through just as the other door broke down and the security room was filling with wild beasts. Eugene could hear them as they ravaged the dead guards. Jim banged the door shut and activated the automatic lock to put the door out of action. Now it would take minutes or hours before this door would be functional again. They breathed a sigh of relief. Eugene looked around. They stood in a room that resembled a labyrinth. The obstacles to finding the exit in this labyrinth, however, were not hedges but wide tall shelves all the way up to the ceiling, full of boxes and undefinable tools. Amazed they looked around. There was only one way they could go and this would guide them through the labyrinth. Something heavy banged against the door behind them but for the moment it proved indestructible.

They stood in front of the entrance to the shelf jungle wondering what might await them in there. After some yards the light was so weak that they could hardly see anything at all. To make it through, they would need a torch, patience and a lot of provisions. Lyon could hear a low whistle that came from the entrance in irregular sounds and intervals and was lost in the darkness behind them. Once they were caught by a gust of wind, not heavy, only very slight so that it could hardly be felt. The longer they stood in front of the big entrance, shelves to the right and left, the less they felt inclined to enter the labyrinth. Who knows why there was no light or why the door Jim had opened had been locked.
"I have a funny feeling."
"Not just you."
They didn't have a choice; they entered the passage that took them into the deep black space. Jim switched on his torch and shone its beam along the path. They walked close together in order not to lose each other. Repeatedly wind gusted into their faces or sounds like the rustling of chains reached their ears. They followed the path, sparingly lit by Jim's torch, for many hours. Jim stayed in touch with Rob virtually all the time. Only occasionally the connection was interrupted but never for more than ten minutes. The constant vigilance and the all-enveloping darkness around them played on their nerves and their will until there was suddenly a loud bang that made them jump.

From one minute to the next they were wide awake. The bang had come from close by, it had come from somewhere behind the shelves to their left. Jim put up his hand signalling them to stop. Silently they listened and they all tried very hard to hold their breath or breathe quietly. There was not a single sound.

"Jim? Report, please," roared Rob's voice into the silence, slightly distorted and hissing. Eugene's heart missed a beat and he was sure that the others' did as well.

"Damn it!" said Jim. "Rob, we're in a labyrinth and every few seconds we hear the same weird noise."

"Yes, I know. I am busy trying to find a way out for you. Strange noises you say?"

"Undefinable. We don't know where they come from and who or what makes them. I hope you'll succeed soon because we are close to going mad in here."

"Now don't wet yourselves, I'll get you out of there, I promise."

Slowly they continued on their way through the labyrinth. The floor was covered in a thick layer of dust that whirled up into the air with every step. In the shine of Jim's torch millions of specks of dust floated around. Eugene's nose itched. Don't sneeze, he thought, and suppressed the urge to sneeze with all his might.

They had walked around for nearly two hours. It was difficult for Rob to help them and they kept ending up in blind alleys or took a wrong turn and had to go back taking up precious time. They had been following a passage now for a while without turn-offs or intersections never mind a bend. The contact with Rob had been interrupted a minute ago and they hoped that they would soon be able to get in touch with him again.

"This bloody dust troubles my sensitive nose quite a bit!" complained Lyon.

179

"Not just yours. I have been struggling against a heavy sneeze for a long time," said Eugene. Lyon rubbed his nose to suppress the tickling.

"I keep thinking about that noise. What could that have been?" remarked Aecey.

"To be honest, I don't really want to know," said Jim who walked at the head of the group and sent the beam of his torch down the black abyss now and then hoping to see the end of the passage in the distance.

"Jim?....ight and ... then...," it came bumbling out of the transmitter.

"Rob, repeat, please," said Jim.

"I sa. ..that you ha.... irst and then left into a tunn........staircase."

"I repeat, we have to turn left into a tunnel that leads us to a staircase."

"First right, then left into the tunn.... and to the staircase."

"Understood," said Jim. "Looks like we're close to the end of this passage," Jim told the others. And really, after a few yards there was a ninety degree turn and finally an intersection. Here they turned right and a little later left into a small passage. And soon they stood at the top of a staircase leading down. Here were shelves, too, connected to the staircase. They went down the stairs in single file. Finally they stood at the bottom of the stairs. Next to them the shelves reached all the way to the ceiling. Down here the ceiling wasn't quite seven feet above them.

"Rob? We're at the bottom."

"...stood. Go to the right till ... intersection," replied Rob. Jim set off and the others followed. Down here humidity was high. There was a musty odour. Eugene looked at the floor, it was damp and dirty. The shelves, here too, were full of boxes. Eugene let his finger glide over one of the boxes and accidentally ripped a hole in it. The boxes were so damp they had nearly turned to mush. Disgusted he threw the mush from his finger to the floor. They walked past the shelves and Eugene didn't notice how much time had passed when they suddenly stopped. They had reached the intersection.

"Okay, Rob, we're at the intersection."

"Guys, I found out something about this labyrinth. Somehow....strange.... and there....looked it up. Important papers are stored there, such as plans, documents or contracts and other precious things, too. And only two people have the right to walk around in there."

"Who?"

"The Dark Ruler and his assistant."

"His assistant?"

"His assistant, I ....about to.....who he is."

"Understood, which way do we go now?"

"To the right."

Jim started to walk.

"What do you think, who is that assistant of the Dark Ruler?" asked Lyon.

"No idea, but somehow I have a feeling that we are going to find out soon," replied Jim.

"Yes, the question is how? Is Rob going to tell us or are we going to meet him," said Lyon.

Without a word they continued walking. The light from Jim's torch became weaker and weaker and bathed everything in an orange glow. There it was again, that strange scratching sound somewhere behind the walls of shelves. Stunned they stopped and listened but there was not a sound. A drop of water fell from the ceiling and burst on the wet floor. Jim signalled to proceed.

"Jim, do you hear me?"

"Rob, I read you."

"I have just found out who the so-called assistant is. It is a hozz, a monster."

"A monster? Charming!"

"Wait, it gets even better. The monster is also called assistant or guardian. Why? Well, because it guards the labyrinth and helps the Dark Ruler by preventing anybody from entering the labyrinth."

"Holy shit! I know now how this will end. Anybody inside the labyrinth without permission will be eliminated," said Lyon.

"Right. But I also have good news for you. If you move quietly....the hozz may not be able to track you down. It has only one real strength, extremely fine hearing."

"Okay, tell me where we have to go next."

"You turn right now and you better hurry up, it will be straight ahead for a while now. You've nearly made it."

Quietly but quickly they rushed on. The shelves flew past them. Eugene looked to one side. What was that? A movement, no, he must have been mistaken. But there it was again, quite clearly, next to them, on the other side of the shelves a creature the size of a big dog followed them.

"Jim!"

"What is it?"

"There is something you ought to know."

"Give it to me!"

"We have been discovered."

"What?"

"The hozz has discovered us. He is following us, over there on the other side of the shelves." While saying these words, Eugene felt sick. His sides ached and the hozz running panting and slobbering next to him didn't improve things.

"Shit, are you serious?"

"Yes, I am," panted Eugene and bent forwards. Aecey had stopped, too, to catch her breath. Jim shone his torch through the gaps in the rows of shelves. There was nothing to be seen.

"Are you sure that you have seen a hozz?"

"I am sure! It was the size of a monster dog."

"Rob?"

"Go on."

"What does a hozz look like?"

"Well, they come in many shapes and sizes. You see that's the thing about these hozz. They are shape-shifters. It can take a while for them to change but there are no limits. It is assumed that they don't have an actual body, only a soul."

"Wonderful."

"Holy shit!" shouted Lyon.

"What happened?" asked Jim.

"A dragonfly just flew past me."

"Are you taking the piss? A dragonfly, down here, in this hole?"

"I am definitely not taking the piss."

"Run! That must be that bloody hozz, it has changed!" called Eugene. They all started running. Aecey stood rooted to the ground.

"Aecey! Come on! We have to get out of here!" Eugene called back. Aecey looked at him. Eugene called to her again. Finally she vanished in the darkness. A staircase came into view in front of Jim. They ran upstairs and reached a heavy iron trapdoor.

"What are we going to do now?"

"We have to go back, Aecey is still down there," called Eugene out of breath.

"No, there is no time for that. According to Rob the hozz will change again soon. We have to get through this trapdoor as quickly as possible!" Jim grabbed Eugene's shoulders. Eugene nodded. Lyon examined the trapdoor.

"The lock can be picked. That's not a problem for me," he said finally, "but pushing up that trapdoor might be a problem."

"We have to try."

Eugene looked back and hoped for Aecey to emerge from

the darkness but she didn't. A monstrous rumbling shook the passage and a little cloud of dust rained down from the shelves to the wet floor.

"I think it's time," said Jim.

"I'm working on it," puffed Lyon. Eugene wanted to run off, back into the darkness to Aecey, to save her. Jim held him back. "Don't do anything stupid. Remember the mission!" Eugene stayed.

"I've got the lock." Behind them they could here loud steps and a hair-raising panting.

"We'll push at three, no at two. One! Two!" With all their strength the three remaining comrades pushed against the trapdoor and opened it just a crack. Lyon went up another step and pushed again. The gap was now nearly wide enough. Eugene squeezed his upper body through and pressed with his hands against the trapdoor from below. Now they could slip through. The creature came closer and closer. Jim looked back and saw two evil eyes glowing red. Eugene stood up and held the trapdoor for Lyon to crawl out and with the help of Jim, who had quickly slipped through, and Lyon, he lowered it slowly till it was closed. The lock clicked shut and with a loud bang the hozz crashed against the lower part of the trapdoor. Aecey...

"Shit!"

"Why didn't she follow us?"

"If you ask me, there is something very odd going on."

"Aecey, holy shit! Damned shit!" Eugene kicked the wall with his foot. Jim put his hand on Eugene's shoulder.

Lyon looked around. They were in a small room, the walls wainscoted with sheet metal. The floor was black and in the middle was the hatch, through which they had just climbed, shining silvery. The room had only one door. Lyon went towards it.

"I guess there is only one way," he said.

Quietly they opened the door while Jim aimed his weapon at possible targets like drads or anything else on the other side. Nobody was in the next room. They entered and closed the door behind them.

"Rob? Do you read me?"

"Yes, please give me a report. You have disappeared from my screen."

"We have left the labyrinth but Aecey stayed behind."

"What?"

"She just stood still, I don't like it."

"What a mess! You better be careful."

"We'll try. Give us directions. We'll go to the engine room now."

"Just a sec, you're back on the screen. I can't see Aecey anywhere. Oh well, first cross the room to the door on the left, then along the corridor to another door again on the left."

"Okay." Jim went to the door. He opened it carefully and with their guns at the ready, they all hoped that there wasn't anyone behind it. They were wrong. There was a robot in the middle of the corridor, his back turned towards them. Jim gave them a sign to be quiet. The robot turned away and stepped through a door. Jim heaved a sigh of relief. They dropped their guns, relieved. They waited for a few more seconds to be sure that the robot wouldn't come back and then stepped into the corridor. It was a very small corridor with red lines along both walls. The ceiling was covered in mirrors and lamps were placed into the floor and were mirrored in the ceiling. Jim saw the door on the left and walked towards it. Something banged behind them. Startled they turned round. A door had opened and an incredible noise came out of it. Eugene guessed that it was the door leading to the kitchen. Quickly they ran to the other door and slipped through. It was pitch-dark and Jim switched on his torch again. Slowly he shone it around the room. It was a pantry. There were shelves everywhere, filled with cans and other food stuffs like fruit and vegetable and boxes of drink.

"I don't have a good feeling about this. If somebody comes from the kitchen where is he likely to go?"

"To the pantry, to get food," replied Eugene. Jim and Lyon nodded.

"Rob? Can you read me?"

"Eugene go to the door and hold it shut with all your strength!" said Lyon.

"Jim, I read you. We are in a room. It's a pantry."

"Okay, it is not far from there. Go straight through the pantry to the fireproof steel door. That'll take you to a staircase. Go left there, then down."

"Shit!" called Eugene. He had to press his whole body against the door to keep everybody out. From outside came loud calling. Lyon joined him and helped to keep the door shut. Jim ran to the door on the other side of the room. When the pushing from outside stopped, Eugene and Lyon dared to leave it and ran as fast as possible across the room to the bright spot of Jim's torch. Behind them the door burst into many small pieces, it had been shot open. The air was misty with the whirling dust. Eugene locked the door.

The staircase was illuminated by a few lamps. It was dark grey and had an iron bannister. Quickly and quietly they ran downstairs. They didn't want to risk being found before having placed the bomb. But that might prove difficult since their action just now had as good as betrayed them. They could only hope that Aecey hadn't been discovered yet.

The others ran away from the dragonfly. Aecey stood there and looked after them. Eugene called to her to come along but she knew better. The light became weaker until she finally stood in the dark. With slow steps she walked back, climbed through one of the rows of shelves and went to a door. In front of her was a small staircase. She climbed it and stepped through another door. She found herself now in a big room strewn with all sorts of machines and tools. She crossed it quickly. How foolish the rebels' boss had been, that old idiot had believed her. Aecey grabbed her blonde hair and pulled it off her head with a jerk. Then she tore off her face and disclosed a robot underneath. It had a sharply cut form and red glowing eyes. She freed herself from the rest of the shell still covering her. Using an elevator she went up to the top floors of the ship. Up here everything was furnished luxuriously. After all, the ruler himself lived on this floor. She followed the hallway to a door. There was more life up here and she kept swerving to avoid bumping into people moving in the other direction. After knocking on the door three times, she entered. Two drads were on guard and she nodded to them as she entered. She was in a big room with tiles shining black. Slowly she went to the desk in the middle of the room. Behind it stood a leather armchair. The Dark Ruler looked at her face. Aecey couldn't see his face. It was all black.

"Aecey," roared his voice sounding like a poorly programmed drad. Aecey nodded.

"There is something to report?"

"Yes, milord. The group succeeded in gaining entrance to the ship. I have left them to warn you. There are three of them and they carry weapons."

"Three? What arrogance. Where are they going?"

"They were in the labyrinth and escaped from the hozz through a trapdoor. It nearly caught them. Their target is the main engine room; they want to place a bomb there."

"Where? It is hardly likely that they will succeed. What

187

else can you tell me?"

"There is a jet on the parking deck where they left a contact."

"Kill that person! And you Aecey, go back to your group, you have to stop them, no matter how."

"Why don't you send your drads?"

"I'll do that as well. But you, Aecey, you are my secret weapon so to speak. And now leave, put on your disguise and wait till I have you called in."

"As you wish, milord." Aecey got up and left the room. Quickly she went to get her disguise and tried to put it back on as well as possible. At last she managed, more or less. When the Dark Ruler had her called, she was ready.

Finally they had arrived at the bottom, it had taken longer than they had expected and Eugene's knees had turned to jelly.

"Rob?"

"Are you at the bottom?"

"Yes, we are all the way down."

"Good, now go through the left door. Do you see it?"

"Yes, I do."

"You'll see an air vent. Go inside and call me once you are there."

"Understood."

When they stepped through the door, they saw the air vent ahead of them. It was as high as it was wide and there was a hatch on the side. Jim kicked it with his foot and with a loud clattering it flew inside. In the vent they had to crawl again. They had to crawl for a long time, round bends, past intersections. Eugene didn't feel his knees anymore and Jim and Lyon suffered, too. Twice they took a wrong turn and had to go back.

"What is this?" called Jim and stopped.

"What do you mean?"

"The air vent goes round a bend but then it goes down," answered Jim.

"That'll be fun."

"We cannot go down here. We don't know how far down that goes and who is waiting there for us."

"What choice have we got?"

"We have to take another way."

"Rubbish. That only wastes time."

Jim looked carefully over the edge.

"It goes down about 20 feet," he said.

"Go on, let's continue."

Jim sighed. He lay down flat on his stomach and slowly slid downhill. He closed his eyes but he realized that he moved ever faster. And finally it was over and he landed hard on the floor.

He quickly got out of the way. Lyon landed next to him and Eugene, too, a moment later. They looked around. The vent was at an end and they had slid into a room. The room was small. In each of the four walls was a door.

"Which door should we take?" Jim asked Rob.

"A door should open, Anjakan is written on it." Jim looked round and found it.

"Yes, we see it."

"Go through and into the next shaft."

Eugene went to the door and opened it. There was an air vent along the ceiling of the room. Eugene smashed one of the many hatches and pulled himself up into the shaft. Lyon followed and then Jim.

"Milord," said the drad.

"What report can you give me, my trusty servant?"

"The group has advanced via staircase 21 into the tenth basement."

"Ah. They are approaching the engine room. Very good, take a team and intercept them. Don't kill them. I want to talk to them. Take them prisoner and put them in a cell. But use a clean one!"

"As you like, milord." The drad turned around. Ten drads followed him as he left the room and they went to the elevators on the right side of the passage.

He wouldn't be able to cope much longer. All this crawling on the metal was hard on Eugene. They had been on board the drad ship for five hours by now. Soon they would reach the engine room. Eugene's thoughts kept wandering to Aecey. Was she still alive? Meanwhile they climbed down a ladder which was bliss for Eugene's knees.

"Rob? We are in a room now with two doors. Which door should we take?"

"The red one. And then straight ahead," replied Rob after a little wait.

"Okay." Lyon went to the red door, put his hand on the handle and pushed. Eugene and Jim didn't believe what they saw.

As soon as Lyon opened the door, he regretted it. In front of him stood at least ten drads. They had a wiry build and a snake-like head. Their eyes shone green, but as Eugene, Lyon, and Jim watched they became red. Lyon lifted his hands, Eugene and Jim did the same. Ten laser pistols that were each connected to a drad arm were pointed at the three comrades at once.

"On the floor!" said the foremost drad. Slowly they lay down on the floor. The floor was icy-cold and Eugene tried not to touch it with his skin. Three drads approached and bound their hands and feet with iron shackles. They did this so expertly, it was frightening.

"Get up," ordered the drad. They got up, hands bound on the back.

"Come along!" The ten drads surrounded them and set off.

They had to keep up their pace in order not to be kicked by the drads walking behind them. They walked through grey, white and black corridors, rooms and halls illuminated by neon lamps, past other drads, creatures and machinery. Eugene wondered what was going to happen to them. Would they have them killed? Or tortured? Eugene was sure that should they try to escape they would definitely be killed. Would they take their guns?

They walked down stairs now. They were grey iron stairs encrusted with dirt. There was bad lighting and one of the drads pressed a light switch that was one of many fixed in a row along the wall. The wall was painted in an ugly brown. After some yards they came into a larger passage that was lined with cell doors on both sides. The doors were thick, heavy and dirty in a silvery colour and without windows but with a serving hatch. The drads walked to one of the big doors. The drad in front unlocked the door, it opened automatically. With an unpleasant kick in the back, the three were pushed into the cell. The floor was made of silvery metal with knobs as were the walls and the ceiling. There was a lamp that illuminated the room that measured three yards by three. The light was reflected a thousand times by the highly polished walls and dazzled them. Eugene was surprised to find the cell so clean whereas the corridors outside had been quite dirty. There was nothing to sit down on therefore they had to sit on the floor.

"They didn't even take our weapons," said Lyon.

"There is a simple enough reason for that. They are no bloody good in this bloody room!" said Jim.

"And what are we going to do now?" asked Eugene.

"Wait. Maybe we will be released again soon. On the other hand, if we are unlucky, we'll be tortured or killed."

"I just wonder what happened to Aecey."

"I guess that Aecey made a good impression by

denouncing us."

"Take that back," shouted Eugene at Lyon.

"Why should I? Look, we all ran away and she stood still. And you, Eugene, didn't you call to her to come along?" Eugene looked at the floor. "And, did she come?" Eugene shook his head.

"But maybe there is a reason for that," he said.

"Which one?"

"I don't know, maybe she thought that there was another exit. I remember that she looked at me when I called to her to run. She looked so hostile," said Eugene.

"You know what? I wouldn't be surprised if we crossed paths with Aecey again on board this ship," predicted Jim.

"Yes, but no longer on our side, but on the side of the dark one," laughed Lyon sarcastically.

"Shut up! You talk about Aecey as if she had really betrayed us and yet she may be dead!" Eugene looked at the others screwing up his eyes. Both of them nodded, embarrassed.

"You are right, of course."

"I am in favour of suggestions about how to get out of here."

"There is really only one chance. We have to wait till they come to get us and then make a run for it," said Lyon.

"You mean when they come to get us to, let's say, torture us we just run away?" asked Eugene.

"That's right if you like it or not." Jim pulled his knees up to his chest.

"Jim? Couldn't you ask Rob for advice?" Jim shook his head. "No, we don't have reception in this cell."

"Then we'll just have to wait."

In the office there was a window giving onto a great hall where there a lot of coming and going, everybody scurrying around busily. The Dark Ruler liked watching how things moved according to the rules and regulations. There was a knock. He slowly turned around to his desk. "Milord!" The drad entered.

"Report!"

"Our team succeeded in catching the three rebels. It was easy."

"Good. I want to talk to them in an hour, take them to the interrogation room. You may leave."

"Thank you, milord."

"I cannot stand this anymore. Can somebody please turn off this bloody light?" Lyon banged against the iron door with his fist.

"How long have we been here?" asked Eugene.

"Nearly an hour," replied Jim.

"It's about time that somebody came to get us. Rob must be worried by now. Plus, time is running out. If the drad transporters leave before we have even placed the bomb we'll have to fight a war after all," moaned Lyon.

"Yes, we'll have to fight it but the bomb is going to take care of the ruler of the UDP and without him the drad armies are as good as defeated," said Jim.

"Never mind what is going to happen. Our mission will be a success, it has to be!"

"I think someone is coming." They listened and, indeed, there were sounds outside the door and a moment later the door of their cell was opened. There were six drads. Eugene studied them, they looked really frightening and a mirror image of their ruler, quite simply incredibly evil.

"Get up!" ordered one of the drads. Lyon, Eugene and Jim did him the favour. Jim looked around. Only two of the drads had their weapons at the ready.

"Step out!" Jim walked through the door, Eugene next, and Lyon last. The drad closed the door and ordered them to start walking. Lyon pulled his gun and shot the drad next to him in the head. There was pandemonium and utter mayhem. The drad beeped and hummed and shouted some orders. Jim and Eugene pulled their guns as well and shot at all drads close by. Laser projectiles whistled through the air. Drads were torn to pieces. None of the three was injured. Panting, they looked at their handiwork. Six drads were lying around them on the floor of the passage, giving off sparks.

"We better hurry. Somebody might have reported this or our shots were heard," said Jim. "Rob? We were caught but we managed to escape."

"Boy, am I glad to hear your voice! Where are you?"

"Somewhere in a corridor with prison cells."

"Okay, there are three dungeons on the ship. You must be in one of them. Give me a hint."

"We came down a staircase leading directly into this corridor. And there is a door at the other end of it."

"I think I've got you. Go to the door, there is a room with five doors."

Jim set off and the others followed. There's was no need now to be careful. With their weapons drawn, they rushed into the room. There was no-one in it. Eugene looked around; it was a room holding instruments of torture. A chair with spikes more than an inch long, whips, crushers, pliers, hammers, and electric appliances.

"Rob? There are only three doors, four if we count ours."

"Okay, I know where you are. Turn right and take the first door."

Eugene couldn't wait to get out of this room. The long room they now entered smelled of metal and when breathing through the mouth, there was a metallic taste on the tongue. The air was damp. Eugene tried to take shallow breaths.

"Rob?"

"There should be a vent underneath you, in the floor." Jim

194

and the others started to search the floor.

"Yes, we've got it."

It was a shaft with a ladder leading into the depth.

"What?" the ruler of the UDP yelled at the bearer of the bad news, "The prisoners have escaped and have destroyed all six drads?"

"Yes, milord."

"Idiots, I am surrounded by idiots! You better see to it that you lock them up again as fast as possible! And send a unit to the main engine room!"

"Instantly, milord."

Jim, Lyon, and Eugene were now in the first part of the engine room.

"Rob? What do we have to do?"

"You are in engine room number 3. Keep walking!"

The noise was deafening and the visibility was bad because the room was full of steam. The engines were huge and pipes were everywhere. Everything shook. They went through a rusty iron door.

"You ar... eng....2."

Jim kept walking, followed by Eugene and Lyon. Engine room 2 was about three times the size of engine room 3 and it took them a long time to cross it. The engines were as tall as houses and twice as noisy as in the previous room. *Engine room 1* was written on a big door. They stepped through.

"Okay, Rob, we are in engine room 1."

"Right. Get go...."

"Wait! I would suggest a small change of plan."

"What?"

"The drads know that we are on board. I suggest that we place the bomb not in engine room 1 itself, but in the minor engine room next to it, close to the fuel tanks."

"Not a bad idea. The tanks will explode and the force of the explosion will tear the ship apart. Rob? We have changed the plan, we're going to explode the fuel tanks of the ship!"

"I…okay…p…you!"

"Raise the alarm! The drads must go to their troopships at once. I expect that in ten minutes there are no more than fifty drads on board. And get me Aecey!"

With a bow the blue-skinned man turned around and left the ruler's office. A moment later Aecey entered.

"Aecey, now you get that task you wanted so much."

"Milord?"

"Find the jet they are in touch with and destroy it including the person inside. And there is no margin for error!"

"Yes, milord."

Lyon pressed against the heavy iron door labelled *Fuel Storage (Authorized personnel only)* and slowly he pushed it open. At last they were able to squeeze through the gap. Lyon left the door ajar to facilitate flight once they had placed the bomb. The room had a high ceiling but was narrow with huge metal tanks reaching to the ceiling on both sides. It smelled of fuel.

"We should place the bomb somewhere where it is difficult to see and, even more importantly where it is difficult to get to," declared Jim and tried to squeeze in between two tanks. He managed to get in about a couple of feet then he pulled the bomb out of his pocket and put it carefully on the floor. It was in the shape of a triangle and had three buttons, one was used to start the countdown, and the others were dummies.

"Get ready to run!" called Jim and put his finger on the button. He pressed and with a quiet click the mechanism engaged and the bomb started counting backwards. They had 30 minutes. Jim squeezed back out of the gap and they started running.

29:55 minutes

"Milord, we are in engine room 1 now but there is nobody here."
"Wait, they are coming. Stay in touch and report anything unusual!"
"Yes, milord."
The Dark Ruler turned to his servant. "How about Aecey? Has she destroyed the jet yet?"
"No, milord, it takes fifteen minutes to get to the parking deck. But she should be ready to act in a few seconds."
"And how are the troops on Xaviera doing?"
"They are nearly complete and ready for action."
"Dismissed."

Eugene, Lyon, and Jim ran back the way they had come, past the dark walls, past the air vent, back to the room with the instruments of torture and through the dungeons. Up the stairs they ran and then guided by Rob through an air vent that would take them to a parking deck one level above the one where their jet was parked. From there they only had to run a little way before they would reach a staircase to run down to the lower level. They made quick progress and Eugene felt those unpleasant stitches again in his side that nearly took his breath away and got worse with every step.

20:38 minutes

Aecey stepped out of the elevator before the door had fully opened. The air on the parking deck always smelled slightly salty, dry and full of exhaust fumes. Quickly she

197

walked past the concrete and steel pillars, walked across the marked parking spaces and approached the jet where Rob sat. With a jerk she pulled her gun and checked it. Everything was in working order. Her steps echoed on the walls and they seemed unnaturally loud to her. She had the feeling that Rob could hear her and escape. That was nonsense, of course. Pull yourself together, she thought. She stood outside the jet now. She went to the hatch and knocked three times. Her mouth twisted in a smile.

"Rob? Which way?" Jim and the other two were in the shaft leading to the parking deck.
"Go straight ahead, then left, then right and then straight ahead to a hatch. That's it. Then you just walk down the staircase and you'll be back here with me."
"See you in a bit."
"Damn!"
"Rob? What is happening?"
"There was a knock at the hatch. What should I do, Jim?"
"Don't open! We're on our way."
As fast as possible they crawled through the shaft. Rob was in trouble and with him their chance to get away from this ship.

14:59 minutes

There was another knock, Rob felt uneasy. It would take the others at least another five minutes, and by then whoever had knocked would lose patience. Rob took his laser pistol from the chair beside him and loaded it. Frightened he went to the corridor leading to the hatch and took aim.
Aecey started to lose her patience. If he didn't open, she would have to break in. She shot at the two hinges to open the hatchway. Rob gave a start when he heard the shots.

Aecey had to fire several shots to break down the hatch because it was made of good material. Clattering loudly, the hatchway fell down at her feet. When the stirred up dust had settled, she saw Rob standing in front of her with a raised gun and staring at her.

"Hi, Rob!" she said and aimed her gun at him.

"Aecey, we thought you were dead," stammered Rob and dropped his gun.

"No, I am very much alive," Aecey kept aiming at him.

"What's going on? Drop your gun!"

"No, I won't. I'll have to kill you now, Rob."

"But why, how, I don't understand."

"You don't understand, Rob? Don't you understand that I am not a living being? I am the same as you! I am a robot!" Aecey pulled the mask off her face again and her red eyes glared at Rob with an evil glimmer.

"You have no chance. Jim and the others are on the way back. The ship will blow up in ten minutes' time."

"Impossible! The Dark Ruler knows where you wanted to place the bomb, in the main engine room. But at this very moment there are at least fifteen drads expecting three rebels right there."

"Aecey, you're wrong! But I tell you one thing. Go to hell!" Rob aimed but Aecey was quicker and fired at his legs. Rob was pulled forward and landed on his knees. His gun was hurled out of his hand and he couldn't reach it anymore. Aecey stepped up to him on the hatchway.

"Oh Rob, I am nearly sorry." And with a well-aimed shot she blew Rob's head to smithereens.

09:46 minutes

Aecey turned around and ran back until there was enough distance between her and the jet. Then she took aim at the windscreen and fired. After a few more shots, the windscreen burst and shattered into a million pieces. Flying into space with this jet would mean instant death. Aecey pushed the button to call the elevator. After a few seconds the door opened. She was about to enter when she heard sounds from the direction of the staircase. There was no-one left on the ship except a few drads, the Dark Ruler and herself. Slowly she turned around and followed the wall to the staircase on the opposite side. This could only be Jim, Eugene, and Lyon. And a moment later the trio stepped through the door and made straight for the jet. Aecey had to smile, they hadn't seen her.

08:23 minutes

They had hardly any strength left and the staircase did for them. Panting, they rushed through the door onto the parking deck and stumbled towards the jet.
They hoped that Rob was fine.
"The hatchway is open!" called Jim.
They stood outside the jet and on the hatchway lay Rob, without head.
"Shit! What are we going to do now?"
"We have to get away as quickly as possible. There isn't much time left!" Eugene and Lyon grabbed Rob and pulled him up the hatchway.
"Damn!" yelled Jim from the cockpit. "Our windscreen has been shattered!" Jim returned to the others and knelt down next to Rob.
"We have to get another jet as fast as possible."
"Are we taking him with us?"
"I'd love to take him with us. Come on, help me to carry him." They took Rob on their shoulders and carefully walked down the hatchway. Eugene looked around for a jet and finally spotted one that looked a bit the worse for wear at the back of the deck. They started heading for it.

Lyon and Jim carried Rob and walked in front. Eugene followed them.

05:57 minutes

"Stop!" Startled they stopped.
"Aecey? Damn it, I knew you had betrayed us!" called Lyon.
"Aecey? Are you nuts? That's not Aecey!" retorted Eugene. Aecey stood in front of them the way she really was, with red eyes.
"Eugene, don't you recognize me?" she asked.
"Aecey, that's not you!"
"Oh yes, it's me! But it won't be you for much longer."
"Wait! First explain to us how you could convince him!" demanded Jim.
"The old fart? That was really easy. Aecey really existed, the old man knew her. My ruler gave me the order to make use of that fact. So I killed the real Aecey and got the disguise. I looked just like Aecey and was very pleased. I was able to talk the old guy into it in no time. And you fools didn't have the least suspicion."
"So? Not bad, really. But you don't convince me!"
"I don't care. It doesn't matter anymore what you find convincing and what you don't!" Aecey's eyes flashed dangerously.
"You do realize that you might have survived if you had stayed with us?" asked Eugene causing Aecey to burst into a spine-chilling tinny laughter.
"What do you mean?" she asked.
"The bomb has been placed."
"No! That is impossible! You didn't have a chance to get past the unit guarding engine room 1!"
"Oh yes, we did! In about three minutes all this will be blown into oblivion!"

"I don't believe it! And even if, it doesn't matter. The drad army is already on its way!" Aecey shot at Jim and hit him. Rob fell down and Lyon stumbled under the weight and the momentum of the falling Jim and fell to the floor. Eugene ducked and aimed in his turn. He shot and hit Aecey in the stomach, she went to her knees and lost her weapon. Eugene rushed towards her and kicked the gun out of reach. Her eyes glowed palely.

"I hate you!" she murmured, then her eyes died and she sank on her back. Eugene got up and ran to Jim lying injured on the floor. Lyon was kneeling beside him.

01:42 minutes

"Everything okay?"

"Not too bad."

"We have to get him on board. There we can take care of him," said Lyon.

"Jim, we'll carry you," said Lyon to warn Jim. Jim nodded and closed his eyes. Lyon and Eugene took him on their shoulders and went slowly to the jet. They had another minute. The jet wasn't locked and they could easily get in through the hatch. There was nobody on board. Eugene ran back to get Rob and put him over his shoulder. Running, he returned and put Rob down beside Jim. After closing the hatch and making sure that Jim was well secured on the floor, Lyon slipped into the cockpit. As quickly as possible he started the jet. Eugene saw the motionless Aecey lying on the floor and was overcome by an undefinable sadness.

00:38 minutes

He needed all his driving skills to steer the jet through the maze of pillars. Finally they reached the exit, Lyon raced through and they were surrounded by the blackness of the universe.

"Another ten seconds!" called Lyon and accelerated even more. In his mind Eugene counted down to ten.

"Milord! We have found the bomb!"

"Very good, can you defuse it?"

"No, we cannot."

"Shit, send it into space in a jet!"

"Impossible! It'll explode in three seconds!"

"What? You damned useless drads! You ungrateful tinny riff-raff! I should never have created you! I must not die! I am too important! No! Where is Aecey! Kill her! It is her fault! It was her job to stop the rebels!"

00:03 minutes
00:02 minutes

"Aecey!"

00:01 minutes

The drad control ship exploded in a gigantic fireball. The fuel tanks increased the force of the bomb so much that within two seconds the entire spaceship was ablaze. Like a living being without a head, the flames crept with incredible speed through the ship and turned everything that stood in their path to ashes.

The ruler of the UDP looked at his office door. It buckled inwards and flew at him, followed by an enormous wall of flames. From one second to the next, he was dead. His dream to rule the universe crumbled to black ashes but the vision lived on....Xaviera existed...

Lyon, Eugene, and Jim didn't hear the explosion but they

could feel it all the more. They had done it! The Dark Ruler had been defeated! Now it would be easy to destroy the drad army.

Through the force of the explosion, the jet had been accelerated even more. Lyon was forced into his seat. Tongues of flames licked the jet. Eugene tried to hold on in order not to be flung through the jet and to secure Jim at the same time. After a while it was over and Lyon switched to autopilot. Lyon left the cockpit to check on Jim. Eugene had knelt down and had covered the wound with some pieces of cloth. Jim had his eyes shut.

"Is he asleep?" asked Lyon.

"I think so," replied Eugene.

"Is it bad?"

"No, it is only superficial. It looks worse than it is."

"Can we treat him here?"

"No, we need qualified medical help."

"What about Rob?"

"We'll have him repaired on the mothership. If his memory chip has not been damaged, and as far as I can see, not being an expert, mind, that is the case, he can be saved."

"Take Jim to a room where he can rest. We better leave Rob here."

Eugene and Lyon sat in the cockpit without talking, looking at the stars. They twinkled yellow and white and brightened the black sky of the universe. The jet hummed quietly and brought them ever closer to the mothership and to safety.

"I don't know why but I feel really safe looking at the stars. I have the feeling that I belong," said Lyon.

"Do you miss your home planet, Mars?"

"Yes, I do. I miss the dry dusty air. The chaotic hustle and bustle in the streets, the wild parties at night and even the hunting for humans. I miss the Colloscoseum and its heart-breaking screams. Not that I approve of what happens there but I miss it all the same."

"I can understand that. I miss Earth even though I don't know why." Lyon nodded, understanding, too. "Shall we go to bed? We had a tough day," he suggested. Eugene nodded, got up and they both left the cockpit.

"I'll just go and check on Jim," said Lyon. Eugene went through one of the two doors and found a room with four beds. He left the door open so Lyon knew where he was. There was even a sink in the room. Eugene went there and turned the tap to the right. When nothing happened, he turned it left, nothing. With a sigh, he sank into one of the beds. They smelled fresh and Eugene was glad about that. He had expected the worst, like a bed smelling of sweat and excrements. The last thing he heard was Lyon coming into the room before he fell asleep.

Floating, Eugene flew over a city. It was bathed in red light and everything glittered. Eugene plunged down, everything was under control. With a loud thud, he landed on the pavement, the streets were empty, there was no-one to be seen. Tall buildings reaching into the red sky rose up near him. Blood..... What had shone red, had been nothing but blood, everything was made of it. He fell into a big black hole, it was cold and his voice started to freeze. Words made of ice streamed out of his mouth and floated out into the eternal blackness. With a heavy bang, he landed in grass. There was a house. The House of Time, laughing, it stood in front of him, it grinned at him, its claws grabbed him and wanted to squash him. He wanted to run away but the grass was alive and yelled at him, "Stay with us, we are not going to hurt you. We are only your grass....your grass...." The windows of the house burst and a torrent of blood poured out of it, it flowed thick and glutinous, getting closer to Eugene. Until it had finally reached him and buried him.

"Eugene! Eugene, wake up! You're having a nightmare!" Lyon stood at his bed and shook him by the shoulders. "Wake up, you're having a nightmare!" he said. He sat down and rubbed his eyes.

"Those damned nightmares. When do we get there?"

"Soon, another ten hours."

"Have you been awake long? How is Jim?"

"He's fine. I have been awake for half an hour."

"Have you eaten?"

"No, I haven't. After checking on Jim, I've had a look over the ship. There is no galley. But don't worry. When we reach the mothership in ten hours' time, they'll prepare a feast for us," Lyon grinned.

"I hope so."

"You can bet your bottom dollar on it!" Lyon got up and left the room. Eugene threw back his blanket and got up himself. Yawning he went through the third door to where Jim lay on a bed.

Jim was on a bed standing in a corner at the end of the room. It was covered with a brown and red blanket. Jim had his eyes closed. Slowly Eugene went to the bed. Jim was still wearing the improvised bandage. He was asleep. Eugene turned around and went to join Lyon in the cockpit.

"Lyon?"

"What's up?"

"I have a question for you."

"Spit it out."

"Well, I am wondering, I don't know how to put it, maybe it sounds a bit daft, if there is a woman somewhere out there, maybe, who is right for me, do you know what I mean?"

"I think I can understand," said Lyon after a while. "You feel lonely. You are the only human being who knows and enjoys the feeling of freedom. You are longing for a partner, preferably a female one." Lyon nodded in Eugene's direction. Eugene looked at him, surprised.

"I've never known you like that at all. Where did you learn to talk like that?"

"Eugene, you know so much and yet so little. And it's the same for me. I am an extremely good soul searcher. That's why I am here. I am the one who was to catch a potential traitor before he can betray us. Unfortunately, I didn't manage to do that with Aecey."

"Incredible! Are there things about Jim I don't know?"

"Of course! Everybody has his private life and his experiences but I know as much about Jim as you do. Well, maybe a bit more."

"And Slow?" asked Eugene and regretted it instantly. Lyon stared into nothing.

"Let's change the subject." Lyon was shattered. Slow and his death still caused him a lot of pain. Eugene looked at the floor; he shouldn't have mentioned this to Lyon. "Sorry!"

"What for? That's okay. I just want to forget about it, you know?" Eugene nodded in agreement.

"You're getting on ok here on your own? I'll go and check on Jim," asked Eugene. Lyon nodded, switched the jet to autopilot and leaned back.

Eugene and Lyon were able to see the mothership from afar, close to a planet shimmering in red and green. In a few minutes they would dock.

"Am I glad to be here at last," said Lyon.

"Do you think it is true what Aecey said?"

207

"What did she say?"

"Well, that the drad army is already on its way."

"Yes, the war isn't over yet. As the saying goes, we have won the battle but not the war - yet," said Lyon and established radio contact with the mothership.

"Access code?" hissed a female voice out of the speaker.

"Lyon, Rob, Eugene, and Jim ask for permission to dock. Access code: 1415900 + 12," said Lyon.

"Access granted. Please go to dock 19. You will be welcomed there in style," it hissed. Lyon guided his jet to dock 19. The mothership was huge and dock 19, a big hatch guarded by many heavy machine guns, seemed small in comparison. Slowly the hatch opened and Lyon approached it equally slowly. Once the hatch had opened completely, Lyon flew into it and landed on a big platform a moment later. They were in a big hangar lined with iron panels. Up above were long windows. Normally there was nobody there but today they were jam-packed with faces pressed against the glass. Everybody wanted to catch a glimpse of the heroes who had defeated the ruler of the UDP.

"Look at that, they are all waiting for us. This is madness. I expected to die in the drad ship. I never dreamed I would be trampled on my return," said Lyon and looked up to the packed windows. Eugene nodded.

"Expected to die quietly as a forgotten almost hero?" They went to Jim, took him on their shoulders and carried him out into the great hall. Then they went back for Rob and carried him outside as well. The door opened and a lot of people rushed towards them. In front were security guards dressed in black suits.

Normally, Lyon thought this was exaggerated, but this time it was necessary. The hall was filled with a cheering crowd. More and more people rushed through the door and tried by all means to catch a glimpse of the heroes. Jim and Rob were taken care of by four doctors dressed in white and carried to the exit. Eugene and Lyon, too, pushed their way through while the security guards tried to keep a path clear for them. That took them a bit longer, however, but finally Lyon and Eugene were able to leave the great hall just to find that outside there were just as many people.

Flanked by an escort, Lyon and Eugene went to see their boss, Hesson Lachopp. Eugene remembered the big and wide, well-lit corridors with their countless doors very well, so different from the cool empty drad control ship. Finally they stopped outside the door where they had stood not so long ago. Lyon knocked. From inside came a "Come in!" Lyon and Eugene entered. Nothing had changed. The office looked exactly the same as it had done the last time. Eugene and Lyon sat down in the leather armchairs opposite the desk behind which Hesson sat.

"Welcome back!" he said and smiled honestly and happily.

"We are happy to be back," said Lyon and Eugene nodded in agreement, "Indeed!"

"I am sure you have noticed with how much enthusiasm you have been welcomed. Naturally, I cannot forbid my people to organize a welcome party in your honour." Hesson looked resigned. "You might also call it the party to end all parties. The whole ship has been invited. The four of you are the guests of honour. But first tell me your story. Have you really done it?"

"Yes, the ship has been destroyed."

"You look downcast, Lyon."

"The drad army fled from the ship before it exploded. The Dark Ruler is dead, yes. But his army is still alive."

"That's not good. We have to expect another battle. But the drads will be weak without their leader."

"But they outnumber us very clearly."

"Yes, that is true. Tell me everything, I want to know everything," said Hesson, and Lyon started to tell their story. He told about their adventure on Mars, the death of Slow. He told about the forest moon of Jupiter and their landing on a chunk of Earth. He told about the discovery of the House of Time and the robots guarding it. He told of their journey into the twenty-first century and of picking up Aecey. He told of the attack of the hunters and the emergency landing on Jaffadurr and the friendly mechanic. Then he told of their experiences on the drad control ship: the air vent, the labyrinth, Aecey's betrayal, the engine room, Rob's destruction and the meeting with Aecey on the parking deck. When he had finished, Lyon breathed heavily. He had talked for nearly three hours without a break. Hesson nodded; he had listened closely, had nodded his head and agreed or asked a question now and then. With a groan, he leaned back into his armchair and looked from Eugene to Lyon and back. Then he said, "You have really earned this party. Enjoy it, party till you drop. There is nothing for you to do tomorrow."

"Thank you, boss," said Lyon and Eugene and went through the door. They were again accompanied by an escort.

"Lyon, what time is it?"

"It's 3pm."

"When does the party start tonight?" Eugene asked one of the security guards.

"At 8pm," replied one of them. Eugene decided to sleep for four hours to be fit for the big party. After all, the party was also given in his honour, so he wanted to stay until the end even if it should last till the morning.

He drove his car over the road as fast as the wind, past trees and rivers. He drove a sporty car, all black. The varnish reflected the sun. A half rotten skull flew against

210

the windscreen and shattered the glass. That's the third one today already, thought Eugene. He sat in an elegant restaurant; the waiter served a plate of beautiful china. Eugene took it and took a bite. The floor caved in beneath his feet, he fell down. He grazed himself on the soil around him and broke his leg. Heavily, he landed on a meadow. It was covered with green grass and flowers. The flowers were particularly beautiful; they had the form of human skulls. He looked up. The House of Time stood in front of him, menacing, black and surrounded by an aura of evil. He wasn't able to get up. The house screamed, louder and louder. Eugene could hardly bear it anymore. It was a shrill sound, first quietly, then louder and louder until the grass went up in flames and his head exploded with a big "splash."

Eugene opened his eyes. He had had another nightmare. Slowly his eyes got used to being awake. The bed he was lying in smelled fresh but was wet with sweat. He looked at the alarm clock. The party would begin in half an hour. With heavy legs, Eugene got up, went to the sink and bathed his face in icy-cold water. There was a knock.
"Come in!" he said while drying his face with a towel. Lyon opened the door and came into the room. "Good evening."
"Hi, Lyon. How long have you been awake?"
"For about ten minutes. We have slept half the afternoon. They've been working all-out. The party will be in the great hall. I've been told that it will be quite impressive."
"I am really looking forward to it."
"Do you have something to wear? You cannot wear your dirty clothes for our party," said Lyon and only now did Eugene notice that Lyon was wearing a clean elegant suit. Eugene shook his head. Lyon went across the room to a wardrobe and opened it. Suits in assorted colours were

211

neatly lined up on coat hangers and swayed back and forth. Eugene gaped. He quickly went to the wardrobe. After some reflection he pulled out a white suit and tried it on. It looked splendid. Now he was ready for the big party. They started heading to the great hall. They were assured that Jim would be present at the party. Since the ship was so big, it took some time to get to the hall. They walked past palm gardens, offices and big doors made of expensive rare woods. They used elevators and walked through hallways laid with carpets. They went through a cafeteria smelling strongly of coffee and bacon. The closer they came to the hall, the denser the crowd became. Some were very busy. Here and there they saw trays with glasses, plates, cakes, roasts and similar things being carried about. There were cries of "Careful!", "Watch out!", "Get out of the way!" Eugene couldn't remember ever having seen anything like it. The background noise was equally incredible, there was a constant humming.

At last they stood outside the big doors of the hall. They stood open and it was possible to see everything that was going on. It was spectacular. Everything was shining and sparkling in all imaginable shades. There were colour organs on all sides, fog machines, flashes and lasers illuminated the room and made it dance. Half the hall had been lined with a platform where there was dancing. Below were tables, counters, bars and food stands. In-between were DJs who did their best to fill the hall with good loud music. There were people everywhere, dancing, shouting, eating, and talking. Everybody aboard ship had to be assembled here! Huge disco balls were hanging from the ceiling in their hundreds.
"Fantastic!" Lyon called into Eugene's ear so he would understand him. Eugene nodded at him.
"I'll plunge myself into the hurly-burly! I'll see you when I

see you!" called Lyon and disappeared among the hopping crowd. Eugene looked around and decided to head across the dancefloor to get to food, drinks and most of all the tables. It took him longer than expected. Moving with the rhythm of the music he weaved his way through the dancers until he finally got there and sat down at the next available table. Many tables were still unoccupied but many others were already taken. The electronic music was animating and encouraged the dancers; the colour organs blinking in time with the music made him feel like he was in another world. Eugene looked around but couldn't see anybody he knew. But that would have been surprising considering that he knew virtually nobody but everybody knew him and total strangers kept coming towards him wishing him all the best or thanking him for everything. A waiter came to his table to take his order. Eugene hadn't even thought of looking at the menu. He ordered something to drink first.

"Water, please."

"Water? Darling, this is your party, you have to have something better to drink, whisky, liqueur, wine, champagne, anything."

"I've never had whisky, liqueur, wine or champagne."

"Oh, oh, wait, I'll bring you some," said the waiter and disappeared between the chairs and tables. The music started to fade away. Everybody looked at the DJs who stood on small pedestals. Now Hesson stood there, too, holding a microphone in his hand. The music faded further and finally stopped altogether.

"Attention, please!" The hall fell silent. "Thank you. We have come together tonight to welcome back and honour some men and to celebrate their achievements. Please put your hands together for Jim. He's down there and he was the leader of the mission!" Hesson pointed into the crowd below him and everybody started to clap and cheer. "And

213

now let's hear it for Lyon who is somewhere in this big hall. He was the weapons specialist and psychotherapist." Again there was cheering and clapping. "And now applaud Eugene who is back there near the food stands and bar!" Everybody turned towards him and they cheered and clapped again, smiling. Eugene thanked them with a smile and a nod. "Unfortunately we also have some bad news. Two of our team members didn't make it. Please applaud with me Slow who stayed behind in the cruel Colloscoseum." They all clapped but nobody cheered this time. "And also Aecey, who was killed before she was able to join the mission." Again everybody clapped. "Well, my friends, the Dark Ruler has been defeated, his drad army won't last much longer! Let's have a party!" They all cheered and the music started to play again at full volume, the colour organs started moving and there was the same happy mood as before.

"Well, Eugene," somebody said; Eugene looked up and looked into a beautiful face. It had green eyes, lightly tanned skin and a beautifully formed mouth with full red lips. "I am Alimada," said the pretty face. Alimada wore a beautiful, figure-hugging black evening dress; her hair was dark and trailing down her back in a ponytail, a small strand straying into her face. "Hello, nice to meet you. Would you like to, I mean, please, sit down."

"Thank you." She sat down opposite Eugene at the round table (Not all the tables were rounding, there were also square ones that could accommodate more than thirty people.)

"How do you like the party?" asked Eugene clumsily.

"Oh, up to now, quite well. I think it is very colourful and light-hearted."

"Would you like a drink? The waiter keeps bringing me things I have never had before in my life."

"Thank you. What does he bring?"

"Wine, champagne, whisky and liqueur, I think."

"Alcohol!"

"What?"

"Alcohol, he brings alcohol. That are drinks that make you drunk if you drink too much of them. You stumble and you are no longer in control of yourself."

"Sounds like one should experience it at least once in a lifetime."

"Yes, I think, that is quite enough." She pulled a package from her handbag and put a light to a stick she had put into her mouth.

Somehow that looked familiar to Eugene. He must have stared at the stick with a wondering look because Alimada said, "Cigarette." Eugene nodded as if he now understood. At that moment the waiter, whom Eugene found quite strange, passed.

"Whisky, liqueur and wine and more!" he said and put a full tray on the table between Eugene and Alimada. Eugene counted; there were five bottles and two appropriate glasses for each drink. The waiter cleared the table. "Have fun," he said and disappeared again. Alimada took one of the bottles and poured its contents into two small glasses. Then she lifted her glass. Eugene did the same. With one gulp she poured the liquid down her throat. Again Eugene did the same. It tasted sharp and sweet at once. Shuddering he put down his glass.

"What is your job on the ship?"

"I am a fortune-teller and doctor though I personally prefer the term healer." She smiled at Eugene.

"That is great." Eugene felt lost.

"You have never flirted with a woman before," she said. Eugen nodded. "You have nightmares, right? At night." Eugene nodded again. "You should come and see me. I have my own practice on the ship. I can interpret your dreams."

215

"I'd like to very much." He took the whisky bottle and poured Alimada and himself another drink. They emptied their glasses together.

"Do you want to dance?" she asked.

"I'd love to but I don't know how."

"Well, in that case, you'll have to learn it!" She took his hand and guided him up to the dance floor using one of the spiral staircases.

They danced, drank and talked all evening deep into the night. Now and then Jim and Lyon joined them at the table and between them emptied the wine bottles. Many of the guests had already left; there was a chaos of plastic cups, paper napkins and other detritus on the floor of the hall. Alimada and Eugene stopped dancing and walked down the spiral staircase, laughing and swaying.

"We should go home soon," said Eugene, his speech was slurred. Alimada nodded.

"Yes, I agree, we should really do that."

They laughed. Staggering and supporting each other they crossed the hall to the big doors.

"I have to give you some medical attention first."

"Absolutely."

Laughing they continued. They were holding hands and walked through the normally heaving corridors on their own.

"Come, Eugene."

"With pleasure."

They stepped into an elevator. It had mirrors and was decorated with wood.

"Eugene, I like you. I really enjoyed this evening."

"I like you a lot as well. This question will probably ruin everything but are you a robot?"

"Oh, Eugene. What do you think? We are on a ship where 85 percent of the population are robots. You are the only human being on board ship. What do you think I am?"

"Yes, I am sorry. I just thought that I might have found someone at last. Someone like me."

"I know, Eugene. I'll take you to my practice now and show you something, okay?"

"I don't think that that is a good idea."

"Trust me, Eugene, please."

"Very well then."

The elevator stopped and they got out holding hands.

"It's over there."

They went to the double door. It read *Doctor's Office: Alimada*. Alimada pulled a key out of her handbag and unlocked the door. They slipped inside. Eugene looked around. It was a very nicely decorated clean office. Glass walls, palm trees, stainless steel furniture and the examination table were the only things in the office. The room had four doors and the layout was quite intricate.

"Sit down on the table."

Eugene sat down, everything was spinning around him. Alimada looked into his eyes for a while.

"I see. You have nightmares, don't you?" Eugene nodded. "Wait a moment." Alimada went to one of the white chests of drawers and pulled out a drawer. She took out a long black item and returned to Eugene.

"Open your mouth. I want to shine a soul searcher into your mouth. That doesn't hurt." Eugene did as he was told and Alimada switched on the soul searcher to shine into his mouth. After a while she pulled it back out again and read what was written on the small lighted display of the instrument.

"It is as I thought. You have a kind of trauma. It's as if you were trying to save yourself into a former life you cannot remember anymore. I don't know your life story, Eugene. But you should tell it to me one of these days."

"I shall, Alimada."

Alimada sat down on the table next to Eugene, both dangling their legs.

"I wanted to show you something, well really tell you," she said. Eugene looked at her face and she smiled shyly.

"Something only you and I will know because I have never told anybody else. I trust you, Eugene, and I hope you will not abuse my trust."

"I won't!" Eugene said it a bit too quickly but Alimada believed him.

"Eugene, I am a real human being. I am made of flesh and blood just like you."

"What?"

"Yes, I am a living being, not a robot."

Eugene took her hand and held it tight.

"I am not going to tell anybody, Alimada."

"I know, the soul searcher displayed it on its screen."

They spend the rest of the night together in the practice and Alimada and Eugene made up for everything that they had missed in their lives so far, lonely lives without another human partner.

Eugene woke up on the examination table of the practice holding Alimada tight in his arms. They were both naked. Eugene put his hand to his head, he had a headache. Carefully he struggled out of Alimada's embrace and got up to look for his clothes.

When he was dressed, he sat down next to Alimada and stroked her soft light brown cheek with the back of his hand. She moaned softly and opened her eyes. Green, they stared at him. She smiled.

"Good morning," he said.

"Morning," she answered tiredly.

"Shall we have breakfast together or something of the sort?"

Alimada nodded, got up, gave Eugene a kiss on the mouth

and collected her pieces of clothing lying around the floor just like Eugene's.

"I think everybody will get together in the hall again, for breakfast this time, however. Are you hungry yet?"

"No, not really."

"Do you have a headache?"

"Yes, I do. How do you know?"

"Alcohol. I have a headache, too. I'll put a couple of aspirins in a glass of water for us, okay?"

"Oh definitely."

Alimada put on her dress and Eugene watched her. How lucky he was. The only free real human beings and they had found each other.

They had drunk the medication dissolved in water in one gulp; it had tasted of nothing. They held hands when they entered the hall. The hall was full of tables, benches and chairs. It smelled of coffee, fresh bread and other culinary delights. Eugene spotted Jim and Lyon at one of the tables and wanted to go and join them. But Alimada held him back.

"I'll go and sit with my friends over there," she said.

"Okay. I'll see you again, won't I?"

"Definitely. See you later."

"Okay."

Alimada walked off in another direction. Eugene headed for Jim and Lyon.

"Good morning," he said.

"Morning, Eugene." Lyon and Jim each sat in front of a cup of coffee and a piece of cake. "Are you hungry?"

"Not much, but I'd like some coffee."

Eugene sat down next to them and told the waiter to bring him a cup of coffee.

"Did you have a good time last night?"

"Yes, I've met a wonderful woman."

"Alimada?"

219

"Yes, how do you know?"

"It wasn't difficult to see last night. You danced all night and you laughed and drank together. Besides you just walked into the hall holding hands with her."

"You're right; we have really got to know each other. Did you two have a good time, too?" asked Eugene and sipped the coffee the waiter had just served.

"Most definitely. I talked all night to Hesson about our future and we finished about six bottles of wine between us," said Jim.

"I spent all night at one of the bars. Things really got going there. Everybody walked around half naked. I haven't had that much fun in a long time, honestly. After a bottle of whisky and a few cocktails I was quite out of it," said Lyon.

"What did Hesson say about our future?" asked Eugene.

"That the war isn't over yet. We'll have to fight one last battle soon."

"Where?"

"We don't know. But we'll have to fight against the drad army. That can only happen on land. Our specialists are working on finding out where the drad troopships have landed. Then we have to raise an army."

"But I thought we had one."

"And so we do. It's here on board, the army of the rebels, about thirty thousand strong. In order to win, we need at least half a million on foot and air support."

"Shit. Where should all this support come from?"

"We're still at the planning stage," said Jim and took a mouthful of coffee. Eugene and Lyon drank from their cups as well. The hall was filling with hungry and thirsty, still somewhat sleepy partygoers. Coffee, orange juice and milk were on offer everywhere. Food was carried around, fried bacon, scrambled eggs, buttered toast, jam rolls and other delights. Slowly the trio got hungry as well and ordered their breakfast from one of the many waiters.

A light shudder went through the hall. Eugene gave Jim an enquiring look, who shrugged his shoulders. With a loud bang, tables crashed burying many. Plates and cups broke with a clatter and there was screaming. Eugene fell on top of Jim and rolled off him next to Lyon who had just avoided being hit by the falling table.

"Damn!" cursed Jim, "Come on, let's go to the command centre," he said to Eugene and Lyon. Swaying they got up. The hall was in a terrible state. No table stood still upright, everybody was down on the floor, cursing or busy freeing themselves form the upturned tables and benches that had landed on top of them. Jim, Lyon, and Eugene wove through the jumble to the exit with careful steps. Eugene looked around for Alimada but didn't see her anywhere. They had problems to get through the door because more and more people came running into the hall to help. Once they finally reached the corridor, they could quickly proceed to the command centre. Jim guided them to an elevator nearby. Eugene saw the key panel in the elevator, one of the buttons was marked *Command Centre*. Jim pressed it.

"Access code or ID code, please," a voice came out of the speaker above the panel.

"Jim109, access code 444 562."

"Access granted."

The door of the elevator closed and with a jolt it started moving downwards. Eugene could feel his stomach give a lurch. As quickly as the ride had started, it ended again and the door opened. The room in front of them was full of panels. There were about twenty people in the room, each sitting in front of their own monitor. At some distance he saw the cockpit behind a glass wall with a glass door. Five pilots sat in the cockpit; Hesson was in the room, too, talking to a man.

"This is General Joe. He is the commander of our army," said Jim quietly to Eugene and Lyon. The mood was tense and the ship had begun to shudder again. Eugene could imagine what it would be like upstairs in the hall. They went down three steps to join Hesson and General Joe.

"Boss, General, can you tell us what is going on?"

"Jim," said Joe.

"We have come under enemy fire by a bunch of hunters."

"What is the situation?"

"Poor. There are so many that our gun turrets are struggling to get them. They're causing major damage. Unless we manage to escape or destroy them, we'll have to evacuate our entire ship." Hesson shook his head with regret.

"Evacuate? Evacuate the entire ship?"

"Indeed, unfortunately."

"Shit. What can we do about it?" asked Lyon.

"Nothing at all," replied Joe.

"But there has to be something we can do!"

"You can get each into a fighter jet and the three of you fight against about thirty hunters. It's hopeless," said Joe to Lyon. Eugene thought of Alimada. The spaceship shook.

"Commander, report, please!" called Joe to one of the men sitting at the monitors.

"There is slight damage to the outer hull. The stern has suffered major damage. There may be a power outage on several decks."

"That doesn't look good. We need to do something. If the lights go out, there will be panic. That is the last thing we need during an attack."

"Shit! Prepare for evacuation!" called Hesson. The alarm was sounded and messages were broadcast all over the ship. Everybody started moving towards the emergency vessels. It was possible to evacuate everybody if there was no more than one empty seat per vessel.

Eugene ran to the elevator, rushed in and pressed the button for the sixth floor. He had to go to Alimada.

"Eugene, come back. You cannot come back down! You do not have an access code!" called Jim. Lyon took a headset and threw it into the elevator just in time before the door closed. The elevator went up and Eugene's stomach seemed to fall into his legs. He picked up the headset from the floor and put it on. Immediately he heard Lyon's voice.

"Eugene? Do you hear me? Eugene, this is Lyon, can you read me?"

"Lyon, here is Eugene. Thank you for the headset."

"My pleasure. I'll stay in touch with you and when you come back, I can give you the access codes. I think I know why you left. But still, why didn't you stay with us down here?"

"I have to go and find Alimada."

"I understand. Good luck and never turn off your headset, otherwise we may not find the right frequency again."

"Okay."

The elevator door opened and hundreds of people streamed past Eugene, all in the same direction. How could he find Alimada? He stepped outside and was instantly carried away by the crowd. Everybody was shouting, the alarm kept on sounding and Eugene was forced to move with the mass since there was no chance to go against the flow. He called for Alimada and did what everybody else did, try and find family and friends. It proved impossible and Eugene decided to step through the next door and wait until the corridors started to empty. Slowly and still moving with the crowd he approached the door, turned the handle and rushed in. He took a deep breath. To keep an eye on the rushing crowd and maybe spot Alimada, he left the door slightly ajar and looked outside.

"Eugene, tell us how things are progressing," Lyon's voice came out of the plug in his ear.

"It's sheer madness. The corridor to the hall is chock-a-block. Everybody is running in the same direction. I got out of it and into a room so they wouldn't carry me off. I'm watching the turmoil through a half-open door."

"I hope all goes well. How is your own search going?"

"Not so good, it is difficult to spot a single person in this crowd. I doubt that I'll find her."

"Best of luck, I'll be in touch."

Screwing up his eyes, Eugene scanned the passing crowd. There was no sign of Alimada. Maybe she had already left, was far ahead somewhere and wouldn't go past him anymore. He had to take that risk. If he left now, he would never find her. He had stood in the room for a total of ten minutes when he saw her. He couldn't believe it and looked again more closely. But it was her, about ten yards away from him. Eugene called her name but she didn't hear him, how could she? Without further ado Eugene decided to intercept her by storming out and running towards her. Stepping out he wondered how he should manage. There were a least fifty people separating them and all heading in one direction. Eugene fought doggedly against the tide in order not to be swept along. To walk was impossible. Alimada had come closer but still hadn't seen him. Suddenly the lights went out. It was pitch-dark and there was panic. Everybody screamed and the so far fairly orderly mass turned into a boiling cauldron. Suddenly the light came back on. The panic started to die down. Eugene looked around for Alimada. He had lost her. She must have moved past him in the dark. He turned around and ran after the crowd calling wildly for Alimada.

"Eugene? Have you found her? The first ships have already undocked," said Lyon's voice in his ear.

224

"I've lost her in the darkness."

"More and more ships are leaving. Hurry up but, honestly, don't you think it would be safer for her to flee?"

"Yes, I agree but I have to say good-bye."

"As you like. I'll be in touch again in a few minutes."

Eugene ran as fast as he was able to, swerving to avoid slower people and scanning the crowd closely. The noise of the alarm rang in his ears. She couldn't have gone that far. It had been dark for a very short time only. Just as this thought crossed his mind and he was close to turning back, he saw her running in the crowd right in front of him. Her brown hair was flapping loosely in her wake. Eugene set off sprinting and caught up with her.

"Alimada!" She turned round towards him. He smiled and she smiled back but it was a frightened smile.

"Eugene, what is happening? Where have you been?"

"I was in the control room with Lyon and Jim. Come with me, I have been looking for you for quite a while." Eugene took her hand and pulled her along struggling against the weakening tide.

"Eugene! Where are we going?"

Eugene stopped.

"Would you rather flee?"

"I want to stay with you but where are we going?"

"To the control room," he said, turned around and continued walking. Alimada followed him. Only a few people were now heading for the hangars. The spaceship swayed under a new attack and Eugene struggled to keep himself and Alimada upright. The lights flickered briefly but didn't go out. Quickly they continued running.

"Eugene?"

"Lyon, how's it going?"

"Badly."

"We are not going to make it. Hesson has been evacuated. There are only five of us down here now, two pilots,

225

General Joe, Jim, and I."

"I've got Alimada with me."

"Perfect. We just have to escape from those blasted hunters. We have destroyed several but there are so many and they are so bloody tiny."

"Is there no other way to destroy them?"

"We could fly into the meteoroid belt to lose them but we don't stand a chance there with our mothership."

"So now what?"

"Fear and trepidation, Eugene, you should flee with Alimada."

"I am not about to do anything of the sort, Lyon. We've nearly reached the elevator; give me the codes in about a minute."

"Sure, talk to you in a bit."

Eugene and Alimada had slowed down from running to walking fast. They were alone in the corridor. Their steps echoed hollowly on the carpet.

"What did Lyon say?" she asked.

"We need a bit of luck to escape the hunters," replied Eugene. Alimada nodded.

"There's the elevator," said Eugene. They stepped up to it and pressed the button. A moment later the door opened. They stepped inside the very moment Lyon came back on.

"Are you in the elevator?"

"Yes, go ahead," said Eugene and pressed the button marked *Command Centre*.

"Guest111 guest code: 22 Eugene and Alimada."

Eugene repeated the codes and the door closed. As before Eugene's stomach lurched and Alimada must have felt the same because she suddenly became tense.

"Thank you for looking for me, Eugene."

"Would you have left without me?"

"No, I was looking for you, too."

The door opened and they entered the command room. Jim

was talking to General Joe. Lyon was with the two pilots in the glass cockpit.

"We could try travelling at the speed of light," Jim was saying when Eugene and Alimada joined him.

"No, there are too many things in the way. In this part of the universe there are plenty of rocks and other junk hurtling around. The probability of hitting one of them is sixty percent."

The light flickered again.

"Can we continue flying without power?" Eugene asked the General.

"Yes, flying and shooting. But we wouldn't be able to use the computers, lights and elevators."

"No elevators? Do you mean to say that when the lights go out we are stuck down here?"

"No, there is an emergency exit down here."

Lyon put his head around the glass door.

"It's looking better and better. If our luck holds, we'll manage to get away!"

"In that case let's hope that our luck holds," said Jim.

There were seven of them in the cockpit and the two pilots did their utmost to save the ship from the hunters who were flying dangerously around the ship, firing. It seemed hopeless. Alimada clung to Eugene. Lyon looked at them doubtfully, changed a meaningful glance with Jim but said nothing. Eugene didn't care. The two pilots did their best to dodge the hunters. At one time they flew slowly, and then accelerated again. They had the advantage that their ship was big and solid as opposed to the small very vulnerable dark hunters. The gun towers had destroyed one or two dozen hunters so far. Their situation started to improve slowly.

"We're approaching a meteoroid belt. Shall we head for it?" asked one of the pilots.

"Yes, maybe we can finally escape them there," said General Joe.

The pilot accelerated and they sped towards the huge meteoroid that moved as if in slow motion.

There were only about five hunters left but they had done a good job. More than a third of the outer hull had been destroyed and the electrical system had been damaged. Expertly the pilot steered the mothership into the meteoroid belt. It was incredibly difficult to avoid the rocks that were sometimes as large as their ship but they did it. Since the meteoroids moved very slowly, they could see at a fair distance which ones they had to avoid. At times they avoided a fateful collision with a monster rock by only a few inches, sometimes by even less. The hunters found it a bit more difficult to avoid the meteoroids because the big ship kept getting in their way. Some grazed a meteoroid and lost their steering or just exploded in a small ball of fire.

"We have nearly made it, according to my computer there are only two hunters left. I'll take us out of this witch's cauldron before we make too close an acquaintance with one of those meteoroids," said the pilot and instantly steered the ship past one of the meteoroids and headed out into the wide open universe. One of the gun towers hit one of the hunters which flew tumbling into a meteoroid, bursting into a thousand pieces. They were beyond the meteoroid belt now. The remaining hunter flew past them and off into space. Soon they lost sight of him.

"I wonder what he is up to."

"Nothing good to be sure. We should get away from here."

"Where to?" asked Eugene.

"We'll fly to Ziguur. That's the planet where the emergency craft are headed. That is where our crew is," said General Joe. The two pilots turned the ship around and soon after they were travelling in the opposite direction.

"The evacuation was a waste of time," said Eugene.

"The evacuation was absolutely appropriate. I am responsible for the safety of the people aboard. I'd rather evacuate unnecessarily then have everybody die on board ship," said Joe.

"You are right," said Eugene after a moment of hesitation. General Joe was too much of a military man for his liking. He was one of those who were guided only by their own opinions and points of view.

The light flickered again.

"I hope the ship will hold until we can land and fix it," said Lyon.

The light flickered alarmingly and it staid dark for some time. Some controls started blinking and beeping.

"Doesn't look good."

The light went out again. There was total silence. After some seconds, one of the pilots sighed and switched off the alarm.

"Right, we don't have electricity anymore. Two of you should go to the emergency generator. We'll stay in touch via radio," General Joe.

"I'll go!" Lyon volunteered.

"I'll come with you, Lyon," said Eugene.

"In that case, I'm coming, too!" Alimada stepped between Eugene and Lyon. Eugene looked at Joe.

"I don't mind," he said. Alimada received a headset as well; Eugene and Lyon already had theirs. They were ready to go.

"Follow me," said Joe and crossed the room. He pressed one of the buttons that were still glowing and quietly, hidden stairs came into view.

"There is a staircase that gives onto every level of the ship. I give you one of the few universal keys. They fit everywhere, so you'll be able to open any door in the

229

whole of the ship. And you'll be given torches." Joe took a bunch of keys from his suit and took off a thick squiggly key and put it into Lyon's hand. Jim supplied them each with a torch.

"The generator is on the eighth level. We'll guide you via radio as soon as you get there," explained Joe.

Eugene, Lyon, and Alimada switched on their headsets and their torches and set off. In front of them was the staircase. It seemed to consist solely of iron bars. Lyon shone his torch upward and the beam cut through the darkness. With echoing steps, they started upstairs. Each level was identified on the wall with the appropriate number. They now were in basement 5. With quick steps they marched upstairs. To Eugene the numbers on the wall seemed like a slow countdown, 4….3….2….1….. Finally they had reached the main level, called the neutral or middle level. They still had eight floors ahead of them, 1…2…3…. Eugene didn't feel his legs anymore and it was as if they were walking by themselves. His brain seemed to have no control over his legs. He had the feeling that even if he had wanted to stop, his legs would have kept on moving. 4….5….6…. They had conquered 11 levels by now and kept ascending, moaning and visibly slower than at the beginning. Eugene's feeling of numbness had yielded to a pain in his knees. Alimada, too, found it hard to keep up with him. Lyon shone his light on the grey wall and the number 7 shone in response. A few more steps and they would be on the eighth and final level. Of course, there were more levels in the ship. The top level was level 23 but for security reasons and convenience the power supply was located on the level in the middle of the ship. A door became visible in the darkness. At last! Lyon stepped up to it and opened it. Behind the door, there was nothing but darkness as well. Lyon shone his light into a corridor like hundreds of others on the ship.

"Seems to be okay, and why shouldn't it be so?" he said to Eugene and Alimada. They stepped outside and Lyon spoke into his headset.

"Joe? We have reached level 8."

"Already? Good. You should be in a passage. Turn to the left."

"Okay."

"Eventually you should reach a black door on the right. It has *No entry* written on it."

They walked down the corridor and Lyon shone his torch on its right wall. Everybody was looking for the black door.

After a while, after nearly having lost all hope of ever reaching it, the beam of Lyon's torch fell on the black door.

"About time, too," said Alimada.

Lyon opened the door with the universal key and they entered. They were on a steel gallery that followed the walls of the room at a height of about seven feet above the floor. The steel floors of the framework rattled and creaked under their steps on the way to the steel stairs. Lyon shone his light around the room. It was full of machinery none of them recognized.

"Joe? We've gone through the black door."

"Very good. You should be on a sort of steel balcony about seven feet above ground level."

"We are."

"Do you see the stairs? Go down into the room."

"Okay and then?"

"There should be another door down there. It's blue if I am not mistaken."

"If you are not mistaken?"

They crossed the room slowly to avoid collision with any of the items lying around and looked for the door. Finally, they found it and it was dark blue. Lyon stepped up to it and turned the handle. The door opened outwards, Lyon shone his light past it. There was a passage in front of them.

"Joe? We have opened the blue door. There is a passage behind it."

"Yes, that is right. Go through to the end of the passage, and then take the last door on the left. There is the generator. I'll give you instructions how to get it going once you are there."

"Okay," said Lyon and beckoned the others to follow him. Eugene wrinkled his nose. It smelled of burnt plastic. Quickly they walked down the passage. Lyon's torch had hardly shown them the way before they had passed. The passage was long but at last they reached its end and the last door on the left. Lyon walked through. The generator stood in front of them. It was about 10 by 7 feet in size and was equipped with several screens and switches.

"Okay, Joe, we're in front of the generator."

"Lyon, do you see a button that says *Emergency*?"

"Yes, I do," said Lyon after a moment's search.

"Press it."

"Done." One of the screens started to glow.

"One of the screens says: CODE."

"Okay, write what I tell you."

"Go ahead."

"1,5,9,6,3,8,8,5,7,1,2,9,3,5,4."

"Okay."

"Now press a long narrow button right beneath the number panel. Then tell me what it shows on the screen."

Lyon pressed the button.

"Access granted. It now wants the code to start the production and flow of electricity."

"Good, enter 5,5,4,1,2,9."

"Got it. It has been confirmed. It is switched on and is working."

"Very good, now return to the cockpit. We're waiting for you."

"See you in a bit."

The generator had started to hum. But there was still no light anywhere in the ship. That would take a few more minutes.

Lyon, Alimada, and Eugene had nearly reached the entrance to the staircase when the lamps started to flicker and then shine, at first weakly but soon brighter and brighter.

"Power is back," stated Alimada.

"Who is up for a second bout of stair racing?" asked Lyon.

"Not me."

"Me neither."

"In that case, let's find an elevator."

They set off for the elevator since none of them felt like repeating their stair marathon in the opposite direction.

"Lyon, we have movement on level 3 and 7. Only weakly but still the computer has picked it up. Jim and I would be grateful if you could check on that. Perhaps there are some of the crew who haven't been evacuated with the others."

"Understood. We'll check. Guys, back to the stairs!"

They returned to the door leading into the staircase. There, too, the lights had come back on. Slowly they walked down to level 7. Lyon was first to step to the equally black door. Here, too, was a corridor. It was covered with carpets and palm trees ensured an atmosphere of well-being. There was total silence.

"Joe, where did you detect that movement?"

"Somewhere in the back part, near the recreation and hobby rooms."

"Do I have to turn left?"

"Yes, stay in the corridor until you get to a big double door. It has *Recreation Area* written on it."

"OK, I'll report."

They set off together and after a short while they reached the big double door.

"Careful. We don't know who might be inside," said Lyon. Eugene and Alimada nodded. Lyon stepped up to the door and opened it slowly. It swung back inside. Shots were heard and hit the wall next to Lyon and the door where there was instant smoke.

"Damn!" Lyon pulled the door shut. "They're shooting at us with laser weapons."

"So now what? What if they are enemies?" asked Alimada.

"Does one of you carry a weapon?" asked Lyon.

"No, we haven't got one."

"Nor do I. We'll have to talk." Lyon stepped up to the door and opened it again a little bit. Again laser projectiles hit the door.

"We are friends!" called Lyon. The shots ceased.

"Prove it!" somebody called from the inside of the room.

"I am Lyon. I was part of the mission to destroy the drad control ship! Next to me are Eugene, a human, and Alimada, one of the ship's doctors."

"Are you armed?"

"No!"

"Open the door so we can see you!"

"Lyon, I am not sure that that is a good idea. He could easily shoot us."

"We'll be all right!" Lyon pushed the door open and showed himself.

"We are friends!" he called again, looking around. The room was big and was furnished with several sofas and tables. Suddenly someone stepped forward from behind a couch.

"It's really you," he said.

"Of course, we are. And who are you?" said Lyon

annoyed.

"I am Rodolf but everybody calls me Ramses. This is my family." He swung his hand around and from behind another couch a woman and a small child appeared.

"I am Isabelle, our child is called Jerephine," she said in a soft voice. The child was no more than three years old.

"I didn't know that robots could have children," said Eugene quietly so only Alimada could hear him.

"Of course, they can. I'll explain to you some other time how it works."

"Why haven't you been evacuated like the others?" Eugene asked Ramses.

"We were asleep when the alarm went off. All the emergency craft on our level had soon left so we went to the next lower level. There was a long queue. We were always too late to get on board because there were three of us. In the end I decided to return to be able to defend my family and myself."

"That wasn't such a good idea."

"I know but I didn't know what else to do."

"General Joe, we have found a family. We'll bring them with us."

"Okay, we'll wait for you."

"Come, let's go to the cockpit," said Lyon. Together they left the room and went back to get into the elevator. Eugene pressed the button to call it. In an instant the steel door opened with a hum and they got in. The woman held the child's hand.

"Joe? Can you give us the password, please."

"Guest 234, guest 255, guest 222, code 98777776." Lyon typed the numbers as radioed by Joe into the number panel and the door closed. With a jolt the elevator started its descent.

The elevator door opened and they stepped into the big room. Jim and General Joe were waiting for them in the middle of the room

"Hey, that thing with the light worked brilliantly," called Jim from afar.

"Yes, it sure did" replied Lyon.

"Would you be so kind as to introduce yourself and your family?" said General Joe.

"Of course. As I've already told the others, we stepped out into the passage and everybody was gone. We went to a lower level but because there were three of us; it was difficult to find a vessel that still had three free places. It was all so complicated. So I decided to take my family back to the recreation room and defend ourselves if necessary."

"That was very stupid of you. And courageous," said Joe.

"Thank you, sir." Ramses didn't know what else to reply, "but why weren't the warriors ordered to remain on board?"

"What a question! Do you really believe that the hunters would have captured the ship? They would have fired at it until it exploded."

"So, what's your plan now?" asked Lyon interrupting Ramses and Joe.

"We're heading for the planet where our crew has gone, Ziguur."

"What kind of a planet is that?" asked Eugene.

"A true paradise. Countless hotels, swimming pools, adventure parks, amusement parks, palm trees and the sea, restaurants." Joe went back to the cockpit. Eugene followed him.

"Sounds good."

Joe stepped through the glass door into the cockpit. "When are we arriving at Ziguur?"

"In about five hours. Speed of light is out of the question," said the pilot who had blond hair and green piercing eyes. General Joe nodded his thanks. Eugene turned around and went back to Alimada sitting lost on one of the steps of the main room. She looked up to him and smiled. He sat down next to her.

"The pilot says we'll arrive in five hours."

"In five hours?" Alimada looked at him with big eyes. Eugene nodded in agreement.

"Can we not fly at the speed of light?"

"The pilot says that's out of the question, don't ask me why."

"And what are we going to do for five hours?"

"Do you know Alimada, I already thought of something. We have the whole ship to ourselves and we could go virtually anywhere we want to. Besides, I am hungry," said Eugene.

"What a wonderful idea! Let's explore the ship," said Alimada with fake sarcasm.

They stood up hand in hand and went to the elevator. Eugene put on a headset and waved good-bye to Lyon. He gave a wave in return; he probably guessed what the two were up to.

Laughing they rushed out of the elevator into the red-carpeted corridor. They were on their way to the cafeteria. They staggered along the corridor as if drunk until they reached the glass door with the blue door handles, the cafeteria. They entered. The cafeteria was nicely furnished. Gleaming steel tables that were half surrounded by upholstered leather benches. Behind a counter all sorts of delicious food were stored. With a jump Eugene was on the other side of the counter.

"What would you like?" he asked Alimada.

"I would like a bit of everything," said Alimada in a mockingly refined manner. Eugene bowed exaggeratedly as he passed her some cakes and rolls. Alimada carried them to one of the tables. Eugene followed her with coffee, honey and jam. They ate until they felt sick. Then they left the cafeteria and walked about aimlessly.

"Eugene, I have to treat you again because of your nightmares," said Alimada suddenly.

"Yes, okay."

"You know I thought about it quite a lot and have reached the conclusion that you are suffering from a time trauma. Inside you are longing for something that you don't know. Or, as I would say in your case, you long for Earth or rather for something specific on Earth. You talk about the House of Time you are visiting in every dream. That is a sign. You are longing for your past."

"But I remember hardly anything; I only have scraps of memory."

"That may be, but I know it nevertheless."

"You know what gets me? Why am I here? I mean Earth was destroyed many years after I must have lived. So, why am I here now?"

"That is something I cannot tell you."

"Yes, nor can I. It is so confusing. If only I could remember! But, you know, sometimes I am quite glad that I don't remember. When I was in the past with Lyon, Rob, and Jim and met myself, I didn't recognize myself. It was as if I had been a different person, you know what I mean?"

Alimada nodded, "I know what you mean." Without thinking about it, they had walked to Alimada's practice and stood outside her door. Alimada opened it and entered holding Eugene's hand.

They had spent the last three hours in Alimada's practice. They had talked and been quiet, they had laughed and joked. Now they were on their way to the elevator because they were due to land on Ziguur in half an hour.

"Lyon? Can you please tell me the code? I am standing outside the elevator with Alimada."

"Yes, wait a moment." Eugene and Alimada stood in the cabin of the elevator. "Eugene, type 123564 98."

"Thank you, see you in a sec," said Eugene and the door closed. With the familiar jerk and the equally familiar lurching of the stomach, the elevator started descending. After a few seconds the door opened.

"Hey, you two, welcome back," Lyon greeted them.

"Hey, Lyon. When will we arrive?" asked Eugene.

"In about half an hour. You can already see the planet." Lyon pointed through the glass door of the cockpit at a planet that stuck blue out of the darkness of the universe. Eugene didn't know what to expect but instinctively he was looking forward to his stay there.

They entered the atmosphere of Ziguur and encountered a sea of clouds. The ship dived into them and soon the blue sea appeared shimmering ahead of them. The pilot steered the ship into a horizontal position and flew over the water surface. Light clouds made the sea shimmer and shine. Land appeared on the horizon, beaches and palm trees gave the impression of incredible peace. Behind the tops of the palm trees a city appeared. Huge hotel complexes with swimming pools and amusement areas. There was excitement everywhere when the big ship appeared. The pilot steered the ship carefully over the hotels and flew to the airport to land.

Expertly the pilot had steered the ship into the parking area. Because of its sheer size they had to take up several parking slots. They could see the multi-storey parking area rising next to the open-air spaces. It was open and they could see the different levels. It was filled with their emergency craft. Over one of the many ramps, the two pilots, General Joe, Jim, Lyon, Ramses with his wife and child, Alimada and Eugene had disembarked. They now stood outside the mothership. It was awesome. Eugene felt like a grain of sand in front of a rock. The ramp closed and they marched off to a small hut from where curious eyes had watched them. Two guards and a parking attendant, the person whose job it was to collect the charges, stood outside the hut.

"A good day to you all," said the person in the black suit and tie.

"Good day. We are here to collect our entire crew. They should have arrived half a day ago. We had to evacuate our ship."

"Yes, that is right. May I know your names?"

"General Joe. Would you be so kind as to tell us the name of the hotel where our people have been put up?"

"Of course, in a minute." The man in the suit disappeared into the hut.

"What is he doing?" asked Ramses.

"He is checking on us and if nothing stupid comes up, we'll learn the name of the hotel where all of our crew are staying in a moment," replied Jim. At last, the man returned.

"You have to go to a hotel called Honeysun; it's not far from here. Go straight ahead on the main road and then left. You can't miss it. It is close enough to walk there. And by the way, you'd better be prepared for a talk with a government representative. You'll have to explain this." He pointed to the mothership and the full parking area. General Joe nodded and Jim thanked the man and they marched off. Eugene looked around. Everything was green. It was as warm as it had been on Tattau but unlike Tattau there was plenty of water and plants grew everywhere. The streets were paved in red and were clean and there were people in bathing clothes all over the place. They went along the main street where there was hardly ever any traffic and turned left where they were soon welcomed by a big sign reading *Honeysun*.

"Very well. We'll soon be in space again," said Joe.

"I quite like it here," stated Alimada.

"Yes, many people like it here but virtually nobody can afford to live here. For the price of a studio apartment here, you can buy a three-bedroom house with large estate on Mars," explained Joe.

"Wow, even though that doesn't mean much to me," said Eugene.

"Not important," said Joe. They were now in front of the hotel Honeysun. It was painted in a honey colour and marble stairs lead up to the entrance. To the left and right were huge palm trees towering up many feet, offering cool shade. They went up the stairs to the entrance and entered. A porter in a smart uniform opened the gilded glass door. The lobby was expensively decorated, luxurious and magnificent, and they stared in wonder. A sea of plants rose in the middle of the lobby, surrounded by reception desks with their employees welcoming the guests. Somewhere a little waterfall bubbled, moistening the cool air and making it pleasant to breathe. Everything glittered golden and was lined with marble. The little jungle grew to a considerable height because the lobby spanned all floors right up to the ceiling. It was possible, safely behind railings, to look down from each floor and to watch the coming and going of the other guests. The elevator went up on one side and was made of glass and gold. The little group stepped up to one of the receptionists.

"A very warm welcome to our luxury hotel Honeysun. My name is Mrs Lima, how can I help you?" the lady at reception greeted them.

"My name is General Joe. We are here in search of our crew. They must have checked in about half a day ago. We had to evacuate them from our spaceship because of severe problems on board."

"Yes, your crew checked in about ten hours ago."

"We managed to fix the problems and landed here to pick up our people."

"I understand. I think considering the number of people involved we have to make an announcement over our public address system." The lady took up a microphone from behind the counter and put it on top. Joe looked at her enquiringly.

"I think you better leave the announcement to me," she said.

"Yes, I think you'll be better at it."

The receptionist nodded.

"Dear hotel guests. Could I have your attention for a moment, please? Would the spaceship crew that has been evacuated and checked in here ten to twelve hours ago please assemble in front of the hotel. Your ship has arrived to meet you. Thank you for your attention and please enjoy your stay in our hotel." She put the microphone back in its place and ignored General Joe.

"Thank you," he said.

"Not at all. We're looking forward to welcoming you again soon," she said without looking up.

Joe and the others turned around and left the hotel to wait outside for their people. Eugene considered what a big mayhem that was going to be.

"General Joe, don't you think that there will be too many people?"

"We'll walk slowly in rows. There is hardly any traffic on the main street as you have seen for yourself. I am sure it'll be okay."

"You are the general," said Eugene and the general nodded. The first people came out of the hotel and walked down the steps to street-level.

"Please line up in rows of ten!" called Joe. Jim helped him give out orders. More and more people streamed out of the hotel and the situation started to become confused. But in the end it all worked out and the trail was so long that the first rows had reached the mothership and entered while the others were still outside the hotel. After three hours, everybody was back on board and in their rooms and apartments.

Once Rob had repeated the movements exactly the way the doctor had shown him, all he had to do was to sign a note. He shook the doctor's hand, thanked him for the umpteenth time, had a look in the mirror and left the repair practice.

"Where are we going?" Eugene put this question to Lyon while walking quickly along the corridors and giving way to on-coming people.
"To the conference room," replied Lyon.
"Do you have any idea why?"
"I guess we should expect a big meeting."
"In what way?"
"There will be war."
Eugene nodded. He hadn't expected anything else. They stopped outside a big black wooden door and Lyon knocked three times. A secretary opened and asked them to come in. She sent them immediately into the conference room that was behind a milky glass wall. Lyon and Eugene entered and saw that half the expected participants were already present. Hesson, General Joe, Rob and one of the pilots sat around an oval table and they each had a piece of paper in front of them and a cup of steaming coffee. Eugene and Lyon greeted briefly, smiled at Rob and told him how happy they were to see him again, and then sat down next to him.
"Rob, you look like new. We already thought, we had lost you," said Eugene after a few minutes. Lyon nodded.

"I was lucky. My memory chip was totally undamaged. The rest is easy to repair."

"Jim, Alimada and the captain of our army will be here soon, too," explained Joe pointing at the empty seats. Not much later, Jim and the captain entered and finally Alimada.

"Well, now that we are complete, we can begin," said Hesson. "I have called this conference to discuss our future movements. General Joe and I have agreed on a plan we would like to present to you now." Hesson folded his hands and General Joe stood up.

"We are going to leave in two days after refuelling and re-stocking of food. We are going to set a straight course for Mars." Joe looked around. Everybody seemed confused, while others already guessed what that would mean.

"We are going to meet with government representatives and negotiate."

"What are you going to negotiate?" asked Lyon.

"Soldiers," was Joe's short reply.

"What do you mean, soldiers?"

"Soldiers means soldiers. We are going to assemble an army."

"To do what? Attack the drads?"

"Precisely. We are going to attack them and defeat them in open battle. They are weak, without energy so to speak. They are no longer trained or instructed."

"That is all very well but what if the negotiations with the government of Mars fail?"

"They are not going to fail."

"Thank you, now I am reassured. When General Joe says, that they will not fail, they will not fail. Good."

"Indeed, they won't fail. The drads are a big threat to Mars as well. The heads of government on Mars won't stand by idly and watch a drad army grow and grow and become an ever greater threat to them. Besides, they still have a bone to pick with the dark ones, or have you forgotten, Lyon, what your home planet looks like?"

Lyon's eyes sparkled angrily at Joe. Then he sighed. "Continue, General."

"The Mars government will visit all planets that have large military forces and invite them for negotiations. That way we should be able to assemble enough warriors not only to fight but also to win the decisive battle."

"Sounds plausible. But how do you know where the drads are?"

"We are in the process of scanning all likely planets and to look for drad concentrations. We will locate them, they cannot go unnoticed. As soon as they have been discovered, which is as I say, just a question of time, we will be informed." General Joe sat down.

"Let's assume we have assembled soldiers from all sorts of planets to form a huge army." Eugene cleared his throat. "We cannot fight the drad armies with soldiers only."

"No, of course not. We have vehicles and fighter jets. Besides, we are going to send out a special destruction squad to infiltrate the enemy camp and to destroy it from within. But so far this is just a pipe dream because we don't know yet what the drad camp looks like."

"Who is going to be a member of this destruction squad?"

"We were hoping Jim and his group could do that," said Hesson.

"We'll see," replied Jim.

"Okay, let's summarize. In two days we'll travel to Mars, talk to their government hoping that we can successfully negotiate a military cooperation and then once we've found the location of the drads we'll send in a destruction squad to destroy the UDP for good," said Rob.

"What about the medical facilities on the battlefield. If I am going with the special force, who is going to do my job?" asked Alimada.

"Nobody said that you were going to be part of the destruction squad. You are going to look after the wounded, of course. Only Lyon, Eugene, Rob, and Jim will form the destruction squad. It would naturally be possible to include another person or two. But don't get up your hopes, Alimada. You are absolutely excluded from participating," declared Hesson.

"Since nobody has any objections, I suggest we'll declare the plan as having been unanimously accepted," said General Joe and got up. The others got up as well and they shook hands.

The meeting was over.

"If necessary, we may call another meeting," said Hesson. They left the conference room one by one.

"Hey, Eugene, I've decided that since we are here I'll use these two days to have some fun. I'm going to one of the local adventure pools. I think it's called Diosson. It is said to have more than twenty slides. So far I've only been to a pool with a slide once in my life."

"Sure, I'll ask Alimada if she's coming along if that's okay."

"Of course, ask her. I'll go and get my swimming trunks and wait for you at the elevator."

Eugene stayed where he was waiting for Alimada who was talking to Jim. Finally she approached him and he asked her. She was enthusiastic about Lyon's idea and they hurried to get their swimming gear and return to the elevator. Once there they entered the elevator with the already impatient Lyon and went down to exit the ship by one of the hatchways. Outside the warmth and the fragrance of the sea welcomed them. A light breeze that carried the smells of chlorine and flowers blew through their hair.

"Where is this adventure pool?" asked Eugene.

"As far as I know, most pools are on the main street. We just walk along and choose the one we like," replied Lyon. They left the parking area. Behind them the emergency vessels were loaded from the multi-storey into the mothership. They turned the corner and walked along the pavement.

"What do you think about it?" asked Alimada.

"The resolution we took at the meeting?" asked Lyon. Alimada nodded.

"I think it's the right thing to do. We have killed their ruler and the drads have been left behind. If we destroy them, it is over once and for all," replied Lyon.

"But what if we lose the war?"

"Losing is not an option. Besides, enough arrangements have been made to minimize the chance of losing or, to put it more positively, to maximize our chances of winning."

"Whenever the question arises what is going to happen if we lose the war, there is the same answer, we mustn't lose. But what if we do lose," said Alimada.

"Our army will be annihilated including the three of us and the ship. The drads will get into the battleships and interceptors and lay waste to the universe, probably. Unless we have destroyed so many of them, that they are no longer able to do so."

"I see. Losing is not an option," said Alimada as if Lyon hadn't said anything.

"Let's not think about it now," interrupted Eugene. "Do you see the pool over there? Let's go there." Eugene pointed to a big tower where countless multi-coloured slides descended into the water. They crossed the street and went to the entrance of the pool. It was separated from the street by a beautifully curved fence. They paid the small entrance fee and entered the pool area. It was very quiet, only a few people were around. They looked for a nice spot on the grass, put down their towels and put on their swimming trunks or swimsuit. They spent several hours sliding, splashing each other with water and jumping off the diving platforms. Slowly it became noticeably cooler and darker. They decided to go and get changed and return to the ship. When they walked back along the pavement, it was already dark and street lamps illuminated the red pavement. They were joking and laughing. Finally they turned a corner and were back at the parking area where the mothership loomed black in the darkness, awaiting them. The emergency craft had all been returned to their hangars.

Once inside the ship they realized how hungry they really were after the long exhausting day and went to the best restaurant of the ship. There they sat down at one of the round tables decorated with candles and flowers. It was a very beautiful restaurant with a counter for self-service salads. A lot of wood had been used as decoration. The ceiling boasting beautifully shaped lamps was made of wood as were the tables and chairs. The floor was made of marble, partly covered by carpets. A waiter took their order. Lyon ordered pasta with cream and vegetable sauce. Eugene wanted a steak with baked potatoes and mayonnaise and Alimada decided on turkey pie and two different types of sauce. They were all looking forward to a decent meal after an exciting day. They talked at length about their day at the pool, laughed a lot and kept an eye out for their food.

"What do you think about this mission, Eugene?" asked Alimada.

"You mean this commando? Well, I find it greatly increases our chances of winning. I don't know yet what we are expected to do but I work on the assumption that it'll have to be very important and absolutely disastrous to the drads," replied Eugene. He thanked the waiter as he was serving his food. Alimada and Lyon, too, were served their meals and started eating ravenously.

"I am sure it will be very dangerous for you," replied Alimada in her turn.

"We were on the drad control ship and managed to place a bomb in the engine room. Drads are stupid," said Lyon.

"Quite possible, but you might get killed."

"Is one life worth more than millions?"

"No, I don't think so." Alimada didn't know what else to say.

"We'll make it. It should be easy enough for us. After all, we've got some experience in dealing with drads." Eugene tried to put her mind at rest.

"I know." Alimada thanked him, smiling.

"The food is great, don't you think?" Lyon changed the subject.

"Yes, it is," replied Eugene and Alimada nodded in agreement.

"What time are we leaving tomorrow?"

"I think in the evening. In the morning the ship will be refuelled and stocks replenished. Besides we all need a good night's rest. But then we'll be ready to go," said Lyon.

They remained in the restaurant for a long time. Most guests had left already when they got up and left the restaurant with well filled stomach. Lyon didn't have the same way back to his quarters as did Eugene and Alimada. Embracing closely Eugene and Alimada walked along the corridors until he gave her a good-night kiss and left her outside her practice door. In his room he fell onto his bed in exhaustion, too weak to brush his teeth or get changed. With a last effort he pulled up his blanket to his chin and arranged his pillow. He closed his eyes and fell asleep at once.

He drove along the road in a car, the wind rushing in his face and tousling his hair. He skidded and became unconscious. When he opened his blood-smeared eyelids, he looked at the House of Time. It stood there, black and staring at him out of red evil eyes. A storm brewed, the sky was black, the shutters banged like gun shots against the wall. The door was swinging open and shut on its hinges and the house gave the impression of wanting to say something. Whistling, the wind swept round the corners. The clouds glittered red in the sky and lightning flashed through the air. Aecey stepped out of the house and said something Eugene didn't understand. Aecey repeated it but again he didn't understand. Aecey repeated it over and over again but he never understood what she said. She became angry, her head was blazing red and she approached him. He was unable to move. But now that she was closer, he could understand her.

"Come with me! To the past! Sool is waiting for you!"
He screamed but Aecey came closer and closer and reached out to him.
"Come with me! To the past! Sool is waiting for you!"
The hand grabbed Eugene's head and squeezed. He screamed and finally his head burst with a loud splashing sound and Aecey pulled back her hand.
"Come with me! To the past! Sool is waiting ... JASON!"

Eugene opened his eyes; another nightmare and what a nightmare. He pulled the blanket over his head and wiped the sweat off his face. He stared at the blanket. What was it Aecey had said? Come with me! Sool is waiting for you! Who was Sool? Sool had never appeared in his dreams before. Hang on, Sool, what had been written on that huge poster? Eugene frowned. *Sool's Time Travels.* Oh my god. Alimada was right after all, unconsciously he longed for his past. He got out of bed and went to the sink to splash cold water into his face. *Sool's Time Travels.* A look at his watch told him that it was lunchtime. A few more hours and they would be headed for Mars. There was a knock.

"Yes," called Eugene and the door opened.

"Good morning," said Alimada.

"Good morning, had a good sleep?"

"Yes, I got up half an hour ago." Alimada closed the door.

"I just did." Eugene kissed her and told her about his nightmare. Once he had finished, Alimada looked at the floor, strained.

"Inside you're longing for your old home. Tell me, are you longing for Earth right now?"

"No, I'm not. It seems like only my subconscious is longing for a former life. I am not that keen to learn who I used to be, you can be sure of that."

"I understand what you're saying. I don't know why but I know what you mean. What about breakfast?"

"Good idea." Eugene was happy to change the subject. Listening to Alimada talking about it sent shivers down his spine although he knew that it was he, who brought up the subject, because he kept telling her about his nightmares. He changed and they went together to the cafeteria for breakfast.

The ship had been refuelled and the storerooms filled with provisions sufficient for a year. Nobody was outside the ship any longer when it took off and disappeared among the clouds made to glow red by the setting sun. Below the spaceship the city with its many hotels and pools looked smaller and smaller. They flew for some time above the sea until they rose into the sky and left the atmosphere behind them. Soon they were back in cold space. They didn't travel at the speed of light. It would take thirty hours to reach Mars.

251

Eugene and Alimada saw Lyon and Jim sitting at one of the tables in the cafeteria and went to join them. Jim and Lyon hadn't eaten yet and so they ate together and talked. Jim told them about the news that they were hot on the trail of the drads. Apparently they had been tracked down. It wasn't confirmed yet but soon they would know more. "Then we'll learn more about our mission," he remarked turning to Eugene and Lyon while sipping his cup of coffee. Eugene had ordered fried eggs on toast and it was delicious.

"I have to get back to my practice. I'll see you," said Alimada. She got up and left giving a quick wave.

"Tell me, Eugene, how long has this been going on with the two of you?" asked Lyon.

"Since the welcome party the other night," he replied. Lyon nodded.

"I take it you know that everybody on board ship knows about it."

"Knows about what?"

"Don't you realize? You are a human being. It is impossible for you to start anything with her and yet the two of you are together. Alimada is without doubt the female partner you have been looking for, Eugene," said Lyon.

"I admire your powers of deduction, Lyon. I for my part think, however, that it is not so noticeable and if it is, who cares?" said Eugene.

"Of course, nobody is stopping you."

"Exactly. How are we going to be protected on Mars, Jim?" asked Eugene, "I mean as we all know, I am human."

"That has been taken care of. There will be no hunt while we're there."

General Joe stood next to the pilot who steered the ship in

a beeline to Mars. Hesson stepped through the glass door into the cockpit.

"Amazing how a planet can still stay in its orbit after such an enormous blow," he said. General Joe nodded.

"What's on your mind?" asked Hesson

"Do you think the Dark Ruler only had this handful of ships?"

"It looks like it. He suffered huge losses on Tattau and later at other battles. I guess that part of the army stayed behind on the control ship. We caught him now that he was at his weakest," explained Hesson.

The pilot held the ship in a horizontal position and slowly allowed it to drop. A moment later, the Colloscoseum came into view, the city around it where somewhere had to be Lyon's house. The ship touched down amid swirling dust.

"Call Jim and his guys, we're going to the government buildings. They are to report to the hall!" said Hesson to one of his subordinates in the control room.

At Hesson's order Jim, Lyon, Rob, and Eugene had made their way to the hall where the hatchways opened to the outside. When they arrived, General Joe and Hesson stood next to the open hatchway waiting for them.

"I assume we're going to see the government of Mars?" asked Lyon.

"Yes, we are," answered Jim.

"Are we going to walk?" asked Eugene who didn't like to remember the last time he had to walk through the city on foot.

"No, we'll ride in a car," said Hesson and at that moment a vehicle was driven up the hatchway and stopped in front of them. It was an SUV with six wheels, no roof and two roll bars. It was red and black and had four headlights. They got in one by one. The driver was a robot who drove off as soon as they were all inside. They drove along a dusty road trailing sand clouds in their wake. The engine hummed loudly. They reached the city and were soon surrounded by the familiar red buildings. Now they had to go more slowly because everybody was walking on the street. They were driven to the city centre. Eugene could make out the Colloscoseum in the distance. Just before they got there, the robot turned right into a wide street and headed for a big building with flags outside. He finally stopped at a staircase that led up to a wooden gate. They got out and climbed the stairs. A security guard was expecting them at the top of the stairs and invited them to enter without a word. Inside the building was a different world. The floor was made of beautiful shiny red stone, the walls were painted white. A chandelier hung from the ceiling and the reception area was decorated with wood. There were some carpets and the air was not dusty at all as it normally was outside on Mars. They headed for the reception desk. Behind it sat another robot, but a female one with long blond hair.

"Good day," greeted General Joe.

"Good day, how can I help you?"

"We would like to talk to the king of Mars. We have an appointment."

"You are the rebels who destroyed the drad ship? The king and his government are expecting you urgently." The lady robot stepped around her desk and beckoned them to follow her. They walked along a short hallway to a big door also made of wood. She opened it and General Joe, Hesson, Jim, Lyon, Rob, and Eugene entered in single file. In front of them was a big wooden conference table. Around the table were seated several people who looked like Lyon in suits and some robots. At the head of the table sat the king. He was dressed the same way as his advisers and yet quite a different kind of power seemed to emanate from him. General Joe and the others bowed deeply.

"A warm welcome to Mars," the king greeted them. "We have heard of your actions and we are most profoundly grateful to be rid of the Dark Ruler for good. My scouts reported a few days ago that you are on your way to see us and I have been wondering ever since what you might want from us."

"Well now, that is a long story," replied Joe.

"Start right at the very beginning, if you please," requested the king.

"Jim, Lyon, Slow, Rob, Aecey, and Eugene had been selected for a secret mission to destroy the drad control ship by means of a bomb placed in the main engine room. After Eugene had been abducted on Mars, Slow met his death in the Colloscoseum but they succeeded in getting to the ship and even to escape the clutches of a traitor in their midst. They blew up the ship. Unfortunately, the Dark Ruler's troops managed to get away. Most likely, they had already relocated to the planet Xaviera days before our attack. We're on our way to Xaviera now to fight the drads in a battle. However, we do not have enough soldiers. That is why we are here. We are asking your support for going to war with the dark ones to expel them from our universe once and for all." General Joe ended his recital. The king looked thoughtful, his black jackal eyes sparkled.

"I'll have to discuss this with my advisers. But I have to tell you right away that I don't have a big army either. If we wage war, we'll need additional help from other planets. Please allow me to discuss this with my advisers in private. The receptionist will show you where you can wait for us in the hall." Thus they were dismissed. With a bow, they left the room. General Joe closed the door and they went back to the hall where the lady robot offered them seats on the many upholstered benches where they sat down thanking her.

"What do you think, will they fight with us?" asked Eugene.

"As I've told you before, they are going to agree," replied General Joe.

"Let's hope that you are right," said Lyon.

They waited in silence for the lady robot to ask them to return to the conference room and hear the decision. Soon the wait was at an end and they were beckoned again to follow her. Without a word, they entered the room.

"I didn't expect that they'd decide so quickly," whispered Lyon.

"We've come to a unanimous decision after our little conference just now. We are going to send our troops to war but not alone. We are going to contact all planets and ask for help. We should be ready within a week. Until then you may move freely on the planet, the humans of your ship, too. You, Hesson and General Joe, I ask to accompany me for my discussions with the leaders of the other planets. I shall call you in good time. Since there are no hotels big enough to accommodate all the inhabitants of your ship, I consider it best for all of you to remain aboard the ship," said the king.

"Of course. Thank you so much, your majesty." They bowed and left the room.

"It really worked out," said Lyon.

"What did you expect?" retorted Joe, annoyed. Rob waved at the receptionist as they walked through the outside door. They were met immediately by dusty hot air and their SUV including their driver. They got in and were taken back through the city to their ship. Lyon insisted on being dropped at his house. After returning to the ship, Eugene went at once in search of Alimada but not before Jim had warned him not to tell her anything unless he was absolutely certain that she would keep mum. Eugene met her in her practice. She had finished with her patients for the day and was about to tidy up and put everything in order. He told her that the government had agreed and that other planets would join the fight, too. When he told her that they had permission to move around on the planet, her face lit up. She thought it would be a shame to be on Mars and only sit around on board ship. But now that she was told she could go anywhere she liked, she didn't know where to start in this city of adventures. She looked out of the window; the sun was setting and bathed the already red Mars in even redder light. It was unique.

"First thing tomorrow, we'll go for breakfast somewhere in the city," she said.

"Fine!"

The next morning Eugene woke up when the sun shone hot and bright into his face. Carefully he pushed Alimada's hand off his naked chest. Yawning quietly he went to the window - Alimada was one of the few who had an apartment with a window - and closed the curtains. The blue curtains that were now backlit bathed the room in a blue light. Quietly Eugene stepped up to the bed and woke Alimada. She opened her eyes and smiled at him.

"You are awake already?"

"The sun has woken me. You're up for breakfast in town?"

"Yummy," mumbled Alimada and sat up. Eugene got dressed and went to the bathroom to freshen up. A moment later, he could hear Alimada getting dressed and following him into the bathroom.

Nearly every day they now had to take part in such conferences. General Joe and Hesson were tired after the three conferences lasting many hours they had to attend that day. Nearly all government leaders of all planets had assured them of their support. They would be able to count on two million soldiers. That ought to be enough to beat the drads. Meanwhile the drad base had been surveyed more closely. They had built a big camp protected by defence artillery, towers, and walls. The plan for Jim's group had been elaborated and was nearly finished. Tomorrow when the last big conference with the allied governments took place, General Joe would explain the plan and report to Jim. General Joe dropped into his bed, exhausted. He fell asleep at once

"Jim," said Hesson when Jim entered the office. General Joe nodded politely. He sat in one of the leather armchairs. "Sit down," Hesson invited him, "We called you because we want to explain to you the plan we decided on after the last conference."
"Okay, I'm curious."
"You and your team have to get into the drad camp. The camp is surrounded by gun towers and walls. There are mountains on one side and they didn't bother to build walls there. You'll have to enter the camp by going over the mountains by night. You'll have to break into the main building and switch off the electricity. That will immobilize the gun towers. Then our troops will storm the camp."
"Sounds incredibly easy."
"Doesn't it? Tell that to your team. Tomorrow the soldiers from the other planets will arrive and then we're heading into battle. This unique project of bringing together all the armies of different planets has been called United Forces.
"That's quite suitable," said Jim. Hesson nodded.
"I hope everything goes well. We'll have another meeting shortly before you cross the mountains. Thank you, Jim."
"We'll see you then. I am sure it'll be okay," Jim got up, nodded to General Joe and said good-bye to Hesson. Immediately he went in search of Rob, Lyon, and Eugene to tell them of the plan.

The week passed very quickly. Eugene had been out and about with Alimada so much that he regretted having to leave this wonderful planet he had grown fond of. After giving it much thought, he didn't fear the coming battle and their mission of destruction. But he was afraid something might happen to Alimada. Through the window of Alimada's apartment, he watched the hustle and bustle outside in the midday sun. Everywhere ships of various nations had landed on the warm red sand. Soldiers were everywhere and the air was filled with fighter jets. The name "United Forces" fitted perfectly. Eugene turned to Alimada and gave her a kiss on the cheek.

"What are we going to do now?"

"Wait. Wait until everybody gets going and then there will be war." She looked into his eyes and nodded thoughtfully.

The fifteen generals were meeting in the big conference room in the Martian government building to discuss the common action one more time. Their meeting lasted well into the night and the bright street lights already shone through the big windows when the conference came to an end. The old building that had been built back in the days of King Lewis IIV was in darkness. Somewhere in the catacombs several lights indicated that the alarm system had been activated. The many soldiers and fighter pilots with their jets had arranged themselves out in the desert and waited for the next day to set out to war. The soldiers had disappeared into the big troopships to get some sleep. The jets were neatly lined up in rows. They would be the first to start the next morning and then circle the troopships to protect them until they had reached Xaviera. Once they had landed there, they would start building their camp.

Swaying from side to side, Eugene and Lyon walked through the rows of parked fighter jets and laughed without knowing why. Lyon said something. The way he talked was so funny and Eugene couldn't help laughing again. That made Lyon laugh again as well and he continued telling his story, mumbling. They closely avoided a collision with the wing of a jet and then walked through the cool desert night. There they could sway from side to side as much as they liked. At last they reached the mothership.

Exhausted, Eugene fell into his bed. When he woke up the next morning, he didn't feel his body anymore. His head seemed to float, his feet were numb. He tried hard to remember the night before. He had gone out to have a drink with Lyon. They had drunk huge amounts of a strange red liquid with a very pleasant taste. Then everything was a blank, he didn't know how he had got back to the mothership. Somehow he had ended up in his bed. How devious that stuff was! Eugene sat up and sat stock still, he had the feeling that his head would explode at the least movement. The numbness in his limbs had vanished, instead he now had the feeling that he had put on several pounds. Carefully he got out of bed, the hands firmly pressed against his temples, and went to the sink. He bent forward, his brain pushed painfully against his eyes, and he splashed a handful of cold water into his face. That didn't improve things. He would go to Alimada and ask her for a painkiller. Groaning, he left his room and set off. The corridors were still empty. Everybody was still asleep. Still holding his head, he entered Alimada's practice. She was busy getting everything ready for the first patients of the day.

"Good morning, Eugene."

"Morning," murmured Eugene.

"You look like death. Last night with Lyon was a bit heavy, wasn't it?" she laughed.

"Very funny, but I am afraid you're right. Do you have some painkillers for me?"

"Yes, hang on. I'll dissolve a pill for you in water." Alimada went to one of her cupboards and started to look through her many drawers. She quickly found what she was looking for, took one pill and held it out to him.

"Take a glass over there, fill it with water and swallow the pill in one go," she ordered. He took the pill and did as he had been told even though she had just contradicted herself but he didn't care.

"Thank you."

"That's alright. Give it half an hour and you'll feel better. Have you looked out of the window yet?"

Eugene shook his head carefully and went to the window. The desert, normally so empty and dusty, was illuminated by little white lights. It was an incredible sight.

"Unique, isn't it?"

Eugene nodded vigorously and regretted it immediately. Alimada joined him; she had finished her preparations for her patients. In ten minutes she'd open her practice and the first patients would arrive. Eugene decided to spend the day in the recreation centre of the ship and perhaps visit the family they had found there.

General Joe and his many colleagues had assembled on the red sand to give a speech to all their soldiers. They stood on a big wooden pedestal emblazoned with the words "The United Forces." General Joe who had been chosen as the spokesperson stepped forward and started to speak to the assembled soldiers. It was a long uplifting speech and when he finished fifteen minutes later, the soldiers felt courageous and hungry for the fight. General Joe was content with his speech. He had spent the whole evening and night working on it.

Eugene had found his way back into his bed after an hour. The painkiller had helped still he didn't feel well. So he decided to rest until they had reached Xaviera. According to Jim they would be taken to the planet by jet. The mothership would not land but remain in orbit. Lyon would come and get him when it was time to go. Eugene closed his tired eyes; he tossed and turned in a fitful sleep.

He opened his eyes when he realized that somebody had grabbed his shoulders and was shaking him violently.
"Wake up!" somebody ordered. Blinking Eugene looked at his living alarm clock, it was Lyon. Had they already arrived at Xaviera?
"What's the matter?" asked Eugene
"We start in an hour."
"We start what?"
"We're flying down to Xaviera. Most of us are already down there. It'll take until late into the night to build the camp."
"I am practically up and dressed." Eugene got up, went to the mirror, did his hair and smoothed down his clothes.
"We'll have to set up our own tent down there. Every team sleeps in its own tent. Everybody is allocated to a group. We're going to share a tent with Jim and Rob."
"That's fine. You're not hungry by any chance?"
"I think I am."
"Shall we go and have something to eat?"
"We don't have much time. This very moment, Jim and Rob are putting their luggage into the jet that'll take us to Xaviera. Do you have any luggage?"
"No, I don't. Do we get our weapons down on the planet?"
"Yes, but most soldiers already have weapons."
"Okay. What about you, do you have any luggage that you

are taking down with you?"

"No, just my laser gun."

"In that case we have time for food."

"I don't mind. Jim's going to bite off our heads anyway."

They set off for the restaurant. When they stepped out of the restaurant with a full stomach three quarters of an hour later, they headed at once for the jet. They walked through several corridors, took the elevator and finally stepped through a steel door. Behind it was a big hangar where the jets were parked. Rob and Jim stood in front of them and talked to each other. Eugene and Lyon joined them. They were going to leave in ten minutes. They walked via the hatchway into the jet.

"Will Hesson be down in the camp?" asked Eugene.

"Yes, he will. He's going to sleep in the generals' tent," replied Jim.

"Is our camp far from the drads' camp?"

"Six miles. We'll have to walk through a petrified forest but that can only be an advantage. After all the drads won't be able to see us."

"Don't they have radar?"

"Yes, of course. But it won't do them much good. A small troop will attack them. There will be chaos at their camp and we can advance from the back undisturbed. And as you know, according to our plan we want to cut their power and without power, no radar. Without radar they won't be able to see the United Forces that are going to attack from all sides. Besides they have no idea that there is a battle ahead."

"Good. Slowly I am getting the feeling that we cannot lose," said Lyon.

"Put on your seatbelts, we're starting," said Jim. The jet engine roared, the gate in front of them opened and Jim flew outside into the wide universe. With an elegant swerve he guided the jet underneath the mothership and back out on the other side. Xaviera appeared ahead on them. It was a grey-green planet that looked like a big marble ball. Jim accelerated and raced through the atmosphere. Eugene noticed that there were many mountains and gorges on the planet but also some stony prairies. Jim steered the jet between steep mountain tops when suddenly a big stony prairie appeared below that had been turned into a parking area for fighter jets and troopships. Soldiers were everywhere. They were erecting tents and building gun towers. Jim aimed for an empty spot between other jets and touched down. The jet engine died down and Jim, Lyon, Rob, and Eugene left down the hatchway. It was unpleasantly cool out there and the air was unusually humid. Eugene, who was still used to the climate of Tattau, found it very unpleasant when after a few steps his hair and clothes stuck damply to his skin.

"This air is lethal!" grumbled Lyon.

"I knew there would be high humidity but I didn't expect that it would feel like walking under water," replied Jim.

"These are not ideal conditions for a good fight," remarked Rob, "it is damned cold. I can only hope for the best."

"Let's put up our tent," stated Jim carrying the rolled-up tent under his arm. They walked between the fighter jets, avoided disoriented soldiers, walked around some recently pitched tents and finally found a suitable spot near the generals' and Hesson's tent.

"I hope there are instructions for putting up that tent," said Lyon.

"What do you think?" commented Jim and let the rolled-up tent fall to the stony ground. He opened the zips and with Lyon's help he pulled out the tent. After some messing about and several crashes, they finally managed to put it up. It was a biggish square tent with a round dome as roof. The colour was dark green. Jim opened the entrance and they went inside. Inside everything was dark green as well. Lyon sniffed, it smelled of plastic but the air was not as damp as outside.

"It's bearable," he commented.

"You are welcome to sleep outside," said Jim.

"No, I definitely prefer this tent reeking of plastic to the underwater feeling of the air outside, thank you kindly," retorted Lyon.

"As you like. Let's get the blankets and sleeping bags from our jet." They went back outside and Eugene carefully closed the entrance of the tent to keep the damp air outside. Back at the jet they carried the four sleeping bags and four blankets. Eugene, Lyon, and Rob who didn't have any had to borrow some from Jim. Quickly they slipped into their tent and Jim closed the entrance. Since the tent was long and wide, they decided to sleep with their feet facing the entrance. Eugene was at the edge, next to Lyon, then Jim and finally Rob.

"Jim? Are you there?"

"Yes, coming," called Jim and opened the entrance. Outside stood General Joe.

"Everything okay?"

"We're fine. Please come in before everything gets damp," Jim invited Joe to enter.

"The climate here is horrible, isn't it? Well, I just wanted to give you your tent number." Joe offered them a piece of paper and a security pin, Jim read: number 129, group: destruction squad.

"Thank you, we'll put it on our tent right away."

"Apart from that I wanted to tell you that you start out tomorrow at noon so you reach the rear of the mountain in the evening. We'll stay in touch via radio. The diversion troops will attack at night. But you'll be told more about that later. I think Hesson will look in, too. I wish you every success on your mission; you have a long and strenuous trip ahead of you."

265

"Okay."

"I'll see you again before you leave."

"Thank you, General Joe," said Jim. Joe nodded once and left the tent.

"I don't think we're going to do much for the rest of the day, are we?" Rob asked the others.

"Apart from sleeping there isn't much planned," answered Lyon. Jim shrugged his shoulders.

"I think I'll go and look for Alimada," said Eugene.

"Has she arrived on Xaviera already? I thought the medical personnel wasn't landing till tomorrow afternoon," said Rob.

"I haven't got the slightest clue."

"I think Rob is right, Eugene, you can look for her tomorrow morning but there won't be much point now," added Jim.

"Perhaps you're right."

"Anybody home?" asked a voice from outside.

"Hesson! Come in," Jim invited the voice. The entrance opened and Hesson entered.

"Everything okay?" he asked. They all nodded. "Good. Has General Joe been here yet?"

"Yes, a minute ago."

"I guess he announced my coming. Eugene, Rob, neither of you has a weapon. You know where the armoury tent is?"

"No, but we'll find out."

"It is next to our tent, not far away. Your mission starts tomorrow at noon. You can expect a longish walk. Have a good night's sleep because you'll have to be awake for a long time."

"Thank you, Hesson."

"You'll get directions tomorrow. You'll get a map as well and a headset each. Well, guys, good night." Hesson turned around and left the tent.

"I'll turn in, good night," said Lyon.

"Good night." Rob twisted himself into his sleeping bag and pulled the blanket over it. Eugene and Jim, too, crept into their sleeping bags. It was dark outside now but everything was lit by floodlights that were put up all over the place. At midnight they were turned off.

Eugene sat on an old wobbly wooden chair. Around him were wooden walls, cobwebs hanging from the ceiling. There were no spiders in sight. He got up and went to the door. Carefully he stepped outside. He fell down into the depth. Green empty depth was around him. It was wet. It was so wet that he could hardly breathe and the deeper he fell the damper it became. He couldn't breathe. He breathed water in and out. He was sick, he spat blood. He hit his head hard. He was inside a house. Out front stood a jeep. He still couldn't breathe, everything was so wet. The jeep became blurred in front of his eyes. He was suffocating.

Eugene turned around and looked at the back of Lyon's head. They were lying in the tent. He breathed deeply, the air was damp. He slowly got up and glanced at Jim's watch. It was four o'clock in the morning. He sank back tiredly. He slept for the rest of the night without any further nightmares.

Eugene opened his eyes, it was daylight already. He rubbed his eyes and looked around. Lyon was no longer in his sleeping bag. Rob and Jim talked standing up.

"Good morning," said Eugene.

"Morning, Eugene," said Jim.

"What time is it?"

"Nine o'clock," said Jim with a quick glance at his watch.

Eugene crept out of his sleeping bag and got up.

"Where is Lyon?"

"He had to follow the call of nature. I told him to hurry up or he would have to wait longer to go to the toilet."

"Why?"

"Because everybody needs to go now and there are so many of us. To the best of my knowledge there are fifty toilets. Do you know how many soldiers there are?"

Eugene nodded. "Have you eaten yet?"

"No, the canteen is being set up right now but I have decided to eat in the jet. I cannot swallow that crap they serve in the soldiers' canteen. Do you know where that comes from? I have heard that it is produced on some slave planet without hygiene rules or anything and when it is a nice yellow mush, it is poured into big tin tanks," said Lyon appearing in the entrance.

"Is that right?"

"That it is a yellow mush is correct. Where it has been produced, I cannot tell you, however, I strongly suspect that Lyon is wrong," explained Jim.

"I think I'll eat with you in the jet," said Eugene.

"Rubbish, you are so fussy!" scolded Rob.

"Look who's talking! You cannot be poisoned by food," retorted Lyon. "Come on, Eugene, I'm hungry." Together Eugene and Lyon left the tent and left Rob and Jim behind. Eugene kept his eyes peeled to spot the field hospital while they were walking to the jet. He couldn't see it.

"Have you seen Alimada?" he asked Lyon finally.

"No, but I met Hesson outside the toilets. He said that the doctors will arrive in three hours and put up their tents. Come now, let's hurry up, I feel like choking in this damned air."

The camp was bustling. Orders were shouted on all sides. Some were still busy pitching their tents. Some had only arrived that day. Soldiers sat on wooden benches and ate their yellow mush from plastic plates. Eugene noticed that there were no clouds on Xaviera. He guessed that that was due to the high humidity everywhere. They walked right in the middle of the clouds. How did the drads cope with the humidity? Eugene and Lyon walked up the hatchway and Lyon quickly closed it again. In the jet it was so much pleasanter than outside.

Eugene avoided some soldiers while looking in vain for Alimada's hospital tent. Where could she be? After several attempts asking soldiers where she might be and getting negative replies, he gave up.

It was noon and Jim, Lyon, Eugene, and Rob were in the generals' tent. In the middle of the big tent was a table with a map on it. General Joe showed them the location of the drad camp and the location of their own camp. Many other generals stood around them and looked on. Then Joe explained the route they had to take to get behind the mountains without drawing the drads' attention. Hesson had been right; it would be quite a long and strenuous march. They checked their weapons, got their headsets, a map on which their planned route was highlighted and which was taken by Jim, a compass and the generals' best wishes before they went outside into the humid air. They checked if radio contact with General Joe had been established and marched off, past the jets, out of the camp. They would be on the move until late in the evening. At seven o'clock in the evening the feint attack on the drad camp would begin. If they hadn't reached the mountains by then, there might be mayhem.

They had left the camp only a few yards behind but Lyon was panting already. The air wasn't good for his lungs. With every breath, the air saturated with water flowed down the windpipe into the bronchial tubes like water.

Eugene was worried whether he would be able to get through the strenuous, long, exhausting march. Jim led their little squad holding the map with their route highlighted in red in his right hand. In the distance they saw the mountains. The air was misty. It all seemed very dramatic to Eugene. The prairie appeared endless. The mountains, their first destination, seemed to stay as distant as they were at the beginning of their march.

"If it goes on like this, I won't make it," moaned Lyon, water dripping off his nose.

"We have to make it, Lyon, we haven't even done a mile yet," said Jim.

"And how many are there to go?"

"Between thirteen and fifteen," said Jim looking at his map. The ground was slightly sloping now, they walked downhill. Ahead there was a path winding through some small rocks. They made somewhat faster progress. Eugene could see the mountains more clearly now. They were enormous; many gaps and holes cut through them, gaping and smiling at the squad, it seemed, telling them how weak they were and how little their chances of conquering them and reaching the other side. Silently they stumbled towards them, and finally had the feeling that they got closer. The path behind them, small and insignificant, wound its way up the little hill. The ground levelled out and their speed slowed again. Lyon panted.

"How long will it take to get to those mountains?" asked Rob.

"We have done about a third of the distance. That means we have some nine miles to go," said Jim.

"Some nine miles? I am dead," groaned Lyon.

"Pull yourself together, man! You behave like a little brat," scolded Jim.

"Yes, yes, the jackal head is in for it. You know, Jim, I am not keen on this underwater planet. I prefer dusty and warm spots."

"Okay, okay, you can turn back and help the soldiers playing at war."

"You know what? I think that is precisely what I am going to do!"

"Be my guest!"

"Oh shut up, both of you!" interrupted Rob. "Another eight miles and we'll be at the foot of the mountains. We can take a short break there and then you'll have time to knock your opinions into each other. But for now shut your traps and save your strength."

Silently they continued walking towards the mountains. Eugene could now see that they were dark grey, in some places even black. They weren't very high but still too high to just walk across them, and their tops were pointed. Strangely enough, they were completely in the shadow and radiated an unpleasantly frightening atmosphere. Rob expressed in words what Eugene had thought.

"I don't like these mountains. You know I have a bad feeling when I look at them as if something evil emanated from them."

"I feel just the same," agreed Eugene.

"Does anyone know what kind of creature lives on this planet?" asked Lyon.

"Yes, I do. They are called Yaggores. Small and ugly creatures, grey like the world around them. They died out about a thousand years ago, at least that's the assumption," said Jim.

"Why did they die out?"

"To the best of my knowledge, the climate changed dramatically to become as it is now. According to myths and legends the climate used to be warmer and there were plants as well."

"No wonder they died out," growled Lyon.

"There are always stories being put about that someone

has seen a Yaggore. If you ask me that's total rubbish. You know, Yaggores sculpted stone statues of themselves, their towns were made of pure stone, too. It is quite possible that in a panic somebody convinces himself that he's seen a real Yaggore but in reality it was only a statue."

"Don't we have to walk through one such deserted town?" asked Rob.

"Indeed. Hesson has planned our route through one of the old Yaggore towns. The town is called Illizio, it had more than a thousand inhabitants, was a big city really."

"A big city?"

"Yes, a big city. More than a thousand years ago, about fifty to a hundred thousand Yaggores lived on the planet. More than a thousand inhabitants in a town was a lot."

"How many lived in the capital?"

"I don't think there was a capital."

"They didn't have a capital?"

"No, but there was a royal palace somewhere on the far side of the planet."

"What a shame, I would have liked to see that," sighed Lyon. The mountains were much closer now. They were huge and seemed to tower like giant nails out of the ground. Jim walked towards one of the small gaps between the mountains. Another two or three miles and they would stand at the foot of the mountains.

"The troops to feign the attack are ready to start. According to our calculations, Jim and his squad should have reached the mountains by now. That means they should be on the other side of the mountains in about two hours, ready to cross the town," said General Joe.

"Okay, I should radio them," said Hesson. Joe nodded and took the headset lying on the table next to the map.

"Jim? Come in, Jim!"

"..."

"Jim? This is General Joe."

"..."

"Jim, do you read me?"

"..."

"Jim, this is General Joe. Please answer"

"..."

"There is no reply."

"I hope they haven't met with any difficulties?"

"Unlikely, nobody has lived on this planet for years. I think it's more likely that this blasted permanent mist swallows our radio waves."

"Can we fix that?"

"No, we can't."

"Damn, we won't be able to arrange when the feint attack takes place and when the destruction squad should cross the mountains."

"We'll do everything according to plan and hope that Jim arrives at the mountains behind the camp in time and attacks."

"We don't have a choice. Hope is all we've got."

"I'll inform the generals about our problem," said Hesson.

"No, don't do that."

"General Joe? The other generals have the right to know that they might send their soldiers to certain death. Explain to me why we should keep it a secret?" asked Hesson, confused.

"They wouldn't order the diversion squad to attack. Jim and his squad would walk to their death; all would have been in vain."

"You are right," said Hesson after a moment's hesitation. Even though he didn't approve of what Joe had said he realized that there was no other way.

Jim, Rob, Lyon, and Eugene stood in front of the impressive mountains. The straight walls towering vertically into the grey sky glistened black with moisture. Ahead of them stretched a long dark tunnel. Jim held his torch in his right hand. He switched it on and shone it into the natural tunnel.

"Sheer suicide," murmured Lyon.

"We are supposed to walk through there?" asked Rob. Jim nodded and entered. Shaking their heads, the other three followed him. Lyon, who had hoped for somewhat drier air, was bitterly disappointed because there was the same climate inside the tunnel. The air was filled with the sound of splashing. The walls of the rocks were wet and water dripped down on them everywhere. They had to avoid stalactites and stalagmites, saving themselves from bumps and bruises. The narrow dark path seemed to have no end. They advanced further and further into the bowels of the mountain. Eugene's legs hurt. Lyon panted exhausted in front of him. After some time the natural cave changed into an artificial tunnel hammered into the stone. In the light of the torch, it was easy to see the places where tools had been used. The ground had been hammered even and they were able to proceed more quickly. Far away a bright white spot of light appeared. The exit. They had nearly crossed the mountains. They speeded up. It would still take a few more minutes before they reached the exit. At last they made it. Relieved, they stepped outside. Ahead was a big valley surrounded by mountains in a semi-circle. In the middle of the valley was Illizio. The town was quite unique. The buildings seemed to have grown out of the rocky ground. Everything was grey, white or black and at times a mixture of these. Some buildings seemed to melt into their surroundings and only became visible at a second glance. Ahead of them the ground sloped steeply. Slipping, they went downhill and reached the first buildings of the town. It seemed to have been built without any pattern. They had all erected their houses where it had pleased them. There were little alleyways, lanes and big, wide streets leading through the wildly assembled houses. The buildings were of different heights; some were rather small, others had several storeys or were some yards in length. There were several big squares where patterns had been etched into the ground. Markets, public speeches or other community events probably took place here. Frequently there were little Yaggore statues in these squares. The squad walked along one of the wider streets towards a square in the centre of town.

"This is quite unusual," said Rob.

"Looks like the Yaggore made everything of stone. They probably even ate stone," opined Lyon and grinned lopsidedly.

"D'you think?" asked Eugene and grinned.

"Have you noticed that all houses have been made out of one piece? They weren't assembled out of lots of small stones but out of one big piece," remarked Jim.

"You're right."

"Do you know what I think? I think they chiselled this town out of a big mountain."

"It looks like it. That would also explain the confusion of houses," said Lyon.

"Wow, impressive, I wonder how long they worked on that."

"At least they managed to finish it before they died out," said Jim. They had reached the big square now. It was surrounded by many buildings and was about thirty yards long and twenty yards wide. In the middle was a statue. Eugene looked at the pattern on the ground. It was angular and wound itself in spirals over the square until it ended at the foot of the statue in the centre.

"I wouldn't like to see what went on here," remarked Lyon.

"I guess that markets took place here," explained Rob.

"I think it's more likely that it was here they swung the

275

robe and dropped the axe," retorted Lyon.

"Nonsense," said Rob.

"General Joe, please come in."

"..."

"General Joe, this is Jim. Please answer."

"..."

"General Joe, do you read me?"

"..."

"We don't have reception," called Jim.

"What do you mean?"

"I mean that we don't have radio contact with General Joe. I cannot reach him."

"That's bad."

"Very bad indeed. There is no possibility to communicate with him. We have to arrive at the rear of the mountains absolutely on time and according to plan, otherwise we send the diversion squad to its death."

"Have you managed to establish contact with Jim?" asked Hesson. Joe shook his head. For an hour he had been trying to reach Jim.

"I cannot even reach our mothership either, this fog is simply too thick for our radio waves."

"Damn. I still had some hope but now we'll have to send off the men without any security. They'll walk through the petrified forest and camp there. When it gets dark, they'll attack. Let's hope that Jim and his squad will attack then, too." Hesson left the tent, avoided a few soldiers and stepped in front of the diversion force. There were six hundred men. They stood in several rows in front of him. Pulling a handkerchief out of his pocket, he wiped the dampness from his face. He gave his speech, emphasizing how important their mission was and gave the captain the command over the force. In step they marched off. Ramses was among them, he had volunteered for this commando.

Their steps didn't reverberate far, the fog swallowed them and soon they couldn't see anybody anymore. They walked over the stony prairie and suddenly the petrified forest appeared in front of them. It was dark grey. The trees looked like columns with long threatening teeth growing out of them. There was no path they could have used. They had no choice but to slip through the trees in confusion. When they reached the middle of the forest, the captain gave the sign to halt. They would wait here until it was dark. Ramses sat down on a tree stump and looked around. The forest was sinister. Faces seemed to hide in the petrified bark of the trees. The silence instilled the feeling that some unknown creature was creeping up on them. The fog wafted between the tree trunks, separating into clouds and assembling again. Ramses leaned back against one of the trees, watched the spectacle for a while and finally closed his eyes.

"This stone town is bigger than it looks," stated Rob.
"We've nearly reached the end," said Jim.
"So what next?"
"We'll follow a little path down a slope, walk some distance and finally we'll be behind the mountains," said Jim.
They walked side by side without a further word. After some time, they reached the slope. It wasn't all that steep, but very long. It was covered in pebbles.
"Where is the path?" asked Lyon.
"I guess we'll have to look for it," said Jim. Together they walked along the top of the slope looking for the small path that would take them down safely. They found it quickly; it was a well trampled path that led diagonally down the slope. Carefully they descended as the ground was wet and slippery. Beneath them spread a grey prairie as far as the eye could see. Far in the distance Eugene was

able to make out the mountains through the fog, mountains bigger than the ones they had already crossed. Eugene's knees turned to jelly because of constantly walking downhill and when, after several minutes, they arrived at the bottom, his legs trembled. Lyon panted worse than ever but he didn't ask for a rest.

"It is getting dark," remarked Eugene. Jim looked at his watch; it was nearly half past seven. The diversion force would attack in an hour and a half.

"Go on, hurry up," said Jim and walked ahead. The others followed.

"Hey! Wake up" somebody shook Ramses' shoulder. He opened his eyes, had he fallen asleep?

"What?"

"Wake up. We're moving on. We'll attack in half an hour," said the soldier who had woken him.

"Did I fall asleep?"

"Looks like it. But that's okay, we're all tired."

"Thank you."

"That's okay. Come on." The soldier held out his hand, Ramses took it and the soldier pulled him up. Together they followed the others through the forest.

"What's your name?" Ramses asked the soldier.

"My name is Horúß."

"I am Ramses."

"Are you afraid of the fight?"

"Not for my sake but for my family if I don't come back."

"You have a family?" Ramses nodded.

"Why did you volunteer?"

"I had an argument with my wife."

"Oh, I see."

They stumbled over tree stumps, branches and other petrified undergrowth for fifteen minutes until they finally stopped. Everyone had come to a halt. The forest was at an end. Suddenly they heard some noise, the jet engines of spaceships. They looked up but couldn't see anything because of the treetops and the thick fog. But then some troopships flew low right above the trees.

"I don't believe it. Those are drad troopships," murmured Horúß and he was right. They heard the captain speaking. "Listen, men! Be quiet! Okay, in five minutes we'll crawl forward, slowly. Once we are close enough, we'll shoot at the wall and then we'll try to break down the gate. I'll give the signal to start. Please pass this message on to those who are at the back and cannot hear me."

They had been walking along the path for some time now leaving the slope behind them; they were on their way towards the mountains. In ten minutes they would be there. They had to slow down a bit. Lyon wasn't well. He had been walking with his head drooping for a while and panted loudly, his breath came bubbling as if there was water in his lungs. His hands were holding his sides. Everybody was seriously worried and feared that he might break down. Jim looked at his watch more and more desperately, the diversion force would attack in a minute. It was impossible to make it in time. They would be late.

"Let's attack!" ordered the captain. Quietly they left the forest and started to crawl. Six hundred men crawled on the stony ground towards the wall surrounding the drad camp. Ramses crawled next to Horúß and both tried very hard not to scratch themselves too much on the rough sharp-edged ground. The captain held up his hand and nobody moved; everybody stared at the hand. Then came the signal for attack. Everybody fired at the big gate in the wall. The big floodlights in the camp were switched on. The gun towers in the wall moved around hectically, sparks flew everywhere and there was a lot of shouting in

279

the camp. Then the gate opened and a lot of drads rushed outside. The captain jumped up and his men followed suit. Everybody rushed at each other. Ramses fired like mad at the gate into the mass of drads while running towards them. Horúß followed him shooting just as wildly. Every second a drad or one of their own men collapsed. Dead bodies were lying in front of Ramses, torn to pieces by fire from the gun towers or by one of the drads. He kicked the drad who suddenly appeared in front of him and made him stagger. Then he shot him in the head that flew off. Quickly he ran on. There were no more drads rushing out of the gate. Things didn't look good. There were two or three drads per man. Horúß kicked a drad in the back so that he bent over by nearly ninety degrees. The red eyes of the drads sparkled everywhere. Ramses pulled one of his comrades out of the firing line behind a little heap of destroyed drads. He looked around, they didn't have a chance and they dropped like flies. Meanwhile there must have been five drads per man.

"We don't have a chance!" Ramses called to Horúß over the fray and noise of the battle.

"What should we do?"

"Let's go into the camp! We'll get them from the inside!"

"Let's hope for the best!"

"Let's go!" Ramses emerged from behind their protective wall and started running for the gate. He shot down a drad aiming at him and then they were in front of the gate. Above them the gun towers incessantly spewed out laser projectiles into the fighting masses.

"Looks like the destruction squad messed up their mission!" shouted Horúß.

"Looks like it. Come on!" They stepped through the gate beneath the wall and were inside the camp. It was a huge camp, there were drad troopships everywhere. Funnily enough, there were no drads in sight.

"Where are they?"

"No idea. Doesn't matter, come on, we go to the back, to the mountains, it is easier to hide there and we are less conspicuous." Under the shadow of the wall they ran past the ships and other gear towards the mountains.

At last they had arrived at the foot of the mountains. Ahead of them their path rose and wound its way up the mountain. Without a break they started to go uphill. Up on the mountain, the air was a bit drier but Lyon didn't seem to feel that anymore. His condition had worsened dramatically, his head drooped and he shuffled his feet along the ground.

"We are already ten minutes late. The battle is already in full swing," said Jim. They climbed the mountain as fast as they could but when they had finally reached the summit, they were so out of breath that they had to sit down. Lyon suffered a coughing fit and lowered himself onto one of the small rocks. From up there, they had an excellent view onto the drad camp. The camp was huge. The battle was swallowed by the thick fog, only now and then could they see the flash of a laser projectile. They couldn't hear the noises of battle.

"Let's go on!" ordered Jim. Groaning, the group got up. They started their descent. Sometimes, rough stairs made progress easier, at other times, they had to clamber but after another then minutes they arrived at the bottom. They were inside the camp.

"Our troops are ready, general," said the soldier and saluted as Joe gave him permission to start. Now it would come to the crunch. The generals had decided after the diversion to send out the first hundred fighter jets and to follow this up with infantry.

"If Jim hasn't managed to cut the drads' power supply,

we're going to lose many soldiers because of the gun towers," said Joe. Hesson nodded. The jets screamed over them and disappeared in the fog. They flew over the petrified forest and reached the battlefield. At once they started firing. Drad bodies exploded and scattered under the salvoes fired by the jets. They flew in a semi-circle over the battlefield and fired again at the remaining drads. Shot down, one of the jets flew over the camp towards the mountains where it exploded in an enormous fireball.

As the burning jet had buzzed over them, Jim, Lyon, Rob, and Eugene had quickly looked for cover behind a troopship. A moment later the jet had crashed into the mountain, exploded and had left a big wave of heat in its wake. Sparks rained down on them and died on their wet clothes.
"The main building should be somewhere around here," said Jim.
"Then let's hurry and look for it." Under cover of the troopship they left their hiding place and went to one of the buildings. It was angular, high and had a cupola on the roof. In the distance they could see the red eyes of the drads. They had to be careful not to be discovered.

"Hey!" Frightened by the voice all four started and turned, guns at the ready. "Calm down, it's me, Ramses. Do you remember me?"
"Bloody idiot! How can you give us such a fright!" scolded Jim whispering.
"Sorry! Tell me, why are you so late?"
"Lyon has problems with the climate, besides we've lost radio contact a long time ago. We couldn't radio in that we wouldn't be able to stick to the plan."
"Yes, that's the fog. This is Horúß," said Ramses nodding in the direction of his comrade. "Nearly our whole squad

282

has been killed; I think maybe only ten might have survived. If the jets hadn't come, it'd look even worse for us. I think we would have been obliterated. We should get going and turn off the electricity."

"That's what we were about to do." They continued towards the building.

"We have to assume that the building is guarded."

"How are we going to proceed?"

"Who'll join me for a reconnaissance tour?" asked Jim.

"I'm coming," said Lyon.

"It'll take five minutes at most. If we're not back by then, you're warned." Jim and Lyon disappeared, with weapons raised, in the fog. Ducking they darted towards the building and disappeared behind it.

They stood in front of an iron double door. Jim stepped up to it and carefully moved the handle. The door was locked.

"Shoot it open," said Lyon.

"We need the others; we don't know how many drads might be waiting for us in there."

Jim and Lyon appeared again in front of them.

"We'll have to open the door by shooting. If we meet drads, we need your help." The six of them walked back to the door. Suddenly ten drads with shining red eyes stood in front of them. Lyon lifted his gun and fired. The first drad lost his head. Jim and Eugene dived to the right as the drads opened fire. Rob let himself drop to the floor. Ramses and Horúß ducked and ran to the left behind a troopship. The laser projectiles hit the metal hull of the ship sending out sparks. The drads separated. Rob and Lyon fired incessantly from the floor and killed three that sank onto their knees while their red eyes went out for ever. Two stormed into Jim's and Eugene's direction, one lost his head as a laser beam from Eugene's gun hit him. The second was cut up by Jim as he jumped from behind a container and separated the drad's trunk from the feet with his gun. Smoking and sparking the drad fell to the ground. Ramses shot down one who had just tried to kill Lyon. Horúß jumped out and wanted to face one of the drads when he was thrown back by a shot. Groaning, he remained lying on the smooth rock. Ramses approached him and killed the drad who had shot down Horúß with a furious salvo. Now it was quiet. Somewhere at the other end of the camp raged the real battle.

"Jim?" called Ramses.
"I am here. Are you okay?"
"Horúß is injured but he's fine." Lyon stepped up to him. Rob, Jim, and Eugene followed.
"I have counted the drads. We shot down eight, two are missing," said Eugene. A shot hit the troopship next to them.
"Duck down!" called Jim. Laser shots exploded virtually everything around them. The drads stood about ten yards away. Jim shot one of them; the other went into hiding behind one of the many containers.

"Be careful, three to the left, the other three to the right. Ramses, Horúß you come with me," said Jim. Horúß held his injured shoulder. They separated and approached slowly from both sides of the container. Virtually at the same time they stepped forward and stood in front of the drad, Lyon dived forward and wrestled him down to the ground. Lyon pressed the arms down; the laser weapon was connected to the drad's hand. Eugene came to his help and shot point blank into the drad's head. Now they had got all ten of them. Jim pulled Lyon to his feet, and quickly they went to the door, which was open. Apparently the ten drads had come through it. Ramses had to support Horúß, his shoulder wound caused him big problems and he was close to losing consciousness. Jim stepped up to the door

284

and listened, there was no sound. Carefully he pushed the door open further, and then they entered the empty room.

In camouflage, three hundred thousand soldiers darted over the prairie as if they were one. They were like living shadows and as soon as they were seen they disappeared again. General Joe led the troops with two other generals. The drad camp appeared ahead of them. Joe saw at once that there weren't many of the diversion force left, none to be precise. Their jets buzzed incessantly over the battlefield where several thousand drads stood and fired constantly, supported by the gun towers that still worked perfectly, as Joe noticed with consternation. What was Jim waiting for? They stepped out of the shadows and rushed towards the drads. The first row fell under the salvoes from the towers but the second row of soldiers attacked the drads furiously. More and more jets crashed, not a few of them in the middle of the battlefield. They slid for many yards and killed everybody who couldn't move out of the way quickly enough. Some crashed into the walls and exploded so that huge pieces of concrete were thrown around and hit their own people decapitating or piercing them. Ever more drads rushed out of the camp gate and entered the battle. If the gun towers weren't turned off soon, nobody would survive.

Jim, Lyon, Rob, Eugene, Ramses, and Horúß stood in front of several monitors and consoles. Rob, Jim, and Lyon had been sitting there for a few minutes trying to hack into the drad system. Their fingers flew over the keyboards and now and then someone called: "I've got it!" and everybody looked at his screen. And inevitably it was a false alarm.
"Guys! I've got it! Power system: camp Yaggo," called Rob. Everybody looked at his screen. He really had done

it. There, in yellow letters was written: Power System: Camp Yaggo. Rob's fingers darted over the keyboard.

"It wants a code."

"Can you get round that?"

"I'll try." Again, his fingers flew, and then he had done it

"Hang on tight; it'll get dark in here in a second!" Rob grinned, stabbing the appropriate button on the keyboard with his finger, the light flickered and went out, just like the monitor and everything else that needed electrical power.

"We did it!"

"Guys, I don't feel so ...." Lyon fell off his chair and landed hard on the concrete floor.

"Shit, that blasted climate. We have to take him to the field hospital. Who knows what his lungs look like," said Eugene. "Jim, turn on your torch." Jim turned it on and shone it at Lyon lying on the floor. Eugene bent down and put his arms under Lyon's shoulders. With Ramses' help he pulled Lyon outside.

Jim grabbed his shoulders and shook him. Lyon murmured something incomprehensible.

"I would shout at him but we'd soon have a herd of drads around us," remarked Rob. Jim shook Lyon again, this time he opened his eyes.

"What is it?"

"You collapsed. The climate doesn't agree with you."

"Hell," Lyon supported himself on his elbows.

"We'd like to take you to the field hospital," said Jim.

"To the field hospital? Why? I am as fit as a fiddle!"

"We're worried about your lungs."

"I'm not going to the field hospital." Supported by Eugene, Lyon got up, swayed for a moment and then took his hand off Eugene's shoulder.

"As good as new," he stated.

"Oh well, if you say so. Rob, just to make sure, can you

install a code to stop the drads from switching electricity back on?"

"Will do," Rob disappeared back into the building.

Meanwhile, the big infantry troops led by Hesson marched to the left side of the camp. There were three hundred thousand soldiers. Hesson, who marched in front, together with some other generals, saw the camp and the battle. The gun towers were out of action. The destruction squad had done it. In step, the United Forces approached the battle. Five minutes later they would be right in the middle of it.

"The code has been installed. They won't be able to crack that." Rob came out again to join the others.

"Let's go then. We're needed up at the gate." Together they hurried off, past troopships and other ships, past containers and all kinds of gear. Drads only came towards them just before they reached the gate. Shooting wildly, they rushed into the tumult of battle. Lyon shot at ten drads at a time and dived behind a crashed, burning jet. He looked to the East, there was something there. Lyon screwed up his eyes, then he saw it, Hesson and the United Forces were advancing. Now their victory was nearly secured. He saw Eugene wrestle with two drads, Jim jumped around and shared out head shots and Ramses who sneaked up to a drad from behind and kicked him so violently that he fell apart. Three jets flew very low over the battlefield and shot several drads to smithereens. Revolving on their own axes several times, they turned round and repeated their manoeuvre with the same success. Lyon looked to the East again, Hesson was coming closer, and soon he would be here.

The number of drads had decreased dramatically in the last two hours. Slowly, they had been pushed back into the camp. Eugene and Jim fought side by side. They had found shelter in the forest as the battlefield had expanded significantly. Eugene and Jim jumped over the petrified branches while laser projectiles kept hitting the trees and sending fountains of dust flying. At least twenty drads were close behind them.

"We'll run an inconspicuous curve and then rush into the battlefield. We'll be safe from them there," called Jim while he avoided a tree that suddenly appeared in front of them. Eugene nodded, "Okay." Deliberately, they began to fight their way to the left. With an effort they managed to keep the drads at a distance. Eugene got a stitch, and he had the feeling that he was breathing water. The sounds of the battle that hadn't been audible for some time could be heard again. They approached the battlefield. Eugene staggered as an unusually low branch appeared in front of him. Weakened, he tried to avoid it. He had nearly succeeded but then he caught his shoulder. His arm was pulled back and he continued sideways for several steps. He would have fallen if he hadn't been able to support himself on a tree. Quickly he ran on. Jim hadn't noticed that he had fallen behind. A shot missed Eugene by a hair's breadth and hit a branch above him. Dust and stones rained down on Eugene. Sheltering his eyes with his hands, he kept on running. Now the noise of battle could be clearly heard, then the battlefield appeared in front of him. He looked around but couldn't see Jim anywhere. The drads came closer, panting they rushed into the tumult, and disappeared among his fighting comrades who now turned round and welcomed the drads emerging from the forest with laser projectiles. He ran through a maze of burnt-out fighter jets and dead bodies. He had discovered Lyon. He was fighting alongside Ramses and Horúß near the gate. Breathing heavily he sank down taking cover behind one of the jets.

"What's the matter?" asked Lyon.

"Jim and I had to flee from twenty or so drads."

"Where is Jim?"

"I lost him when I collided with a branch."

"A branch?"

"We went through the forest," said Eugene and looked at his shoulder. It bore a deep scratch and was bleeding heavily. "Jim is quite capable of looking after himself."

"I know," stated Lyon.

"How are things? Are we winning?"

"I would say we have a lead. However, we haven't managed yet to get into the camp but that's just a question of time."

"Yes, I think you're right. Oh damn it!"

"What's up?"

"Look," Eugene pointed at Horúß. Lyon followed the line of his finger.

"Shit!" Horúß was surrounded by five drads and held up his gun into the air, and then he threw it at the drads' feet.

"Damned drads, they know that they are going to lose and want to take hostages." Lyon took aim, Eugene did the same. They fired at the same time. Now Ramses had noticed Horúß' dilemma, too, and rushed towards him. Two drads were brought down by Eugene's and Lyon's shots. Another was finished by Ramses but one of the other two hit Horúß in the stomach and he sank to the ground. Lyon shot and killed him a second later and Ramses did for the last one just in time before he could fire. Quickly they ran to Horúß who lay motionless between all the dead drads. Jim knelt down next to him, silently the others stood around him. Shots buzzed past but time seemed to stand still. The noise died down, they could hear the wind rustling through the branches and leaves. Laughing and crying at the same time, Horúß closed his eyes. Jim stood up.

"He is dead. The shot killed him fast."

Without a word, they left the body behind and went back to the fight. Full of anger they struck down and shot and killed the drads. Heads were sent flying; drad bodies broke down and remained motionless on the ground. The ubiquitous red eyes increasingly lost their light. The United Forces pushed back the drads. One of the fighter jets flew low over the battlefield when a laser shot penetrated the windscreen. At full throttle the jet hurtled into one of the gun towers of the drads. With a huge bang it exploded into a thousand pieces. Pieces of metal buzzed deadly over the battlefield, pieces of stone rained on everybody, and those who didn't pay attention, were struck down. More and more the drads were pushed back and the size of the battlefield got smaller. Soon the battle was reduced to the area around the gate that could not be locked without electricity. But even if the drads had been able to lock it, many other points of entry had been blasted open by the crashing jets. Under cover of the wrecks the soldiers advanced. Hardly any were hit by drad projectiles.

"Attack the camp!" called Hesson, standing in the middle of the turmoil, smeared with blood and sweat. Everybody cheered and shouted, and then they attacked, overran the few remaining drads and were inside the camp where they didn't stop. They attacked the troopships and containers and shot and killed all drads that were still left. The fighter jets sprayed the camp with permanent fire and riddled the troopships. Some drads tried to flee but the jets didn't allow them to get far. Like stones they crashed back into the camp where they exploded. Engines and fuel were close together in the troopships, both in the fuselage. The huge heat waves that were released swept through the camp in a lethal storm. Some soldiers who were too close had their faces torn away.

"Careful!" called Eugene. He and Lyon jumped behind a

container. A moment later, a troopship nearby went up in flames and exploded.

The fire wall swept past the container.

"That was close," remarked Lyon.

Bit by bit the army made their way through the camp. None of the remaining drads had a chance. Lyon, Eugene, Jim and Rob arrived at the rearward end of the camp. There were no drads left. They had eliminated them. Once and for all! They flung their arms in the air and yelled. All the others soldiers followed their example. Everybody cheered. There were no more shots. Smoke rose from the troopships, bodies of dead drads lay everywhere, in places even on top of each other. Hesson held up his hands and everybody fell silent.

"Last night we marched, uncertain what to expect. Many men have been lost. But now we have won. I don't have much to say, we're exhausted. Let's take care of our fallen comrades and mourn them. Afterwards let's celebrate and rock the planet." Again everybody burst out cheering.

Jim, Ramses, Rob, Lyon, and Eugene walked back to the camp together. For the moment they wanted to get out of cleaning up. They would help eventually but first they wanted to take Lyon to Alimada for a check-up.

"I am glad that this is finally over," said Rob.

"We're all glad," stated Jim.

"What are you going to do now? I mean now that we have accomplished our mission?" asked Eugene.

"I live on the mothership," said Ramses. "I'll return there."

"Me, too," said Jim.

"I am going to fly back to Mars. You have no idea how much I miss the climate there," said Lyon.

"I am going back, too, back to the forest moon, to Hio," said Rob dreamily.

"What about you, Eugene? What are you going to do?"

asked Jim.

"I don't know. I didn't have a home, I was on the run."

"Hesson would allow you to live on the mothership straightaway."

"You think so? I don't know."

"You could move to a planet," suggested Rob.

"I have to think about it for a bit and talk to Alimada, too." They left the petrified forest and soon they entered the camp. There weren't many people about. Most of them were in their tents or the troopships. With Lyon in tow they went to the field hospital and entered. It was white and inside equipped with all the instruments necessary for operations or the treatment of the badly wounded or whatever else was needed when the soldiers returned from battle. Alimada sat on a chair leaning over a book.

"Hello," said Eugene. Alimada looked up and started to grin.

"Eugene! The battle is over?" Eugene nodded. "I was so worried about you."

Alimada came towards them, gave Eugene a big hug and kissed him.

"Alimada, Lyon isn't well. The climate is too humid for him. He even collapsed earlier," said Jim. Alimada nodded.

"Sit down on the examination table," she ordered Lyon. Lyon sat down. With a stethoscope she listened at his chest and gave him a few instructions like, "Breathe in, hold your breath, breathe out. Breathe in quickly, breathe out quickly or breathe in slowly, breathe out slowly." Then she put stethoscope aside. "He has some water in his lungs and, if I am not mistaken, that will develop into a bad cold." Lyon sighed.

"I give you two kinds of pills. Take one in the morning, the other one before you go to bed."

She took two packages from her desk drawer and gave

them to Lyon who was back on his feet now.

"Thank you for not having to die," he said smiling and put them into this pocket.

"I'll see you. Eugene, we'll be in our jet," said Jim and left the tent with Lyon and Rob.

"Are you okay?" asked Alimada.

"Yes, I'm fine."

"You look awful. What happened to your arm?"

"That's a long story."

"Tell me." They sat down together on the examination table and Eugene started talking. He told her how he and the others put up their tent, walked through the mountains and traversed the town, how they got into the camp, cut the power supply and finally ended by admitting how he and the others had sneaked away so they wouldn't have to help with cleaning up the dead and instead had gone to see her to have Lyon treated.

"I am glad nothing happened to you. Show me your arm." Eugene put his, by now, numb arm in Alimada's outstretched hand. She felt it carefully and disinfected it before dressing the wound.

"Have you thought about what to do next?" asked Eugene while she was dressing his arm. She shook her head.

"I don't know either. But I would like to stay with you," said Eugene.

"We are going to stay together and you will have to live on the ship. After all, I am a doctor there," stated Alimada.

"I know, but have you ever thought about leaving, living somewhere else, where it is more beautiful."

"Sure, but that is my home. It is not easy to take a decision like that."

"Think about it. I just remembered a wonderful planet, Ziguur. You know, the luxury planet."

"You're daydreaming. Do you know how expensive it is to live there?"

"No, not really but I am still owed the reward for my efforts and for the destruction of the UDP."

"That is true." Alimada looked into Eugene's eyes and smiled. "I'll think about it."

"I'll see you." Eugene turned around and went towards the exit.

"Where are you going?"

"To join the others. I think we should help with the clean-up now. Soon your first patients are going to arrive as well, I guess."

"See you soon." Eugene left the tent and went to their jet.

2 days later

They had cleaned up in shifts. Day and night they had buried the dead. This morning they had finally finished. The last drad bodies and their own fallen soldiers had been placed in the houses of the stone city. Now the preparations for the celebrations had begun. Hesson would hand out medals and a colourful rich buffet would be served. The feast was to be held in a huge tent that was specially flown down from the mothership and set up. Big air conditioning systems should make sure that humidity was reduced to a pleasant level inside. Soldiers were already working to put up the iron frame. Lyon, Ramses, Rob, Jim, and Eugene ambled through the maze of tents and talked about what they would do with the money they would receive as a reward for the destruction of the drad ship.

"I hope Alimada approves of my plan," remarked Eugene.

"Why should she refuse the offer?" asked Rob.

"Because the mothership is her home."

"Why don't you want to stay on the ship?"

"I want to live on a planet, I think."

"You know, Eugene, you just have to take it as it comes," said Lyon. "The future is unfathomable. You never know what it holds for you. Who knows where life will take you."

"You're right."

"Hey, there is Hesson over there. Come, let's go and say hi," said Jim and walked between two tents to where Hesson was sitting on a bench talking to one of the soldiers. When he saw Jim, he got up. The soldier saluted and left.

"Jim, Eugene, Rob, Lyon, Ramses. Nice to see you," said Hesson.

"Nice to see you, too. How are things progressing?" asked Jim.

"Very well. The tent should be ready by tonight. We can accommodate most people in here; the others will have to stand."

"Amazing! When does the big party begin?"

"Tomorrow night. You will be the guests of honour, of course. Think about a few words of thanks you might want to say when I present you with your reward."

"Will we be on stage?"

"Sure."

"Great," said Lyon sarcastically.

"What's so bad about that?" asked Hesson.

"To find the right words in front of so many people is very difficult. And it can even end in total embarrassment."

"I am sure you'll know how to avoid an embarrassing situation. I have to talk to all of you individually anyway. This evening from six o'clock in my office."

"Your office? On the ship? But the ship is in space."

"It is going to land, in two hours. After the party we'll all go aboard. Then the war will be over at last, it will all be over."

"Okay, this evening at six," said Jim.

Eugene walked through the familiar corridors on his way

to see Hesson. It was five minutes to six. Using the elevator, he went to the executive suites. Slowly he ambled along the wide corridor towards the door behind which lay Hesson's office. Lyon was already waiting.

"What do you think? What does he want to talk about with each of us, alone?" asked Lyon as Eugene joined him.

"I haven't got a clue," said Eugene. Lyon breathed in the air noisily.

"I love this air. You have no idea how I've missed it."

"I can imagine. How are you, how's the cold?"

"Not too bad. Alimada's pills worked well. My limbs ache, I have a slight headache and I'm feeling awfully tired but apart from that I feel splendid."

"Hi, guys," said Rob joining them. They hadn't even noticed him. Soon Jim arrived as well. Now they were all together. At six o'clock sharp the office door opened.

"You have all come. Very good. First I would like to talk to Jim," said Hesson. Jim nodded and entered. Hesson closed the door.

"I wonder what they are talking about," remarked Rob.

"I think we'll learn that soon enough."

"Tell me, has anything struck you as odd about Jim? He has changed so much lately," said Lyon.

"Since he was appointed leader of the destruction squad, I would say," said Rob. Soon they got tired of standing around and sat down leaning against the opposite wall. After another ten minutes, Jim came out of the office. Without a word, he sat down next to Lyon.

"Eugene? Could you please come in next?" Eugene got up and went past Hesson into the latter's office.

"Sit down," said Hesson closing the door. Eugene sat down in the leather armchair while Hesson took his seat behind the desk.

"I am sure you are wondering why I want to talk to each one of you individually." Eugene nodded. "Well, the reason is your reward. I have thought about it for a while and finally concluded that now that the dark ones have been defeated each of you must have some dream for the future." Hesson folded his hands and looked into Eugene's eyes. "I know about you and Alimada and I am sure that many things still lie ahead of you. I've been wondering what you might wish for and then suddenly it hit me." Hesson paused.

"And what was it that hit you?" asked Eugene after a few seconds.

"A wedding."

"A wedding?"

"Yes, a wedding. You and Alimada, I am going to pay for a big luxurious wedding on a planet of your choice."

"Are you serious?"

"Dead serious! You have done so much for the peoples of the universe and I think a reward is more than necessary. In addition, you will receive a large sum of money in a currency of your choosing."

"Thank you so much! I have to talk about this with Alimada. Thank you, that is totally incredible." Eugene grinned and no matter how hard he tried he couldn't stop himself. So he kept grinning at Hesson.

"All right, all right. The others are getting equally valuable rewards. You know, Eugene, not many people know, but we own the largest goldmine in our galaxy," said Hesson.

"I am impressed. I am going to talk to Alimada tonight."

"Will you come and see me to tell me her answer?"

"Definitely."

"Good. You can tell me tomorrow at the celebrations, that'll do. Oh and keep the bit about the goldmine to yourself."

"Sure thing," said Eugene. Hesson got up and they shook hands. Eugene went outside, he felt dazed. Hesson asked Rob into his office. Slowly Eugene slid down the wall next to Lyon.

Eugene entered Alimada's apartment and gave her a long kiss by way of greeting. Then he lifted her up and carried her to the bed. They started talking. Eugene told her everything. Tears welled up into her eyes.
"Alimada, will you marry me?"
"Yes, I will."
They kissed again.

The air was redolent with many different and wonderful smells. Lyon, Alimada, and Eugene walked towards the white tent towering up into the sky. It smelled of roast meat, cake, pizza and other culinary delights. They made Eugene's mouth water. He had deliberately eaten very little all day in order to be able to eat as much as possible on that special night. The sounds of music wafted towards them and an exuberant mood set in. They were looking forward to the party immensely. When they passed through the entrance consisting of plastic sheets that had to be pushed aside, they were overwhelmed. The ceiling was raised high by means of wooden beams to make it taper. It all looked very abstract and gave the impression of safety. The tent was full of wooden tables and the corresponding benches. Far in the background Eugene could just make out the colourfully decorated stage. The food was served at a long counter with the kitchen right behind it and it was possible to watch your own food being prepared. Lyon, Alimada, and Eugene walked down between the tables along the main aisle until they were close to the stage. They discovered Jim, Rob, General Joe, and all the other generals and joined them.
"Are you hungry?" asked Jim.
"Hungry as a hunter," replied Lyon and grabbed one of the menus. Eugene and Alimada did the same and studied the

many interesting dishes.

"What would you like to eat and drink?" asked a waitress. "I'd like a pizza and a glass of water," said Eugene instantly.

"I'll have the fillet steak with two potatoes and pepper sauce," said Lyon.

"And to drink?"

"Red wine," replied Lyon.

"I'll have a mixed salad and the seafood pasta followed by the greogasi fish steak," said Alimada.

"And to drink?"

"White wine, please." The waitress nodded and disappeared amongst the tables.

"I am really excited," said Lyon.

"Because you have to go on stage?" asked Alimada. Lyon nodded.

"I am nervous, too. Have you thought about a speech?" asked Eugene.

"Not really. I thought I might just say 'Thank you' or 'Many thanks'," said Lyon.

"I guess I'll do the same then."

"You might have bothered to think about it a bit more," opined Alimada.

"Oh rubbish! 'Thank you' will do fine." Lyon leaned back to make it easier for the waitress to serve their drinks.

"I think you should at least say a whole sentence."

"We'll say the right thing," stated Lyon and that was that. The tent filled up slowly but steadily. Many table rows were already occupied. The air hummed with the sounds of conversations. Every second new guests arrived through the plastic entrance. Finally Eugene's, Lyon's and Alimada's food arrived. Glad to be able to fill their stomachs, they started eating.

Eugene didn't look up from his plate until it was empty.

The tent was full of people. It was virtually impossible to move along the aisles because they were full of those who hadn't found a seat.

"Unbelievable. I hope this strange roof holds out," said Lyon over the noise of the crowd and the music and directed a sceptical glance at the sharp gable.

"Are you ready?" Hesson had appeared behind them.

"Hesson, where have you sprung from?"

"You wouldn't believe how long it took me to get here. Your show will be on in ten minutes."

"Okay, we're coming." They got up and had their work cut out getting past the crowd. Jim, Lyon, Rob, and Eugene followed Hesson through the crowded aisle. They passed to the left of the stage through a small side entrance and finally stood at the bottom of the stairs leading up to the stage.

"Okay, listen. I'll go up first and ask for silence. Then I'll give my speech and when I've finished, I'll first call Jim onto the stage. He'll get his award and then I'll call the next one and so on. That's it."

"Understood," said Jim. Hesson nodded once again, turned around and walked up the wooden steps to the stage.

"Attention, please." Hesson's voice echoed through the tent and the crowd fell silent almost instantly. Somewhere there was the clanging of plates.

"I am glad that you have all come to this celebration of our victory. This party marks the beginning of a new era in our universe. The UDP have been defeated." The audience began to cheer and punched their fists into the air. Hesson raised his hands and the crowd fell silent.

"The United Forces fought bravely and it is well deserved that they emerged victorious. The drads didn't stand a chance against us! Nevertheless, we also owe our victory to our diversion force; sadly, only two members of that force survived. A true tragedy, but what's done, is done.

For the victory and the fact that there haven't been many more victims, we also have to thank our team that destroyed the drad control ship, our destruction squad. Jim, come onto the stage, please." The crowd applauded and Jim climbed the steps to the stage.

For a while, Lyon, Rob, and Eugene couldn't hear anything. Then the crowd applauded again.

"Thank you so much, thank you. I am very grateful. It's been a real honour to have been chosen as the leader of this squad. We got to know each other quite well during our mission and they are a great team. I'd like to thank Lyon, Rob, Slow, and Eugene. I'd like to thank Aecey as well, although she never took part," they heard Jim's voice sweep through the tent.

"Damn it, he did prepare a speech after all," said Lyon. Eugene nodded.

"I prepared one as well," stated Rob.

"Thank you, Jim. Next I'd like to ask Eugene onto the stage. He is the first human ever to have escaped from the clutches of drad slavery," they heard Hesson say. Again the crowd cheered. Eugene in his turn climbed the stairs; he thought of nothing. The whole situation was dreamlike as if he wasn't in his body but just controlled it. He took the last step and stood inside the tent. Everybody clapped. Eugene put on his wide grin and went to Hesson, who shook his hand and put a golden medal round his neck. Eugene stepped up to the microphone.

"Thank you," Eugene cleared his throat. "Ahem, as my friend Jim has just said, I, too, feel honoured to have been a member of this squad. It is our, or rather my, farewell from you because I am not going to stay here with you but I'll move to Ziguur and marry Alimada." This time the crowd cheered even louder. Eugene stepped back and took his position next to Jim.

"My congratulations!"

301

"Thank you, Jim."

Next Hesson called Lyon to the stage, who really gave his speech as he had announced at dinner.

"Thank you, thank you so much. Thanks, thank you."

"You really put a lot of thought into your speech, didn't you?" remarked Jim when Lyon joined them.

"Indeed," replied Lyon.

"Thank you, thank you very much. I feel very privileged that I was invited to fight with this tremendous squad. And I'd like to thank them for everything not least for saving my life," said Rob.

When the audience had calmed down again, the four bowed and left the stage. Next the many generals of the United Forces would take the stage to give their various speeches.

Lyon, Rob, Jim, Ramses, Hesson, and General Joe wished Eugene and Alimada all the best on their wedding. They walked down the aisle arm in arm, rice was thrown and petals lined their path to their wedding jet. They waved for a long time and then got in. Eugene hugged Jim, Rob, and Lyon, shook hands with Ramses and promised to visit them before he got on board. A moment later, the jet took off. After a five-hour flight they landed on Ziguur just as the sun was setting. They got off and walked along the street, Eugene in a black suit, Alimada in a tight white dress surrounded by the familiar odours of chlorine and flowers.

Yes, life would be good here.

In the end, Eugene had received nearly twenty million Guldias from Hesson, the equivalent of about half a ton of pure gold.

"What do you think of a house on the beach with a garden, some trees and our own yacht?" asked Eugene.

"I don't mind, but right now I'd like to go for dinner with

you. What about the hotel 'Honeysun'? They say food's really nice there."
"Yes, I've heard that, too. Let's go."

Lyon returned to Mars and used his money to buy a large piece of land where he built a splendid villa. After some years he entered the race to become king and was duly elected. He abolished the hunt for humans and replaced it with many entertaining, amusing and attractive games held in the Colloscoseum. He wanted to be re-elected after all.

Rob returned to his forest moon and died only a few years later due the long term effects of his fight with Aecey. He was found months later in his apartment, the battery liquid having leaked. His memory chip had been corroded.

Jim was soon made Hesson Lachopp's successor. And on Hesson's death some years later, he inherited his seat on the ship.

Ramses and his family lived on the ship for a long time until he finally decided to leave. He left his wife and child behind. It is said that he became a musician on Jaffadurr but nobody really knew anything for certain.

Eugene and Alimada did buy a house on the beach. It was a beautiful villa, not as big as Lyon's but quite presentable. Their yacht lay at their own jetty and their lawn was always immaculate. The whole estate was surrounded by woodland. Soon Alimada became pregnant and had their first child. Eugene called him Jason. It was the first free born human child since Earth had been destroyed. Soon there was another one and then a third, the only girl. They stayed on Ziguur for good, often visiting Lyon or else he came to see them. They never visited Rob's grave again, neither did they visit Ramses. Jim came to see them twice, but in his new job he was very busy. Eugene never thought about his past again, he lived in the here and now.

On Earth, somewhere 3rd August, 2001

It was sunny and the convertible sped over the straight dusty road, past trees, fields and lakes. At last, it stopped at the roadside and Jason Hanks got out. He wiped the tears from his cheeks. He couldn't believe that Sool had killed his little brother. No, Eugene hadn't deserved that. It was he who would have deserved it, but not Eugene. Faltering, he headed off across the fields and meadows. His mind was a blank, he had switched off. His fingers touched the bump on his trouser pocket. Did he load it? He didn't know. Woodland came into view in front of him. As he entered among the trees, he was surrounded by the odours of damp wood and cool air. A few rays of sunlight pierced through the branches. A path appeared in front of him. He slowly walked along until he reached a small wooden bridge crossing a bubbling stream. He smiled. His hand slid into his pocket and pulled out the pistol. He looked at it for a long time and put it into his mouth.

After a while, Jason came out of the wood again, got into his Mercedes and drove off. The pistol lay in the stream, sparkling silvery. Sool's people wouldn't cow him. They would never find him. At a hundred miles an hour Jason cruised along the road to the House of Time. When he arrived, he marched through the entrance hall, by-passed the security controls, knocked down a scientist who tried to stop him and finally stood outside the big time gate. He ran towards it and jumped....